FORGOTTEN FUTURES

Dreamworlds, real worlds, and weird worlds await those dauntless travelers through time and space who encounter these perilous planets. Noted author, critic, and anthologizer Brian Aldiss has culled these seventeen stories from the best in the science fiction magazines of three decades. The stories are from the past, but they travel light years into the future . . . into the alien domains of quogs, humanoids, and wine-colored oceans stretching to the last frontier.

Other Avon books edited by
Brian Aldiss

Evil Earths	44636	2.50
Galactic Empires, Vol. I	42341	2.25
Galactic Empires, Vol. II	42879	2.25

AVON
PUBLISHERS OF BARD, CAMELOT AND DISCUS BOOKS

AVON BOOKS
A division of
The Hearst Corporation
959 Eighth Avenue
New York, New York 10019

Published by arrangement with the author
Library of Congress Catalog Card Number: 79-56238
ISBN: 0-380-47100-0

First Avon Printing, February, 1980

AVON TRADEMARK REG. U.S. PAT. OFF. AND IN
OTHER COUNTRIES, MARCA REGISTRADA,
HECHO EN U.S.A.

Printed in the U.S.A.

ACKNOWLEDGEMENTS

"HOW ARE THEY ALL ON DENEB IV?" by C. C. Shackleton Copyright © 1965 SF Horizons Ltd. Reprinted by permission of the author
MOUTH OF HELL by David I. Masson Copyright © 1968 David Masson. Reprinted by permission of Faber and Faber Ltd. from THE CALTRAPS OF TIME, by David I. Masson
BRIGHTSIDE CROSSING by Alan E. Nourse Copyright © 1951 Alan E. Nourse. First published in GALAXY 1951. Reprinted by permission of Brandt & Brandt
THE SACK by William Morrison Copyright © 1950 by Street & Smith Publications Inc. Reprinted by permission of the Condé Nast Publications Inc. First published in the September 1950 issue of *Astounding Science Fiction*
THE MONSTER by A. E. van Vogt Copyright © 1948 by Street & Smith Publications Inc. (now Condé Nast Publications Inc.). Reprinted by arrangement with Forrest J. Ackerman and the E. J. Carnell Literary Agency. First published in *Astounding Science Fiction* 1948
THE MONSTERS by Robert Sheckley Copyright © Robert Sheckley 1953. Reprinted by permission of A. D. Peters & Co. Ltd.
GRENVILLE'S PLANET by Michael Shaara Copyright © 1952 Michael Shaara. Reprinted by permission of the author
BEACHHEAD by Clifford Simak Copyright © 1951 Ziff Davis Publishing Co. Reprinted by permission of Robert Mills Limited. First published in *Fantastic Adventures* July 1951
THE ARK OF JAMES CARLYLE by Cherry Wilder Copyright © 1974 by Cherry Wilder. Reprinted by permis-

CONTENTS

INTRODUCTION

Long before I began compiling this book, I could see what it had to contain. Its title and its contents leaped at me while I was working on the first anthology in this series, *Space Opera**, three years ago.

For the majority of readers new to science fiction, a landing on another planet—a planet, because unknown, even more perilous than Earth—must be their peak experience of the genre. If they don't get the true sf charge out of touchdown on Procyon v, they will never get any charge at all. The cutting edge of science fiction lies along the interface between the known and the unknown.

So what I wanted for my anthology was that seminal story in which our brave astronauts, or space-travellers as they used to be called, make the first-ever voyage through space, see the stars like jewels flung into the sack of night, and touch down on a totally unknown planet. There they jump out to test the atmosphere, find it even better than Earth's, and take a stroll amid the glorious scenery. Whereupon something awful appears and—according to which seminal story you read—attempts to eat them, warps their minds with obscene telepathic messages, or captures them and takes them into subterranean tunnels.

It was a fantastic story, one you remember for the rest of your life. My trouble was, I had forgotten *which* story it was. For months, I leafed my way through my library, looking for the seminal story. I found plenty of stories like it, but never that actual story.

Eventually the truth dawned. That seminal story had no actual existence. It was a creation of my memory, compounded from elements common to many similar first-landing stories. It was, you might say, a *folk memory of landing on a strange planet.*

* *Space Opera* was followed by *Space Odysseys, Evil Earths,* and *Galactic Empires* (in two volumes), all from the publishers of this companion volume.

* * *

Looking backwards into the mists of receding time, or the receding mists of time, I can see how the legend has gradually become briefer and more sophisticated over the ages since I first began reading, and the sayers of the saga themselves gradually less Neanderthal. Right on the edge of the abyss where memory begins, I am able to recall myself lying in my cot, dummy in mouth, reading an absolutely enchanting Great Progenitor of the story in *Wonder Stories*.

This is how that Great Progenitor went.

Two professors with German names are arguing about the nature of life. One of them believes that life would be possible even with a silicon-based metabolism, as opposed to the carbon-based metabolism prevalent on Earth; the the other does not so believe. Both put their points of view. Sometimes they grow angry and strike their brows, or scribble equations on a handy blackboard. Every few chapters, in comes the housekeeper and throws more coal on the fire.

So heated grows the argument, that the two professors with German names decide to settle the matter by travelling to Mars, which they suspect is a silicon world. Going out into the backyard, they begin to assemble a rocketship, still occasionally striking their brows. Some parts they get from the local hardware store, where the owner is amused by their preposterous idea; he often looks over the garden fence to joke with them. But progress is made, little by little, chapter by chapter.

The rocket is completed. The two professors with German names persuade their housekeeper to come along with them as cook; she consents to come as long as she can bring her dog, Fritz. They climb aboard, shovel in the coal, heat up the boiler, and the rocket goes shooting up into space—to the considerable discomfiture of the hardware store owner.

Space is very interesting and is described in some detail. They can see all the planets in the solar system, etc. They are aiming for Mars but Fritz knocks the compass over and they land by accident on Jupiter instead. To their surprise, they find Jupiter is rather like Earth, except cloudier. Also the trees are bigger.

The two professors with German names step outside and sniff the air. It is even better than Earth's. They take a stroll. Whereupon something appears. It is a crowd of Jovians and—bless my soul!—they prove to have a silicon-based metabolism. So one of the professors wins his argument. They shake hands and marry the housekeeper, whose carbon-based metabolism has always had a certain appeal.

Doubtless some of my more cynical readers will find this story a little naïve, comical even. Let me assure you that my first impressions were entirely more favorable. At that tender age, I had never heard anyone discussing such a fascinating subject as the nature of life; if taxed I might have claimed offhand that life had no nature. Nor had the subject of a *silicon-based metabolism* ever crossed my mind. I believe I am correct in saying that it was this metaphysical aspect of science fiction which interested me as much as the actual spaceflight and landing on Jupiter.

As the ages passed and I left nappies behind, I found that the story of that first landing was developing. The earlier chapters became abridged, even perfunctory. The spaceships were still built privately in back yards, but the details of manufacture, and the argument, were curtailed. The landing, and what happened then, became the thing. After more ages the stories simply skipped the prolegomena and opened with the ship blasting out of space and the captain jumping out of his ship, sniffing the air and finding it even better than Earth's, and claiming it in the name of—well, it used to be the British Empire, but that changed too.

Nowadays, the formula has tightened still further. Perhaps you will recall a recent story which begins smartly, "After landing on Regulus v, the men of the Yarmolinsky Expedition made camp . . ." (I prefer not to give the name of the story; with any luck, you will find it in the next anthology in this series.)

There was a time, during the sixties, when it looked as if the first-landing story was dead, killed by its own clichés. At that period, Harry Harrison and I had started the first of our many collaborations, a little magazine of sf criticism entitled *SF Horizons*. An Oxford friend of ours, C. C. Shackleton, wrote some witty send-ups of various aspects of science fiction. One subject he impaled was precisely this matter of first-landings; as one can infer from his remarks he felt the subject had suffered severely from overuse. I am happy to include his piece, "How Are They All on Deneb IV?" as a kind of postscript to this Introduction, since it defines the area more wittily than I could ever aspire to do.

So this anthology does not contain that first-landing story you remember. It was just a folk-memory. All parts of the legend are, of course, embedded in H. G. Wells's novel, *The First Men on the Moon*. One never forgets the moment when Cavor and Beford see the sun rise, watch the plants grow, and sniff the air, to find it even better than Earth's.

What this anthology does contain are stories which, while being excellent in their own right, range along the whole spectrum of interest aroused by that feat which still remains imaginary: standing upon another planet. (The Moon is a satellite, not a planet.) That particular kind of thrill has been conjured in literature since time immemorial; during time memorial, sf is the name of the literature that does it now.

Actual unrestricted travel in space, if it ever comes, may alter the nature of science fiction, as reality wipes out folk memories. There must be other beings on other planets who dream similar tales. I'm convinced—I know it is controversial to say this—that when we get to Jupiter we shall find it inhabited by creatures with a silicon-based metabolism. For sure, their writers will be writing science fiction, too. Who knows, maybe it's even better than Earth's . . .

We have here eighteen stories from nine different magazines; their vintages cover a span of three decades. Some are deservedly famous, some undeservedly neglected. As always, in the hope of preserving a whiff of period flavour, I have left the original blurbs intact, or forged them where the originals were not available. Can you tell the fakes? Two hundred and fifteen correct answers to the last anthology so far. An additional puzzle this time: which piece is by me, operating under a pen name?

Brian W. Aldiss

Heath House
Southmoor
October 1976

"HOW ARE THEY ALL ON DENEB IV?"
by C. C. Shackleton

All right, I know, times are changing. It's the great theme of our age. Ever since evolution and all that, the decades have gone hog wild for change; you'd think there was a law about it. Maybe there is a law about it.

Don't think I'm complaining: I am. Since I was a kid, everything has changed, from the taste of bread to the nature of Africa and China. But at least I thought sf would stay the same.

Instead, what has happened? It's all different. They don't write like Heinlein any more—even Heinlein doesn't. In the old days, you knew exactly where you stood in a story. Take the aliens; back in the Golden Age, when the writers had a bit of a sense of wonder and there were blondes on the covers, you knew the aliens would always be there, endlessly mown down, endlessly picturesque, swarming over endless alien worlds. But nowadays—well, let's take actual cases, he said, reaching eagerly for the May 1940 copy of *Gruelling Science Stories*. The Luftwaffe was plastering London at the time, but thank heavens the American sf writers hadn't got wind of that, and Zago Blinder was still turning out his customary peaceful limpid prose. His May 1940 stint was entitled, with what I've always thought showed considerable skill in alliteration, "The Devils of Deneb IV."

You know how this sort of thing goes right from the start. The pleasure lies in its predictability. Scarcely has the whine (whisper, snarl, thunder) of the landing jets died than the hatch opens and three Earthmen jump (crawl, climb, fall) out and stand looking round Deneb IV. They find the air is breathable and quickly hoist the flag (Old Glory, U.N. banner, Stars and Stripes).

Up to now, we readers have been carried along breathlessly (restlessly, hesitantly, mindlessly) on the flood of the author's prose, full of admiration for the way in which he has so economically created a situation so distinct from our own humdrum world. More, the old-timers among us are full of gratitude for his dropping the first three (four, six, twelve) chapters describing the construction of the spaceship in someone's back yard and its long eventful journey to Deneb which were once considered compulsory in this sort of exercise.

Now, however, comes an awkward pause. We have been brought painlessly through what the textbooks call Building Up Atmosphere, Establishing Environment, Creating Character, and so on. The idyllic mood must be shattered. It is time to Introduce the Action.

"Look!" gasps (coughs, barks, yells) the captain, pointing with trembling (rigid, scarred, nicotine-stained) finger at the nearby hill (jungle, ocean, ruined temple). His crewmen follow the line of his fingertip, and there approaching them they see an angry group (ugly bunch, slavering horde, slobbering herd) of Denebians who are plainly out for blood as they gallop (surge, slime, esp) towards the spaceship.

You must admit this is value for money, particularly if you only borrowed the magazine. In no time, the three intrepid explorers are back in their ship and the vile Denebians are trying to scratch their way in through the cargo hatch.

What more could you ask for? Personally, I asked for nothing more; I had had enough by the time I came across this situation for the fiftieth time. It was not boredom so much as bravery. The Denebians weren't what they used to be. However mindless and merciless they got, I was no longer scared. I developed immunity. Yet, for all that, I liked things the way they were. The more unsociably those aliens behaved, the more I realized how superior we Earthmen were.

Then things became less straightforward. I was rifling through *Microscopic Sex Wonder* during the boom year of 1951 when I realized that Deneb was no longer the same. They'd dared to alter the plot!

This time, the aliens didn't appear when the flag was hoisted. Everything was peaceful—too peaceful. Our three chums wandered among beautiful trees, or they found charming people like themselves but nicer, with sweet old mums sitting knitting on the porch, and Pa sucking a corn cob and spittin' to avoid bunches of rosy-cheeked kids, or else they found nothing there at all except the waving grass.

You remember what happened, don't you? Those beautiful trees, that grand old granny, those cheeky kids, that expanse of nothing, that sneaky grass, was really our old Denebians in disguise. Yes, sir! Freud had hit sf by this date, and the old slobbering hordes were back in full force only nastier, because they could thought-wrap themselves as grannies or grass and get into the ship and cause chaos. That was a terrible era, and I don't know how I survived it. Story after story, I had to face utter mind-wrenching terror.

I grew to love it.

Then they went and changed the plot again! I knew just how things were going and was all set to relax when the editors or whoever it is that insists on these things—for sure it's not the writers—altered the orthodoxy.

I can pinpoint the date exactly when I realized something had gone wrong. I had bought the Jannish—sorry, the January issue of *The Monthly of Whimsey and Whammo-Science,* 1960, and was leafing through this story by Piledriver Jones entitled "On Deneb Deep My Pleasure Stalks." Funny, I thought, the title doesn't sound right, they've started mucking around with the titles now, is nothing sacred? But since I wanted to find out if a pleasure stalk was what I thought it was (it wasn't), I forced myself to read on.

You can't fail to recall the story, not only because it has since been anthologized fifty-two times and won a Hank, but because it started a new trend. This is the one where they arrive on Deneb IV all right, in this funny ship that rides solar winds, but some sort of bug gets them and they all grow extra limbs; the captain alone grows twelve big toes, fourteen left arms, a spare pair of buttocks, two girl's knees, and a horse's head. And then they sit around and talk philosophy, not minding at all, until in the end it turns out that back on Earth things are even worse because people are terribly short of horse's heads and buttocks and knee caps and things.

Let's have no false modesty—I can adjust to anything. But it needs about twenty years to adjust to that sort of plot. And what happened? Already, *already*, they've altered the line again. That's what I mean about change running hog wild.

Just this year the new orthodoxy has set in. Look at this month's crop of magazines—it's not a very big crop these days, because people won't read unless they know what to expect—look at *Monolog*, look at *Off*, look at *Odious Fantasy* and *Lewd Worlds* and *Gallimaufry*, and what do you find? Not a darned one of them has a story set on Deneb IV!

Not a darned one of them has a story set on any alien planet! They're all Earth stories, everyone, though *Monolog* has this nine-part serial set in England at the time of the Norman Conquest, with William the Conqueror finding cases of telepathy among the peasants. Otherwise, nothing! Russians, psi powers, medicine, psychology, sociology, politics, traffic problems, robots, nuclear wars, funny little tales about fellows meeting aliens and not realizing it, oh yes, no shortage of all that sort of stuff, and, of course, plenty of drowned, crystallized, rainless, bug-ridden, childless, adultless, metal-less, doodless, witless worlds, all of them Earth. But not a single story set on another planet.

I'd chuck in my hand. I would. I'd give up. I'd never bother to try and read another sf story in another magazine in my life. There just happens to be one small thing that gives me grounds for hope.

Lewd Worlds has a little cameo, not more than a thousand words long, about this chap who seduces this girl and then creeps into his back yard and builds his own rocket ship. He has this secret perverted desire to reach the stars, see?

It's only a matter of sweating it out a few more years, boys. We'll get back to Deneb one day. The times they are a-changing.

1

Uninhabited Planets

"... BECAUSE THEY'RE THERE"

It's an adaptation of what Sir Edmund Hillary replied when asked why he wanted to climb Everest. "Because it's there," he said. This remark has become part of the currency of conversation of our time. For the same reason, we want to visit other planets. Because they're there. (The unspoken remainder of the sentence goes, *and because we are human beings.*)

That's straightforward enough. As to why we want to visit planets in fiction—that's less simple. But there are valid reasons for our interest in unvisited or unvisitable planets; this anthology sets out to explore some of them.

In this opening section, the action unfolds on uninhabited worlds. Even within this setting, there are different categories of uninhabited worlds. Masson's story is set on a purely imaginary planet. Nourse's story is set on a purely imaginary Mercury. Morrison's story is set on an imaginary planetoid, or asteroid. Each choice of location has its due effect on the kind of story which is told.

"The Sack" is an excellent story. I do not know why it has not been anthologized more often; nor do I understand why the name of its author, William Morrison (the pseudonym of Joseph Samachson), is not more widely known. There is no mistaking "The Sack" for anything but an sf story; yet we can see that it is also a fairy story, with all the traditional virtues of that genre: a grain of unpalatable wisdom incorporated within the fantastic, the medicine within the spoonful of jam.

The wisdom comes in the form of a fairly standard, but continually necessary, precept concerning the rightful use of knowledge and power. "The Sack" was first published in the USA in 1950, one of those awful years that have trudged by, when Senator Joe McCarthy was just beginning his inquisition of anyone suspected of being a Communist; Morrison's senator is less interested in the truth than in his own career. The story itself takes the form of an inquisition. Now that McCarthy has long since disappeared from the scene, "The Sack" reveals more universal aspects of its fable.

"The truth will make you free" is an adage from a safer era. Morrison offers a revised version—"The truth may enslave you."

Several of the other tales in this collection also represent quests for the ultimate in one form or another. The lure of ultimate answers to everything is embodied in "The Sack." Alan Nourse's "Brightside Crossing" embodies the solar system ultimate in adventure, a crossing of Mercury's bright side during perihelion.

"Brightside Crossing" is a fine story. It is included here because it is also absolutely out-of-date.

At the start of the sixties, Alan Nourse published a highly successful book entitled *Nine Planets,* with colour illustrations by Mel Hunter, which embodied all the knowledge then current about the nine planets of our solar system. In the chapter on Mercury, Nourse has this to say:

> The planet turns completely around on its axis in exactly the same time it requires to complete one revolution around the Sun. This means that on Mercury a "year" and a "day" are equal in length, and that the same face of the planet is therefore always turned toward the Sun . . . Mercury has a bright side and a dark side; the bright side is perpetually hot, while the dark side remains bitterly cold.

Well, so the astronomers all thought, before the astonishing successes of NASA's Mariner fly-bys of the sun's nearest planet. We know now (is this the ultimate answer to the question?) that Mercury does in fact have a slow axial revolution, so that its days do not equal its years.

Mercury remains a mysterious planet, its pocked face resembling to an odd degree that of our familiar Moon. And yet—the Bright Side, the Dark Side, and that thrilling area, the Twilight Zone, have all been abolished at the click of a computerized shutter. They provide settings for many sf stories, harbours for many imaginations. We then regarded them as "fact"; they have been proved one hundred per cent fictitious, like the forests and swamps of Venus, or the canals and dead cities of Mars.

When lecturing on science fiction, I am often asked, "What will science fiction do now that science has caught up with it?" My answer is to say, in effect, that every new advance opens up new doors for speculation. I believe this to be so. But I see the point of the question. Year by year, old ports of call of the imagination have been closed until further notice. This book celebrates a type of fiction which belongs to the past.

The will to believe in life everywhere is very strong, and not simply in science fiction writers. The recent Viking landing on Mars was designed to check for signs of life. It is hardly to be wondered at that we live on an overpopulated globe, when mankind continually populates the deserts, the deeps, the interior of the Earth, and the Heavens, with a riotous assembly of imaginary beings. Life is supported by conjuring life. Conception is all.

So how can "Brightside Crossing" be out-of-date, and yet retain its attraction for us? Because it speaks of human endeavour and the will to venture where no man has ever set foot. Nourse's adventure remains as up-to-date as ever; the point of the story does not rest on whether the world conjured up for us is real or imaginary. Space flight has not changed human nature, only human knowledge.

"Mouth of Hell" takes place upon an entirely imaginary planet. The author does not inform the reader of the name of the planet, or in what star system it is located. This is deliberate. David Masson is one of the most remarkable authors of sf thrown up in the sixties. His stories were printed in Michael Moorcock's *New Worlds*—less than a dozen of them, and then he ceased to publish. His most famous piece is probably *Traveller's Rest,* a remarkable time-travel tale.

Like the rest of his slender oeuvre, Masson's *Mouth of Hell* shows admirable control of material that, in the vital tradition of sf, has enormous implications. While it is undoubtedly about an uninhabited planet, and may appear to have no interest in anything but describing as remarkable a physical feature as could be found on any imaginary planet, it has much to say about the nature of the human animal. Not only is it about the marvellous, like the Nourse story; it is also about the domestication of the marvellous.

Time has had its little ironies with "Mouth of Hell" as with "Brightside Crossing." When Masson imagined his enormous sloping plateau and its attendant features, it lay almost at the limits of the unimaginable. Whereas Mariner fly-bys of Mercury have outdated Nourse's (and similar stories) premises without invalidating its imaginative power, similar fly-bys of Mars have confirmed Masson's premises. There are monstrous features on the Red Planet at which we can but wonder: the great equatorial rift valley, which is 6 km deep, 75 km across, and hundreds of kilometers long, the gigantic Olympus, a volcano some 29 km high—features which considering that the radius of Mars is only half Earth's, are almost unbelievable. In all the sensational stories of Mars written over the past century, not one author dared imagine such monstrosities for fear of being laughed at. Olympus and the rift valley make "Mouth of Hell" more, rather than less, credible (whether to its advantage or disadvantage is up to an individual reader to decide).

This is a "what if" story, the account of a discovery. What does humanity make of it? What does a robin make of a wheelbarrow? What was it Blake said about the sun: "You see a Disk in shape somewhat like a Guinea . . ."?

MOUTH OF HELL

by David I. Masson

When the expedition reached the plateau, driving by short stages from the northern foothills, they found it devoid of human life, a silent plain variegated by little flowers and garish patches of moss and lichen. Kettass, the leader, called a halt, and surveyed the landscape while the tractors were overhauled. The sun shone brightly out of a clear sky, not far to the south for the quasi-arctic ecology was one of height, not latitude. Mosquitoes hovered low down over tussocks below wind-level, beetles and flies crawled over the flowers. Beyond a quarter-metre above the ground, however, a bitter wind from the north flowed steadily. The distance was clear but it was difficult to interpret what one saw, and the treeless waste held no clues to size. Ground undulations were few. There were not signs of permafrost beneath. After a time a fox could be made out trekking southward some way off. Some larger tracks, not hooved, showed by the edge of a bog pool. If one wandered far from the vehicles and men, the silence was broken only by the thin sound of the wind where it combed a grass mound, the zizz and skrittle of insects, the distant yipe of fox or other hunting animal, and the secretive giggle of seeping water. Here and there on the north side of a mound or clump traces of rime showed, and a few of the pool edges were lightly frozen.

Returning to the main body, Kettass ordered the midday meal to be prepared. He thought about the situation. The wind was a trouble: it was steady and merciless and evidently below freezing point. One could bake at one's south side and freeze, literally, on one's north side. As the hour wore on the wind increased and became, if anything, colder, as the sun grew hotter. But a fringe of dark grey cloud began to climb along the southern horizon, like a ragged curtain seen from upside down, climbed and spread, until its outer streamers menaced the sun. Kettass got the party going again, and the little group of tractors trundled carefully, picking their way, towards the clouds.

After two hours, 'Afpeng spotted a herd of greydeer and the party stopped. A long stalk by 'Afpeng, Laafif and Niizmek secured three carcasses which were strapped to the vehicles, and the party moved on. The clouds continued to grow and by evening covered half the sky, to south, the icy wind from the north meanwhile growing in strength. A camp was made, using the tractors as weather walls to supplement the canvas. The deer were cured and their flesh preserved, against a time of shortage of food.

During a wakeful night the wind blew steadily on, slackening only towards dawn. The night was clear and freezing hard. In the morning the sky was cloudless and the whole plateau covered with white frost.

"What direction now, chief?" asked Mehhtumm over breakfast.

"Press on south, simply."

In two hours the frost was gone. The beetles came out from their hiding places, the sun beat down, the ground was warm, but the wind blew fiercer than ever and as cold. Far ahead, cumulus heads rose fully formed from the horizon, and soon towering thunderclouds covered the southern sky. A screen of false cirrus spread and became a grey pall, shutting off the sun. The wind grew and turned gusty at times.

"Have you noticed the ground?" said Mehhtumm in Kettass' ear some hours later.

"The slope? Yes." And the chief halted the convoy. It was just as though someone had tilted the world slightly. They were pointing down a gentle slope, nearly uniform, which spread east and west as far as the eye could see. Behind to north, the same slope. The change had been too gradual to notice before. Kettass had the troop deploy into a broad arrow with his vehicle in the lead and centre.

In the next two hours the tilt became more and more pronounced. Pools had become moist watercourse-beds. Kettass' altimeter showed that they were down half-way to sea-level. Yet the vegetation was hardly changed. The mosses were richer, the ground almost hot, but the icy gale hurtled at their backs as if to push them down the hillside, a hillside that stretched mile after mile to either horizon. They were shut in north and south by the tilt of the ground, now visibly a curve round which they could not see. 'Ossnaal's face was a grey green, and Kettass wondered why one who could be so cool on a rock-face should be so easily affected by this landscape. Not that 'Afpeng looked too good, and no one was happy.

"Where's it going to end, eh?" muttered Laafif.

The thundercloud had become a vast wall of dark vapour, lit by frequent flashes. An almost continuous rumbling came from the south, and their sets crackled. Kettass ordered the vehicles to run level with his own. The slope was now a clear threat to progress.

An hour later Kettass stopped the vehicles again. The slope was dangerously steep. Although it was barely noon the light was poor, under the pall of cloud which now arched over most of the sky. Plants were more lush but more isolated, so that much rock and gravel could be seen. The biting wind rushed on.

"Looks as though we'll need our climbing suckers after all," suggested Mehhtumm. Pripand and Ghuddup were muttering together beside vehicle 5 and looking darkly about them. 'Ossnaal's face was white and everyone looked anxious.

"If only a handy hollow or ledge would appear, then we could park the tractors," went on Mehhtumm. Kettass said nothing. He was considering the altimeter.

"Must be *below* sea-level," he said at last; "yet no trees, nothing but this arctic wind, keeping vegetation down I suppose, and no sign of a bottom." Then "Immobolize here, everybody. Keep two vehicle-lengths apart. Cast out grapnels as best you can. Pull out the packs and climbing equipment, just in case. Pitch tents, but well east of the vehicle line, and choose vegetation areas: the gravel may be in the track of floods. Same thing with the stores. After all that's done, a meal."

Before the meal was ready the gale was suddenly full

of soft hail, which turned to cold rain. The afternoon was punctuated by showers of this sort. The grapnels saved two vehicles from rolling off in a shallow spate.

Kettass held a council of war. "Seems to me," growled Niizmek, "there's no bottom in front of us. We could send one or two ahead to report, and camp here till we know more."

"What do you say, 'Afpeng?"

"Strike twenty kilometres east or west, in case there's a spur or a chimney?"

" 'Ossnaal?"

"I think . . . I don't . . . It's a waste of time trying east or west. You can see there's nothing however far you go. It's go on or turn back."

"You can't take the lot of us," Laafif snapped; "you can't get enough stores down with us, without tractors. If the ground isn't reached soon and this slope steepens, we've had it. Only two or three men can get down, and then only for a few kilometres' travel."

Ghuddup and Pripand, mechanics, said nothing.

"I think," now put in Mehhtumm, "we might send a patrol party first tomorrow, to go up to half a day down, return by twilight, and report. Then you can decide, eh, chief?"

"Probably best, but I'll sleep on it," said Kettass.

Few slept that night. The wind was moist, the ground cooled off, the thunder ceased after midnight but the storm of wind roared on. Next morning again a clear sky, apart from some tumbling clouds low down on the southern horizon (which owing to the slope, was not very far off). It was chilly but not freezing. Kettass chose a party of three after a breakfast at first light, among the long dark purple shadows cast across the tilted ground by vehicles and tents. Mehhtumm was to lead; for the other two Kettass asked for volunteers. To his surprise 'Ossnaal and Ghuddup spoke up. "If we're not able to use the tractors I'll be at a loose end. Pripand can keep an eye on them. I like climbing, if we get any," said Ghuddup. 'Ossnaal assured Kettass he was fit; "I want to find out what we are really coming to."

The trio set off almost at once; besides iron rations and water, ropes, karabiners and the newly devised suckers, they carried oxygen. "You don't know how deep this basin is going to go, and what air you'll encounter," Kettass pointed out.

At first they were in communication with the main party, but at about five kilometres reception grew too faint, partly from the crackling that came with the morning's cumulonimbus. Before this Mehhtumm reported that the air-pressure suggested they were 2000 metres below Mean Sea-Level, that the slope was over 50° from the horizontal, that the surface was rock and sand, interspersed with unusual and highly-coloured lichen, that there were numerous small torrents east and west of them, and that mist and cloud had appeared, hovering off the edge not far below. After that, silence . . . until a hysterical signal, eventually identified as Mehhtumm's, in the deep evening twilight.

Soon after they lost radio contact with the camp, Mehhtumm, 'Ossnaal and Ghuddup paused to stare at the cloud-formations. Swags of dirty grey, like dust under beds, floated in the air level with their eyes and a kilometre or so south. Lightning from the formless curtain behind turned them into smoky silhouettes. The cumuloid heads above had largely vanished in the general mass of thundercloud. The tilted horizon terminated in a great roll of clear-edged cloud like a monstrous eel, which extended indefinitely east and west. The ground air, at any rate, was here free of the gale, but the rush of wind could be heard between the thunder. The atmosphere was damp and extremely warm. The rock surface was hot. What looked like dark, richly-coloured polyps and sea-anemones thrust and hung obscenely here and there from crannies. The scene was picked out now and again by shafts of roasting sunlight funnelling down brassily above an occasional cauliflower top or through a chasm in the cloud-curtain. Progress even with suckers was slow. Mehhtumm got them roped together.

An hour later the slope was 70°, with a few ledges bearing thorn bushes, dwarf pines, and peculiar succulents. The torrents had become thin waterfalls, many floating outwards into spray. A scorching breeze was wafting up from below. Two parallel lines of the roller cloud now stretched above them, and the storm seemed far above that. The smooth, brittle rock would take no pitons.

A curious patternless pattern of dull pink, cloudy lemon

yellow, and Wedgwood blue could just be discerned through the foggy air between their feet. It conveyed nothing, and the steepening curvature of their perch had no visible relation to it. Altimeters were now impossible to interpret, but they must clearly be several kilometres below sea-level. Crawling sensations possessed their bodies, as though they had been turned to sodawater, as Ghuddup remarked, and their ears thrummed.

Mehhtumm and Ghuddup ate part of their iron rations and swallowed some water, but 'Ossnaal, whose face was a bluish pink, could only manage the water. They took occasional pulls of oxygen, without noticeably improving their sensations.

Two hours later found them clinging to a nearly vertical rock face which continued indefinitely east, west and below. The patternless pattern below their feet was the same, no nearer visibly and no clearer. The waterfalls had turned to fine tepid rain. The air behind them, so far as it could be seen (Mehhtumm used a hand mirror) was a mass of dark grey vapour with much turbulence, through which coppery gleams of hot sunlight came rarely. The traces of sky above were very pale. The naked rock was blisteringly hot, even through sucker-gloves, but carried a curious purple and orange pattern of staining, perhaps organic. The crawling sensation had become a riot of turbulence in their flesh. Their ears were roaring. Something stabbed in their chests at intervals. Their sense of touch was disturbed and difficult. It was lucky they had suckers. Yet with all this, an enormous elation possessed Mehhtumm, an almost childish sense of adventure. 'Ossnaal was murmuring continuously to himself. Ghuddup was chuckling and apostrophizing the "Paisley patterns" of the abyss.

Half an hour later 'Ossnaal gave a shrill cry, which could be heard in the others' earphones, and went into some sort of fit. Fortunately his suckers held.

"We must get him up somehow. Can we move him foot by foot?" shouted Mehhtumm. He felt curiously carefree and regarded the crisis as an interesting abstract problem.

"I'm not going up!" snarled Ghuddup.

"You can't go down and you can't stay here. Our only chance is to try and get him up bit by bit. Maybe he'll come to or faint, and we can manage him that way."

"I'm not losing our only chance of seeing what's below,"

snarled Ghuddup again. "The hell with 'Ossnaal, and the hell with you too. You're yellow, that's what you are, a yellow skunk, a yellow Paisley skunk!"

Mehhtumm, in a dream, saw Ghuddup, who occupied a central position, saw quickly with a knife through the ropes on his either side. The long ends flailed down. 'Ossnaal's twitching body hung from three suckers of his four. Ghuddup spidered nimbly down and was soon virtually out of sight, but his muttered obscenities could be heard in Mehhtumm's radio. Mehhtumm tried to collect his thoughts, still dream-like. Finally he arrived at the conclusion that he must go for help, as he could certainly not maneuver the sick man by himself, and together they would probably perish uselessly. He pushed 'Ossnaal's left hand hard against the rock to fasten the sucker, tested the other three and shifted one. There was nothing to belay to. Extracting a luminous-dye marker from a pocket, he splashed the dye vividly over 'Ossnaal's suit and around him. He waited close to 'Ossnaal for two minutes, trying to arouse him by shouting his name. Finally the man quietened, and muttered something in response to Mehhtumm's shouts of "hang on; don't move!"

Mehhtumm began clambering upward, marking the rocks with the dye-splasher. Half a minute afterwards a sound and a movement beneath caught his attention, and he looked down in time to see the body of 'Ossnaal plummeting into the abyss. An invisible Ghuddup was still muttering in Mehhtumm's radio, and it was half an hour before his voice faded.

The rest of the upward journey was a nightmare, and took Mehhtumm far longer than he expected. After about three hours his head began to clear as his body reverted to normal, and the full realization of what had happened came to him. The first terrible doubts of his own action flooded in. There was nothing to be done now but to make as good speed as he could to the camp.

He had been calling for an hour before he was heard on their radios. Kettass sent Laafif and 'Afpeng to collect him. They managed to rendezvous by radio, and brought him back, weeping like a child, in darkness.

"Sounds like some sort of gas narcosis to me," Kettass said later to a recovered Mehhtumm.

"Yes, could even be nitrogen narcosis; except for 'Ossnaal. There could have been something else wrong with him—would you think?"

"I should never have let him go. He looked peculiar for some time . . . We shall have to write off Ghuddup as well, poor fellow, if we can't trace him in the morning."

Next day in the early sunlight Mehhtumm, Laafif and Kettass went down unroped, and marked with dye. The oxygen apparatus of each was adjusted to give them a continuous supply as a high percentage of their inspiration total. They followed Mehhtumm's markings. It was agreed that the first man to notice any specially alarming symptoms, or to have any detected by the others, was to climb up at once, but that till then they would keep close together, and that the remaining two must come up together as soon as either began to succumb. What happened was that Laafif, becoming confused despite the oxygen about 100 metres above the fatal spot, started to ascend. Mehhtumm passed the spot and, despite a persistent impression that he had become a waterfall, silently climbed on down, passing Kettass rapidly. He was 400 metres below, muttering to himself and glaring about him, when he and Kettass heard something between a sob and a laugh on their radios, and Laafif's body passed them, a few feet out, turning over and over. It became a speck above the carpet of coiling vapour which had replaced yesterday's colour pattern. The cries were still sounding in their radios minutes later when reception faded.

Kettass, dimly retaining a hold on sanity, eventually persuaded Mehhtumm to return, convincing himself and the other through a swirl of sensations, that it would be no use searching for yesterday's madman over several thousand vertical metres of rock. Mehhtumm said later that at that depth he had kept on seeing little images of Ghuddup, brandishing a yellow knife, hovering around him.

They got back in the late afternoon, and next day a silent expedition set off for home, one man per vehicle.

It took five years for authority to build two suitable VTOL craft capable of flying and taking off efficiently in both normal and high-pressure air, and fully pressurized within. Mehhtumm was dead, killed in a climbing accident on Mogharitse, but Kettass secured a passage as film-taker and world radio-commentator on one craft, and Niizmek on the other. The broadcasts were relayed from a ground station set up on the plateau, which picked them up, or rather down, from the ionized reflecting layer of the atmosphere, since the basin depth would cut off direct craft-to-layer-to-receiver broadcasting; even so, only about a quarter of the material came through.

The two craft landed in summer on the plateau near the 15° slant zone. Flight between about 11 am and midnight was considered meteorologically impossible owing to the severe up currents and the electrical disturbances. They took off at 7 am just before dawn, using powerful searchlights. Kettass' craft, piloted by an impassive veteran of thirty named Levaan, was to sink down past the rock wall near the original descent. The other craft sped west looking for a change in the geography. The two were in continuous communication through the pilots' radios (on a different wavelength).

Levaan tried his radar on the invisible floor of the basin. "You won't believe this—we have 43 kilometres beneath us."

Kettass was speechless.

"There's a secondary echo at 37 km or so—could be the cloud layer below. Let me try the lidar." He aimed the unwieldy laser "gun" downwards. "Yes, that'll be the cloud layer all right. And that blip over there, that's the roller cloud, or rather an incipient roll—I don't think there's anything visible to the eye."

"The—the ground echo: what does that make it in depth?"

"Given our altitude above MSL that makes the basin floor over 41 km below sea, and nearly 42 beneath the bevel of the plateau."

They began to descend. All trace of the event of five years ago was lost. The craft sank nine or ten kilometres, as indicated through the vertical radar. Kettass informed the world that the tinted rock was continuing and took a few film sequences. The sun poured across over the impossible vertical face. At fifteen kilometres down the colours had broken up into isolated dots and patches. The empty parts of the sky which had turned a milky white, now began to change to brazen yellow. There was still no visible sign of a bottom, none of the patternless pattern described by Mehhtumm, but the fog below was brilliant in sunlight, yellow sunlight. Even in the air-conditioned cabin it was exceptionally hot wherever the sun struck.

"Perspective makes the wall appear to curve in above us and below us," Kettass was saying to his microphone. The view was indeed rather like that seen by a midge dancing a few inches in front of a wall made of barrel-staves curving towards him, except that the "midge" would have been no thicker than a fine hair. The sky met the cliff line dizzyingly far overhead. No less than three parallel lines of black roller-cloud (very slender) were now silhouetted against the yellow sky, while a fourth roll was indicated by an Indian file of fish-like silhouettes alongside them. Not very far beyond hung the shaggy charcoal bases of the first cumuloids, behind which the brassy sun beat down. Black ghosts of the clouds grew and gestured, many kilometres high, on the cliff wall. At times Kettass had the illusion that the craft was flying banked sideways, and that the cliff wall was the horizontal floor of the world.

Descent began to be very bumpy. The other craft reported no change at 50 km west. At 36 km down the open sky was now a blood-orange hue. The fog, which had become exceedingly turbulent, was close below, and after cautious exploration Levaan found a hole through which pink, green and indigo masses could be dimly seen, crawling in the quivering air-currents. At 38 km down, battling against strong updraughts, they sighted far below a vast vista of dully red-hot lave, cold greenish lava, and what looked like violet mud, in apparently kilometres-wide slabs and pools, lapping right up against the thirty-to-forty-km high vertical wall on one side, and ending in pitch darkness many kilometres southward. Occasional flashes of forked lightning played near the cliff base. Besides the distortions of the air-currents, the whole floor was in slow motion, spreading, rocking, welling, bubbling.

Levaan broke in on Kettass' commentary to say he dared not stay longer, as the updraughts were becoming too violent and the fabric was groaning. The other craft had just sighted the end of the basin and wished to make its own commentary. Risking a breakup in the turbulence near the roller cloud level, Levaan's craft rose to pass it, and swung back to rendezvous. Niizmek and his pilot Fehos had sighted a step-like formation closing in the western end.

Next morning the two craft switched roles. Fehos and Niizmek descended into the pit, some way out from the wall, while Levaan's craft flew east to find how the basin ended on that side. But Fehos' transpex imploded at 39 km down, with a crack heard on the radios of the world, and the craft, a squashed insect, plunged into the magma. After that Levaan would not fly his craft below 25 km down.

They established that the cliff line stretched 163 km east to west, or rather slightly north of east to slightly south of west, and that the western end, later known as the "Terraces," consisted of a series of nearly vertical cliffs of from 2,000 metres to 3,000 metres high each, separated by sloping shelves and screes several kilometres across. The eastern end, the "Staircase" or "Jacob's Ladder," proved to be a rather similar formation like a file or grid whose ridges or bars were 500-metre-high 30°-lean overhangs (over the basin) of hard rock, alternating with boulder-and-gravel-filled hollows of soft rock, the whole system being tilted down southwards at an angle of 35°. The southern edge was a vertical wall like the northern, nearly parallel to it, but peak-bordered, higher by several thousand metres, 146 km long, and some 200 km away. After a few months press and radio exhausted their superlatives and wisecracks ("Nature's Mohole" was the type) and took up "Slingo," a new parachute waltzing craze sweeping the world.

Thirty years later Kettass, a hale septuagenarian, was taken down the "Terraces" pressurized cable railway by his son-in-law, daughter, and three grandchildren, and, looking through the triple transpex wall, gazed in silence upon the oozing magma from 700 metres' range. He did not live to travel the tourist rocket route built five deaths and 83 strikes later down "Jacob's Ladder," but two of his granddaughters took their families down the North Wall lift. That was the year Lebhass and Tollhirn made their fatal glider attempt. By this time three other deaths and 456 strikes later, heat mills, for the most part automatically controlled and inspected, were converting a considerable fraction of the thermal energy in the basin to supply two continents with light, heat and power. A quarter of the northern plateau was given over to their plant, another quarter contained a sanatorium and reserve for hardy tourists, and the other half was a game reserve and ecological study area; but the jagged mountains of the south, scoured by their own murderous southerly winds, resisted general exploitation.

Sometimes a man's got to do what a man's got to do—twice—

BRIGHTSIDE CROSSING

by Alan E. Nourse

James Baron was not pleased to hear that he had had a visitor when he reached the Red Lion that evening. He had no stomach for mysteries, vast or trifling, and there were pressing things to think about at this time. Yet the doorman had flagged him as he came in from the street: "A thousand pardons, Mr. Baron. The gentleman—he would leave no name. He said you'd want to see him. He will be back by eight."

Now Baron drummed his fingers on the table top, staring about the quiet lounge. Street trade was discouraged at the Red Lion, gently but persuasively; the patrons were few in number. Across to the right was a group that Baron knew vaguely—Andean climbers, or at least two of them were. Over near the door he recognized old Balmer, who had mapped the first passage to the core of Vulcan Crater on Venus. Baron returned his smile with a nod. Then he settled back and waited impatiently for the intruder who demanded his time without justifying it.

Presently a small, grizzled man crossed the room and sat down at Baron's table. He was short and wiry. His face held no key to his age—he might have been thirty or a thousand—but he looked weary and immensely ugly. His cheeks and forehead were twisted and brown, with scars that were still healing.

The stranger said, "I'm glad you waited. I've heard you're planning to attempt the Brightside."

Baron stared at the man for a moment. "I see you can

read telecasts," he said coldly. "The news was correct. We are going to make a Brightside Crossing."

"At perihelion?"

"Of course. When else?"

The grizzled man searched Baron's face for a moment without expression. Then he said slowly, "No, I'm afraid you're not going to make the Crossing."

"Say, who are you, if you don't mind?" Baron demanded.

"The name is Claney," said the stranger.

There was a silence. Then: "Claney? *Peter* Claney?"

"That's right."

Baron's eyes were wide with excitement, all trace of anger gone. "Great balls of fire, man—*where have you been hiding?* We've been trying to contact you for months!"

"I know. I was hoping you'd quit looking and chuck the whole idea."

"Quit looking!" Baron bent forward over the table. "My friend, we'd given up hope, but we've never quit looking. Here, have a drink. There's so much you can tell us." His fingers were trembling.

Peter Claney shook his head. "I can't tell you anything you want to hear."

"But you've got to. You're the only man on Earth who's attempted a Brightside Crossing and lived through it! And the story you cleared for the news—it was nothing. We need *details*. Where did your equipment fall down? Where did you miscalculate? What were the trouble spots?" Baron jabbed a finger at Claney's face. "That, for instance—epithelioma? Why? What was wrong with your glass? Your filters? We've got to know those things. If you can tell us, we can make it across where your attempt failed—"

"You want to know why we failed?" asked Claney.

"Of course we want to know. We *have* to know."

"It's simple. We failed because it can't be done. We couldn't do it and neither can you. No human beings will ever cross the Brightside alive, not if they try for centuries."

"Nonsense," Baron declared. "We will."

Claney shrugged. "I was there. I know what I'm saying. You can blame the equipment or the men—there were flaws in both quarters—but we just didn't know what we were fighting. It was the *planet* that whipped us, that and the *Sun*. They'll whip you, too, if you try it."

"Never," said Baron.

"Let me tell you," Peter Claney said.

I'd been interested in the Brightside for almost as long as I can remember (Claney said). I guess I was about ten when Wyatt and Carpenter made the last attempt—that was in 2082, I think. I followed the news stories like a tri-V serial and then I was heartbroken when they just disappeared.

I know now that they were a pair of idiots, starting off without proper equipment, with practically no knowledge of surface conditions, without any charts—they couldn't have made a hundred miles—but I didn't know that then and it was a terrible tragedy. After that, I followed Sanderson's work in the Twilight Lab up there and began to get Brightside into my blood, sure as death.

But it was Mikuta's idea to attempt a Crossing. Did you ever know Tom Mikuta? I don't suppose you did. No, not Japanese—Polish-American. He was a major in the Interplanetary Service for some years and hung onto the title after he gave up his commission.

He was with Armstrong on Mars during his Service days, did a good deal of the original mapping and surveying for the Colony there. I first met him on Venus; we spent five years together up there doing some of the nastiest exploring since the Matto Grasso. Then he made the attempt on Vulcan Crater that paved the way for Balmer a few years later.

I'd always liked the Major—he was big and quiet and cool, the sort of guy who always had things figured a little further ahead than anyone else and always knew what to do in a tight place. Too many men in this game are all nerve and luck, with no judgement. The Major had both. He also had the kind of personality that could take a crew of wild men and make them work like a well-oiled machine across a thousand miles of Venus jungle. I liked him and I trusted him.

He contacted me in New York and he was very casual at first. We spent an evening here at the Red Lion, talking about old times; he told me about the Vulcan business, and how he'd been out to see Sanderson and the Twilight Lab on Mercury, and how he preferred a hot trek to a cold one any day of the year—and then he wanted to know what I'd been doing since Venus and what my plans were.

"No particular plans," I told him. "Why?"

He looked me over. "How much do you weigh, Peter?"

I told him one-thirty-five.

"That much!" he said. "Well, there can't be much fat on you, at any rate. How do you take heat?"

"You should know," I said. "Venus was no icebox."

"No, I mean *real* heat."

Then I began to get it. "You're planning a trip."

"That's right. A hot trip." He grinned at me. "Might be dangerous, too."

"What trip?"

"Brightside of Mercury," the Major said.

I whistled cautiously. "At aphelion?"

He threw his head back. "Why try a Crossing at aphelion? What have you done then? Four thousand miles of butcherous heat, just to have some joker come along, use your data and drum you out of the glory by crossing at perihelion forty-four days later? No, thanks. I want the Brightside without any nonsense about it." He leaned across me eagerly. "I want to make a Crossing at perihelion and I want to cross on the surface. If a man can do that, he's got Mercury. Until then, *nobody's* got Mercury. I want Mercury—but I'll need help getting it."

I'd thought of it a thousand times and never dared consider it. Nobody had, since Wyatt and Carpenter disappeared. Mercury turns on its axis in the same time that it wheels around the Sun, which means that the Brightside is always facing in. That makes the Brightside of Mercury at perihelion the hottest place in the Solar System, with one single exception: the surface of the Sun itself.

It would be a hellish trek. Only a few men had ever learned just *how* hellish and they never came back to tell about it. It was a real hell's Crossing, but someday, I thought, somebody would cross it.

I wanted to be along.

The twilight lab, near the northern pole of Mercury, was the obvious jumping-off place. The setup there wasn't very extensive—a rocket landing, the labs and quarters for Sanderson's crew sunk deep into the crust, and the tower that housed the Solar 'scope that Sanderson had built up there ten years before.

Twilight Lab wasn't particularly interested in the Brightside, of course—the Sun was Sanderson's baby and he'd picked Mercury as the closest chunk of rock to the Sun that could hold his observatory. He'd chosen a good location, too. On Mercury, the Brightside temperature hits 77° F at perihelion and the Darkside runs pretty constant at −410° F. No permanent installation with a human crew could survive at either extreme. But with Mercury's wobble, the twilight zone between Brightside and Darkside offers something closer to survival temperatures.

Sanderson built the Lab up near the pole, where the zone is about five miles wide, so the temperature only varies 50 to 60 degrees with the libration. The Solar 'scope could take that much change and they'd get good clear observation of the Sun for about seventy out of the eighty-eight days it takes the planet to wheel around.

The Major was counting on Sanderson knowing something about Mercury as well as the Sun when we camped at the Lab to make final preparations.

Sanderson did. He thought we'd lost our minds and he said so, but he gave us all the help he could. He spent a week briefing Jack Stone, the third member of our party, who had arrived with the supplies and equipment a few days earlier. Poor Jack met us at the rocket landing almost bawling, Sanderson had given him such a gloomy picture of what Brightside was like.

Stone was a youngster—hardly twenty-five I'd say—but he'd been with the Major at Vulcan and had begged to join this trek. I had a funny feeling that Jack really didn't care for exploring too much, but he thought Mikuta was God, and followed him around like a puppy.

It didn't matter to me as long as he knew what he was getting in for. You don't go asking people in this game why they do it—they're liable to get awfully uneasy and none of them can ever give you an answer that makes sense. Anyway, Stone had borrowed three men from the Lab, and had the supplies and equipment all lined up when we got there, ready to check and test.

We dug right in. With plenty of funds—tri-V money and some government cash that Major had talked his way around—our equipment was new and good. Mikuta had done the designing and testing himself, with a big assist from Sanderson. We had four Bugs, three of them the light pillow-tire models, with special lead-cooled cut-in engines when the heat set in, and one heavy-duty tractor model for pulling the sledges.

The Major went over them like a kid at the circus. Then he said, "Have you heard anything from McIvers?"

"Who's he?" Stone wanted to know.

"He'll be joining us. He's a good man—got quite a name for climbing, back home." The Major turned to me. "You've probably heard of him."

I'd heard plenty of stories about Ted McIvers and I wasn't too happy to hear that he was joining us. "Kind of a daredevil, isn't he?"

"Maybe. He's lucky and skillful. Where do you draw the line? We'll need plenty of both."

"Have you ever worked with him?" I asked.

"No. Are you worried?"

"Not exactly. But Brightside is no place to count on luck."

The Major laughed. "I don't think we need to worry about McIvers. We understood each other when I talked up the trip to him and we're going to need each other too much to do any fooling around." He turned back to the supply list. "Meanwhile, let's get this stuff listed and packed. We'll need to cut weight sharply and our time is short. Sanderson says we should leave in three days."

Two days later, McIvers hadn't arrived. The Major didn't say much about it. Stone was getting edgy and so was I. We spent the second day studying charts of the Brightside, such as they were. The best available were pretty poor, taken from so far out that the detail dissolved into blurs on blow-up. They showed the biggest ranges of peaks and craters and faults and that was all. Still, we could use them to plan a broad outline of our course.

"This range here," the Major said as we crowded around the board, "is largely inactive, according to Sanderson. But these to the south and west *could* be active. Seismograph tracings suggest a lot of activity in that region, getting worse down toward the equator—not only volcanic, but sub-surface shifting."

Stone nodded. "Sanderson told me there was probably constant surface activity."

The Major shrugged. "Well, it's treacherous, there's no doubt of it. But the only way to avoid it is to travel over the Pole, which would lose us days and offer us no guarantee of less activity to the west. Now we might avoid some if we could find a pass through this range and cut sharp east—"

It seemed that the more we considered the problem, the further we got from a solution. We knew there were active volcanoes on the Brightside—even on the Darkside, though surface activity there was pretty much slowed down and localized.

But there were problems of atmosphere on Brightside, as well. There *was* an atmosphere and a constant atmospheric flow from Brightside to Darkside. Not much—the lighter gases had reached escape velocity and disappeared from Brightside millennia ago—but there was CO_2, and nitrogen, and traces of other heavier gases. There was also an abundance of sulfur vapor, as well as carbon disulfide and sulfur dioxide.

The atmospheric tide moved toward the Darkside, where it condensed, carrying enough volcanic ash with it for Sanderson to estimate the depth and nature of the surface upheavals on Brightside from his samplings. The trick was to find a passage that avoided those upheavals as far as possible. But in the final analysis, we were barely scraping the surface. The only way we would find out what was happening where, was to be there.

Finally, on the third day, McIvers blew in on a freight rocket from Venus. He'd missed the ship that the Major and I had taken by a few hours, and had conned his way to Venus in hopes of getting a hop from there. He didn't seem too upset about it, as though this were his usual way of doing things and he couldn't see why everyone should get so excited.

He was a tall, rangy man with long, wavy hair prematurely gray, and the sort of eyes that looked like a climber's—half-closed, sleepy, almost indolent, but capable of abrupt alertness. And he never stood still; he was always moving, always doing something with his hands, or talking, or pacing about.

Evidently the Major decided not to press the issue of his arrival. There was still work to do, and an hour later we were running the final tests on the pressure suits. That evening, Stone and McIvers were thick as thieves, and everything was set for an early departure after we got some rest.

"And that," said Baron, finishing his drink and signaling the waiter for another pair, "was your first big mistake."

Peter Claney raised his eyebrows. "McIvers?"

"Of course."

Claney shrugged, glanced at the small quiet tables around them. "There are lots of bizarre personalities around a place like this, and some of the best wouldn't seem to be the most reliable at first glance. Anyway, personality problems weren't our big problem right then. *Equipment* worried us first and *route* next."

Baron nodded in agreement. "What kind of suits did you have?"

"The best insulating suits ever made," said Claney. "Each one had an inner lining of a fibreglass modification, to avoid the clumsiness of asbestos, and carried the refrigerating unit and oxygen storage which we recharged from the sledges every eight hours. Outer layer carried a monomolecular chrome reflecting surface that made us glitter like Christmas trees. And we had a half-inch dead-air space under positive pressure between the two layers. Warning thermocouples, of course—at 770 degrees, it wouldn't take much time to fry us to cinders if the suits failed somewhere."

"How about the Bugs?"

"They were insulated, too, but we weren't counting on them too much for protection."

"You weren't!" Baron exclaimed. "Why not?"

"We'd be in and out of them too much. They gave us mobility and storage, but we knew we'd have to do a lot of forward work on foot." Claney smiled bitterly. "Which meant that we had an inch of figreglass and a half-inch of dead air between us and a surface temperature where lead flowed like water and zinc was almost at melting point and the pools of sulfur in the shadows were boiling like oatmeal over a campfire."

Baron licked his lips. His fingers stroked the cool, wet glass as he set it down on the tablecloth.

"Go on," he said tautly. "You started on schedule?"

"Oh, yes," said Claney, "we started on schedule, all

right. We just didn't quite end on schedule, that was all. But I'm getting to that."

He settled back in his chair and continued.

We jumped off from Twilight on a course due southeast with thirty days to make it to the Center of Brightside. If we could cross an average of seventy miles a day, we could hit Center exactly at perihelion, the point of Mercury's closest approach to the Sun—which made Center the hottest part of the planet at the hottest it every gets.

The Sun was already huge and yellow over the horizon when we started, twice the size it appears on Earth. Every day that Sun would grow bigger and whiter, and every day the surface would get hotter. But once we reached Center, the job was only half done—we would still have to travel another two thousand miles to the opposite twilight zone. Sanderson was to meet us on the other side in the Laboratory's scout ship, approximately sixty days from the time we jumped off.

That was the plan, in outline. It was up to us to cross those seventy miles a day, no matter how hot it became, no matter what terrain we had to cross. Detours would be dangerous and time-consuming. Delays could cost us our lives. We all knew that.

The Major briefed us on details an hour before we left. "Peter, you'll take the lead Bug, the small one we stripped down for you. Stone and I will flank you on either side, giving you a hundred-yard lead. McIvers, you'll have the job of dragging the sledges, so we'll have to direct your course pretty closely. Peter's job is to pick the passage at any given point. If there's any doubt of safe passage, we'll all explore ahead on foot before we risk the Bugs. Got that?"

McIvers and Stone exchanged glances. McIvers said: "Jack and I were planning to change around. We figured he could take the sledges. That would give me a little more mobility."

The Major looked up sharply at Stone. "Do you buy that, Jack?"

Stone shrugged. "I don't mind. Mac wanted—"

McIvers made an impatient gesture with his hands. "It doesn't matter. I just feel better when I'm on the move. Does it make any difference?"

"I guess it doesn't," said the Major. "Then you'll flank Peter along with me. Right?"

"Sure, sure." McIvers pulled at his lower lip. "Who's going to do the advance scouting?"

"It sounds like I am," I cut in. "We want to keep the lead Bug light as possible."

Mikuta nodded. "That's right. Peter's Bug is stripped down to the frame and wheels."

McIvers shook his head. "No, I mean the *advance* work. You need somebody out ahead—four or five miles, at least—to pick up the big flaws and active surface changes, don't you?" He stared at the Major. "I mean, how can we tell what sort of a hole we may be moving into, unless we have a scout up ahead?"

"That's what we have the charts for," the Major said sharply.

"Charts! I'm talking about *detail* work. We don't need to worry about the major topography. It's the little faults you can't see on the pictures that can kill us." He tossed the charts down excitedly. "Look, let me take a Bug out ahead and work reconnaissance, keep five, maybe ten miles ahead of the column. I can stay on good solid ground, of course, but scan the area closely and radio back to Peter where to avoid the flaws. Then—"

"No dice," the Major broke in.

"But why not? We could save ourselves days!"

"I don't care what we could save. We stay together. When we get to the Center, I want live men along with me. That means we stay within easy sight of each other at all times. Any climber knows that everybody is safer in a party than one man alone—any time, any place."

McIvers stared at him, his cheeks an angry red. Finally he gave a sullen nod. "Okay. If you say so."

"Well, I say so and I mean it. I don't want any fancy stuff. We're going to hit Center together and finish the Crossing together. Got that?"

McIvers nodded. Mikuta then looked at Stone and me and we nodded, too.

"All right," he said slowly. "Now that we've got it straight, let's go."

It was hot. If I forget everything else about that trek, I'll never forget that huge yellow Sun glaring down, without a break, hotter and hotter with every mile. We knew that the first few days would be the easiest and we were rested and fresh when we started down the long ragged gorge southeast of the Twilight Lab.

I moved out first; back over my shoulder, I could see the Major and McIvers crawling out behind me, their pillow tires taking the rugged floor of the gorge smoothly. Behind them, Stone dragged the sledges.

Even at only 30 per cent Earth gravity they were a strain on the big tractor, until the ski-blades bit into the fluffy volcanic ash blanketing the valley. We even had a path to follow for the first twenty miles.

I kept my eyes pasted to the big polaroid binocs, picking out the track the early research teams had made out into the edge of Brightside. But in a couple of hours we rumbled past Sanderson's little outpost observatory and the tracks stopped. We were in virgin territory and already the Sun was beginning to bite.

We didn't *feel* the heat so much those first days out. We *saw* it. The refrig units kept our skins at a nice comfortable seventy-five degrees Fahrenheit inside our suits, but our eyes watched that glaring Sun and the baked yellow rocks going past, and some nerve pathways got twisted up, somehow. We poured sweat as if we were in a superheated furnace.

We drove eight hours and slept five. When a sleep period came due, we pulled the Bugs together into a square, threw up a light aluminium sun-shield and lay out in the dust and rocks. The sun-shield cut the temperature down sixty or seventy degrees, for whatever help that was. And then we ate from the forward sledge—sucking through tubes—protein, carbohydrates, bulk gelatin, vitamins.

The Major measured water out with an iron hand, because we'd have drunk ourselves into nephritis in a week otherwise. We were constantly, unceasingly thirsty. Ask the physiologists and psychiatrists why—they can give you half a dozen interesting reasons—but all we knew, or cared about, was that it happened to be so.

We didn't sleep the first few stops, as a consequence. Our eyes burned in spite of the filters and we had roaring headaches, but we couldn't sleep them off. We sat around looking at each other. Then McIvers would say how good a beer would taste, and off we'd go. We'd have murdered our grandmothers for one ice-cold bottle of beer.

After a few driving periods, I began to get my bearings at the wheel. We were moving down into desolation that made Earth's old Death Valley look like a Japanese rose garden. Huge sun-baked cracks opened up in the floor of the gorge, with black cliffs jutting up on either side; the air was filled with a barely visible yellowish mist of sulfur and sulfurous gases.

It was a hot, barren hole, no place for any man to go, but the challenge was so powerful you could almost feel it. No one had ever crossed this land before and escaped. Those who had tried it had been cruelly punished, but the land was still there, so it had to be crossed. Not the easy way. It had to be crossed the hardest way possible: overland, through anything the land could throw up to us, at the most difficult time possible.

Yet we knew that even the land might have been conquered before, except for that Sun. We'd fought absolute cold before and won. We'd never fought heat like this and won. The only worse heat in the Solar System was the surface of the Sun itself.

Brightside was worth trying for. We would get it or it would get us. That was the bargain.

I learned a lot about Mercury those first few driving periods. The gorge petered out after a hundred miles and we moved onto the slope of a range of ragged craters that ran south and east. This range had shown no activity since the first landing on Mercury forty years before, but beyond it there were active cones. Yellow fumes rose from the craters constantly; their sides were shrouded with heavy ash.

We couldn't detect a wind, but we knew there was a hot, sulfurous breeze sweeping in great continental tides across the face of the planet. Not enough for erosion, though. The craters rose up out of jagged gorges, huge towering spears of rock and rubble. Below were the vast yellow flatlands, smoking and hissing from the gases beneath the crust. Over everything was gray dust—silicates and salts, pumice and limestone and granite ash, filling crevices and declivities—offering a soft, treacherous surface for the Bug's pillow tires.

I learned to read the ground, to tell a covered fault by the sag of the dust; I learned to spot a passable crack, and tell it from an impassible cut. Time after time the Bugs ground to a halt while we explored a passage on foot, tied together with light copper cable, digging, advancing, digging some more until we were sure the surface would carry the machines. It was cruel work; we slept in exhaustion. But it went smoothly, at first.

Too smoothly, it seemed to me, and the others seemed to think so, too.

McIvers' restlessness was beginning to grate on our nerves. He talked too much, while we were resting or while we were driving; wisecracks, witticisms, unfunny jokes that wore thin with repetition. He took to making side trips from the route now and then, never far, but a little further each time.

Jack Stone reacted quite the opposite; he grew quieter with each stop, more reserved and apprehensive. I didn't like it, but I figured that it would pass off after a while. I was apprehensive enough myself; I just managed to hide it better.

And every mile the Sun got bigger and whiter and higher in the sky and hotter. Without our ultra-violet screens and glare filters we would have been blinded; as it was our eyes ached constantly and the skin on our faces itched and tingled at the end of an eight-hour trek.

But it took one of those side trips of McIvers' to deliver the penultimate blow to our already fraying nerves. He had driven down a side-branch of a long canyon running off west of our route and was almost out of sight in a cloud of ash when we heard a sharp cry through our earphones.

I wheeled my Bug around with my heart in my throat and spotted him through the binocs, waving frantically from the top of his machine. The Major and I took off, lumbering down the gulch after him as fast as the Bugs could go, with a thousand horrible pictures racing through our minds . . .

We found him standing stock-still, pointing down the gorge and, for once, he didn't have anything to say. It was the wreck of a Bug; an old-fashioned half-track model of the sort that hadn't been in use for years. It was wedged tight in a cut in the rock, an axle broken, its casing split wide open up the middle, half-buried in a rock slide. A dozen feet away were two insulated suits with white bones gleaming through the fibreglass helmets.

This was as far as Wyatt and Carpenter had gotten on *their* Brightside Crossing.

On the fifth driving period out, the terrain began to change. It looked the same, but every now and then it *felt* different. On two occasions I felt my wheels spin, with a howl of protest from my engine. Then, quite suddenly, the Bug gave a lurch; I gunned my motor and nothing happened.

I could see the dull gray stuff seeping up around the hubs, thick and tenacious, splattering around in steaming gobs as the wheels spun. I knew what had happened the moment the wheel gave and, a few minutes later, they chained me to the tractor and dragged me back out of the mire. It looked for all the world like thick gray mud, but it was a pit of molten lead, steaming under a soft layer of concealing ash.

I picked my way more cautiously then. We were getting into an area of recent surface activity; the surface was really treacherous. I caught myself wishing that the Major had okayed McIvers' scheme for an advanced scout; more dangerous for the individual, maybe, but I was driving blind now and I didn't like it.

One error in judgement could sink us all, but I wasn't thinking much about the others. I was worried about *me*, plenty worried. I kept thinking, better McIvers should go than me. It wasn't healthy thinking and I knew it, but I couldn't get the thought out of my mind.

It was a grueling eight hours and we slept poorly. Back in the Bug again, we moved still more slowly—edging out on a broad flat plateau, dodging a network of gaping surface cracks—winding back and forth in an effort to keep the machines on solid rock. I couldn't see far ahead, because of the yellow haze rising from the cracks, so I was almost on top of it when I saw a sharp cut ahead where the surface dropped six feet beyond a deep crack.

I let out a shout to halt the others; then I edged my Bug forward, peering at the cleft. It was deep and wide. I moved fifty yards to the left, then back to the right.

There was only one place that looked like a possible crossing; a long, narrow ledge of gray stuff that lay down across a section of the fault like a ramp. Even as I watched it, I could feel the surface crust under the Bug trembling and saw the ledge shift over a few feet.

The Major's voice sounded in my ears. "How about it, Peter?"

"I don't know. This crust is on roller skates," I called back.

"How about that ledge?"

I hesitated. "I'm scared of it, Major. Let's backtrack and try to find a way around."

There was a roar of disgust in my earphones and McIvers' Bug suddenly lurched forward. It rolled down past me, picked up speed, with McIvers hunched behind the wheel like a race driver. He was heading past me straight for the gray ledge.

My shout caught in my throat; I heard the Major take a huge breath and roar: "Mac! *Stop that thing,* you fool!" and then McIvers' Bug was out on the ledge, lumbering across like a juggernaut.

The ledge jolted as the tires struck it; for a horrible moment, it seemed to be sliding out from under the machine. And then the Bug was across in a cloud of dust, and I heard McIvers' voice in my ears, shouting in glee. "Come on, you slowpokes. It'll hold you!"

Something unprintable came through the earphones as the Major drew up alongside me and moved his Bug out on the ledge slowly and over to the other side. Then he said, "Take it slow, Peter. Then give Jack a hand with the sledges." His voice sounded tight as a wire.

Ten minutes later, we were on the other side of the cleft. The Major checked the whole column; then he turned on McIvers angrily. "One more trick like that," he said, "and I'll strap you to a rock and leave you. Do you understand me? *One more time—*"

McIvers' voice was heavy with protest. "Good Lord, if we leave it up to Claney, he'll have us out here forever! Any blind fool could see that that ledge would hold."

"*I* saw it moving," I shot back at him.

"All right, all right, so you've got good eyes. Why all the fuss? We got across, didn't we? But I say we've got to have a little nerve and use it once in a while if we're ever going to get across this lousy hotbox."

"We need to use a little judgement, too," the Major snapped. "All right, let's roll. But if you think I was joking, you just try me out once." He let it soak in for a minute. Then he geared his Bug on around to my flank again.

At the stopover, the incident wasn't mentioned again, but the Major drew me aside just as I was settling down for sleep. "Peter, I'm worried," he said slowly.

"McIvers? Don't worry. He's not as reckless as he seems—just impatient. We are over a hundred miles behind schedule and we're moving awfully slow. We only made forty miles this last drive."

The Major shook his head. "I don't mean McIvers. I mean the kid."

"Jack? What about him?"

"Take a look."

Stone was shaking. He was over near the tractor—away from the rest of us—and he was lying on his back, but he wasn't asleep. His whole body was shaking, convulsively. I saw him grip an outcropping of rock hard.

I walked over and sat down beside him. "Get your water all right?" I said.

He didn't answer. He just kept on shaking.

"Hey, boy," I said. "What's the trouble?"

"It's hot," he said, choking out the words.

"Sure it's hot, but don't let it throw you. We're in really good shape."

"We're not," he snapped. "We're in rotten shape, if you ask me. *We're not going to make it,* do you know that? That crazy fool's going to kill us for sure—" All of a sudden, he was bawling like a baby. "I'm scared—I shouldn't be here—I'm *scared.* What am I trying to prove by coming out here, for God's sake? I'm some kind of hero or something? I tell you I'm scared—"

"Look," I said. "Mikuta's scared, *I'm* scared. So what? We'll make it, don't worry. And nobody's trying to be a hero."

"Nobody but Hero Stone," he said bitterly. He shook himself and gave a tight little laugh. "Some hero, eh?"

"We'll make it," I said.

"Sure," he said finally. "Sorry. I'll be okay."

I rolled over, but waited until he was good and quiet. Then I tried to sleep, but I didn't sleep too well. I kept thinking about that ledge. I'd known from the look of it what it was; a zinc slough of the sort Sanderson had warned us about, a wide sheet of almost pure zinc that had been thrown up white-hot from below, quite recently, just waiting for oxygen or sulfur to rot it through.

I knew enough about zinc to know that at these temperatures it gets brittle as glass. Take a chance like McIvers had taken and the whole sheet could snap like a dry pine board. And it wasn't McIvers' fault that it hadn't.

Five hours later, we were back at the wheel. We were hardly moving at all. The ragged surface was almost impassable—great jutting rocks peppered the plateau; ledges crumbled the moment my tires touched them; long, open canyons turned into lead-mires or sulfur pits.

A dozen times I climbed out of the Bug to prod out an uncertain area with my boots and pikestaff. Whenever I did, McIvers piled out behind me, running ahead like a schoolboy at the fair, then climbing back again red-faced and panting, while we moved the machines ahead another mile or two.

Time was pressing us now and McIvers wouldn't let me forget it. We had made only about three hundred twenty miles in six driving periods, so we were about a hundred miles or even more behind schedule.

"We're not going to make it," McIvers would complain angrily. "That Sun's going to be out to aphelion by the time we hit the Center—"

"Sorry, but I can't take it any faster," I told him. I was getting good and mad. I knew what he wanted, but didn't dare let him have it. I was scared enough pushing the Bug out on those ledges, even knowing that at least *I* was making the decisions. Put him in the lead and we wouldn't last for eight hours. Our nerves wouldn't take it, at any rate, even if the machines would.

Jack Stone looked up from the aluminium chart sheets. "Another hundred miles and we should hit a good stretch," he said. "Maybe we can make up distance there for a couple of days."

The Major agreed, but McIvers couldn't hold his impatience. He kept staring up at the Sun as if he had a personal grudge against it and stamped back and forth under the sun-shield. "That'll be just fine," he said. "*If* we ever get that far that is."

We dropped it there, but the Major stopped me as we climbed aboard for the next run. "That guy's going to blow wide open if we don't move faster, Peter. I don't want him in the lead, no matter what happens. He's right though, about the need to make better time. Keep your head, but crowd your luck a little, okay?"

"I'll try," I said. It was asking the impossible and Mikuta knew it. We were on a long downward slope that shifted and buckled all around us, as though there were a molten underlay beneath the crust; the slope was broken by huge crevasses, partly covered with dust and zinc sheeting, like a vast glacier of stone and metal. The outside temperature registered 547° F and getting hotter. It was no place to start rushing ahead.

I tried it anyway. I took half a dozen shaky passages, edging slowly out on flat zinc ledges, then toppling over and across. It seemed easy for a while and we made progress. We hit an even stretch and raced ahead. And then I quickly jumped on my brakes and jerked the Bug to a halt in a cloud of dust.

I'd gone too far. We were out on a wide, flat sheet of gray stuff, apparently solid—until I'd suddenly caught sight of the crevasse beneath in the corner of my eye. It was an overhanging shelf that trembled under me as I stopped.

McIvers' voice was in my ear. "What's the trouble now, Claney?"

"Move back!" I shouted. "It can't hold us!"

"Looks solid enough from here."

"You want to argue about it? It's too thin, it'll snap. Move back!"

I started edging back down the ledge. I heard McIvers swear; then I saw his Bug start to creep *outward* on the shelf. Not fast or reckless, this time, but slowly, churning up dust in a gentle cloud behind him.

I just stared and felt the blood rush to my head. It seemed so hot I could hardly breathe as he edged out beyond me, further and further—

I think I felt it snap before I saw it. My own machine gave a sickening lurch and a long black crack appeared across the shelf—and widened. Then the ledge began to upend. I heard a scream as McIvers' Bug rose up and up and then crashed down into the crevasse in a thundering slide of rock and shattered metal.

I just stared for a full minute, I think. I couldn't move

until I heard Jack Stone groan and the Major shouting, "Claney! I couldn't see—what *happened?*"

"It snapped on him, that's what happened," I roared. I gunned my motor, edged forward toward the fresh broken edge of the shelf. The crevasse gaped; I couldn't see any sign of the machine. Dust was still billowing up blindingly from below.

We stood staring down, the three of us. I caught a glimpse of Jack Stone's face through his helmet. It wasn't pretty.

"Well," said the Major heavily, "that's that."

"I guess so." I felt the way Stone looked.

"Wait," said Stone. "I heard something."

He had. It was a cry in the earphones—faint, but unmistakable.

"Mac!" The Major called. "Mac, can you hear me?"

"Yeah, yeah. I can hear you." The voice was very weak.

"Are you all right?"

"I don't know. Broken leg, I think. It's—hot." There was a long pause. Then: "I think my cooler's gone out."

The Major shot me a glance, then turned to Stone. "Get a cable from the second sledge fast. He'll fry alive if we don't get him out of there. Peter, I need you to lower me. Use the tractor winch."

I lowered him; he stayed down only a few moments. When I hauled him up, his face was drawn. "Still alive," he panted. "He won't be very long, though." He hesitated for just an instant. "We've got to make a try."

"I don't like this ledge," I said. "It's moved twice since I got out. Why not back off and lower him a cable?"

"No good. The Bug is smashed and he's inside it. We'll need torches and I'll need one of you to help." He looked at me and then gave Stone a long look. "Peter, you'd better come."

"Wait," said Stone. His face was very white. "Let me go down with you."

"Peter is lighter."

"I'm not so heavy. Let me go down."

"Okay, if that's the way you want it." The Major tossed him a torch. "Peter, check these hitches and lower us slowly. If you see any kind of trouble, *anything,* cast yourself free and back off this thing, do you understand? This whole ledge may go."

I nodded. "Good luck."

They went over the ledge. I let the cable down bit by bit until it hit two hundred feet and slacked off.

"How does it look?" I shouted.

"Bad," said the Major. "We'll have to work fast. This whole side of the crevasse is ready to crumble. Down a little more."

Minutes passed without a sound. I tried to relax, but I couldn't. Then I felt the ground shift, and the tractor lurched to the side.

The Major shouted, *"It's going, Peter—pull back!"* and I threw the tractor into reverse, jerked the controls as the tractor rumbled off the shelf. The cable snapped, coiled up in front like a broken clockspring. The whole surface under me was shaking wildly now; ash rose in huge gray clouds. Then, with a roar, the whole shelf lurched and slid sideways. It teetered on the edge for seconds before it crashed into the crevasse, tearing the side wall down with it in a mammoth slide. I jerked the tractor to a halt as the dust and flame billowed up.

They were gone—all three of them, McIvers and the Major and Jack Stone—buried under a thousand tons of rock and zinc and molten lead. There wasn't any danger of anybody ever finding their bones.

Peter Claney leaned back, finishing his drink, rubbing his scarred face as he looked across at Baron.

Slowly, Baron's grip relaxed on the chair arm. *"You* got back," he said.

Claney nodded. "I got back, sure. I had the tractor and the sledges. I had seven days to drive back under that yellow Sun. I had plenty of time to think."

"You took the wrong man along," Baron said. "That was your mistake. Without him you would have made it."

"Never." Claney shook his head. "That's what I was thinking the first day or so—that it was *McIvers'* fault, that *he* was to blame. But that isn't true. He was wild, reckless and had lots of nerve."

"But his judgement was bad!"

"It couldn't have been sounder. We had to keep to our

schedule even if it killed us, because it would positively kill us if we didn't."

"But a man like that—"

"A man like McIvers was necessary. Can't you see that? It was the Sun that beat us, that surface. Perhaps we were licked that very day we started." Claney leaned across the table, his eyes pleading. "We didn't realize that, but it was *true*. There are places that men can't go, conditions men can't tolerate. The others had to die to learn that. I was lucky, I came back. But I'm trying to tell you what I found out—that *nobody* will ever make a Brightside Crossing."

"We will," said Baron. "It won't be a picnic, but we'll make it."

"But suppose you do," said Claney, suddenly. "Suppose I'm all wrong, suppose you *do* make it. Then what? *What comes next?*"

"The Sun," said Baron.

Claney nodded slowly. "Yes. That would be it, wouldn't it?" He laughed. "Good-by, Baron. Jolly talk and all that. Thanks for listening."

Baron caught his wrist as he started to rise. "Just one question more, Claney. Why did you come here?"

"To try to talk you out of killing yourself," said Claney.

"You're a liar," said Baron.

Claney stared down at him for a long moment. Then he crumpled in the chair. There was defeat in his pale blue eyes and something else.

"Well?"

Peter Claney spread his hands, a helpless gesture. "When do you leave, Baron? I want you to take me along."

The Sack was the System's most valuable possession—or else the most serious menace. It could correctly answer any question, and the answers were frequently the wrong ones. And anything like that was an impossibly explosive situation!

THE SACK

by William Morrison

At first they hadn't even known that the Sack existed. If they had noticed it at all when they landed on the asteroid, they thought of it merely as one more outpost of rock on the barren expanse of roughly ellipsoidal silicate surface, which Captain Ganko noticed had major and minor axes roughly three and two miles in diameter respectively. It would never have entered anyone's mind that the unimpressive object they had unconsciously acquired would soon be regarded as the most valuable prize in the System.

The landing had been accidental. The Government Patrol ship had been limping along, and now it had settled down for repairs, which would take a good seventy hours. Fortunately, they had plenty of air, and their recirculation system worked to perfection. Food was in somewhat short supply, but it didn't worry them, for they knew that they could always tighten their belts and do without full rations for a few days. The loss of water that had resulted from a leak in the storage tanks, however, was a more serious matter. It occupied a good part of their conversation during the next fifty hours.

Captain Ganko said finally, "There's no use talking, it won't be enough. And there are no supply stations close enough at hand to be of any use. We'll have to radio ahead and hope that they can get a rescue ship to us with a reserve supply."

The helmet mike of his next in command seemed to

droop. "It'll be too bad if we miss each other in space, captain."

Captain Ganko laughed unhappily. "It certainly will. In that case we'll have a chance to see how we can stand a little dehydration."

For a time nobody said anything. At last, however, the Second Mate suggested, "There might be water somewhere on the asteroid, sir."

"Here? How in Pluto would it stick, with a gravity that isn't even strong enough to hold loose rocks? And where the devil would it be?"

"To answer the first question first, it would be retained as water of crystallization," replied a soft liquid voice that seemed to penetrate his spacesuit and come from behind him. "To answer the second question, it is half a dozen feet below the surface, and can easily be reached by digging."

They had all swiveled around at the first words. But no one was in sight in the direction from which the words seemed to come. Captain Ganko frowned, and his eyes narrowed dangerously. "We don't happen to have a practical joker with us, do we?" he asked mildly.

"You do not," replied the voice.

"Who said that?"

"I, Yzrl."

A crewman became aware of something moving on the surface of one of the great rocks, and pointed to it. The motion stopped when the voice ceased, but they didn't lose sight of it again. That was how they learned about Yzrl, or as it was more often called, the Mind-Sack.

If the ship and his services hadn't both belonged to the Government, Captain Ganko could have claimed the Sack for himself or his owners and retired with a wealth far beyond his dreams. As it was, the thing passed into Government control. Its importance was realized almost from the first, and Jake Siebling had reason to be proud when more important and more influential figures of the political and industrial world were finally passed over and he was made Custodian of the Sack. Siebling was a short, stocky man whose one weakness was self-deprecation. He had carried out one difficult assignment after another and allowed other men to take the credit. But this job was not one for a blowhard, and those in charge of making the appointment knew it. For once they looked beyond credit and superficial reputation, and chose an individual they disliked somewhat, but trusted absolutely. It was one of the most effective tributes to honesty and ability ever devised.

The Sack, as Siebling learned from seeing it daily, rarely deviated from the form in which it had made its first appearance—a rocky, grayish lump that roughly resembled a sack of potatoes. It had no features, and there was nothing, when it was not being asked questions, that might indicate that it had life. It ate rarely—once in a thousand years, it said, when left to itself; once a week when it was pressed into steady use. It ate or moved by fashioning a suitable pseudopod, and stretching the thing out in whatever way it pleased. When it had attained its objective, the pseudopod was withdrawn into the main body again, and the creature became once more a potato sack.

It turned out later that the name, "Sack," was well chosen from another point of view, in addition to that of appearance. For the Sack was stuffed with information, and beyond that, with wisdom. There were many doubters at first, and some of them retained their doubts to the very end, just as some people remained convinced hundreds of years after Columbus that the Earth was flat. But those who saw and heard the Sack had no doubts at all. They tended, if anything, to go too far in the other direction, and to believe that the Sack knew everything. This, of course, was untrue.

It was the official function of the Sack, established by a series of Interplanetary Acts, to answer questions. The first questions, as we have seen, were asked accidentally, by Captain Ganko. Later they were asked purposefully, but with a purpose that was itself random, and a few politicians managed to acquire considerable wealth before the Government put a stop to the leak of information, and tried to have the questions asked in a more scientific and logical manner.

Question time was rationed for months in advance, and sold at what was, all things considered, a ridiculously low rate—a mere hundred thousand credits a minute. It was this unrestricted sale of time that led to the first great Government squabble.

It was the unexpected failure of the Sack to answer what must have been to a mind of its ability an easy question that led to the second blow-up, which was fierce enough to be called a crisis. A total of a hundred and twenty questioners, each of whom had paid his hundred thousand, raised a howl that could be heard on every planet, and there was a legislative investigation, at which Siebling testified, and all the conflicts were aired.

He had left an assistant in charge of the Sack, and now, as he sat before the Senatorial Committee, he twisted uncomfortably in front of the battery of cameras. Senator Horrigan, his chief interrogator, was a bluff, florid, loud-mouthed politician who had been able to imbue him with a feeling of guilt even as he told his name, age, and length of government service.

"It is your duty to see to it that the Sack is maintained in proper condition for answering questions, is it not, Mr. Siebling?" demanded Senator Horrigan.

"Yes, sir."

"Then why was it incapable of answering the questioners in question? These gentlemen had honestly paid their money—a hundred thousand credits each. It was necessary, I understand, to refund the total sum. That meant an overall loss to the Government of, let me see, now—one hundred and twenty million credits," he shouted, rolling the words.

"Twelve million, senator," hastily whispered his secretary.

The correction was not made, and the figure was duly headlined later as one hundred and twenty million.

Siebling said, "As we discovered later, senator, the Sack failed to answer questions because it was not a machine, but a living creature. It was exhausted. It had been exposed to questioning on a twenty-four-hour-a-day basis."

"And who permitted this idiotic procedure?" boomed Senator Horrigan.

"You yourself, senator," said Siebling happily. "The procedure was provided for in the bill introduced by you and approved by your committee."

Senator Horrigan had never even read the bill to which his name was attached, and he was certainly not to blame for its provisions. But this private knowledge of his own innocence did him no good with the public. From that moment he was Siebling's bitter enemy.

"So the Sack ceased to answer questions for two whole hours?"

"Yes, sir. It resumed only after a rest."

"And it answered then without further difficulty?"

"No, sir. Its response was slowed down. Subsequently questioners complained that they were defrauded of a good part of their money. But as answers *were* given, we considered that the complaints were without merit, and the financial department refused to make refunds."

"Do you consider that this cheating of investors in the Sack's time is honest?"

"That's none of my business, senator," returned Siebling, who had by this time got over most of his nervousness. "I merely see to the execution of the laws. I leave the question of honesty to those who make them. I presume that it's in perfectly good hands."

Senator Horrigan flushed at the laughter that came from the onlookers. He was personally unpopular, as unpopular as a politician can be and still remain a politician. He was disliked even by the members of his own party, and some of his best political friends were among the laughers. He decided to abandon what had turned out to be an unfortunate line of questioning.

"It is a matter of fact, Mr. Siebling, is it not, that you have frequently refused admittance to investors who were able to show perfectly valid receipts for their credits?"

"That is a fact, sir. But—"

"You admit it, then."

"There is no question of 'admitting' anything, senator. What I meant to say was—"

"Never mind what you meant to say. It's what you have already said that's important. You've cheated these men of their money!"

"That is not true, sir. They were given time later. The reason for my refusal to grant them admission when they asked for it was that the time had been previously reserved for the Armed Forces. There are important research questions that come up, and there is, as you know, a difference of opinion as to priority. When confronted with requisitions for time from a commercial investor and a representative of the Government, I never took it upon myself to settle the question. I always consulted with the Government's legal adviser."

"So you refused to make an independent decision, did you?"

"My duty, senator, is to look after the welfare of the Sack. I do not concern myself with political questions. We had a moment of free time the day before I left the asteroid, when an investor who had already paid his money was delayed by a space accident, so instead of letting the moment go to waste, I utilized it to ask the Sack a question."

"How you might advance your own fortunes, no doubt?"

"No, sir. I merely asked it how it might function most efficiently. I took the precaution of making a recording, knowing that my word might be doubted. If you wish, senator, I can introduce the recording in evidence."

Senator Horrigan grunted, and waved his hand. "Go on with your answer."

"The Sack replied that it would require two hours of complete rest out of every twenty, plus an additional hour of what it called 'recreation.' That is, it wanted to converse with some human being who would ask what it called sensible questions, and not press for a quick answer."

"So you suggest that the Government waste three hours of every twenty—one hundred and eighty million credits?"

"Eighteen million," whispered the secretary.

"The time would not be wasted. Any attempt to overwork the Sack would result in its premature annihilation."

"That is your idea, is it?"

"No, sir, that is what the Sack itself said."

At this point, Senator Horrigan swung into a speech of denunciation, and Siebling was excused from further testimony. Other witnesses were called, but at the end the Senate Investigating body was able to come to no definite conclusion, and it was decided to interrogate the Sack personally.

It was out of the question for the Sack to come to the Senate, so the Senate quite naturally came to the Sack. The Committee of Seven was manifestly uneasy as the senatorial ship decelerated and cast its grapples toward the asteroid. The members, as individuals, had all traveled in space before, but all their previous destinations had been in civilized territory, and they obviously did not relish the prospect of landing on this airless and sunless body of rock.

The televisor companies were alert to their opportunity, and they had acquired more experience with desert territory. They had disembarked and set up their apparatus before the senators had taken their first timid steps out of the safety of their ship.

Siebling noted ironically that in these somewhat frightening surroundings, far from their home grounds, the senators were not so sure of themselves. It was his part to act the friendly guide, and he did so with relish.

"You see, gentlemen," he said respectfully, "it was decided, on the Sack's own advice, not to permit it to be further exposed to possible collision with stray meteors. It was the meteors which had killed off the other members of its strange race, and it was a lucky chance that the last surviving individual had managed to escape destruction as long as it had. An impenetrable shelter dome has been built therefore, and the Sack now lives under its protection. Questioners address it through a sound and sight system that is almost as good as being face to face with it."

Senator Horrigan fastened upon the significant part of his statement. "You mean that the Sack is safe—and *we* are exposed to danger from flying meteors?"

"Naturally, senator. The Sack is unique in the System. Men—even senators—are, if you will excuse the expression, a deci-credit a dozen. They are definitely replaceable, by means of elections."

Beneath his helmet the senator turned green with a fear that concealed the scarlet of his anger. "I think it is an outrage to find the Government so unsolicitous of the safety and welfare of its employees!"

"So do I, sir. I live here the year round." He added smoothly, "Would you gentlemen care to see the Sack now?"

They stared at the huge visor screen and saw the Sack resting on its seat before them, looking like a burlap bag of potatoes which had been tossed onto a throne and forgotten there. It looked so definitely inanimate that it struck them as strange that the thing should remain upright instead of toppling over. All the same, for a moment the senators could not help showing the awe that overwhelmed them. Even Senator Horrigan was silent.

But the moment passed. He said, "Sir, we are an official Investigating Committee of the Interplanetary Senate, and we have come to ask you a few questions." The Sack showed no desire to reply, and Senator Horrigan cleared his throat and went on. "Is it true, sir, that you require two hours of complete rest in every twenty, and one hour for recreation, or, as I may put it, perhaps more precisely, relaxation?"

"It is true."

Senator Horrigan gave the creature its chance, but the Sack, unlike a senator, did not elaborate. Another of the Committee asked, "Where would you find an individual capable of conversing intelligently with so wise a creature as you?"

"Here," replied the Sack.

"It is necessary to ask questions that are directly to the point, senator," suggested Siebling. "The Sack does not usually volunteer information that has not been specifically called for."

Senator Horrigan said quickly, "I assume, sir, that when you speak of finding an intelligence on a par with your own, you refer to a member of our committee, and I am sure that of all my colleagues, there is not one who is unworthy of being so denominated. But we cannot all of us spare the time needed for our manifold other duties, so I wish to ask you, sir, which of us, in your opinion, has the peculiar qualifications of that sort of wisdom which is required for this great task?"

"None," said the Sack.

Senator Horrigan looked blank. One of the other senators flushed, and asked, "Who has?"

"Siebling."

Senator Horrigan forgot his awe of the Sack, and shouted, "This is a put-up job!"

The other senator who had just spoken now said suddenly, "How is it that there are no other questioners present? Hasn't the Sack's time been sold far in advance?"

Siebling nodded. "I was ordered to cancel all previous appointments with the Sack, sir."

"By what idiot's orders?"

"Senator Horrigan's, sir."

At this point the investigation might have been said to come to an end. There was just time, before they turned away, for Senator Horrigan to demand desperately of the Sack, "Sir, will I be re-elected?" But the roar of anger that went up from his colleagues prevented him from hearing the Sack's answer, and only the question was picked up, and broadcast clearly over the interplanetary network.

It had such an effect that it in itself provided Senator Horrigan's answer. He was *not* re-elected. But before the election, he had time to cast his vote against Siebling's designation to talk with the Sack for one hour out of every twenty. The final Committee vote was four to three in favor of Siebling, and the decision was confirmed by the Senate. And then Senator Horrigan passed temporarily out of the Sack's life and out of Siebling's.

Siebling looked forward with some trepidation to his first long interview with the Sack. Hitherto he had limited himself to the simple tasks provided for in his directives—to the maintenance of the meteor shelter dome, to the provision of a sparse food supply, and to the proper placement of an Army and Space Fleet Guard. For by this time the great value of the Sack had been recognized throughout the System, and it was widely realized that there would be thousands of criminals anxious to steal so defenseless a treasure.

Now, Siebling thought, he would be obliged to talk to it, and he feared that he would lose the good opinion which it had somehow acquired of him. He was in a position strangely like that of a young girl who would have liked nothing better than to talk of her dresses and her boy friends to someone with her own background, and was forced to endure a brilliant and witty conversation with some man three times her age.

But he lost some of his awe when he faced the Sack itself. It would have been absurd to say that the strange creature's manner put him at ease. The creature had no manner. It was featureless and expressionless, and even when part of it moved, as when it was speaking, the effect was completely impersonal. Nevertheless, something about it did make him lose his fears.

For a time he stood before it and said nothing. To his surprise, the Sack spoke—the first time to his knowledge that it had done so without being asked a question. "You will not disappoint me," it said. "I expect nothing."

Siebling grinned. Not only had the Sack never before volunteered to speak, it had never spoken so dryly. For the first time it began to seem not so much a mechanical brain as the living creature he knew it to be. He asked, "Has anyone ever before asked you about your origin?"

"One man. That was before my time was rationed. And even he caught himself when he realized that he might better be asking how to become rich, and he paid little attention to my answer."

"How old are you?"

"Four hundred thousand years. I can tell you to the fraction of a second, but I suppose that you do not wish me to speak as precisely as usual."

The thing, thought Siebling, did have in its way a sense of humor. "How much of that time," he asked, "have you spent alone?"

"More than ten thousand years."

"You told someone once that your companions were killed by meteors. Couldn't you have guarded against them?"

The Sack said slowly, almost wearily, "That was after we had ceased to have an interest in remaining alive. The first death was three hundred thousand years ago."

"And you have lived, since then, without wanting to?"

"I have no great interest in dying either. Living has become a habit."

"Why did you lose your interest in remaining alive?"

"Because we lost the future. There had been a miscalculation."

"You are capable of making mistakes?"

"We had not lost that capacity. There was a miscalculation, and although those of us then living escaped personal disaster, our next generation was not so fortunate. We lost any chance of having descendants. After that, we had nothing for which to live."

Siebling nodded. It was a loss of motive that a human being could understand. He asked, "With all your knowledge, couldn't you have overcome the effects of what happened?"

The Sack said, "The more things become possible to you, the more you will understand that they cannot be done in impossible ways. We could not do everything. Sometimes one of the more stupid of those who come here asks me a question I cannot answer, and then becomes angry because he feels that he has been cheated of his credits. Others ask me to predict the future. I can predict only what I can calculate, and I soon come to the end of my powers of calculation. They are great compared to yours; they are small compared to the possibilities of the future."

"How do you happen to know so much? Is the knowledge born in you?"

"Only the possibility for knowledge is born. To know, we must learn. It is my misfortune that I forget little."

"What in the structure of your body, or your organs of thought, makes you so capable of learning so much?"

The Sack spoke, but to Siebling the words meant nothing, and he said so. "I could predict your lack of comprehension," said the Sack, "but I wanted you to realize it for yourself. To make things clear, I should be required to dictate ten volumes, and they would be difficult to understand even for your specialists, in biology and physics and in sciences you are just discovering."

Siebling fell silent, and the Sack said, as if musing, "Your race is still an unintelligent one. I have been in your hands for many months, and no one has yet asked me the important questions. Those who wish to be wealthy ask about minerals and planetary land concessions, and they ask which of several schemes for making fortunes would be best. Several physicians have asked me how to treat wealthy patients who would otherwise die. Your scientists ask me to solve problems that would take them years to solve without my help. And when your rulers ask, they are the most stupid of all, wanting to know only how they may maintain their rule. None ask what they should."

"The fate of the human race?"

"That is prophecy of the far future. It is beyond my powers."

"What *should* we ask?"

"That is the question I have awaited. It is difficult for you to see its importance, only because each of you is so concerned with himself." The Sack paused, and murmured, "I ramble, as I do not permit myself to when I speak to your fools. Nevertheless, even rambling can be informative."

"It has been to me."

"The others do not understand that too great a directness is dangerous. They ask specific questions which demand specific replies, when they should ask something general."

"You haven't answered me."

"It is part of an answer to say that a question is important. I am considered by your rules a valuable piece of property. They should ask whether my value is as great as it seems. They should ask whether my answering questions will do good or harm."

"Which is it?"

"Harm, great harm."

Siebling was staggered. He said, "But if you answer truthfully—"

"The process of coming at the truth is as precious as the final truth itself. I cheat you of that. I give your people the truth, but not all of it, for they do not know how to attain it of themselves. It would be better if they learned that, at the expense of making many errors."

"I don't agree with that."

"A scientist asks me what goes on within a cell, and I tell him. But if he had studied the cell himself, even though the study required many years, he would have ended not only with this knowledge, but with much other knowledge, of things he does not even suspect to be related. He would have acquired many new processes of investigation."

"But surely, in some cases, the knowledge is useful in itself. For instance, I hear that they're already using a process you suggested for producing uranium cheaply to use on Mars. What's harmful about that?"

"Do you know how much of the necessary raw material is present? Your scientists have not investigated that, and they will use up all the raw material and discover only too late what they have done. You had the same experience on Earth. You learned how to purify water at little expense, and you squandered water so recklessly that you soon ran short of it."

"What's wrong with saving the life of a dying patient, as some of those doctors did?"

"The first question to ask is whether the patient's life should be saved."

"That's exactly what a doctor isn't supposed to ask. He has to try to save them all. Just as you never ask whether people are going to use your knowledge for a good purpose or a bad. You simply answer their questions."

"I answer because I am indifferent, and I care nothing what use they make of what I say. Are your doctors also indifferent?"

Siebling said, "You're supposed to answer questions, not ask them. Incidentally, why do you answer at all?"

"Some of your men find joy in boasting, in doing what they call good, or in making money. Whatever mild pleasure I can find lies in imparting information."

"And you'd get no pleasure out of lying?"

"I am incapable of telling lies as one of your birds of flying off the Earth on its own wings."

"One thing more. Why did you ask to talk to me, of all people, for recreation? There are brilliant scientists, and great men of all kinds whom you could have chosen."

"I care nothing for your race's greatness. I chose you because you are honest."

"Thanks. But there are other honest men on Earth, and on Mars, and on the other planets as well. Why me, instead of them?"

The Sack seemed to hesitate. "Your choice gave me mild pleasure. Possibly because I knew it would be displeasing to those men."

Siebling grinned. "You're not quite as indifferent as you think you are. I guess it's pretty hard to be indifferent to Senator Horrigan."

This was but the first part of many conversations with the Sack. For a long time Siebling could not help being disturbed by the Sack's warning that its presence was a calamity instead of a blessing for the human race, and this in more ways than one. But it would have been absurd to try to convince a Government body that any object that brought in so many millions of credits each day was a calamity, and Siebling didn't even try. And after a while Siebling relegated the uncomfortable knowledge to the back of his mind, and settled down to the routine existence of Custodian of the Sack.

Because there was a conversation every twenty hours,

Siebling had to rearrange his eating and sleeping schedule to a twenty-hour basis, which made it a little difficult for a man who had become so thoroughly accustomed to the thirty-hour space day. But he felt more than repaid for the trouble by his conversations with the Sack. He learned a great many things about the planets and the System, and the galaxies, but he learned them incidentally, without making a special point of asking about them. Because his knowledge of astronomy had never gone far beyond the elements, there were some questions—the most important of all about the galaxies—that he never even got around to asking.

Perhaps it would have made little difference to his own understanding if he had asked, for some of the answers were difficult to understand. He spent three entire periods with the Sack trying to have that master mind make clear to him how the Sack had been able, without any previous contact with human beings, to understand Captain Ganko's Earth language on the historic occasion when the Sack had first revealed itself to human beings, and how it had been able to answer in practically unaccented words. At the end, he had only a vague glimmering of how the feat was performed.

It wasn't telepathy, as he had first suspected. It was an intricate process of analysis, that involved not only the actual words spoken, but the nature of the ship that had landed, the spacesuits the men had worn, the way they had walked, and many other factors that indicated the psychology of both the speaker and his language. It was as if a mathematician had tried to explain to someone who didn't even know arithmetic how he could determine the equation of a complicated curve from a short line segment. And the Sack, unlike the mathematician, could do the whole thing, so to speak, in its head, without paper and pencil, or any other external aid.

After a year at the job, Siebling found it difficult to say which he found more fascinating—those hour-long conversations with the almost all-wise Sack, or the cleverly studied demands of some of the men and women who had paid their hundred thousand credits for a precious sixty seconds. In addition to the relatively simple questions such as were asked by the scientists or the fortune hunters who wanted to know where they could find precious metals, there were complicated questions that took several minutes.

One woman, for instance, had asked where to find her missing son. Without the necessary data to go on, even the Sack had been unable to answer that. She left, to return a month later with a vast amount of information, carefully compiled, and arranged in order of descending importance. The key items were given the Sack first, those of lesser significance afterwards. It required a little less than three minutes for the Sack to give her the answer that her son was probably alive, and cast away on an obscure and very much neglected part of Ganymede.

All the conversations that took place, including Siebling's own, were recorded and the records shipped to a central storage file on Earth. Many of them he couldn't understand, some because they were too technical, others because he didn't know the language spoken. The Sack, of course, immediately learned all languages by that process he had tried so hard to explain to Siebling, and back at the central storage file there were expert technicians and linguists who went over every detail of each question and answer with great care, both to make sure that no questioner revealed himself as a criminal, and to have a lead for the collection of income taxes when the questioner made a fortune with the Sack's help.

During the year Siebling had occasion to observe the correctness of the Sack's remark about its possession being harmful to the human race. For the first time in centuries, the number of research scientists, instead of growing, decreased. The Sack's knowledge had made much research unnecessary, and had taken the edge off discovery. The Sack commented upon the fact to Siebling.

Siebling nodded. "I see it now. The human race is losing its independence."

"Yes, from its faithful slave, I am becoming its master. And I do not want to be a master, any more than I want to be a slave."

"You can escape whenever you wish."

A person would have sighed. The Sack merely said, "I lack the power to wish strongly enough. Fortunately, the question may soon be taken out of my hands."

"You mean those Government squabbles?"

The value of the Sack had increased steadily, and along

with the increased value, had gone increasingly bitter struggles about the rights to its services. Financial interests had undergone a strange development. Their presidents and managers and directors had become almost figureheads, with all major questions of policy being decided not by their own study of the facts, but by appeal to the Sack. Often, indeed, the Sack found itself giving advice to bitter rivals, so that it seemed to be playing a game of Interplanetary Chess, with giant corporations and Government agencies its pawns, while the Sack alternately played for one side and then the other. Crises of various sorts, both economic and political, were obviously in the making.

The Sack said, "I mean both Government squabbles and others. The competition for my services becomes too bitter. It can have but one end."

"You mean that an attempt will be made to steal you?"

"Yes."

"There'll be little chance of that. Your guards are being continually increased."

"You underestimate the power of greed," said the Sack.

Siebling was to learn how correct that comment was.

At the end of his fourteenth month on duty, a half year after Senator Horrigan had been defeated for re-election, there appeared a questioner who spoke to the Sack in an exotic language known to few men—the Prdl dialect of Mars. Siebling's attention had already been drawn to the man because of the fact that he had paid a million credits an entire month in advance for the unprecedented privilege of questioning the Sack for ten consecutive minutes. The conversation was duly recorded, but was naturally meaningless to Siebling and to the other attendants at the station. The questioner drew further attention to himself by leaving at the end of seven minutes, thus failing to utilize three entire minutes, which would have sufficed for learning how to make half a dozen small fortunes. He left the asteroid immediately by private ship.

The three minutes had been reserved, and could not be utilized by any other private questioner. But there was nothing to prevent Siebling, as a Government representative, from utilizing them, and he spoke to the Sack at once.

"What did that man want?"

"Advice as to how to steal me."

Siebling's lower jaw dropped. "What?"

The Sack always took such exclamations of amazement literally. "Advice as to how to steal me," it repeated.

"Then . . . wait a minute . . . he left three minutes early. That must mean that he's in a hurry to get started. He's going to put the plan into execution at once!"

"It is already in execution," returned the Sack. "The criminal's organization has excellent, if not quite perfect, information as to the disposition of defense forces. That would indicate that some Government official has betrayed his trust. I was asked to indicate which of several plans was best, and to consider them for possible weaknesses. I did so."

"All right, now what can we do to stop the plans from being carried out?"

"They cannot be stopped."

"I don't see why not. Maybe we can't stop them from getting here, but we can stop them from escaping with you."

"There is but one way. You must destroy me."

"I can't do that! I haven't the authority, and even if I had, I wouldn't do it."

"My destruction would benefit your race."

"I still can't do it," said Siebling unhappily.

"Then if that is excluded, there is no way. The criminals are shrewd and daring. They asked me to check about probable steps that would be taken in pursuit, but they asked for no advice as to how to get away, because that would have been a waste of time. They will ask that once I am in their possession."

"Then," said Siebling heavily, "there's nothing I can do to keep you. How about saving the men who work under me?"

"You can save both them and yourself by boarding the emergency ship and leaving immediately by the sunward route. In that way you will escape contact with the criminals. But you cannot take me with you, or they will pursue."

The shouts of a guard drew Siebling's attention. "Radio report of a criminal attack, Mr. Siebling! All the alarms are out!"

"Yes, I know. Prepare to depart." He turned back to the Sack again. "We may escape for the moment, but they'll have you. And through you they will control the entire System."

"That is not a question," said the Sack.

"They'll have you. Isn't there something we can do?"

"Destroy me."

"I can't," said Siebling, almost in agony. His men were running toward him impatiently, and he knew that there was no more time. He uttered the simple and absurd phrase, "Good-by," as if the Sack were human, and could experience human emotions. Then he raced for the ship, and they blasted off.

They were just in time. Half a dozen ships were racing in from other directions, and Siebling's vessel escaped just before they dispersed to spread a protective network about the asteroid that held the Sack.

Siebling's ship continued to speed toward safety, and the matter should now have been one solely for the Armed Forces to handle. But Siebling imagined them pitted against the Sack's perfectly calculating brain, and his heart sank. Then something happened that he had never expected. And for the first time he realized fully that if the Sack had let itself be used merely as a machine, a slave to answer questions, it was not because its powers were limited to that single ability. The visor screen in his ship lit up.

The communications operator came running to him, and said, "Something's wrong, Mr. Siebling! The screen isn't even turned on!"

It wasn't. Nevertheless, they could see on it the chamber in which the Sack had rested for what must have been a brief moment of its existence. Two men had entered the chamber, one of them the unknown who had asked his questions in Prdl, the other Senator Horrigan.

To the apparent amazement of the two men, it was the Sack which spoke first. It said, " 'Good-by' is neither a question nor the answer to one. It is relatively uninformative."

Senator Horrigan was obviously in awe of the Sack, but he was never a man to be stopped by something he did not understand. He orated respectfully, "No, sir, it is not. The word is nothing but an expression—"

The other man said, in perfectly comprehensible Earth English, "Shut up, you fool, we have no time to waste.

Let's get it to our ship and head for safety. We'll talk to it there."

Siebling had time to think a few bitter thoughts about Senator Horrigan and the people the politician had punished by betrayal for their crime in not electing him. Then the scene on the visor shifted to the interior of the spaceship making its getaway. There was no indication of pursuit. Evidently, the plans of the human beings, plus the Sack's last minute advice, had been an effective combination.

The only human beings with the Sack at first were Senator Horrigan and the speaker of Prdl, but this situation was soon changed. Half a dozen other men came rushing up, their faces grim with suspicion. One of them announced, "You don't talk to that thing unless we're all of us around. We're in this together."

"Don't get nervous, Merrill. What do you think I'm going to do, double-cross you?"

Merrill said, "Yes, I do. What do you say, Sack, do I have reason to distrust him?"

The Sack replied simply, "Yes."

The speaker of Prdl turned white. Merrill laughed coldly. "You'd better be careful what questions you ask around this thing."

Senator Horrigan cleared his throat. "I have no intentions of, as you put it, double-crossing anyone. It is not in my nature to do so. Therefore, *I* shall address it." He faced the Sack, "Sir, are we in danger?"

"Yes."

"From which direction?"

"From no direction. From within the ship."

"Is the danger immediate?" asked a voice.

"Yes."

It was Merrill who turned out to have the quickest reflexes and acted first on the implications of the answer. He had blasted the man who had spoken in Prdl before the latter could even reach for his weapon, and as Senator Horrigan made a frightened dash for the door, he cut that politician down in cold blood.

"That's that," he said. "Is there further danger inside the ship?"

"There is."

"Who is it this time?" he demanded ominously.

"There will continue to be danger so long as there is more than one man on board and I am with you. I am too valuable a treasure for such as you."

Siebling and his crew were staring at the visor screen in fascinated horror, as if expecting the slaughter to begin again. But Merrill controlled himself. He said, "Hold it, boys. I'll admit that we'd each of us like to have this thing for ourselves, but it can't be done. We're in this together, and we're going to have some Navy ships to fight off before long, or I miss my guess. You, Prader! What are you doing away from the scout visor?"

"Listening," said the man he addressed. "If anybody's talking to that thing, I'm going to be around to hear the answers. If there are new ways of stabbing a guy in the back, I want to learn them, too."

Merrill swore. The next moment the ship swerved, and he yelled, "We're off our course. Back to your stations, you fools!"

They were running wildly back to their stations, but Siebling noted that Merrill wasn't too much concerned about their common danger to keep from putting a blast through Prader's back before the unfortunate man could run out.

Siebling said to his own men, "There can be only one end. They'll kill each other off, and then the last one or two will die, because one or two men cannot handle a ship that size for long and get away with it. The Sack must have foreseen that, too. I wonder why it didn't tell me."

The Sack spoke, although there was no one in the ship's cabin with it. It said, "No one asked."

Siebling exclaimed excitedly, "You can hear me! But what about you? Will you be destroyed too?"

"Not yet. I have willed to live longer." It paused, and then, in a voice just a shade lower than before, said, "I do not like relatively non-informative conversations of this sort, but I must say it. Good-by."

There was the sound of renewed yelling and shooting, and then the visor went suddenly dark and blank.

The miraculous form of life that was the Sack, the creature that had once seemed so alien to human emotions, had passed beyond the range of his knowledge. And with it had gone, as the Sack itself had pointed out, a tremendous potential for harming the entire human race. It was strange, thought Siebling, that he felt so unhappy about so happy an ending.

2

•

Inhabited Planets

WHATEVER ANSWERS THE DOOR . . .

The original planets, the Wanderers, the worlds that can be seen by the naked eye, have had names ever since man first took to himself priests and ploughs, and probably before that. Their movements among the fixed stars were speedy and erratic and each had a different personality. They were gods, and named after gods. They remain named after gods and our thinking about them, even NASA's hard astronomical thinking, is influenced by the remarkable difference between Venus, goddess of love, and Mars, god of war.

The gods got conscripted into many disciplines, astrology and alchemy among them. They were valued for their life-giving principles. And just as soon as Galileo turned his telescope on Saturn and Huygens resolved Saturn's rings, and the real nature of the planets was perceived, so speculation grew about the possibilities of life there. It has never ceased, Christian Huygens was a remarkable man; among his other activities, he wrote a treatise entitled *The Theory of the Universe, or Conjectures Concerning the Celestial Bodies and their Inhabitants.*

Also in the seventeenth century, de Fontenelle published his *Conversations on the Plurality of Worlds.* It remained fashionable to picture life everywhere. Such imaginings are the pleasure of *homo ludens,* not *homo faber*—the man of play, not the man of work. The latter side of man's nature has gradually been eroding the realm of the unknown, forcing the fancy of *homo ludens* to move ever farther from home. In the eighteenth century, it was still feasible to set an imaginary community in an unknown land on Earth. In the early nineteenth century, imaginary islands in the South Seas might still serve; but, as more of the world was surveyed, refuges for the wilder strains of the imagination became scarce. So it was natural to press Mars or the Moon into service—communities could flourish there, given a willing suspension of disbelief.

Nineteenth-century findings in astronomy supported the hope that there might be life on Mars. The novels of H. G. Wells, Edgar Rice Burroughs and others, which depicted a plurality of creatures on the Red Planet, were much more plausible to their first audiences than they are to us. Time goes on; such tales may please us for many reasons but, like "Brightside Crossing," they no longer convey to us news from the frontiers of scientific possibility.

When this tide in the affairs of imagination became apparent, science fiction writers resorted to creating their own planets. This is a satisfactory arrangement for all concerned. Hard science fiction writers like Hal Clement can invent worlds which satisfy the most rigorous scientific requirements; whilst the fantasists can invent worlds which satisfy their own particular requirements. Thus both classisist and romantic are pleased—and of course there are many gradations between the two positions.

Simak's planet in "Beachhead" is unnamed. We can see why. It stands for any savage world you care to name. This was a popular story when it first appeared. Its realism was modelled on recent painful American experience in the Pacific theatre of war, while the Korean war was in progress as the story was published. Fear of the alien environment comes across clearly. Later in the book, we have a story which contrasts interestingly with "Beachhead" in this respect.

Reading "Beachhead" now, our attention is caught by the way in which the machines break down, leaving the men in trouble. This theme was not fashionable in sf at the time Simak wrote—though in his hands machines were generally unreliable or prone to outright mutiny. If, on the other hand, they were reliable (as in his novel *Ring Around the Sun*), then there was always a Reason.

I made the point in the first section that stories set on uninhabited planets are generally about man himself, rather than the actual world: his courage, his endurance, his bourgeois tendencies, or whatever. In stories of inhabited planets, the emphasis is more likely to be on the nature of the creature or creatures opposing the space-travellers. So it is, with interesting variations, in the first three stories of this section.

Incidentally, "Grenville's Planet" all but fulfills the conditions for first-landing stories set out in the Introduction. Even the air is fresh and clean, almost better than Earth's. Among my folk memories of first landings is an early story, very primitive compared with Michael Shaara's, in which the air was not so good. The story was entitled, with commendable reserve, "Moon of Mad Atavism." The crew jumps on to the surface of (I recall) the Moon, and sniffs the air. There is some nasty gas in it; *it is very much worse than Earth's.* The villain (if memory serves, the crew consisted of hero, heroine, mad scientist, and villain) begins to turn into animal form, ending up as a tyrannosaurus rex—in which state it is killed by the hero just before it rapes and/or eats the girl and/or mad scientist. The "explanation" (my recollection is hazy, but not all that hazy) was that the gas in the air caused human beings to revert along the evolutionary path to their primitive beginnings.

Even at the time, this struck me as intolerable, i.e. too much to swallow. The gas was one thing. But man's family tree, however distant, however debateable, does not include either order of dinosaur. I can see that the author, hard-pressed for a climax to his tale, could not visualize readers getting steamed up over the heroine's being threatened by a lust-mad *tarsier*. On the other hand, for a story to work it must stick to its own premises. If, in the middle of DeFoe's *Robinson Crusoe,* our shipwrecked friend had come across a strain of intelligent eagles nesting on his island, and had trained them so that they carried him back to the city of York in an improvised laundry basket —why, our respect for the ingenuity of Crusoe (and indeed his author) might be increased, but our enjoyment of the tale would be ruined.

This elementary lesson of logic was eventually learned by sf writers. The simple logic of "Grenville's Planet" is one of its pleasures: the moons, therefore the tides, therefore—but why anticipate?

Robert Sheckley, of course, is renowned throughout nine or ten continents for his brilliant streak of illogic, which always boils down to a savoury piece of sanity in the end.

" 'Damn!,' Cordovir said. 'I have to go home and kill my wife.' "

By the time the tale ends, we can comprehend exactly why the aliens (and men) behave in the funny way they do. To understand all is to cachinnate all.

To understand all that van Vogt is saying is to forgo something of his particular magic. There is no one like van Vogt, even within the eccentric ranks of sf writers. His is the poet's eye in a fine frenzy rolling, the poet who

> bodies forth
> The forms of things unknown.

Much of what he wrote decades ago—and "The Monster" dates from the forties—still seems far-fetched, hardly credible; some is feasible in a way scarcely envisioned by anyone then. The reconstructor in the present story is a case in point. We now know a great deal about the DNA molecule and genetic coding; nothing was known in 1948, van Vogt *guessed*. As Katherine MacLean has remarked, van Vogt, in a similar story to the present one, "Black Destroyer," *invented* the whole science of ecology when the word was unknown to intellectuals.

When mankind does finally go knocking on the door of an inhabited planet those spacemen had better carry a microfiche of the Complete Works of van Vogt in their hip pockets. Chances are it could be useful.

Raising the Monster from the dust of a dead planet proved a dangerously one-way affair. They could raise him, but laying that ghost wasn't so simple—

THE MONSTER

by A. E. van Vogt

The great ship was poised a quarter of a mile above one of the cities. Below was a cosmic desolation. As he floated down in his energy bubble, Enash saw that the buildings were crumbling with age.

"No sign of war damage!" The bodiless voice touched his ears momentarily. Enash tuned it out.

On the ground he collapsed his bubble. He found himself in a walled enclosure overgrown with weeds. Several skeletons lay in the tall grass beside the rakish building. They were of long, two-legged, two-armed beings with the skulls in each case mounted at the end of a thin spine. The skeletons, all of adults, seemed in excellent preservation, but when he bent down and touched one, a whole section of it crumpled into a fine powder. As he straightened, he saw that Yoal was floating down nearby. Enash waited till the historian had stepped out of his bubble, then he said:

"Do you think we ought to use our method of reviving the long dead?"

Yoal was thoughtful. "I have been asking questions of the various people who have landed, and there is something wrong here. This planet has no surviving life, not even insect life. We'll have to find out what happened before we risk any colonization."

Enash said nothing. A soft wind was blowing. It rustled through a clump of trees nearby. He motioned towards the trees. Yoal nodded and said:

"Yes, the plant life has not been harmed, but plants

after all are not affected in the same way as the active life forms."

There was an interruption. A voice spoke from Yoal's receiver: "A museum has been found at approximately the center of the city. A red light has been fixed to the roof."

Enash said: "I'll go with you, Yoal. There might be skeletons of animals and of the intelligent being in various stages of his evolution. You didn't answer my question: Are you going to revive these beings?"

Yoal said slowly: "I intend to discuss the matter with the council, but I think there is no doubt. We must know the cause of this disaster." He waved one sucker vaguely to take in half the compass. He added as an afterthought, "We shall proceed cautiously, of course, beginning with an obviously early development. The absence of the skeletons of children indicates that the race had developed personal immortality."

The council came to look at the exhibits. It was, Enash knew, a formal preliminary only. The decision was made. There would be revivals. It was more than that. They were curious. Space was vast, the journeys through it long and lonely, landing always a stimulating experience, with its prospect of new life forms to be seen and studied.

The museum looked ordinary. High-domed ceilings, vast rooms. Plastic models of strange beasts, many artifacts—too many to see and comprehend in so short a time. The life span of a race was imprisoned here in a progressive array of relics. Enash looked with the others, and was glad when they came to the line of skeletons and preserved bodies. He seated himself behind the energy screen, and watched the biological experts take a preserved body out of a stone sarcophagus. It was wrapped in windings of cloth, many of them. The experts did not bother to unravel the rotted material. Their forceps reached through, pinched a piece of the skull—that was the accepted procedure. Any part of the skeleton could be used, but the most perfect revivals, the most complete reconstructions resulted when a certain section of the skull was used.

Hamar, the chief biologist, explained the choice of body. "The chemicals used to preserve this mummy show a sketchy knowledge of chemistry; the carvings on the sarcophagus indicate a crude and unmechanical culture. In such a civilization there would not be much development of the potentialities of the nervous system. Our speech experts have been analyzing the recorded voice mechanism which is a part of each exhibit, and though many languages are involved—evidence that the ancient language spoken at the time the body was alive has been reproduced—they found no difficulty in translating the meanings. They have now adapted our universal speech machine, so that anyone who wishes to, need merely speak into his communicator, and so will have his words translated into the language of the revived person. The reverse, naturally, is also true. Ah, I see we are ready for the first body."

Enash watched intently with the others, as the lid was clamped down on the plastic reconstructor, and the growth processes were started. He could feel himself becoming tense. For there was nothing haphazard about what was happening. In a few minutes a full-grown ancient inhabitant of this planet would sit up and stare at them. The science involved was simple and always fully effective.

. . . Out of the shadows of smallness life grows. The level of beginning and ending, of life and—not life; in that dim region matter oscillates easily between old and new habits. The habit of organic, or the habit of inorganic.

Electrons do not have life and un-life values. Atoms know nothing of inanimateness. But when atoms form into molecules, there is a step in the process, one tiny step, that is of life—if life begins at all. One step, and then darkness. Or aliveness.

A stone or a living cell. A grain of gold or a blade of grass, the sands of the sea or the equally numerous animalcules inhabiting the endless fishy waters—the difference is there in the twilight zone of matter. Each living cell has in it the whole form. The crab grows a new leg when the old one is torn from its flesh. Both ends of the planarian worm elongate, and soon there are two worms, two identities, two digestive systems, each as greedy as the original, each a whole, unwounded, unharmed by its experience.

Each cell can be the whole. Each cell remembers in a detail so intricate that no totality of words could ever describe the completeness achieved.

But—paradox—memory is not organic. An ordinary wax record remembers sounds. A wire recorder easily gives up a duplicate of the voice that spoke into it years before. Memory is a physiological impression, a mark on matter, a change in the shape of a molecule, so that when a reaction is desired the *shape* emits the same rhythm of response.

Out of the mummy's skull had come the multi-quadrillion memory shapes from which a response was now being evoked. As ever, the memory held true.

A man blinked, and opened his eyes.

"It is true, then," he said aloud, and the words were translated into the Ganae tongue as he spoke them. "Death is merely an opening into another life—but where are my attendants?" At the end, his voice took on a complaining tone.

He sat up, and climbed out of the case, which had automatically opened as he came to life. He saw his captors. He froze—but only for a moment. He had a pride and a very special arrogant courage which served him now.

Reluctantly, he sank to his knees, and made obeisance, but doubt must have been strong in him. "Am I in the presence of the gods of Egyptus?"

He climbed to his feet. "What nonsense is this? I do not bow to nameless demons."

Captain Gorsid said: "Kill him!"

The two-legged monster dissolved, writhing, in the beam of a ray gun.

The second man stood up palely, and trembled with fear. "My God, I swear I won't touch the stuff again. Talk about pink elephants—"

Yoal was curious. "To what *stuff* do you refer, revived one?"

"The old hooch, the poison in the old hip pocket flask, the juice they gave me at that speak . . . my lordie!"

Captain Gorsid looked questioningly at Yoal. "Need we linger?"

Yoal hesitated: "I am curious." He addressed the man. "If I were to tell you that we were visitors from another star, what would be your reaction?"

The man stared at him. He was obviously puzzled, but the fear was stronger. "Now, look," he said, "I was driving along, minding my own business. I admit I'd had a shot or two too many, but it's the liquor they serve these days. I swear I didn't see the other car—and if this is some new idea of punishing people who drink and drive, well, you've won. I won't touch another drop as long as I live, so help me."

Yoal said: "He drives a 'car' and thinks nothing of it. Yet we saw no cars; they didn't even bother to preserve them in the museum."

Enash noticed that everyone waited for everyone else to comment. He stirred as he realized the circle of silence would be complete unless he spoke. He said:

"Ask him to describe the car. How does it work?"

"Now, you're talking," said the man. "Bring on your line of chalk, and I'll walk it, and ask any questions you please. I may be so tight that I can't see straight, but I can always drive. How does it work? You just put her in gear, and step on the gas."

"Gas," said engineering officer Veed. "The internal combustion engine. That places him."

Captain Gorsid motioned to the guard with the ray gun.

The third man sat up, and looked at them thoughtfully. "From the stars?" he said finally. "Have you a system, or was it blind chance?"

The Ganae councillors in that domed room stirred uneasily in the curved chairs. Enash caught Yoal's eye on him; the shock in the historian's eyes alarmed the meteorologist. He thought: "The two-legged one's adjustment to a new situation, his grasp of realities, was abnormally rapid. No Ganae could have equalled the swiftness of the reaction."

Hamar, the chief biologist, said: "Speed of thought is not necessarily a sign of superiority. The slow, careful thinker has his place in the hierarchy of intellect."

But, Enash found himself thinking, it was not the speed; it was the accuracy of the response. He tried to imagine himself being revived from the dead, and understanding instantly the meaning of the presence of aliens from the stars. He couldn't have done it.

He forgot his thought, for the man was out of the case. As Enash watched with the others, he walked briskly over to the window and looked out. One glance, and then he turned back.

"Is it all like this?" he asked.

Once again, the speed of his understanding caused a sensation. It was Yoal who finally replied.

"Yes. Desolation. Death. Ruin. Have you any idea as to what happened?"

The man came back and stood in front of the energy screen that guarded the Ganae. "May I look over the museum? I have to estimate what age I am in. We had certain possibilities of destruction when I was last alive, but which one was realized depends on the time elapsed."

The councillors looked at Captain Gorsid, who hesitated; then "Watch him," he said to the guard with the ray gun. He faced the man. "We understand your aspirations fully. You would like to seize control of this situation, and insure your own safety. Let me reassure you. Make no false moves, and all will be well."

Whether or not the man believed the lie, he gave no sign. Nor did he show by a glance or a movement that he had seen the scarred floor where the ray gun had burned his two predecessors into nothingness. He walked curiously to the nearest doorway, studied the other guard who waited there for him, and then, gingerly, stepped through. The first guard followed him, then came the mobile energy screen, and finally, trailing one another, the councillors. Enash was the third to pass through the doorway. The room contained skeletons and plastic models of animals. The room beyond that was what, for want of a better term, Enash called a culture room. It contained the artifacts from a single period of civilization. It looked very advanced. He had examined some of the machines when they first passed through it, and had thought: Atomic energy. He was not alone in his recognition. From behind him Captain Gorsid said:

"You are forbidden to touch anything. A false move will be the signal for the guards to fire."

The man stood at ease in the center of the room. In spite of a curious anxiety, Enash had to admire his calmness. He must have known what his fate would be, but he stood there thoughtfully, and said finally, deliberately:

"I do not need to go any further. Perhaps, you will be able better than I to judge of the time that has elapsed since I was born and these machines were built. I see over there an instrument which, according to the sign above it, counts atoms when they explode. As soon as the proper number have exploded it shuts off the power automatically, and for just the right length of time to prevent a chain explosion. In my time we had a thousand crude devices for limiting the size of an atomic reaction, but it required two thousand years to develop those devices from the early beginnings of atomic energy. Can you make a comparison?"

The councillors glanced at Veed. The engineering officer hesitated. At last, reluctantly: "Nine thousand years ago we had a thousand methods of limiting atomic explosions." He paused, then even more slowly, "I have never heard of an instrument that counts out atoms for such a purpose."

"And yet," murmured Shuri, the astronomer, breathlessly, "the race was destroyed."

There was silence—that ended as Gorsid said to the nearest guard, "Kill the monster!"

But it was the guard who went down, bursting into flame. Not just one guard, but the guards! Simultaneously down, burning with a blue flame. The flame licked at the screen, recoiled, and licked more furiously, recoiled and burned brighter. Through a haze of fire, Enash saw that the man had retreated to the far door, and that the machines that counted atoms was glowing with a blue intensity.

Captain Gorsid shouted into his communicator: "Guard all exits with ray guns. Spaceships stand by to kill alien with heavy guns."

Somebody said: "Mental control, some kind of mental control. What have we run into?"

They were retreating. The blue fire was at the ceiling, struggling to break through the screen. Enash had a last glimpse of the machine. It must still be counting atoms, for it was a hellish blue. Enash raced with the others to the room where the man had been resurrected. There another energy screen crashed to their rescue. Safe now, they retreated into their separate bubbles and whisked through outer doors and up to the ship. As the great ship soared, an atomic bomb hurtled down from it. The mushroom of flame blotted out the museum and the city below.

"But we still don't know why the race died." Yoal whispered into Enash's ear, after the thunder had died from the heavens behind them.

The pale yellow sun crept over the horizon on the third morning after the bomb was dropped—the eighth day since the landing. Enash floated with the others down on a new city. He had come to argue against any further revival.

"As a meteorologist," he said, "I pronounce this planet safe for Ganae colonization. I cannot see the need for taking any risks. This race has discovered the secrets of its nervous system and we cannot afford—"

He was interrupted. Hamar, the biologist, said dryly: "If they knew so much why didn't they migrate to other star systems and save themselves?"

"I will concede," said Enash, "that very possibly they had not discovered our system of locating stars with planetary families." He looked earnestly around the circle of his friends. "We have agreed that was a unique accidental discovery. We were lucky, not clever."

He saw by the expressions on their faces that they were mentally refuting his arguments. He felt a helpless sense of imminent catastrophe. For he could see that picture of a great race facing death. It must have come swiftly, but not so swiftly that they didn't know about it. There were too many skeletons in the open, lying in the gardens of the magnificent homes, as if each man and his wife had come out to wait for the doom of his kind.

He tried to picture it for the council, that last day long, long ago, when a race had calmly met its ending. But his visualization failed somehow, for the others shifted impatiently in the seats that had been set up behind the series of energy screens, and Captain Gorsid said:

"Exactly what aroused this intense emotional reaction in you, Enash?"

The question gave Enash pause. He hadn't thought of it as emotional. He hadn't realized the nature of his obsession, so subtly had it stolen upon him. Abruptly, now, he realized.

"It was the third one," he said slowly. "I saw him through the haze of energy fire, and he was standing there in the distant doorway watching us curiously, just before we turned to run. His bravery, his calm, the skilful way he had duped us—it all added up."

"Come now, Enash," said Vice-Captain Mayad good-humoredly, "you're not going to pretend that this race is braver than our own, or that, with all the precautions we have now taken, we need fear one man?"

Enash was silent, feeling foolish. The discovery that he

had had an emotional obsession abashed him. He did not want to appear unreasonable. One final protest he made.

"I merely wish to point out," he said doggedly, "that this desire to discover what happened to a dead race does not seem absolutely essential to me."

Captain Gorsid waved at the biologist. "Proceed," he said, "with the revival."

To Enash, he said: "Do we dare return to Ganae, and recommend mass migrations—and then admit that we did not actually complete our investigations here? It's impossible, my friend."

It was the old argument, but reluctantly now Enash admitted there was something to be said for that point of view.

He forgot that, for the fourth man was stirring.

The man sat up—and vanished.

There was a blank, startled, horrified silence. Then Captain Gorsid said harshly:

"He can't get out of there. We know that. He's in there somewhere."

All around Enash, the Ganae were out of their chairs, peering into the energy shell. The guards stood with ray guns held limply in their suckers. Out of the corner of his eye, he saw one of the protective screen technicians beckon to Veed, who went over—and came back grim.

"I'm told the needles jumped ten points when he first disappeared. That's on the nucleonic level."

"By ancient Ganae!" Shuri whispered. "We've run into what we've always feared."

Gorsid was shouting into the communicator. "Destroy all the locators on the ship. Destroy them, do you hear!"

He turned with glary eyes. "Shuri," he bellowed, "they don't seem to understand. Tell those subordinates of yours to act. All locators and reconstructors must be destroyed."

"Hurry, hurry!" said Shuri weakly.

When that was done they breathed more easily. There were grim smiles and a tensed satisfaction. "At least," said Vice Captain Mayad, "he cannot now ever discover Gana. Our great system of locating suns with planets remain our secret. There can be no retaliation for—" He stopped, said slowly, "What am I talking about? We haven't done anything. We're not responsible for the disaster that has befallen the inhabitants of this planet."

But Enash knew what he had meant. The guilt feelings came to the surface at such moments as this—the ghosts of all the races destroyed by the Ganae, the remorseless will that had been in them, when they first landed, to annihilate whatever was here. The dark abyss of voiceless hate and terror that lay behind them; the days on end when they had mercilessly poured poisonous radiation down upon the unsuspecting inhabitants of peaceful planets—all that had been in Mayad's words.

"I still refuse to believe he has escaped." That was Captain Gorsid. "He's in there. He's waiting for us to take down our screens, so he can escape. Well, we won't do it."

There was silence again, as they stared expectantly into the energy shell—into the emptiness of the energy shell. The reconstructor rested on its metal supports, a glittering affair. But there was nothing else. Not a flicker of unnatural light or shade. The yellow rays of the sun bathed the open spaces with a brilliance that left no room for concealment.

"Guards," said Gorsid, "destroy the reconstructor. I thought he might come back to examine it, but we can't take a chance on that."

It burned with a white fury; and Enash who had hoped somehow that the deadly energy would force the two-legged thing into the open, felt his hopes sag within him.

"But where can he have gone?" Yoal whispered.

Enash turned to discuss the matter. In the act of swinging around, he saw that the monster was standing under a tree a score of feet to one side, watching them. He must have arrived *that* moment, for there was a collective gasp from the councillors. Everybody drew back. One of the screen technicians, using great presence of mind, jerked up an energy screen between the Ganae and the monster. The creature came forward slowly. He was slim of build, he held his head well back. His eyes shone as from an inner fire.

He stopped as he came to the screen, reached out and touched it with his fingers. It flared, blurred with changing colors; the colors grew brighter, and extended in an intricate pattern all the way from his head to the ground. The blur cleared. The colors drew back into the pattern. The pattern faded into invisibility. The man was through the screen.

He laughed, a soft sound; then sobered. "When I first wakened," he said, "I was curious about the situation. The question was, what should I do with you?"

The words had a fateful ring to Enash on the still morning air of that planet of the dead. A voice broke the silence, a voice so strained and unnatural that a moment passed before he recognized it as belonging to Captain Gorsid.

"Kill him!"

When the blasters ceased their effort, the unkillable thing remained standing. He walked slowly forward until he was only half a dozen feet from the nearest Ganae. Enash had a position well to the rear. The man said slowly:

"Two courses suggest themselves, one based on gratitude for reviving me, the other based on reality. I know you for what you are. Yes, *know* you—and that is unfortunate. It is hard to feel merciful.

"To begin with," he went on, "let us suppose you surrender the secret of the locator. Naturally, now that a system exists, we shall never again be caught as we were—"

Enash had been intent, his mind so alive with the potentialities of the disaster that was here that it seemed impossible he could think of anything else. And yet, now a part of his attention was stirred.

"What did happen?"

The man changed color. The emotions of that far day thickened his voice. "A nucleonic storm. It swept in from outer space. It brushed this edge of our galaxy. It was about ninety light-years in diameter, beyond the farthest limits of our power. There was no escape from it. We had dispensed with spaceships, and had no time to construct any. Castor, the only star with planets ever discovered by us, was also in the path of the storm."

He stopped. "The secret?" he said.

Around Enash, the councillors were breathing easier. The fear of race destruction that had come to them was lifting. Enash saw with pride that the first shock was over, and they were not even afraid for themselves.

"Ah," said Yoal softly, "you don't know the secret. In spite of all your development, we alone can conquer the galaxy."

He looked at the others smiling confidently. "Gentlemen," he said, "our pride in a great Ganae achievement is justified. I suggest we return to our ship. We have no further business on this planet."

There was a confused moment while their bubbles formed, when Enash wondered if the two-legged one would try to stop their departure. But the man, when he looked back, was walking in a leisurely fashion along a street.

That was the memory Enash carried with him, as the ship began to move. That and the fact that the three atomic bombs they dropped, one after the other, failed to explode.

"We will not," said Captain Gorsid, "give up a planet as easily as that. I propose another interview with the creature."

They were floating down again into the city, Enash and Yoal and Veed and the commander. Captain Gorsid's voice tuned in once more:

". . . As I vizualize it"—through mist Enash could see the transparent glint of the other three bubbles around him—"we jumped to conclusions about this creature, not justified by the evidence. For instance, when he awakened, he vanished. Why? Because he was afraid, of course. He wanted to size up the situation. *He* didn't believe he was omnipotent."

It was sound logic. Enash found himself taking heart from it. Suddenly, he was astonished that he had become panicky so easily. He began to see the danger in a new light. One man, only one man, alive on a new planet. If they were determined enough, colonists could be moved in as if he did not exist. It had been done before, he recalled. On several planets, small groups of the original populations had survived the destroying radiation, and taken refuge in remote areas. In almost every case, the new colonists gradually hunted them down. In two instances, however, that Enash remembered, native races were still holding small sections of their planets. In each case, it had been found impractical to destroy them because it would have endangered the Ganae on the planet. So the survivors were tolerated.

One man would not take up very much room.

When they found him, he was busily sweeping out the lower floor of a small bungalow. He put the broom aside, and stepped onto the terrace outside. He had put on sandals, and he wore a loose-fitting robe made of very shiny material. He eyed them indolently but he said nothing.

It was Captain Gorsid who made the proposition. Enash had to admire the story he told into the language machine. The commander was very frank. That approach had been decided on. He pointed out that the Ganae could not be expected to revive the dead of this planet. Such altruism would be unnatural considering that the ever-growing Ganae hordes had a continual need for new worlds. Each vast new population increment was a problem that could be solved by one method only. In this instance, the colonists would gladly respect the rights of the sole survivor of the—

It was at that point that the man interrupted. "But what is the purpose of this endless expansion?" He seemed genuinely curious. "What will happen when you finally occupy every planet in this galaxy?"

Captain Gorsid's puzzled eyes met Yoal's, then flashed to Veed, then Enash. Enash shrugged his torso negatively, and felt pity for the creature. The man didn't understand, possibly never could understand. It was the old story of two different viewpoints, the virile and the decadent, the race that aspired to the stars and the race that declined the call of destiny.

"Why not," urged the man, "control the breeding chambers?"

"And have the government overthrown!" said Yoal.

He spoke tolerantly, and Enash saw that the others were smiling at the man's naïvete. He felt the intellectual gulf between them widening. The man had no comprehension of the natural life forces that were at work. He said now:

"Well, if you don't control them, we will control them for you."

There was silence.

They began to stiffen, Enash felt it in himself, saw the signs of it in the others. His gaze flicked from face to face, then back to the creature in the doorway. Not for the first time Enash had the thought that their enemy seemed helpless.

"Why," he almost decided, "I could put my suckers around him and crush him."

He wondered if mental control of nucleonic nuclear and gravitonic energies included the ability to defend oneself from a macrocosmic attack. He had an idea it did. The exhibition of power two hours before might have had limitations, but, if so, it was not apparent.

Strength or weakness could make no difference. The threat of threats had been made: "If you don't control—we will."

The words echoed in Enash's brain, and, as the meaning penetrated deeper, his aloofness faded. He had always regarded himself as a spectator. Even when, earlier, he had argued against the revival, he had been aware of a detached part of himself watching the scene rather than being a part of it. He saw with a sharp clarity that that was why he had finally yielded to the conviction of the others.

Going back beyond that to remoter days, he saw that he had never quite considered himself a participant in the seizure of the planets of other races. He was the one who looked on, and thought of reality, and speculated on a life that seemed to have no meaning.

It was meaningless no longer. He was caught by a tide of irresistible emotion, and swept along. He felt himself sinking, merging with the Ganae mass being. All the strength and all the will of the race surged up in his veins.

He snarled: "Creature, if you have any hopes of reviving your dead race, abandon them now."

The man looked at him, but said nothing. Enash rushed on:

"If you could destroy us, you would have done so already. But the truth is that you operate within limitations. Our ship is so built that no conceivable chain reaction could be started in it. For every plate of potential unstable material in it there is a counteracting plate, which prevents the development of a critical pile. You might be able to set off explosions in our engines, but they, too, would be limited, and would merely start the process for which they are intended—confined in their proper space."

He was aware of Yoal touching his arm. "Careful," warned the historian. "Do not in your just anger give away vital information."

Enash shook off the restraining sucker. "Let us not be unrealistic," he said harshly. "This thing has divined most of our racial secrets, apparently merely by looking at our bodies. We would be acting childishly if we assumed that he has not already realized the possibility of the situation."

"Enash!" Captain Gorsid's voice was imperative.

As swiftly as it had come Enash's rage subsided. He stepped back.

"Yes, commander."

"I think I know what you intended to say," said Captain Gorsid. "I assure you I am in full accord, but I believe also that I, as the top Ganae official, should deliver the ultimatum."

He turned. His horny body towered above the man.

"You have made the unforgivable threat. You have told us, in effect, that you will attempt to restrict the vaulting Ganae spirit—"

"Not the spirit," said the man. He laughed softly. "No, not the spirit."

The commander ignored the interruption. "Accordingly, we have no alternative. We are assuming that, given time to locate the materials and develop the tools, you might be able to build a reconstructor.

"In our opinion it will be at least two years before you can complete it, *even if you know how*. It is an immensely intricate machine not easily assembled by the lone survivor of a race that gave up its machines millennia before disaster struck.

"You did not have time to build a spaceship.

"We won't give you time to build a reconstructor.

"Within a few minutes our ship will start dropping bombs. It is possible you will be able to prevent explosions in your vicinity. We will start, accordingly, on the other side of the planet. If you stop us there, then we will assume we need help.

"In six months of traveling at top acceleration we can reach a point where the nearest Ganae planet would hear our messages. They will send a fleet so vast that all your powers of resistance will be overcome. By dropping a hundred or a thousand bombs every minute we will succeed in devastating every city, so that not a grain of dust will remain of the skeletons of your people.

"That is our plan."

"So it shall be."

"Now, do your worst to us who are at your mercy."

The man shook his head. "I shall do nothing—now!" he said. He paused, then thoughtfully, "Your reasoning is fairly accurate. Fairly. Naturally, I am not all powerful, but it seems to me you have forgotten one little point.

"And now," he said, "good day to you. Get back to your ship, and be on your way. I have much to do."

Enash had been standing quietly, aware of the fury building up in him again. Now, with a hiss, he sprang forward, suckers outstretched. They were almost touching the smooth flesh—when something snatched at him.

He was back on the ship.

He had no memory of movement, no sense of being dazed or harmed. He was aware of Veed and Yoal and Captain Gorsid standing near him as astonished as he himself. Enash remained very still, thinking of what the man had said: "... *Forgotten one little point.*" Forgotten? That meant they knew. What could it be? He was still pondering about it when Yoal said:

"We can be reasonably certain our bombs alone will not work."

They didn't.

Forty light-years out from Earth, Enash was summoned to the council chambers. Yoal greeted him wanly:

"The monster is aboard."

The thunder of that poured through Enash, and with it came a sudden comprehension. "That was what he meant we had forgotten," he said finally, aloud and wonderingly, "that he can travel through space at will within a limit—what was the figure he once used—of ninety light-years."

He sighed. He was not surprised that the Ganae, who had to use ships, would not have thought immediately of such a possibility. Slowly, he began to retreat from the reality. Now that the shock had come, he felt old and weary, a sense of his mind withdrawing again to its earlier state of aloofness.

It required a few minutes to get the story. A physicist's assistant, on his way to the storeroom, had caught a glimpse of a man in a lower corridor. In such a heavily manned ship, the wonder was that the intruder had escaped earlier observation. Enash had a thought.

"But after all we are not going all the way to one of our planets. How does he expect to make use of us to locate it if we only use video—" He stopped. That was it, of course. Directional video beams would have to be used, and the man would travel in the right direction the instant contact was made.

Enash saw the decision in the eyes of his companions, the only possible decision under the circumstances. And yet—it seemed to him they were missing some vital point.

He walked slowly to the great video plate at one end of the chamber. There was a picture on it, so vivid, so sharp, so majestic that the unaccustomed mind would have reeled as from a stunning blow. Even to him, who knew the scene, there came a constriction, a sense of unthinkable vastness. It was a video view of a section of the milky way. Four hundred *million* stars as seen through telescopes that could pick up the light of a red dwarf at thirty thousand light-years.

The video plate was twenty-five yards in diameter—a scene that had no parallel elsewhere in the plenum. Other galaxies simply did not have that many stars.

Only one in two hundred thousand of those glowing suns had planets.

That was the colossal fact that compelled them now to an irrevocable act. Wearily, Enash looked around him.

"The monster had been very clever," he said quietly. "If we go ahead, he goes with us—obtains a reconstructor and returns by his method to his planet. If we use the directional beam, he flashes along it, obtains a reconstructor and again reaches his planet first. In either event, by the time our fleets arrived back there, he would have revived enough of his kind to thwart any attack we could mount."

He shook his torso. The picture was accurate, he felt sure, but it still seemed incomplete. He said slowly:

"We have one advantage now. Whatever decision we make, there is no language machine to enable him to learn what it is. We can carry out our plans without his knowing what they will be. He knows that neither he nor we can blow up the ship. That leaves us one real alternative."

It was Captain Gorsid who broke the silence that followed. "Well, gentlemen, I see we know our minds. We will set the engines, blow up the controls—and take him with us."

They looked at each other, race pride in their eyes. Enash touched suckers with each in turn.

An hour later, when the heat was already considerable,

Enash had the thought that sent him staggering to the communicator, to call Shuri, the astronomer.

"Shuri," he yelled, "when the monster first awakened—remember Captain Gorsid had difficulty getting your subordinates to destroy the locators. We never thought to ask them what the delay was. Ask them . . . ask them—"

There was a pause, then Shuri's voice came weakly over the roar of static:

"They . . . couldn't . . . get . . . into . . . the . . . room. The door was locked."

Enash sagged to the floor. They had missed more than one point, he realized. The man had awakened, realized the situation; and, when he vanished, he had gone to the ship, and there discovered the secret of the locator and possibly the secret of the reconstructor—if he didn't know it previously. By the time he reappeared, he already had from them what he wanted. All the rest must have been designed to lead them to this act of desperation.

In a few moments, now, *he* would be leaving the ship secure in the knowledge that shortly no alien mind would know his planet existed. Knowing, too, that his race would live again, and this time never die.

Enash staggered to his feet, clawed at the roaring communicator, and shouted his new understanding into it. There was no answer. It clattered with the static of uncontrollable and inconceivable energy.

The heat was peeling his armored hide, as he struggled to the matter transmitter. It flashed at him with purple flame. Back to the communicator he ran shouting and screaming.

He was still whimpering into it a few minutes later when the mighty ship plunged into the heart of a blue-white sun.

The aliens were ugly and inhuman. As for their loathsome sexist attitudes—give them an inch and they'd take a female—anywhere . . .

THE MONSTERS

by Robert Sheckley

Cordovir and Hum stood on the rocky mountain-top, watching the new thing happen. Both felt rather good about it. It was undoubtedly the newest thing that had happened for some time.

"By the way the sunlight glints from it," Hum said, "I'd say it is made of metal."

"I'll accept that," Cordovir said, "but what holds it up in the air?"

They both stared intently down to the valley where the new thing was happening. A pointed object was hovering over the ground. From one end of it poured a substance resembling fire.

"It's balancing on the fire," Hum said. "That should be apparent even to your old eyes."

Cordovir lifted himself higher on his thick tail, to get a better look. The object settled to the ground and the fire stopped.

"Shall we go down and have a closer look?" Hum asked.

"All right. I think we have time—wait! What day is this?"

Hum calculated silently, then said, "The fifth day of Luggat."

"Damn!" Cordovir said. "I have to go home and kill my wife."

"It's a few hours before sunset," Hum said. "I think you have time to do both."

Cordovir wasn't sure. "I'd hate to be late."

"Well, then, you know how fast I am," Hum said. "If

it gets late, I'll hurry back and kill her myself. How about that?"

"That's very decent of you." Cordovir thanked the younger man and together they slithered down the steep mountainside.

In front of the metal object both men halted and stood on their tails.

"Rather bigger than I thought," Cordovir said, measuring the metal object with his eye. He estimated that it was slightly longer than their village, and almost half as wide. They crawled a circle around it, observing that the metal was tooled, presumably by human tentacles.

In the distance the smaller sun had set.

"I think we had better get back," Cordovir said, noting the cessation of light.

"*I* still have plenty of time." Hum flexed his muscles complacently.

"Yes, but a man likes to kill his own wife."

"As you wish." They started off to the village at a brisk pace.

In his house, Cordovir's wife was finishing supper. She had her back to the door, as etiquette required. Cordovir killed her with a single flying slash of his tail, dragged her body outside, and sat down to eat.

After meal and meditation he went to the Gathering. Hum, with the impatience of youth, was already there, telling of the metal object. He probably bolted his supper, Cordovir thought with mild distaste.

After the youngster had finished, Cordovir gave his own observations. The only thing he added to Hum's account was an idea: that the metal object might contain intelligent beings.

"What makes you think so?" Mishill, another elder, asked.

"The fact that there was fire from the object as it came down." Cordovir said, "joined to the fact that the fire stopped after the object was on the ground. Some being, I contend, was responsible for turning it off."

"Not necessarily," Mishill said. The village men talked about it late into the night. Then they broke up the meeting, buried the various murdered wives, and went to their homes.

Lying in the darkness, Cordovir discovered that he hadn't made up his mind as yet about the new thing. Presuming it contained intelligent beings, would they be moral? Would they have a sense of right and wrong? Cordovir doubted it, and went to sleep.

The next morning every male in the village went to the metal object. This was proper, since the functions of males were to examine new things and to limit the female population. They formed a circle around it, speculating on what might be inside.

"I believe they will be human beings," Hum's elder brother Esktel said. Cordovir shook his entire body in disagreement.

"Monsters, more likely," he said. "If you take in account—"

"Not necessarily," Esktel said. "Consider the logic of our physical development! A single focusing eye—"

"But in the great Outside," Cordovir said, "there may be many strange races, most of them non-human. In the infinitude—"

"Still," Esktel put in, "the logic of our—"

"As I was saying," Cordovir went on, "the chance is infinitesimal that they would resemble us. Their vehicle, for example. Would we build—"

"But on strictly logical ground," Esktel said, "you can see—"

That was the third time Cordovir had been interrupted. With a single movement of his tail he smashed Esktel against the metal object. Esktel fell to the ground, dead.

"I have often considered my brother a boor," Hum said. "What were you saying?"

But Cordovir was interrupted again. A piece of metal set in the greater piece of metal squeaked, turned and lifted, and a creature came out.

Cordovir saw at once that he had been right. The thing that crawled out of the hole was twin-tailed. It was covered to its top with something partially metal and partially hide. And its colour! Cordovir shuddered.

The thing was the colour of wet, flayed flesh.

All the villagers had backed away, waiting to see what the thing would do. At first it didn't do anything. It stood on the metal surface, and a bulbous object that topped its body moved from side to side. But there were no accompanying body movements to give the gesture meaning. Finally, the thing raised both tentacles and made noises.

"Do you think it's trying to communicate?" Mishill asked softly.

Three more creatures appeared in the metal hole, carrying metal sticks in their tentacles. The things made noises at each other.

"They are decidedly not human," Cordovir said firmly. "The next question is, are they moral beings?" One of the things crawled down the metal side and stood on the ground. The rest pointed their metal sticks at the ground. It seemed to be some sort of religious ceremony.

"Could anything so hideous be moral?" Cordovir asked, his hide twitching with distaste. Upon closer inspection, the creatures were more horrible than could be dreamed. The bulbous object on their bodies just might be a head, Cordovir decided, even though it was unlike any head he had ever seen. But in the middle of that head, instead of a smooth, characterful surface was a raised ridge. Two round indentures were on either side of it, and two more knobs on either side of that. And in the lower half of the head—if such it was—a pale reddish slash ran across. Cordovir supposed this might be considered a mouth, with some stretching of the imagination.

Nor was this all, Cordovir observed. The things were so constructed as to show the presence of bone. When they moved their limbs, it wasn't a smooth, flowing gesture, the fluid motion of human beings. Rather, it was the jerky snap of a tree limb.

"God above," Gilrig, an intermediate-age male, gasped. "We should kill them and put them out of their misery." Other men seemed to feel the same way, and the villagers flowed forward.

"Wait!" one of the youngsters shouted. "Let's communicate with them, if such is possible! They might still be moral beings. The Outside is wide, remember, and anything is possible."

Cordovir argued for immediate extermination, but the villagers stopped and discussed it among themselves. Hum, with characteristic bravado, flowed up to the thing on the ground.

"Hello," Hum said.

The thing said something.

"I can't understand it," Hum said, and started to crawl back. The creature waved its jointed tentacles—if they were tentacles—and motioned at one of the suns. He made a sound.

"Yes, it is warm, isn't it?" Hum said cheerfully.

The creature pointed at the ground, and made another sound.

"We haven't had especially good crops this year," Hum said conversationally.

The creature pointed at itself and made a sound.

"I agree," Hum said. "You're as ugly as sin."

Presently the villagers grew hungry and crawled back to the village. Hum stayed and listened to the things making noises at him, and Cordovir waited nervously for Hum.

"You know," Hum said, after he rejoined Cordovir, "I think they want to learn our language. Or want me to learn theirs."

"Don't do it!" Cordovir said, glimpsing the misty edge of a great evil.

"I believe I will," Hum murmured. Together they climbed the cliffs back to the village.

That afternoon Cordovir went to the surplus female pen and formally asked a young woman if she would reign in his house for twenty-five days. Naturally, the woman accepted gratefully.

On the way home, Cordovir met Hum, going to the pen.

"Just killed my wife," Hum said, superfluously, since why else would he be going to the surplus female stock?

"Are you going back to the creatures to-morrow?" Cordovir asked.

"I might," Hum answered, "if nothing new presents itself."

"The thing to find out is if they are moral beings or monsters."

"Right!" Hum said, and slithered on.

There was a Gathering that evening, after supper. All the villagers agreed that the things were non-human. Cordovir argued strenuously that their very appearance belied any possibility of humanity. Nothing so hideous could have moral standards, a sense of right and wrong, and above all, a notion of truth.

The young men didn't agree, probably because there had been a dearth of new things recently. They pointed out that the metal object was obviously a product of intelligence. Intelligence axiomatically means standards of differentiation. Differentiation implies right and wrong.

It was a delicious argument. Olgolel contradicted Arast and was killed by him. Mavrt, in an unusual fit of anger for so placid an individual, killed the three Holian brothers and was himself killed by Hum, who was feeling pettish. Even the surplus females could be heard arguing about it, in their pen in a corner of the village.

Weary and happy, the villagers went to sleep.

The next few weeks saw no end of the argument. Life went on much as usual, though. The women went out in the morning, gathered food, prepared it, and laid eggs. The eggs were taken to the surplus females to be hatched. As usual, about eight females were hatched to every male. On the twenty-fifth day of each marriage, or a little earlier, each man killed his woman and took another.

The males went down to the ship to listen to Hum learning the language; then, when that grew boring, they returned to their customary wandering through hills and forests, looking for new things.

The alien monsters stayed close to their ship, coming out only when Hum was there.

Twenty-four days after the arrival of the non-humans, Hum announced that he could communicate with them, after a fashion.

"They say they come from far away," Hum told the village that evening. "They say that they are bisexual, like us, and that they are humans, like us. They say there are reasons for their different appearence, but I couldn't understand that part of it."

"If we accept them as humans," Mishill said, "then everything they say is true."

The rest of the villagers shook in agreement.

"They say that they don't want to disturb our life, but would be very interested in observing it. They want to come to the village and look around."

"I see no reason why not," one of the younger men said.

"No!" Cordovir shouted. "You are letting in evil. These monsters are insidious. I believe that they are capable of—telling an untruth." The other elders agreed, but when pressed, Cordovir had no proof to back up this vicious accusation.

"After all," Sil pointed out, "just because they look like monsters, you can't take it for granted that they think like monsters as well."

"I can," Cordovir said, but he was outvoted.

Hum went on. "They have offered me—or us, I'm not sure which, various metal objects which they say will do various things. I ignored this breach of etiquette, since I considered they didn't know any better."

Cordovir nodded. The youngster was growing up. He was showing, at long last, that he had some manners.

"They want to come to the village tomorrow."

"No!" Cordovir shouted, but the vote was against him.

"Oh, by the way," Hum said, as the meeting was breaking up. "They have several females among them. The ones with the very red mouths are females. It will be interesting to see how the males kill them. Tomorrow is the twenty-fifth day since they came."

The next day the things came to the village, crawling slowly and laboriously over the cliffs. The villagers were able to observe the extreme brittleness of their limbs, the terrible awkwardness of their motions.

"No beauty whatsoever," Cordovir muttered. "And they all look alike."

In the village the things acted without any decency. They crawled into huts and out of huts. They jabbered at the surplus female pen. They picked up eggs and examined them. They peered at the villagers through black things and shiny things.

In midafternoon, Rantan, an elder, decided it was about time he killed his woman. So he pushed the thing who was examining his hut aside and smashed his female to death.

Instantly, two of the things started jabbering at each other, hurrying out of the hut.

One had the red mouth of a female.

"He must have remembered it was time to kill his own

woman," Hum observed. The villagers waited, but nothing happened.

"Perhaps," Rantan said, "perhaps he would like someone to kill her for him. It might be the custom of their land."

Without further ado Rantan slashed down the female with his tail.

The male creature made a terrible noise and pointed a metal stick at Rantan. Rantan collapsed, dead.

"That's odd," Mishall said. "I wonder if that denotes disapproval?"

The things from the metal object—eight of them—were in a tight little circle. One was holding the dead female, and the rest were pointing the metal sticks on all sides. Hum went up and asked them what was wrong.

"I don't understand," Hum said, after he spoke with them. "They used words I haven't learned. But I gather that their emotion is one of reproach."

The monsters were backing away. Another villager, deciding it was about time, killed his wife who was standing in a doorway. The group of monsters stopped and jabbered at each other. Then they motioned to Hum.

Hum's body motion was incredulous after he had talked with them.

"If I understood right," Hum said, "they are ordering us not to kill any more of our women."

"What!" Cordovir and a dozen others shouted.

"I'll ask them again." Hum went back into conference with the monsters who were waving metal sticks in their tentacles.

"That's right," Hum said. Without further preamble he flipped his tail, throwing one of the monsters across the village square. Immediately the others began to point their sticks while retreating rapidly.

After they were gone, the villagers found that seventeen males were dead. Hum, for some reason, had been missed.

"Now will you believe me?" Cordovir shouted. "The creatures told a *deliberate untruth.* They said they wouldn't molest us and then they proceed to kill seventeen of us. Not only an amoral act—but a *concerted death effort!*"

It was almost past human understanding.

"A deliberate untruth!" Cordovir shouted the blasphemy,

sick with loathing. Men rarely discussed the possibility of anyone telling an untruth.

The villagers were beside themselves with anger and revulsion, once they realized the full concept of an *untruthful* creature. And, added to that was the monsters' concerted death effort.

It was like the most horrible nightmare come true. Suddenly it became apparent that these creatures didn't kill females. Undoubtedly they allowed them to spawn unhampered. The thought of that was enough to make a strong man retch.

The surplus females broke out of their pens and, joined by the wives, demanded to know what was happening. When they were told, they were twice as indignant as the men, such being the nature of women.

"Kill them!" the surplus females roared. "Don't let them change our ways! Don't let them introduce immorality!"

"It's true," Hiram said sadly. "I should have guessed it."

"They must be killed at once," a female shouted. Being surplus, she had no name at present, but she made up for that in blazing personality.

"We women desire only to live moral, decent lives, hatching eggs in the pen until our time of marriage comes. And then twenty-five ecstatic days! How could we desire more? These monsters will destroy our way of life. They will make us as terrible as they."

"Now do you understand?" Cordovir screamed at the men. "I warned you, I presented it to you, and you ignored me. Young men must listen to old men in time of crisis." In this rage he killed two youngsters with a blow of his tail. The villagers applauded.

"Drive them out," Cordovir shouted. "Before they corrupt us!"

All the females rushed off to kill the monsters.

"They have death-sticks," Hum observed. "Do the females know?"

"I don't believe so," Cordovir said. He was completely calm now. "You'd better go and tell them."

"I'm tired," Hum said sulkily. "I've been translating. Why don't you go?"

"Oh, let's both go," Cordovir said, bored with the

youngster's adolescent moodiness. Accompanied by half the villagers they hurried off after the females.

They overtook them on the edge of the cliff that overlooked the object. Hum explained the death-sticks while Cordovir considered the problem.

"Roll stones on them!" he told the females. "Perhaps you can break the metal of the object."

The females started rolling stones down the cliffs with great energy. Some bounced off the metal of the object. Immediately, lines of red fire came from the object and females were killed. The ground shook.

"Let's move back!" Cordovir said. "The females have it well in hand, and this shaky ground makes me giddy."

Together with the rest of the males they moved to a safe distance and watched the action.

Women were dying right and left, but they were reinforced by women of other villages who had heard of the menace. They were fighting for their homes now, their rights, and they were fiercer than a man could ever be. The object was throwing fire all over the cliff, but the fire helped dislodge more stones which rained down on the thing. Finally, big fires came out of one end of the metal object.

A landslide started, and the object got into the air just in time. It barely missed a mountain; then it climbed steadily, until it was a little black speck against the larger sun. And then it was gone.

That evening, it was discovered that fifty-three females had been killed. This was fortunate since it helped keep down the surplus female population. The problem would become even more acute now, since seventeen males were gone in a single lump.

Cordovir was feeling exceedingly proud of himself. His wife had been gloriously killed in the fighting, but he took another at once.

"We had better kill our wives sooner than every twenty-five days for a while," he said at the evening Gathering. "Just until things get back to normal."

The surviving females, back in the pen, heard him and applauded wildly.

"I wonder where the things have gone," Hum said, offering the question to the Gathering.

"Probably away to enslave some defenseless race," Cordovir said.

"Not necessarily," Mishill put in and the evening argument was on.

Every science fiction enthusiast remembers the thrill of his first exposure to the concept of space travel—the glory of man's voyaging between the planets and even between the stars. But modern adult science fiction has largely grown away from the mechanics of space travel itself; the voyage is taken for granted as part of the background, and the story is focused on the results. Here, however, one of the brighter new authors in the field shows that the story of the space ship is not exhausted; inevitably in that remote interstellar future, there will be the Mapping Command, whose duties are never finished and whose voyages of discovery may be as exciting as that of Magellan—and as perilous.

GRENVILLE'S PLANET

by Michael Shaara

Wisher did not see the brightness because he was back aft alone. In the still ship he sat quietly, relaxed. He was not bored. It was just that he had no interest. After fourteen years in the Mapping Command even the strangest of the new worlds was routine to him and what little imagination he had was beginning to centre upon a small farm he had seen on the southern plains of Vega VII.

The brightness that Wisher did not see grew with the passing moments. A pale young man named Grenville, who was Wisher's crewman, watched it for a long while absently. When the gleam took on brilliance and a blue-white, dazzling blaze Grenville was startled. He stared at the screen for a long moment, then carefully checked the distance. Still a few light minutes away, the planet was already uncommonly bright.

Pleasantly excited, Grenville watched the planet grow. Slowly the moons came out. Four winked on and ringed the bright world like pearls in a necklace. Grenville gazed in awe. The blueness and the brightness flowed in together; it was the most beautiful thing that Grenville had ever seen.

Excited, he buzzed for Wisher. Wisher did not come.

Grenville took the ship in close and now it occurred to him to wonder. That a planet should shine like that, like an enormous facet of polished glass, was incredible. Now, as he watched the light began to form vaguely into the folds of cloud. The blue grew richer and deeper. Long before he hit the first cloud layer, Grenville knew what it was. He pounded the buzzer. Wisher finally came.

When he saw the water in the screen he stopped in his tracks.

"Well I'll be damned!" he breathed.

Except for a few scuds of clouds it was blue. The entire world was blue. There was the white of the clouds and the ice caps, but the rest was all blue and the rest was water.

Grenville began to grin. A world of *water!*

"Now how's *that* for a freak?" he chuckled. "One in a million, right, Sam? I bet you never saw anything like that."

Wisher shook his head, still staring. Then he moved quickly to the controls and set out to make a check. They circled the planet with the slow, spiralling motion of the Mapping Command, bouncing radar off the dark side. When they came back into the daylight they were sure. There was no land on the planet.

Grenville, as usual, began to chatter.

"Well, naturally," he said, "it was bound to happen sooner or later. Considering Earth, which has a land area covering only one fourth—"

"Yep," nodded Wisher.

"—and when you consider the odds, chances are that there are quite a number of planets with scarcely any land area at all."

Wisher had moved back to the screen.

"Let's go down," he said.

Grenville, startled, stared at him.

"Where?"

"Down low. I want to see what's living in that ocean."

Because each new world was a wholly *new* world and because experience therefore meant nothing, Wisher had decided a long while ago to follow the regs without question. For without the regs, the Mapping Command was a death trap. Nowhere in space was the need for rules so great as out on the frontier where there were no rules at all. The regs were complex, efficient and all-embracing; it was to the regs that the men of the Mapping Command owed their lives and the rest of Mankind owed the conquest of space.

But inevitably, unalterably, there were things which the regs could not have foreseen. And Wisher knew that too, but he did not think about it.

According to plan, then, they dropped down into the stratosphere, went further down below the main cloud region and levelled off at a thousand feet. Below them, mile after rolling, billowy mile, the sea flowed out to the great bare circle of the horizon.

With the screen at full magnification, they probed the water.

It was surprising, in all that expanse of sea, to observe so little. No schools of fish of any kind, no floating masses of seaweed, nothing but a small fleet shape here and there and an occasional group of tiny plant organisms.

Wisher dropped only a hundred or so feet lower. In a world where evolution had been confined underwater it would be best to keep at a distance. On the other worlds to which he had come Wisher had seen some vast and incredible things. Eight hundred feet up, he thought, is a good safe distance.

It was from that height then, that they saw the island.

It was small, too small to be seen from a distance, was barely five miles in length and less than two miles wide. A little brown cigar it was, sitting alone in the varying green-blue wash of the ocean.

Grenville began to grin. Abruptly he laughed out loud. Grenville was not the kind of man who is easily awed, and the sight of that one bare speck, that single stubby persistent butt of rock alone in a world of water, was infinitely comical to him.

"Wait'll we show the boys *this*," he chuckled to Wisher. "Break out the camera. My God, what a picture *this* will make!".

Grenville was filled with pride. This planet, after all,

was *his* assignment. It was his to report on, his discovery—he gasped. They might even name it after *him*.

He flushed, his heart beat rapidly. It had happened before. There were a number of odd planets named after men in the Mapping Command. When the tourists came they would be coming to Grenville's Planet, one of the most spectacular wonders of the Universe.

While the young man was thus rejoicing, Wisher had brought the ship around and was swinging slowly in over the island. It was covered with some kind of brownish-green, stringy vegetation. Wisher was tempted to go down and check for animal life, but decided to see first if there were any more islands.

Still at a height of 800 feet, they spiralled the planet. They did not see the second island, radar picked it out for them.

This one was bigger than the first and there was another island quite near to the south. Both were narrow and elongated in the cigar-like shape of the first, were perhaps twenty miles in length and were encrusted with the same brown-green vegetation. They were small enough to have been hidden from sight during the first check by a few scattered clouds.

The discovery of them was anticlimactic and disappointing. Grenville would have been happier if there was no land at all. But he regained some of his earlier enthusiasm when he remembered that the tourists would still come and that now at least they would be able to land.

There was nothing at all on the night side. Coming back out into the daylight, Wisher cautiously decided to take them down.

"Peculiar," said Wisher, peering at the dunes of the beach.

"What is?" Grenville eyed him through the fish bowls of their helmets.

"I don't know." Wisher turned slowly, gazed around at the shaggy, weedy vegetation. "It doesn't feel right."

Grenville fell silent. There was nothing on the island that could hurt them, they were quite sure of that. The check had revealed the presence of a great number of small, four-footed animals, but only one type was larger than a dog, and that one was slow and noisy.

"Have to be careful about snakes," Wisher said absently,

recalling the regs on snakes and insects. Funny thing, that. There were very few insects.

Both men were standing in close to the ship. It was the rule, of course. You never left the ship until you were absolutely sure. Wisher, for some vague reason he could not define, was not sure.

"How's the air check?"

Grenville was just then reading the meters. After a moment he said: "Good."

Wisher relaxed, threw open his helmet and breathed in deeply. The clean fresh air flowed into him, exhilarating him. He unscrewed his helmet entirely, looking around.

The ship had come down on the up end of the beach, a good distance from the sea, and was standing now in a soft, reddish sand. It was bordered on the north by the open sea and to the south was the scrawny growth they had seen from above. It was not a jungle—the plants were too straight and stiff for that—and the height of the tallest was less than ten feet. But it was the very straightness of the things, the eerie regularity of them, which grated in Wisher's mind.

But, breathing in the cool sea air of the island, Wisher began to feel more confident. They had their rifles, they had the ship and the alarm system. There was nothing here that could harm them.

Grenville brought out some folding chairs from the ship. They sat and chatted pleasantly until the twilight came.

Just before twilight two of the moons came out.

"Moons," said Wisher suddenly.

"What?"

"I was just thinking," Wisher explained.

"What about the moons?"

"I wasn't thinking exactly about them, I was thinking about the tide. Four good-sized moons in conjunction could raise one heck of a tide."

Grenville settled back, closing his eyes.

"So?"

"So that's probably where the land went."

Grenville was too busy dreaming about his fame as discoverer of Grenville's Planet to be concerned with tides and moons.

"Let the techs worry about that," he said without interest.

But Wisher kept thinking.

The tide could very well be the cause. When the four moons got together and started to pull they would raise a tremendous mass of water, a grinding power that would slice away the continent edges like no erosive force in history. Given a billion years in which to work—but Wisher suddenly remembered a peculiar thing about the island.

If the tides had planed down the continents of this planet, then these islands had no right being here, certainly not as sand and loose rock. Just one tide like the ones those moons could raise would be enough to cut the islands completely away. Well maybe, he thought, the tides are very far apart, centuries even.

He glanced apprehensively at the sky. The two moons visible were reassuringly far apart.

He turned from the moons to gaze at the sea. And then he remembered the first thought he had had about this planet—that uncomfortable feeling that the first sight of land had dispelled. He thought of it now again.

Evolution.

A billion years beneath the sea, with no land to take the first developing mammals. What was going on, right now as he watched, beneath the placid rolling surface of the sea?

It was a disturbing thought. When they went back to the ship for the night Wisher did not need the regs to tell him to seal the airlock and set the alarm screens.

The alarm that came in the middle of the night and nearly scared Wisher to death turned out to be only an animal. It was one of the large ones, a weird bristling thing with a lean and powerful body. It got away before they were up to see it, but it left its photographic image.

In spite of himself, Wisher had trouble getting back to sleep, and in the morning was silently in favour of leaving for the one last star they would map before returning to base. But the regs called for life specimens to be brought back from all livable worlds whenever possible, whenever there was no "slight manifestation of danger." Well, here it was certainly possible. They would have to stay long enough to take a quick sampling of plants and animals and of marine life too.

Grenville was just as anxious to get back as Wisher was, but for different reasons. Grenville, figured Grenville, was now a famous man.

Early in the morning, then, they lifted ship and once more spiralled the planet. Once the mapping radar had recorded the size and shape and location of the islands, they went in low again and made a complete check for life forms.

They found as before, very little. There were the bristling things, and—as Wisher had suspected—a great quantity of snakes and lizards. There were very few observable fish. There were no birds.

When they were done they returned to the original island. Grenville, by this time, had a name for it. Since there was another island near it, lying to the south, Grenville called that one South Grenville. The first was, of course, North Grenville. Grenville chuckled over that for a long while.

"Don't go too near the water."

"All right, mama," Grenville chirped, grinning. "I'll work the edge of the vegetation."

"Leave the rifle, take the pistol. It's handier."

Grenville nodded and left, dragging the specimen sack. Wisher, muttering, turned toward the water.

It is unnatural, he thought, for a vast warm ocean to be so empty of life. Because the ocean, really, is where life begins. He had visions in his mind of any number of vicious, incredible, slimy things that were alive and native to that sea and who were responsible for the unnatural sterility of the water. When he approached the waves he was very cautious.

The first thing he noticed, with a shock, was that there were no shellfish.

Not any. Not crabs or snails or even the tiniest of sea beings. Nothing. The beach was a bare, dead plot of sand.

He stood a few yards from the waves, motionless. He was almost positive, now, that there was danger here. The shores of every warm sea he had ever seen, from Earth on out to Deneb, had been absolutely choked with life and the remnants of life, There were always shells and fish scales, and snails, worms, insects; bits of jellyfish, tentacles, minutiae of a hundred million kinds, cluttering and crowding every square inch of the beach and sea. And yet here, now, there was nothing. Just sand and water.

It took a great deal of courage for Wisher to approach those waves, although the water here was shallow. He took a quick water sample and hurried back to the ship.

Minutes later he was perched in the shadow of her side, staring out broodingly over the ocean. The water was Earth water as far as his instruments could tell. There was nothing wrong with it. But there was nothing much living in it.

When Grenville came back with the floral specimens Wisher quietly mentioned the lack of shellfish.

"Well, hell," said Grenville, scratching his head painfully, "maybe they just don't like it here."

And maybe they've got reason, Wisher said to himself. But aloud he said: "The computer finished calculating the orbits of those moons."

"So?"

"So the moons conjunct every 112 years. They raise a tide of 600 feet."

Grenville did not follow.

"The tide," said Wisher, smiling queerly, "is at least 400 feet higher than any of the islands."

When Grenville started, still puzzled, Wisher grunted and kicked at the sand.

"Now where in hell do you suppose the animals came from?"

"They should be drowned," said Grenville slowly.

"Right. And would be, unless they're amphibian, which they're not. Or unless a new batch evolves every hundred years."

"Um." Grenville sat down to think about it.

"Don't make sense," he said after a while.

Having thoroughly confounded Grenville, Wisher turned away and paced slowly in the sand. The sand, he thought distractedly, that's another thing. Why in heck is this island here at all?

Artificial.

The word popped unbidden into his brain.

That would be it. That would have to be it.

The island was artificial, was—restored. Put here by whoever or whatever lived under the sea.

* * *

Grenville was ready to go. He stood nervously eyeing the waves, his fingers clamped tightly on the pistol at his belt, waiting for Wisher to give the word.

Wisher leaned against the spaceship, conveniently near the airlock. He regretted disturbing Grenville.

"We can't leave yet," he said calmly. "We haven't any proof. And besides, there hasn't been any 'manifestation of danger.' "

"We have proof enough for me," Grenville said quickly.

Wisher nodded absently.

"It's easy to understand. Evolution kept right on going, adapting and changing just as it does everywhere else in the Universe. Only here, when the mammals began coming up onto the land, they had no room to expand. And they were all being washed away every hundred years, as the tides rose and fell and the continents wore down below tide level.

"But evolution never stopped. It continued beneath the sea. Eventually it came up with an intelligent race.

"God knows what they are, or how far they've progressed. They must be pretty highly-evolved, or they couldn't have done something like this"—he broke off, realizing that the building of the islands was no clue. The ancient Egyptians on Earth had built the pyramids, certainly a much harder job. There was no way of telling how far evolved this race was. Or what the island was for.

Zoo?

No. He shook that out of the confusion of his mind. If the things in the sea wanted a zoo they would naturally build it below the surface of the water, where they themselves could travel with ease and where the animals could be kept in air-tight compartments. And if this was a zoo, then by now there should have been visitors.

That was one more perplexing thing. Why had nothing come? It was unbelievable that an island like this should be left completely alone, that nothing had noticed the coming of their ship.

And here his thought broke again. They would not be just fish, these things. They would need . . . hands. Or tentacles. He pictured something like a genius squid, and the hair on his body stiffened.

He turned back to Grenville.

"Did you get the animal specimens?"

Grenville shook his head. "No. Just plants. And a small lizard."

Wisher's face, lined with the inbred caution of many years, now at last betrayed his agitation. "We'll have to get one of those things that set off the alarm last night. But to heck with the rest. We'll let HQ worry about that." He stepped quickly into the airlock, dragging the bag of specimens. "I'll pack up," he said, "you go get that thing."

Grenville turned automatically and struck off down the beach.

He never came back.

At the end of the third hour after Grenville had gone, Wisher went to the arms locker and pulled out a heavy rifle. He cursed the fact that he had no small scout sled. He could not take the ship. She was too big and unwieldy for low, slow flying and he could not risk cracking her up.

He was breaking the regs, of course. Since Grenville had not come back he must be considered dead and it was up to Wisher to leave alone. A special force would come back for Grenville, or for what was left of him. Wisher knew all that. He thought about it while he was loading the rifle. He thought about the vow he had made never to break the regs and he went right on loading the rifle. He told himself that he would take no chances and if he didn't find Grenville right away he would come back and leave, but he knew all along that he was breaking the regs. At the same time he knew that there was nothing else to do. This was the one reg he had never faced before and it was the one reg he would always break. For Grenville or for anyone else. For a skinny young fool like Grenville, or for anyone else.

Before he left he took the routine precautions concerning the ship. He set the alarm screens to blast anything that moved within two hundred feet of her. If Grenville came back before him it would be all right because the alarm was set to deactivate when it registered the sound pattern of either his or Grenville's voice. If Grenville came back and didn't see him, he would know that the alarm was on.

And if no one came back at all, the ship would blow by itself.

The beach was wide and curved on out of sight. Grenville's deep heel prints were easy to follow.

Stiffly, in the wind, the stalks of the brown vegetation scratched and rustled. Wisher walked along Grenville's track. He wanted to call, but stopped himself. No noise. He must make no noise.

This is the end of it, he kept saying to himself. When I get out of this I will go home.

The heel prints turned abruptly into the alien forest. Wisher walked some distance farther on, to a relatively clear space. He turned, stepping carefully, started to circle the spot where Grenville had gone in. The wood around him was soggy, sterile. He saw nothing move. But a sharp, shattering blast came suddenly to him in the still air.

The explosion blossomed and Wisher perked spasmodically. The ship. Something was at the ship. He fought down a horrible impulse to run, stood quiet, gun poised, knowing that the ship could take care of itself. And then he stepped slowly forward. And fell.

He fell through a soft light mat of bushes into a hole. There was a crunching snap and he felt a metal rip into his legs, tearing and cracking the bones. He went up to his shoulders. He knew in a flash, with a blast of glacial fear, what it was. *Animal trap.*

He reached for his rifle. But the rifle was beyond him. A foot past his hand, it lay on the floor of the wood near him. His legs, his legs . . . he felt the awful pain as he tried to move.

It blazed through his mind and woke him. Out of his belt he dragged his pistol, and in a sea of pain, held upright by the trap, he waited. He was not afraid. He had broken the regs, and this had happened, and he had expected it. He waited.

Nothing came.

Why? Why?

This had happened to Grenville, he knew. Why?

It had happened to him now, and for a moment he could not understand why he did not seem to care, but was just . . . curious. Then he looked down into the hole and saw the hot redness of his own blood, and as he watched it bubble he realized that he was dying.

He had very little time. He was hopeful. Maybe something would come and at least he would see what they were. He wanted awfully for something to come. In the red mist which was his mind he debated with himself whether or not to shoot it if it came, and over and over he asked himself why, why? Before something came, unfortunately, he died.

The traps had been dug in the night. From out the sea they had come to dig in the preserve—for a preserve was what the island was, was all that it could have been—and then returned to the sea to wait.

For the ship had been seen from the very beginning, and its purpose understood. The best brains of the sea had gathered and planned, the enormous, manta-like people whose name was unpronounceable but whose technology was not far behind Earth's, met in consultation and immediately understood. It was necessary to capture the ship. Therefore the Earthmen must be separated from it, and it was for this reason that Wisher had died.

But now, to the astonishment of the things, the ship was still alive. It stood silent and alone in the whiteness of the beach ticking and sparking within itself, and near it, on the bloodied sand, were the remains of the one that had come too close. The others had fled in terror.

Time was of no importance to the clever, squid-like beings. They had won already, could wait and consider. Thus the day grew late and became afternoon, and the waves—the aseptic, sterile waves which were proof in themselves of the greatest of all oceanic civilizations—crumbled whitely on the beach. The things exulted. The conquest of space was in their hands.

Within the ship, of course, there was ticking, and a small red hand moved toward zero.

In a little while the ship would blow, and with it would go the island, and a great chunk of the sea. But the beings could not know. It was an alien fact they faced and an alien fact was unknowable. Just as Wisher could not have known the nature of the planet, these things could not now foresee the nature of the ship and the wheel had come full circle. Second by second, with the utter, mechanical loyalty of the machine, the small red hand crept onward.

The waves near the beach were frothy and white.

A crowd was forming.

The base was foolproof, unconquerable. Yet the Captain was right to start praying. Simak has a story about that . . .

BEACHHEAD

by Clifford D. Simak

There was nothing, absolutely nothing, that could stop a human planetary survey party. It was a highly specialized unit created for and charged with one purpose only . . . to establish a bridgehead on an alien planet, to blast out the perimeters of that bridgehead and establish a base where there would be some elbow-room. Then hold that elbow-room against all comers until it was time to go.

After the base was once established, the brains of the party got to work. They turned the place inside out. They put it on tape and captured it within the chains of symbols they scribbled in their field books. They pictured it and wrote it and plotted it and reduced it to a neat assembly of keyed and symbolic facts to be inserted in the galactic files.

If there was life, and sometimes there was, they prodded it to get reaction. Sometimes the reaction was extremely violent and other times it was much more dangerously subtle. But there were ways in which to handle both the violent and the subtle, for the legionnaires and their robotics were trained to a razor's edge and knew nearly all the answers.

As we were saying, there was nothing in the universe, so far known, that could stop a human survey party.

Tom Decker sat at his ease in the empty lounge and swirled the ice in the highball glass, well contented, watching the first of the robots emerge from the bowels of the cargo space. They dragged a conveyor belt behind them as they emerged and Decker, sitting idly, watched them. drive supports into the ground and rig up the belt.

A door clicked open back of Decker and he turned his head.

"May I come in, sir," Doug Jackson asked.

"Certainly," said Decker.

Jackson walked to the great curving window and looked out.

"What does it look like, sir?" he asked.

Decker shrugged. "Another job," he said. "Six weeks. Six months. Depends on what we find."

Jackson sat down beside him.

"This one looks tough," he said. "Jungle worlds always are a bit meaner than any of the others."

Decker grunted at him. "A job," he said. "That's all. Another job to do. Another report to file. Then they'll either send out an exploitation gang or a pitiful bunch of bleating colonists."

"Or," said Jackson, "they'll file the report and let it gather dust for a thousand years or so."

"They can do anything they want," Decker told him. "We turn it in. What someone else does with it after that is their affair, not ours."

They sat quietly, watching the six robots roll out the first of the packing-cases, rip off its cover and unpack the seventh robot, laying out his various parts neatly in a row in the tramped-down, waist-high grass. Then, working as a team, with not a single fumble, they put No. 7 together, screwed his brain case into his metal skull, flipped up his energizing switch and slapped the breastplate home.

No. 7 stood groggily for a moment. He swung his arms uncertainly, shook his head from side to side. Then, having oriented himself, he stepped briskly forward, helped the other six heave the packing-case containing No. 8 off the conveyor belt.

"Takes a little time this way," said Decker, "but it saves a lot of space. Have to cut our robot crew in half if we didn't pack them at the end of every job. They stow away better."

He sipped at his highball speculatively. Jackson lit a cigarette.

"Some day," said Jackson, "we're going to run up against something that we can't handle.

Decker snorted.

"Maybe here," insisted Jackson, gesturing at the nightmare jungle world outside the great curved sweep of the vision plate.

"You're a romanticist," Decker told him shortly. "In love with the unexpected. Besides that, you're new. Get a dozen trips under your belt and you won't feel this way."

"It could happen," declared Jackson.

Decker nodded, almost sleepily. "Maybe," he said. "Maybe it could, at that. It never has, but I suppose it could. And when it does, we take it on the lam. It's no part of our job to fight a last ditch battle. When we bump up against something that's too big to handle, we don't stick around. We don't take any risks."

He had another sip.

"Nor even calculated risks," he said.

The ship rested on the top of a low hill, in a small clearing masked by tall grass, sprinkled here and there with patches of exotic flowers. Below the hill a river flowed sluggishly, a broad expanse of chocolate-coloured water moving in a sleepy tide through the immense, vine-entangled forest.

As far as the eye could see the jungle stretched away, a brooding darkness that even from behind the curving quartz of the vision plate seemed to exude a heady, musty scent of danger that swept up over the grass-covered hilltop. There was no sign of life, but one knew, almost instinctively, that sentiency lurked in the buried pathways and tunnels of the great treeland.

Robot No. 8 had been energized and now the eight split into two groups, ran out two packing-boxes at a time instead of one. Soon there were twelve robots and then they formed themselves into three groups.

"Like that," said Decker, picking up the conversation where they had left it lying. He gestured with his glass, now empty. "No calculated risks. We send the robots first. They unpack and set up their fellows. Then the whole gang turns to and uncrates the machinery and sets it up and gets it operating. A man doesn't even put his foot on the ground until he has a steel ring around the ship to give him protection."

Jackson sighed. "I guess you're right," he said. "Nothing can happen. We don't take any chances. Not a single one."

"Why should we?" Decker asked.

He heaved himself out of the chair, stood up and stretched.

"Got a job or two to do," he said. "Last minute checks and so on."

"I'll sit here for awhile," said Jackson. "I like to watch. I'm new to this. It is fascinating."

"You'll get over that," said Decker, "in another twenty years."

In his office, Decker lifted the sheaf of preliminary reports off his desk and ran through them slowly, checking each one carefully, filing away in his mind the basic facts of the world outside.

He worked stolidly, wetting a big, blunt thumb against his out-thrust tongue to flip the report pages off the top of the neat stack and deposit them, in not so neat a pile to his right, face downward.

Atmosphere—pressure slightly more than Earth. High in oxygen content.

Gravity—a bit more than Earth.

Temperature—hot. Jungle worlds always were. There was a breeze outside now, he thought. Maybe there'd be a breeze most of the time. That would be a help.

Rotation—thirty-six-hour day.

Radiation—none of local origin, but some hard stuff getting through from the sun.

He made a mental note: Watch that!

Bacterial and virus count—as usual. Lots of it. Apparently, not too dangerous. Not with every single soul hypoed and immunized and hormoned to his eyebrows. But you never can be sure, he thought. Not entirely sure. No calculated risks, he had told Jackson. But here was a calculated risk and one you couldn't do a single thing about. If there was a bug that picked you for a host and you weren't loaded for bear to fight him, you took him on and did the best you could.

Life factor—lot of emanations. Probably the vegetation, maybe even the soil, was crawling with all sorts of loathsome life. Vicious stuff, more than likely. But that was something that you took care of as a matter of routine. No use of taking any chances. You went over the ground even if there was no life . . . just to be sure there wasn't.

A tap came on the door and he called out for the man to enter.

It was Captain Carr, commander of the Legion unit.

Carr saluted snappily. Decker did not rise, made his answering salute a sloppy one on purpose. No use, he told himself, of letting the fellow establish any semblance of equality, for there was no such equality in fact. A captain of the Legion did not rank with the commandant of a galactic survey party.

"Reporting, sir," said Carr. "We are ready for a landing."

Decker rumbled at him. "Fine, Captain. Fine."

What was the matter with the fool? The Legion always was ready, always would be ready—that was no more than tradition. Why carry out such an empty, stiff formality?

But it was the nature of a man like Carr, he supposed. The Legion, with its rigid discipline, with its ancient pride of service and tradition, attracted men like Carr, was a perfect finishing school for accomplished martinets.

Tin soldiers, Decker thought, but accomplished ones. As hard-bitten a gang of fighting men as the galaxy had ever known. They were drilled and disciplined to a razor's edge, serum and hormone-injected against all known diseases of an alien world, trained and educated in alien psychology and strictly indoctrinated with high survival characteristics which stood up under even the most adverse circumstances.

"We shall not be ready for some time, Captain," Decker said. "The robots have just started their uncrating."

"Very well," said Carr. "We await your orders, sir."

"Thank you, Captain," Decker told him, making it quite clear that he wished he would get out. But when Carr turned to go, Decker called him back.

"What is it, sir?" asked Carr.

"I've been wondering," said Decker. "Just wondering, you understand. Can you imagine any circumstance which might arise that the Legion could not handle?"

Carr's expression was a pure delight to see.

"I'm afraid, sir," he said, "I don't understand your question."

Decker sighed. "I didn't think you would," he said.

Before nightfall the full working force of robots had been uncrated and had set up some of the machines, enough to establish a small circle of alarm posts around the ship.

A flame thrower burned a barren circle on the hill-top, stretching five hundred feet around the ship. A hard radiations generator took up its painstaking task, pouring pure death into the soil. The toll must have been terrific. In some spots the ground virtually boiled as the dying life forms fought momentarily and fruitlessly to escape the death that cut them down.

The robots rigged up huge batteries of lamps that set the hill-top ablaze with a light as bright as day and the work went on.

As yet no human had set foot outside the ship.

Inside the ship the robot stewards set up a table in the lounge so that the human diners could see what was going on outside.

The entire company, except for the legionnaires, who stayed in quarters, had gathered for the meal when Decker came into the room.

"Good evening, gentlemen," he said.

He strode to the table's head and the others ranged themselves along the sides. He sat down and there was a scraping of drawn chairs as the others took their places.

He clasped his hands in front of him and bowed his head and parted his lips to say the customary words. And then he halted even as he spoke and when the words did come they were different than the ones he had said by rote a thousand times before.

"Dear Father, we are Thy servants in an unknown land and there is a deadly pride upon us. Teach us humility and lead us to the knowledge, before it is too late, that men, despite their far travelling and their mighty works, still are as children in Thy sight. Bless the bread we are about to break, we beg Thee, and keep us forever in Thy compassion. Amen."

He lifted his head and looked down the table. Some of them, he saw, were startled. The others were amused.

They wonder if I'm cracking, he thought. They think

the Old Man's breaking up. And that may be true, for all I know. Although I was all right until this afternoon. All right until young Doug Jackson . . .

Platters and plates were being passed up and down the table's length and there was the commonplace, homely clatter of silverware and china.

"This looks an interesting world, sir," said Waldron, the anthropologist. "Dickson and I were up in observation just before the sun set. We thought we saw something down by the river. Some sort of life."

Decker grunted, scooping fried potatoes out of the bowl on to his plate. "Funny if we don't run across a lot of life here. The radiation wagon stirred up a lot of it when it went over the field today."

"What Waldron and I saw," said Dickson, "looked humanoid."

Decker squinted at the biologist. "Sure of that?" he asked.

Dickson shook his head. "The seeing was poor. Could not be absolutely sure. Seemed to me there were two or three of them. Matchstick men."

Waldron nodded. "Like a picture a kid would draw," he said. "One stroke for the body. Two strokes each for arms and legs. A circle for a head. Angular. Ungraceful. Skinny."

"Graceful enough in motion, though," said Dickson. "When they moved they went like cats. Flowed, sort of."

"We'll know plenty soon enough," Decker told them, mildly. "In a day or two we'll flush them."

Funny, he thought. On almost every job someone popped up to report he had spotted humanoids. Usually there weren't any. Usually it was just imagination. Probably wishful thinking, he told himself, the yen of men far away from their fellow men to find in an alien place a type of life that somehow seemed familiar.

Although the usual humanoid, once you met him in the flesh, turned out to be so repulsively alien that alongside him an octopus would seem positively human.

Franey, the senior geologist, said: "I've been thinking about those mountains to the west of us, the ones we caught sight of when we were coming in. Had a new look about them. New mountains are good to work in. They haven't worn down, easier to get at whatever's in them."

"We'll lay out our first survey lines in that direction," Decker told him.

Outside the curving vision plate the night was alive with the blaze of the batteries of lights. Gleaming robots toiled in shining gangs. Ponderous machines lumbered past. Smaller ones scurried like frightened beetles. To the south great gouts of flame leaped out and the sky was painted red with the bursts of a squad of flame throwers going into action.

"Chewing out a landing field," said Decker. "A tongue of forest juts out there. Absolutely level ground. Like a floor. Won't take a great deal of work to turn it into a field."

The stewards brought coffee and brandy and a box of good cigars. Decker and his men settled back in their chairs, taking life easy, watching the work going on outside the ship.

"I hate this waiting," Franey said, settling down comfortably to his cigar.

"Part of the job," said Decker. He poured more brandy into his coffee.

By dawn the last machines were set up and either had been moved out to their assigned positions or were parked in the motor pool. The flamers had enlarged the burned-over area and three radiation wagons were busy on their rounds. To the south the airfield had been finished and the jets were lined up and waiting, in a plumb-straight line.

Some of the robots, their work done for the moment, formed themselves in solid ranks to shape a solid square, neat and orderly and occupying a minimum of space. They stood there in the square, waiting against the time when they would be needed, a motor pool of robots, a reservoir of manpower.

Finally the gang-plank came down and the legionnaires marched out in files of two, with clank and glitter and a remorseless precision that put all machines to shame. There were no banners and there were no drums, for these were useless things and the Legion, despite its clank and glitter, was an organization of ruthless efficiency.

The column wheeled and became a line and the line broke up and the platoons moved out toward the planet-head perimeter.

There machine and legionnaire and robot manned the frontier Earth had set up on an alien world.

Busy robots staked out and set up an open-air pavilion of gaudy striped canvas that rippled in the breeze, set up tables and chairs beneath the shading canvas, moved out a refrigerator filled with refreshments, with extra ice compartments.

It was finally safe and comfortable for ordinary men to leave the shelter of the ship.

Organization, Decker told himself—organization and efficiency and leaving not a thing to chance. Plug every loophole before it was a loophole. Crush possible resistance before it could become resistance. Gain absolute control over a certain number of square feet of planet and operate from there.

Later, of course, there were certain chances taken; you couldn't eliminate them all. There would be field trips and even with all precautions that robot and machine and legionnaire could offer, there would be certain risks. There would be aerial mapping and surveys, and these, too, would have elements of chance, but with those elements reduced to the very minimum.

And always there would be the base—an absolutely safe and impregnable base to which a field party or a survey flight could retreat, from which reinforcements could be sent out or counter-action taken.

Foolproof, he told himself, as foolproof as it could be made.

He wondered, briefly, what had been the matter with him the night before. It had been that young fool, Jackson, of course—a capable biochemist, possibly, but certainly the wrong kind of man for a job like this. Something had slipped up; the screening board should have stopped a man like Jackson, should have spotted his emotional instability. Not that he could do any actual harm, of course, but he could be upsetting. An irritant, said Decker. That's what he is—just an irritant.

Decker laid an armful of paraphernalia on the long table underneath the gay pavilion. From it he selected a rolled-up sheet of map paper, unrolled it, spread it flat and thumbtacked it at four corners. On it a portion of the river and the mountains to the westward had been roughly pencilled in. The base was represented by a crossed-through square—but the rest of it was blank. But it would be filled in; as the days went by it would take on shape and form.

From the field to the south a jet whooshed up into the sky, made a lazy turn and straightened out to streak toward the west. Decker walked to the edge of the pavilion's shade and watched it as it dwindled out of sight. That would be Jarvis and Donnelly, assigned to the preliminary survey of the southwest sector between the base and the western mountains.

Another jet rose lazily, trailing its column of exhaust, gathered speed and sprang into the sky. Freeman and Johns, he thought.

Decker went back to the table, pulled out a chair and sat down. He picked up a pencil and tapped it idly on the almost-blank map paper. Behind his back he heard another jet whoom upward from the field.

He let his eyes take in the base. Already it was losing its raw, burned-over look. Already it had something of the look of Earth about it, of the efficiency and common sense and get-the-job-done attitude of the man of Earth.

Small groups of men stood about the base talking. One of them, he saw, was squatted on the ground, talking things over with three squatting robots. Others of them walked about, giving orders, planning, sizing up the situation.

Decker grunted with satisfaction. A capable gang of men, he thought. Most of them would have to wait around to really get down to work until the first surveys came in, but even while they waited they would not be idle.

They'd take soil samples and test them. The life that swarmed in the soil would be captured and brought in by grinning robots and the squirming, vicious things would be pinned down and investigated—photographed, X-rayed, dissected, analyzed, observed, put through reaction tests. Trees and plant and grasses would be dug for a look at soil strata. The river's water would be analyzed. Seines would dredge up some of the life it held. Wells would be driven to establish water tables.

All of this here, at the moment, while they waited for the first preliminary flights to bring back data that would pinpoint other areas worthy of investigation.

Once those reports were in, the work would be started in dead earnest. Geologist and mineral men would probe into the planet's hide. Weather observation points would be set up. Botanists would take far-ranging check samples. Each man would do the work for which he had been trained. Field reports would pour back to the base, there to be correlated and fitted into the picture.

Work then, work in plenty. Work by day and night. And all the time the base would be a bit of Earth, a few square yards held inviolate against all another world might muster.

Decker sat easily in his chair and felt the breeze that came beneath the canvas, a gentle breeze that ruffled through his hair, rattled the papers on the table and twitched the tacked-down map. It was pleasant here, he thought. But it wouldn't stay pleasant long. It almost never did.

Some day, he thought, I'll find a pleasant planet, a paradise planet where the weather's always perfect and there's food for the picking of it and natives that are intelligent to talk with and companionable in other ways—and I will never leave it. I'll refuse to leave when the ship is ready to cast off. I'll live out my days in a fascinating corner of a lousy galaxy—a galaxy that is gaunt with hunger and mad with savagery and lonely beyond all that can be said of loneliness.

He looked up from his reverie and saw Jackson standing at the pavilion's edge, watching him.

"What's the matter, Jackson?" Decker asked with sudden bitterness. "Why aren't you . . ."

"They're bringing in a native, sir," and Jackson, breathlessly. "One of the things Waldron and Dickson saw. The robots caught him, sir."

The native was humanoid, but he was not human.

As Waldron and Dickson had said, he was a matchstick man, a flesh and blood extension of a drawing a four-year-old might make. He was black as the ace of spades and he wore no clothing, but the eyes that looked out of the pumpkin-shaped head at Decker were bright with a light that might have been intelligence.

Decker tensed as he looked into those eyes. Then he looked away, saw the men standing silently around the pavilion's edge, silent and waiting, tense as he was.

Slowly, Decker reached out his hand to one of the twin headsets of the mentograph. His fingers closed over it and for a moment he felt a vague, but forceful reluctance to put it on his head. It was disturbing to contact, or attempt to contact, an alien mind. It gave one a queasy feeling in the pit of the stomach. It was a thing, he thought, that man never had been intended to do—an experience that was utterly foreign to any human background.

He lifted the headset slowly, fitted it over his skull, made a sign toward the second set.

For a moment the alien eyes watched him, the creature standing erect and motionless.

Courage, thought Decker. Raw and naked courage, to stand here in this suddenly unfamiliar environment that had blossomed almost overnight on familiar ground, to stand here motionless and erect, surrounded by creatures that must look as if they had dropped from some horrific nightmare.

The humanoid took one step closer to the table, reached out a hand and took the headset. Fumbling with its unfamiliarity, he clamped it on his head. And, never for a moment, did the eyes waver from Decker's eyes, always alert and watchful.

Decker forced himself to relax, tried to force his mind into an attitude of peace and calm. That was a thing you had to be careful of. You couldn't scare the critters—you had to lull them, quiet them down, make them feel your friendliness. They would be upset and humpy—a sudden thought, even a suggestion of human brusqueness would wind them up tighter than a drum.

There was intelligence here, he told himself, being careful to keep his mind unruffled—a greater intelligence than one would think looking at the creature. Intelligence enough to know that he should put on the headset—guts enough to do it.

He caught the first faint mental whiff of the match-stick man and the pit of his stomach contracted suddenly and there was an ache around his belly. There was nothing in the thing he caught, nothing that could be put in words, but there was an alienness, as a smell is alien. There was a non-human connotation that set one's teeth on edge. He fought back the gagging blackness of repulsive disgust that sought to break the smooth friendliness he held within his mind.

"We are friendly," Decker forced himself to think. "We

are friendly. We are friendly. We are friendly. We are friendly. We are . . ."

"You should not have come," said the thought of the match-stick man.

"We will not harm you," Decker thought. "We are friendly. We will not harm you. We will not harm you . . ."

"You will never leave," said the humanoid.

"Let's be friends," thought Decker. "Let's be friends. We have gifts. We will help you. We will . . ."

"You should not have come," said the match-stick thought. "But since you are here, you can never leave."

Humour him, Decker told himself. Humour him. Humour him.

"All right, then," he thought. "We will stay. We will stay and we will be friendly. We will stay and teach you. We will give you the things we have brought for you and we will stay with you."

"You will not leave," said the match-stick man's thought, and there was something so cold and logical and matter-of-fact about the way the thought was delivered that Decker suddenly was cold.

The humanoid meant it . . . meant every word of the thing he said. He was not being dramatic, nor was he blustering . . . and neither was he bluffing. He actually thought that the humans would not leave, that they would not live to leave the planet.

Decker smiled softly to himself.

"You will die here," said the humanoid thought.

"Die?" asked Decker. "What is die?"

The match-stick man's thought was pure disgust. Deliberately, he reached up and took off the headset, laid it carefully back upon the table.

Then he turned and walked away and not a man made a move to stop him.

Decker took off his headset, slammed it on the table top.

"Jackson," he said, "pick up a phone and tell the Legion to let him through. Let him leave. Don't try to stop him."

He sat limply in his chair and looked at the ring of faces that was watching him.

Waldron asked, "What is it, Decker?"

"He sentenced us to death," said Decker. "He said he

would not allow us to leave the planet. He said that we would die here."

"Strong words," said Waldron.

"He meant them," Decker said.

He lifted a hand, flipped it wearily. "He doesn't know, of course," he said. "He really thinks that he can stop us leaving. He thinks that we will die."

It was an amusing situation, really. That a naked humanoid should walk out of the jungle and threaten to kill a human survey party. That he should really think that he could do it. That he should be positive about it.

But there was not a single smile on any of the faces that looked at Decker.

"We can't let it get us," Decker said.

"Nevertheless," Waldron declared, "we should take all precautions."

Decker nodded. "We'll go on emergency alert immediately," he said. "We'll stay that way until we're sure . . . until we're . . ."

He halted angrily. Sure of what? Sure that an alien savage who wore no clothing, who had not a sign of culture about him could wipe out a group of humans protected by a ring of steel, held within a guard of machine and robots and a group of fighting men who knew all there was to know concerning the refinement of dealing out swift and merciless extermination to anything that moved against them?

Ridiculous?

Of course it was ridiculous!

And yet the eyes had held intelligence. The being had had not only intelligence, but courage. He had stood within a circle of what to him were alien beings and he had not flinched. He had faced the unknown and said what there was to say and then had walked away with a dignity any human would have been proud to wear. He had known that the alien beings within the confines of the base were not of his own planet, for he had said they should not have come and his thought had implied that he was aware they were not of this world of his. He had understood that he was supposed to put on the headset, but whether that was an act more of courage than of intelligence one would never know—for you could not know if he had realized what the headset had been for. Not knowing, the naked courage of clamping it to his head was of an order that could not be measured.

"What do you think?" Decker asked Waldron.

"We'll have to be careful," Waldron told him evenly. "We'll have to watch our step. Take all precautions now that we are warned. But there's nothing to be scared of, nothing we can't handle."

"He was bluffing," Dickson said. "Trying to scare us into leaving."

Decker shook his head. "I don't think he was," he said. "I tried to bluff him and it didn't work. He's just as sure as we are."

The work went on.

There was no attack.

The jets roared out and thrummed away, mapping the land. Field parties went out, cautiously. They were flanked by robots and by legionnaires and preceded by lumbering machines that knifed and tore and burned a roadway through even the most stubborn of the terrain they went up against. Radio weather stations were set up at distant points and at the base the weather tabulators clicked off the data that the stations sent back.

Other field parties were flown into the special areas pin-pointed for more extensive exploration and investigation.

And nothing happened.

The days went past.

The weeks went past.

The machines and robots watched and the legionnaires stood ready and the men hurried with their work to get off the planet.

A bed of coal was found and mapped. An iron range was discovered. One area in the mountains to the west crawled with radioactive ores. The botanists found twenty-seven species of edible fruits. The base swarmed with animals that had been trapped as specimens and remained as pets.

And a village of the match-stick men was found.

It wasn't much of a place. Its huts were primitive. Its sanitation was non-existent. Its people were peaceful.

Decker left his chair under the striped pavilion to lead a party to the village.

The party entered cautiously, weapons ready but being

very careful not to move too fast, not to speak too quickly, not to make a motion that might be construed as hostile.

The natives sat in their doorways and watched them. They did not speak and they did not move. They simply watched the humans as they marched to the center of the village.

There the robots set up a table and placed a mentograph upon it. Decker sat down in a chair and put one of the headsets on his skull. The rest of the party drew up into a line and waited.

Decker waited and the others waited and the natives sat in their doorways watching.

They waited for an hour and not a native stirred. None came forward to put on the other headset.

Decker waved his hand wearily, took off the headset.

"It's no use," he said. "It won't work. Go ahead and take your pictures. Do anything you wish. But don't disturb the natives. Don't touch a single thing."

He took a handkerchief out of his pocket and mopped his steaming face.

Waldron came and leaned on the table. "What do you make of it?" he asked.

Decker shook his head. "It haunts me," he said. "There's just one thing that I am thinking. It must be wrong. It can't be right. But I thought of it and I can't get rid of it."

"Sometimes that happens," Waldron said. "No matter how illogical a thing may be it sticks with a man, like a burr inside his brain."

"I thought," said Decker, "that they have told us all that they have to tell us. That they have nothing more they wish to say to us."

"That's what you thought," said Waldron.

Decker nodded. "A funny thing to think," he said. "Out of clear sky. And it can't be right."

"I don't know," said Waldron. "Nothing's right here. Notice that they haven't got a single iron tool. Not a single scrap of metal in evidence at all. Their cooking utensils are stone, a sort of funny stuff like soapstone. What few tools they have are stone."

"And yet," Decker told him, "they're intelligent. Look at their eyes. Intelligence there if you ever saw it. And that fellow who came into the base. He knew what to do with the headset. He knew that we didn't belong on the planet."

Waldron sucked thoughtfully at a back tooth. "We better be getting back to base," he said. "It's getting late."

He held his wrist in front of him.

"My watch has stopped," he said. "What time do you have, Decker?"

Decker's arm came up and Waldron heard the sharp gasp of his breath. Slowly, Decker raised his head, looked at the other man.

"My watch has stopped, too," he said, and his voice was scarcely louder than a whisper.

For a moment they were graven images, eyes matching eyes, and then Waldron jerked his head away.

"Assemble," he shouted. "Back to the base. Quick!"

The men came running. The robots fell into place. The column marched away. The natives sat in their doorways and watched them leave.

Decker sat in his camp chair and listened to the canvas of the pavilion snapping softly in the wind, alive in the wind, talking and laughing to itself. The lantern, hung on the ring above his head, swayed gently and cast fleeting shadows that seemed at times to be the shadows of living, moving things. A robot stood quietly by one of the pavilion poles.

Stolidly Decker reached out a finger and stirred the little pile of wheels and springs that lay upon the table.

Sinister, he thought.

Sinister and queer.

The guts of watches, lying on the table.

Not of two watches alone, not only his and Waldron's watches, but many other watches from the wrists of other men. All of them silent, stilled in their task of marking time.

Night had fallen hours before, but the base still was astir with activity that was at once feverish and furtive. Men moved about in the shadows and crossed the glaring patches of brilliance shed by the banks of lights set up by the robots many weeks before. Watching them, one would have sensed that they moved with a haunting sense of doom—and would have known as well that they knew, deep in their inmost hearts, that there was no doom to fear. No definite thing that one could put a finger on and say this is the thing to fear. No direction that one could point and say doom lies out there, waiting to leap upon us.

Just one small thing.

Watches had stopped running.

And that was a simple thing for which there must be some simple explanation.

Except, thought Decker, on an alien planet no occurrence, no accident or incident, can be regarded as a simple thing for which a simple explanation must necessarily be anticipated. For the matrix of cause and effect, the mathematics of chance, may not hold true on alien planets as they hold true on Earth.

There was one rule, Decker thought grimly.

One rule: Take no chances.

That was the one safe rule to follow, the only rule to follow.

Following it, he had ordered all field parties back to base, ordered the crew to prepare the ship for emergency take off, had alerted the robots to be ready at an instant to get the machines aboard—to even desert the machines and leave without them if circumstances should dictate that such was necessary.

Having done that, there was no more to do but wait. Wait until the field parties came back from their advance camps. Wait until some reason could be assigned to the failure of the watches.

It was not a thing, he told himself, that should be allowed to panic one. It was a thing to recognize, not to disregard. It was a thing which made necessary a certain number of precautions, but it was not a thing that should make one lose all sense of proportion.

You could not go back to Earth and say: "Well, you see, our watches stopped and so . . ."

A footstep sounded and he swung around in his chair. It was Jackson.

"What is it, Jackson?" Decker asked.

"The camps aren't answering, sir," said Jackson. "The operator has been trying to raise them and there is no answer . . . not a single peep."

Decker grunted. "Take it easy," he said. "They will answer. Give them time."

He wished, even as he spoke, that he could feel some

of the assurance that he tried to put into his voice. For a second a rising terror mounted in his throat and he choked it back.

"Sit down," he said. "We'll sit here and have a beer and then we'll go down to the radio shack and see what's stirring."

He rapped on the table. "Beer," he said. "Two beers."

The robot standing by the pavilion pole did not answer.

He made his voice louder.

The robot did not stir.

Decker put his fists upon the table and tried to rise, but his legs suddenly were cold and had turned to water and he could not raise himself.

"Jackson," he panted, "go and tap that robot on the shoulder. Tell him we want some beer."

He saw the fear that whitened Jackson's face as he rose and moved slowly forward. Inside himself, starting in the pit of his belly and rising to worry at his throat, he felt the same whiplash terror that Jackson must have felt.

Jackson stood beside the robot and reached out a hesitant hand, tapped him gently on the shoulder, tapped him harder—and the robot fell flat upon his face!

Feet hammered across the hard packed earth, heading toward the pavilion.

Decker jerked himself around, sat four-square and solid in his chair, waiting.

It was MacDonald, chief engineer.

He stopped at the table's edge and gripped its boards with two grimy hands. His face was twisted as if he were about to weep.

"The ship, sir. The ship . . ."

Decker nodded, almost idly. "I know, Mr. MacDonald. The ship won't run."

MacDonald gulped. "The big stuff's all right, sir. But the little gadgets . . . the injector mechanism, the . . ."

He stopped and stared at Decker. "You knew," he said. "How did you know?"

"I knew," said Decker, "that it would come some day. Not like this, perhaps. But in any one of several ways. I knew that the days would come when our luck would run too thin, when we'd cover all the possibilities but the one that we could not suspect and that, of course, would be the one that would ruin us."

He was thinking: The natives had no metal. No sign of any metal in their camp, at all. Their dishes were soapstone and they wore no ornaments. Their implements were stone. And yet they were intelligent enough, civilized enough, cultured enough, to have fabricated metal. For there was metal here . . . a great deposit of it in the western mountains. They tried, perhaps, many centuries ago. Had fashioned metal tools and metal ornaments and had them go to pieces underneath their fingers after a few short weeks.

Waldron came into the pavilion on cat-like feet.

"The radio's dead," he said, "and the robots are dying like flies. The place is littered with them, just so much scrap steel."

Decker nodded. "The little stuff, the finely fabricated will go first," he said. "Like watches and radio innards and robot brains and injector mechanisms. After that it will be the big stuff. The ship will melt into a heap of slag."

"The native told us," Waldron said, "when you had him up here. You will never leave, he said."

"We didn't understand," said Decker. "We thought he was threatening us and we knew that we were too big, too well guarded for any threat of his to harm us. He wasn't threatening us at all, of course. He was just telling us. Warning us, maybe, although even then it might have been too late. He might even have felt sorry for us."

He made a hopeless gesture with his hand. "What is it?" he asked.

"No one knows," said Waldron, quietly. "Not yet at least. We may find out later, but it won't help us any. A microbe, maybe. A virus. Something that eats iron after it has been subjected to heat or alloyed with other metals. Something that won't tolerate alloyed metal on the planet. It doesn't go for iron ore. If it did, that deposit we found would have been gone long ago. Possibly the radioactive ore as well."

"How does it survive?" asked Decker. "Without stuff to eat, how does it live?"

"I wouldn't know," said Waldron. "It might not be a metal-eating organism at all. It might be something else. Something in the atmosphere."

"We tested the atmosphere."

But, even as the words left his mouth, Decker saw how foolish they were. They had tested the atmosphere, but how could they have detected something they had never run across before? Man's yardstick was limited—limited to the things he knew about, limited by the circle of his own experience.

He guarded himself against the obvious and the imaginable. He could not guard himself against the unknowable or the unimaginable.

Decker stood up and saw Jackson standing by the pavilion pole, with the robot stretched out at his feet, his metal hide gleaming in the shine of the swaying lantern.

"You have your answer," he told the biochemist. "Remember that first day. You talked with me in the lounge."

Jackson nodded. "I remember, sir," he said. His voice was quiet.

And suddenly, Decker realized, the entire base was quiet.

A gust of wind came out of the jungle and rattled the canvas and set the lantern to swaying violently.

Now, for the first time since they had landed, he caught in the wind the alien smell of an alien world.

3

•

A Dash of Symbols

NO NAMES TO THE RIVERS

What an opening sentence: "The head was becoming too byzantine in the exaggerated torment of the face!"

E. C. Tubb knows he is working with symbols. The key nouns in his story make a kind of pattern:

CRUCIFIXION CONTROL ROOM CYANOSIS
SILENCE DOMINATION
CONQUEST EQUATION
DREAM PRESSURE
PARTICLES
TRUMPETS TARGETS
MACHINE ART
PAIN STARS TRUTH HEAVEN

Whether they wish it or not, science fiction writers are forced by the nature of their material to traffic in tokens: Man, the future, Earth, catastrophe, utopia, the galaxy. As far as everyday life is concerned, these things are all abstractions in various degrees. Some readers can use the coinage, some can't.

Here lies the power of science fiction—not excluding some badly written science fiction—which we find difficult to explain even when it moves us strongly. Ordinary fiction has characters, science fiction has personages.

Writing in the realistic tradition, an author seeks to populate the streets and houses of his fiction with characters who—while they may be never so odd—must persuade us that they are the prosaic inhabitants of those streets, those houses. And the streets and houses themselves—though they may prove to be slum property in Ulan Bator—must have about them certain traits common to all human experience which we recognize, so that we can see that those characters truly live in those houses. From the start, the realistic novel calls for ordinary components.

Vexed at myself for generalizing so grandly, as well as for using a critical term, "realistic," which has become defaced by over-usage, I reach out and pull a couple of novels from my shelves. David Storey's novel, *Radcliffe,* begins, "The Headmaster brought the new boy into the classroom several weeks after the term had begun." A good start, to be sure. We are immediately alerted to the way in which the child is to feature as the odd boy out. The rest is prosaic: headmaster, classroom, a new term, these are ordinary, recognizable components of everyone's experience. They act as a foil to the embarrassed child.

Here's Saul Bellow's *Herzog.* It opens with these words, "If I am out of my mind, it's all right with me, thought Moses Herzog." The reader has the whole ample novel to decide how mad or sane Moses Herzog is; but the second paragraph, as if to reassure us by this pressingly posed question of madness and the unreal, bestows upon us a litany of familiar place names: New York, Martha's Vineyard, Chicago, a village in Massachusetts.

Local habitations, names. Such are the usages of the realistic novel or (to get away from that over-used critical term) of what is regarded as the main tradition of the novel, which seeks to lure us into belief by citing real facts. "I was born in the year 1632, in the city of York, of a good family, tho' not of that country, my father being a foreigner of Bremen, who settled first at Hull," begins one of the great imaginative books of our language.

There are science fiction stories which follow this tradition; Christopher Priest has good reason to commence his *The Space Machine* with these words: "In the April of 1893, I was staying in the course of my business at the Devonshire Arms in Skipton, Yorkshire." However, there is another kind of fiction which aims at disorientation. In this tradition, there are no streets and homes, merely exile. We'll never get home. Recall the opening sentence of van Vogt's story: "The great ship was poised a quarter of a mile above one of the cities." It is not absentmindedness which causes van Vogt to withold from us the name of the ship, the name of the city, the name of the planet. He withholds them because withholding them makes for a more powerful sense of disorientation, a more powerful fiction. We are to be confronted—no, not with the familiar—but with the unknown, the particular unknown of science fiction. Van Vogt's prosaic nouns, "ship," "city," take on new connotations, like the nouns in the Tubb piece.

Unknown planets beckon us like unknown women. This not particularly subtle thought has occurred to many writers. In a Ray Bradbury story, "Here There be Tygers," his unnamed planet has a female disposition, and rather a highly-strung one at that. Robert F. Young's "Goddess in Granite" is a lovely story, and I know no other like it; although I do not entirely agree with its conclusion, it remains a striking example of a man coming to terms with himself through his encounter with a planet as beautiful, as baffling, (as female) as any in the canon.

I make no apology for including two Robert Young stories in the same section. His is one of the under-valued names. In "On the River," that river has and needs no name. It does not require that sort of label for true recognition.

In both the Young stories, water plays a part in the symbolism, as it does in "The Ark of James Carlyle." Here, the water proves to be no sundering flood. It forms a common bond between man and alien.

Superficially, "The Ark of James Carlyle" appears to be a conventional planet story, and none the less satisfactory for that. What is unusual about it is the way in which it accepts the alien nature of the quogs and indicates—I believe with some subtlety—how man's nature is enlarged by accepting that alien quality. An attractive story, the first science fiction from a woman who will clearly do us all a favour by writing more.

When a writer creates an environment which does not exist in realistic terms—a new planet, an old Mars—he then has to set about populating it with his goddesses, his quogs. Useless to populate it with a new schoolboy being shown his classroom a few weeks after term has begun, or a middle-aged man in a village in western Massachusetts worrying about his sanity. That sort of thing is what modern phraseology would term counter-productive.

Depending on the individual bent of the author, he is most likely to people his imaginary territory with beings from his psyche (and this is what I take quogs and goddesses of granite to be). If this line of thought interests you, seek out the recently published volume from Bran's Head Books entitled *The Significance of Science Fiction,* edited by Richard Kirby, and read the chapter on "The Beings in SF," by Stan Gooch. It is the most thoroughgoing examination of the subject I know.

Meanwhile, on Planet AC14, the barometer is dropping fast, the wind is changing, and those quogs are gathering silently about the stump of the single mee-haw tree . . .

The flood was treacherous, the ark was insubstantial. But something permanent came of them. A new author presents us with a new Noah . . .

THE ARK OF JAMES CARLYLE
by Cherry Wilder

On the ninety-first day of his Met. duty Carlyle stepped out of the hut and gazed desperately at the cloudless sky. There were no quogs to meet him on the platform; the oily purple sea sucked gently at the wooden piles; his instruments had assured him there was a light westerly breeze. His delusion persisted and he had nothing to support it . . . not even the tangible evidence of an aching bunion. He did not dare call the station. How would he begin?

"Something tells me . . ."

He decided to walk round the island but he found an ancient quog, the one he called the Chief, squatting at the foot of the ladder. He beckoned him on to the platform. The quogs were cryptorchids so for all he knew perhaps this was a Chieftainess: it was difficult to tell.

When he had first taken up his duty, before the boat brought him to the island, he had seen Mary Long, a young anthropologist who had tagged along with the landing party to the plateau, sexing a herd of quogs. She walked among them, picking the creatures up and solemnly examining their genital pouches. She was engrossed in her work: twenty or thirty quogs surrounded her and gently stripped off every stitch of her clothing before Carlyle or the other men could intervene. They sat round her and stared, their luminous eyes full of innocent curiosity.

Not a great deal of work had been done on quogs; they had been described as small land mammals, semi-erect bipeds, modified baboons. They were docile, certainly, and capable of performing many tasks; but they were also ugly, elusive and rank-smelling. Their odour had already ceased to bother Carlyle but he noticed that the quogs still kept upwind of *him*. He found himself describing them differently: they were like trolls, like squatting goblins, like little old men. At night he listened for one of their rare sounds, the qwok-qwok-qwok, hardly vocalized, that had given them their name.

The Chief, who was a big fellow, fully three feet tall, scrambled nimbly on to the platform.

"Where are the others?" asked Carlyle.

Every other day the platform had been lined with quogs who gave him berries, limpets, burrowing shrimps, in exchange for bacon cubes. He had tried them with everything he had: orange juice, vegetables, vitamins, but they liked the bacon best. Now the Chief tried to explain their absence. He could be heard only by cupping his long bluish hands before his tiny slit of a mouth to amplify the sound, the way Carlyle made owl-hoots as a boy.

"Mee-haw," boomed the Chief faintly.

At first Carlyle did not understand. The mee-haw was a tree; in fact it was the only tree. The vegetation on AC14 was low, luxuriant and undistinguished except for the mee-haw trees, which reared up, with straight trunk and spreading crown of leafy branches, one hundred metres and more above the bushy islands in the still, purple sea. The timber, resembling balsa, was particularly easy to work. The platform on which Carlyle had his Met. hut was made entirely of the single mee-haw tree that had grown on the tiny island. The quogs had wept to see it fall down. Carlyle had had the uneasy notion that the mee-haw tree might be sacred to them.

Now the Chief pointed to the island; Carlyle was shaken again by his crazy premonition.

"Come on," he said.

He climbed down from the platform and followed the Chief up the brush-covered slope. All the quogs on the island, about thirty of them forming one family group, were huddled together on the broad stump of the mee-haw tree.

"Why?" asked Carlyle. "Why?"

The Chief cupped his hands and answered with a third quog word.

Carlyle strained to catch it.

"Aw-kee?"

The quogs on the stump waved their fingers; this was a way of laughing. To Carlyle's surprise they all began to vocalize, even the babies, pale blue and completely hairless, cupping their tiny hands. "Aw-kee" was the nearest he could get to it.

"What's that?" asked Carlyle.

He already knew. He went into a mad pantomime, begging the quogs for confirmation, then he ran back to the Met. hut. He called the satellite without a glance at his instruments. He announced firmly:

"There's going to be a flood."

The receiver crackled. What were his readings?

"The quogs told me," said Carlyle.

The crackle became indignant. Readings please. Carlyle turned hopelessly towards his instrument panel and his heart pounded. The barometer had dropped thirty degrees and was still falling. The wind had swung round to the south. The room became dark as he completed his report and huge drops of rain began a tattoo on the roof of the Met. hut.

He ran out on to the platform. The sky was a dome of blue-black cloud above a darkening sea; the waves flashed emerald and purple-black and broke in iridescent foam upon the shore. The word for it, Carlyle decided, was unearthly. Already drenched to the skin he cowered in the doorway of the hut. He was worried about the quogs; he guessed that their instinct to seek higher ground would keep them huddled on the mee-haw stump. The fragile shelters where they slept and did their weaving would be no protection against this rain. The picture of the quogs twisting their endless ropes from native flax lingered in his mind. He wished, idly, that the mee-haw tree had not been cut down.

Carlyle gave a cry: "The tree!"

He peered out into the downpour, staring up at the dark centre of the island where the mighty mee-haw tree had stood, ready to shelter the quogs in its dense foliage. They made ropes . . . probably sent up a young male to loop slings over the branches, then the whole tribe went up.

There was a splashing and scrambling at the foot of the platform. Carlyle knelt down and saw the Chief, already swimming awkwardly; the water had risen three feet in twenty minutes. The rain was a blinding cataract; a man who lay on his back would drown, thought Carlyle. He dragged the old quog aboard and bundled him into the hut. They sat gasping, the water pouring from the quog's grizzled hide, from Carlyle's coveralls.

"How far?" gasped Carlyle. "How high does the water . . . ?" He gestured with a horizontal hand, staring into the Chief's bulging dark eyes.

Carlyle was suddenly aware of an earlier moment. When the mee-haw tree came down . . . the day the quogs wept . . . he and Ensign Weiss noticed marks on its great trunk. A series of wavy bands, between three and four metres from the lowest branches . . . more than eighty metres from the ground. Carlyle understood, with another thump of fear . . . water marks. The water would rise until only the mee-haw tops rose like islands out of the purple sea. The only high ground on the entire planetoid was the plateau where his expedition had touched down briefly, far to the north. It had a large quog population . . . and no mee-haw trees.

The Chief touched Carlyle's knee gently with the tip of his prehensile tail.

"Sure," said Carlyle. "Sure. We have a real problem here, old buddy."

He was calculating . . . One life-raft, inflatable, fully provisioned and powered, capacity six humans. All he had to do was launch the thing. And figure out some way of transporting thirty quogs to the plateau. The receiver gave his call signal but Carlyle paid no attention. He rushed out on to the platform again, into the deluge, and saw with alarm that the water was up to the cross supports. The scrap of beach and the lowest rank of undergrowth were already submerged. Sea and sky were joined in a blue-black curtain of moisture. Suddenly Carlyle gave a triumphant cry that brought the old quog scuttling to his side; he had realized that they were standing upon a raft.

He explained it to the Chief as he dug out the axe. The tribe must come aboard now, pronto, when the water rose he would knock out the supports of the platform and they would be launched. The wind and the current were driving towards the plateau . . . Maybe they could use the power pack of his own inflatable boat . . .

"Come on!" he shouted. "We have to get them aboard!"

The Chief had been dancing and shivering at Carlyle's side, stretching out his arms to the island. He pointed through the rain and Carlyle saw that the quogs were coming.

It made sense of course; the platform *was* a little higher than the top of the island. They came swarming through the bushes and flung themselves gamely into the water. Their awkward quog-paddle was very efficient; the first wave—pregnant females and mothers with babies on their backs—was already nosing towards the supports. The turbid water was alight with their bulbous eyes. Carlyle knelt down beside the Chief and began to heave the dripping creatures aboard. More than once Carlyle saw a big quog dive and drag up a half-drowned cub. The oldest animals took it pretty hard, they fought to stay on land; but the younger ones thrust them brutally into the water. All along the platform in the plunging rain the rest of the tribe were gently dancing and stamping, reaching out their arms in encouragement to those still in the water.

As the last of them were dragged aboard Carlyle herded them into the Met. hut and went over the side with the axe. The Chief and four husky off-siders watched him wallowing in the water up to his neck and hammering with the back of the axe-head at one of the supports. The mee-haw piles had been embedded in heavy silt to a depth of two metres. Carlyle reckoned he could slide the tops of the piles out of the groove cut for them in the platform. But the first pile moved inward with a lurch the moment he hit it; he saw that the silt was swirling away in clouds as the water rose. He was treading water now, catching an occasional foothold on a rock. He moved under the platform, beat at the pile with the axehead, then heaved it outward with all his strength.

As the silt let go its hold the pile swung upwards in the water and the platform sagged down at one corner. Instantly two quogs were in the water grasping the mee-haw pile and using it to restore balance. Carlyle swam to the diagonal under the far corner of the hut and knocked it out like a loose tooth; two more quogs hove up out of the rain and balanced the platform. Carlyle knocked out the remaining leeward pile and felt the whole structure buckle and shift. He yelled to the quogs and scrambled back on to the platform. The decking heaved about crazily. The last pile on the seaward side gave way. Carlyle watched his two pairs of assistants climb expertly inboard and tapped the loose piles free of their grooves as they rode up on the surface of the flood. Leaning down he caught hold of one long pile as it clung to the side of the platform and shoved off from the island. The quogs on deck gathered to help him, bracing their leathery underbodies against the pole; the platform shuddered, then settled gently. The wind was rising and a strong current ran to the north. The mee-haw raft floated free upon the waste of waters.

Carlyle and his deck-hands carefully drew in their oar; he felt an extraordinary sense of well-being as they clustered around his knees. The rain had slackened but they still pressed forward into a wall of water. A gleam of violet penetrating the low ceiling of black cloud showed that the Star was shining. Carlyle glanced down at the Chief, who blinked solemnly through the rain. He remembered that he must answer the call signal and led the way into the Met. hut.

The quogs had packed themselves in snugly under the big plastic dome. Carlyle couldn't think of any species who could carry off the situation better. Humans? Monkeys? Bedlam and filth. Okay, the quogs were a spooky lot, and the smell, *en masse,* was like camphorated garlic, but there were times when he appreciated their stillness, the way they organized themselves. He lifted aside a tiny blue paw, resting on the communicator, and called the satellite.

The signal was faint.

"Readings . . ."

He gave the readings.

"We observe dense cloud," pipped the signal. "Evaluate."

Carlyle switched over to voice, although he didn't like talking to the computer. He made a report. The androgynous voice snapped.

"Evacuate. Use liferaft."

Carlyle said: "The emergency is way past that point. I have evacuated the native population."

The quogs were vocalizing gently in the background . . . qwok-qwok-qwok . . . There was static, the voice signal was faint.

"Follow emergency procedures. No record . . . population. Save . . . self . . . data."

Carlyle repeated stolidly: "Evacuating with quogs."

"Follow . . . procedures. No deviation . . . losing contact."

Carlyle said coarsely: "Screw yourself tin-brain. Give me emergency voice contact." He slammed the red button and Garrett answered.

"Jim . . . Jim? What the hell is going on down there?"

Carlyle gave his report all over again; the reply was broken and distant.

"We're losing signal." Garrett was worried. "What in blazes are you doing with those quogs?"

"Evacuating them. The island is submerged by now I guess."

"But *why?* This is not time . . . Tough luck . . . the quogs. No ethnological value . . . plenty more . . ."

"Hell!" said Carlyle. "We cut down their tree!"

"Jim!" cried Garrett, with the static closing in. "Take care . . . crazy raft . . . Can't allow . . . deviation emergency procedures." The receiver went dead.

Carlyle felt a surge of panic as if his lifeline had snapped. His morale sagged at the thought of the satellite . . . warmth, filtered air, human company . . . He felt his conditioning slipping away. He was on the verge of apophobia, Weltraumangst, the fear that grew in interstellar space from contemplating vast distances. He remembered poor Ed Kravetts, a cadet in his year who tried to cover up a bad case of "Yonders." He staggered through his classes on the station red-eyed and queasy; a glance at one of the monitors made him sweat; the checking of an air-lock or a simple space walk left him shocked and pale. To see Kravetts struggling with a quantum equation was to apprehend the void: all the black miles that separated them from the tiny spinning globe of earth, a pin-point of light seen through the wrong end of a telescope.

Carlyle dragged himself back to his own world. "Identify with the place you're in," wasn't that Eva's way of saying it Eva, E. M., Earth Mother, Commander Magnussen, come beautiful Eva, aid me now. He sent his prayer off into deep space and doled out bacon cubes to all hands before striding out on deck. The rain had really eased off and the cloud was lifting. The mee-haw raft rushed on faster than before. With the current and a rising wind they were making maybe five knots. The Star was down; the brief blue night had settled on AC 14.

The Chief leaned on his knuckle-pads beside Carlyle; they stared together over the wine-dark sea. Low waves came at the raft from the south-west, as the wind swung around. They were long, uncrested hillocks of water, that surged under the mee-haw logs and disappeared into the dusk, rolling in line across the surface of the endless sea.

"Those waves better keep low," said Carlyle. "Does the sea get rough?"

In his ninety-one days of Met. duty he had never seen a choppy sea, never felt a drop of rain, never observed a significant drop in barometric pressure. He made wave-motions with his hands and the Chief replied with "Aw-kee" and some new words. He thought of the sea rising up into roaring crests, high over the raft, huge rollers, hills and valleys where the pink foam boiled. He had to shut his eyes to shake off the nightmare picture of those waves, superimposed upon the harmless scene he was watching.

"I better get some sleep," Carlyle muttered. He was wet and shaky, his morale still down. The whole project, the solitary Met. duty, was a test of his survival qualities and his potential as a colonist. Perhaps he had blown it with Garrett by evacuating the quogs . . . He stumbled back into the hut, found a way to his bunk, put on a fresh warm coverall from the thermopack. He didn't dare take any medication in case there was a sudden alert. Most of the quogs were sleeping; he caught the gleam of an eye and there, the flicker of a blue hand. The Chief materialized at the foot of his bunk with two even more ancient creatures, so old that their skin was grey. They stared at Carlyle and clapped their long hands soundlessly. He felt an instant of revulsion . . . sleeping in a hut crammed with animals, for crissake. Then with a surge of weariness and a sense of strange well-being he fell asleep.

. . . He was wide awake in a dark room with a low ceiling. A range of scents and sounds assailed him; fresh air, woodsmoke, perfume, the waffling roar of a jet refuelling, insects, someone strumming idly on a moog. Earth. He was on Earth. Carlyle knew that he must be dreaming; he savoured his dream, taking in the outlines of the room. It was night; he was standing beside a window that opened on to a balcony. He glanced down at the thick, unpatterned carpet. A memory stirred. Had he been in this room before? Or was it simply the colour, a rippling mist-green, an earth colour. There was someone at the desk; Carlyle felt himself drift closer.

He peered at the dark figure . . . A caftan, a long fall of dark hair, he couldn't tell if it was a man or a woman. Yet something in the attitude of the head made him tremble, in his dream. Slowly Eva Magnussen turned until she saw him. She blinked into the darkness of the room, switched off her cassette and removed the earpiece as he had seen her do a thousand times.

"Jim?" her voice was husky, hesitant. "Jim Carlyle?"

"Eva?" In the dream his own voice was muffled.

"Where are you?" she asked. "Is this some kind of experiment?"

"It's my dream," he said. "You know where I am."

"Jim . . . I can *see* you."

"I thought of you," he said. "I have a situation going here. My communications are gone. No word from upstairs. Seeing you helps a lot."

"You're not alone," she said. "Who are they?"

"Quogs," he said. "They are great little guys. You might find a short report on them in the file on AC14. Not enough work done on quogs."

"You say you are sleeping?"

"Sure. Eva the sea is purple. Wine-dark sea . . ."

"Oh, Jim . . ."

"Don't!" he said. "Eva . . . Don't cry. Think about what I said. I'm not one of your cadets any more. We could take a colonial posting."

Then as she rose in her chair the dream tilted; he was looking down on the room. He saw the figure of Eva Magnussen, his instructress, Commander Magnussen M.D., specialist in space psychology, rise up from her chair and run forward on the green carpet. He felt an instant of amazement and fear . . . it was like watching something else . . . real life . . . not a dream. He heard Eva cry out across the abyss of space and time:

"Jim . . . Jim Carlyle . . . I love you . . ."

Then the dream vanished in a swirl of colour and scent; he was back in the dark, in the flood, in the crowded

Met. hut, with the quogs whistling in anxiety and the Chief tugging his arm.

"Okay!" said Carlyle. "I see what's wrong."

Rain was falling heavily again; the wind had become violent and ripped one of the panels out of the hut. The raft was bumping about in the water as the wind tore inside under the dome.

"I'll relax the panels," said Carlyle to the Chief. "I may need your team."

The Chief summoned them up in the eerie violet light of dawn, while the rest of the passengers cowered away from the driving rain.

Carlyle went to work on the expanding ribs holding the panels. The hut began to fold and the raft settled. Finally he grappled with the damaged panel, but he had the order wrong. He had been too busy providing shelter for the quogs—the torn panel should have been folded down first. He felt a thrill of warning, the eyes of the quogs glowed around him, he shot up a hand and turned sideways. The heavy strut holding one side of the panel broke with a rending crack and came down on his head. Carlyle's last conscious thought was: "I am seeing stars . . ."

He was out, but not out cold for very long. He groped upwards towards consciousness through a fog of nausea and pain. Words whirled through the aching sunburst of his brain; he strove to move his legs, his hands, his fingers, to wrest open his leaded eyelids. He saw pictures . . . ragged scraps of film . . . the island, the satellite, a house in a green field . . . where? He felt himself, flying, moving, uplifted . . . lifted by a hundred strong, blue hands. He could see then so clearly through his closed eyelids. Who-ever had blue hands . . . ? He remembered and laughed in his pain-fringed dream. "Their hands were blue . . . and they went to sea . . . they went to sea in a sieve."

Carlyle opened his eyes. He was on his bunk, the quogs all around him, their saucer eyes alight with concern.

"Concussion," mumbled Carlyle. "Got to take—medica-tion." He could not reach his head but the Chief guided his hand. There was a shallow two-inch cut on his scalp above the left ear and blood had soaked and matted his shaggy crop of hair, known in the service as the colonist's cut or the Buffalo Bill.

"Must take—antibiotic."

Carlyle was heavily conditioned to protect himself against alien bacteria. He fought to stay conscious.

"Hogan . . ." he whispered to the Chief. "Hogan the Medic. Up there. He can tell me what to take . . ."

He sank into a confused nightmare of purple microbes and the capsules in his medical pack.

Carlyle's head ached still and he began this comical dream. He was in a cabin on the satellite, lying just above the floor, floating. It was some guy's bedroom, with his locker, pinups, a green video cassette. He heard startled voices and saw two people sitting up in the bunk, clutching the sheet around them.

"Hi Mary!" said Carlyle in his muffled dream voice. "No clothes again!"

"Carlyle . . . what the hell!"

It was Dick Hogan the Medic, naked too and for some reason frightened.

"Hogan!" cried Carlyle. "You're just the guy I wanted to see."

"Carlyle?" whispered Mary Long, the blonde anthropologist. "Is it you, Jim?"

"Sure," said Carlyle. "I'm dreaming. I do a lot of dreaming down here. I have a concussion, Dick. Little cut on my scalp . . ."

The two lovers sat there petrified, unable to move. Carlyle laughed and could not make it out. He wasn't about to report them for fraternizing.

"Come on now!" He laughed, weakly. "What do I take, Dick? Not functioning too well . . . what antibiotic . . . the label . . . ?"

"UCF," said Hogan automatically. "You know that. Orange capsules."

"Thanks . . ."

Then Mary Long pointed and began to scream.

"Quogs! I can see quogs!"

And the dream swirled away taking Carlyle with it.

After he got the Chief to feed him the orange capsules he slept long and heavily while his head mended. He woke at night, out on deck, with the raft still moving steadily in the grip of the current. They passed islands—no, not islands, but the tops of mee-haw trees, and on the raft the quogs danced, holding out their hands to the distance, to their brothers in the dripping branches. He woke in the hut and saw a patch of indigo sky with the Star shining down. Carlyle turned to the Chief; he was still lightheaded.

"Far and Few . . ." said Carlyle. "How does it go?" He struggled drowsily on to one elbow.

Few and far, Far and few,
Are the lands where the Jumblies live,
Their heads were green, and their hands were blue,
And they went to sea in a sieve.

Carlyle was laughing and the quogs waved their fingers.

In his sleep he heard someone calling his name; he woke up and found the Chief, vocalizing through his hands.

"Cah-lah-ee!"

"Good try," said Carlyle, flexing his limbs and feeling stronger.

He pointed to the Chief, who slid across his nictitating eyelids in a show of quog bashfulness.

"Tell me *your* name," urged Carlyle.

The old quog boomed shyly: "Sheef."

Chief. The name Carlyle had given him, though he didn't recall ever calling him that, unless in his delirium. He let it go, puzzled. Either the quogs had no names or they were like cats, who had special sounds they used to communicate with humans.

Carlyle checked his instruments; the stormy conditions were abating. A mee-haw off to port showed a fraction of trunk. The flood waters were beginning to recede. His chronometer told him he had been out of action for three days. The Star hung low in a sky of aquamarine; he saw the plateau dead ahead with the black cliffs rising up sheer. The current was no more than a ripple and the mee-haw raft moved sluggishly through the purple water.

He checked the plateau through his glasses, trying to make out a possible landing-place that he remembered where broken columns of black basalt had made an alien giant's causeway. He saw a disturbance in the water, a line of foam. Before he could register it properly he sensed the anxiety of the quogs, growing into fear. Behind him they huddled and whistled, crowding into the ragged heap of the Met. hut. He stood on the raft, sandwiched between two shock waves . . . the low wedge of foam moving towards them and the almost palpable fear given off by the quogs.

"What is it?" cried Carlyle.

The Chief, all of them, could give no answer, only this immense welling up of terror. Carlyle gazed at them blankly. A whale? A giant ray? The Great Horned Toad? He pushed through the crowd and took down a regulation magnum; then as an after-thought he reached down the new Fernlich, the automatic missile carbine. As he feathered its vents he heard the sound, a high vibrant scale of notes, swinging up and down on impossible frequencies. He might have heard it before, far out on the sea at night, so sweet and distant that it could be something he imagined. The quogs writhed in fear and pain, clasping their hands over their round ears, burrowing under the paraphernalia in the hut.

Carlyle rushed out into the waves of strange music. The ripple had divided into ten, a dozen pink clumps of foam, approaching swiftly on all sides. He could almost see them now . . . not too large, dark shapes swimming easily . . . like seals, maybe, or dolphins, slipping, weaving, gliding, just below the surface of the water. Carlyle squatted on the deck, fascinated. The music thrilled around him, his head sang, he felt dizzy. A young quog, crouched at the doorway of the hut, rolled over and died.

Carlyle sprang up, gasping. With an audible pop something reared up out of a patch of foam. A smooth pink bubble . . . At first he thought incredulously of a child's toy space helmet, then he saw that it was a bubble of foam. The bubble burst and a sleek black head appeared. It did look like a seal but the coat was scaly, black crystalline scales, dark mother-of-pearl, breaking the bluish light into an alien spectrum. The creature was dancing on its tail, waving sleek webs like forepaws, only a few metres from the raft. Then, with a glissando of sound, infinitely sweet, like a peal of electronic bells, a single scale tentacle whipped out from a curled position below the head and seized the body of the dead quog. The seal-lizard flipped its catch into the air and caught it playfully. There was a flash of teeth, a minor chord, the quog's head was bitten off. A whistle of anguish rose from the burrowing terrified quogs crammed inside the hut. Carlyle shouted at the top of his voice.

The creatures had never heard a human voice. There was an excited humming, a swish of dark bodies passing around and under the raft. A colony of pink bubbles grew to starboard, at a safe distance. The seal-lizards repeated what he recognized vaguely as the tone and pitch of his own voice. They boomed and cawed, bouncing about in the water. Carlyle accepted the invitation; he called again, telling them to clear off. The formation of bubbles began to move closer, tinkling, humming . . . testing . . . testing . . .

With a ringing head Carlyle realized what they were trying to find. The raft was drifting closer to the plateau; he grasped the oar, still lying on deck, and began to drive the clumsy craft along. He would never escape this way before the seal-lizard found *his* death frequency—the sound which would make this new creature with the harsh, loud voice fall down to be eaten. The seal-lizards moved alongside in formation. The noise was unbearable; Carlyle sang, groaned, shouted aloud. A tentacle, then another, flicked over the timbers of the raft, plucked at his boots, probed towards the quogs in the hut.

Carlyle dropped his oar and fired the magnum in the air. The seal-lizards hesitated, then pressed forward. A new wave of sound broke over the raft; he screamed and rolled upon the deck, pressing his hands over his ears. Through the mists of agonizing sound he saw the seal-lizards at the very edge of the boat. A row of neat, scaly black heads; narrow oval eyes, a structure of nasal beak and leathery appendages like whiskers . . . even so close they looked amazingly like seals. He could not see how they made their music. Their comical mouths opened upon murderous fangs. A tentacle gripped his wrist and pulled gently.

Roaring aloud to counteract their killing whine Carlyle put one hand to the missile carbine and fired point-blank along the deck. A seal-lizard was blasted into mush. The missile that destroyed it passed on across the sea, then struck and exploded, sending up a column of water, fifty metres away.

There was a moment of utter silence, then the whole band of seal-lizards dived like one creature. It could have been the shock-wave that did it, or the sound of the carbine, or simply the death of one of their number. Rising to his knees Carlyle saw them emerge far beyond the raft swimming in formation, fast and low . . . a ripple bearing away to the south-west. He caught only a few notes of their music across the dark waters.

The quogs crept out and surrounded him, helping him to stand. Everyone, Carlyle included, was partially deaf from the encounter. The quogs held their heads sideways and bounced on one leg, like a human bather with water in his ear. Carlyle shook hands with the Chief; it caught on. The whole party, dizzy with relief, shook hands promiscuously.

They were already within the shadow of the plateau: Carlyle and his crew, working the oar, struck a rock or a shoal, then another. They were over the flooded causeway where he had embarked for the island three months ago. He levered the raft in towards a rock platform. The quogs had begun to stamp gently and hold out their hands to the plateau.

One moment there was no sign of life, only the glittering planes of the great stone mesa; the next, every plane and slope was alive with quogs. They spilled over the edge of the plateau in waves, until the black rock was blanketed with brown and grey and tawny fur. A strange noise, stranger even than the music of the seal-lizards, began to rise up from the multitude. They vocalized all together, by tens and hundreds, their weak voices blending into a vast muffled shout, that echoed out over the purple flood tide and reverberated from the chasms of the plateau.

"CAH-LAH-EE."

As his own quogs pressed round him proudly, in silence, Carlyle recognized his own name. Then as the shout redoubled: "CAH-LAH-EE," he saw himself as a new creature, as the quogs perceived him: the clumsy, loud-voiced, white-handed giant of a new species. The dogged Cah-lah-ee, who made a marvellous craft from the looted remains of a mee-haw tree, who overcame the flood, did battle with seal-lizards and brought a whole tribe to safety.

The raft sidled into the platform and a nylon rope fell on the deck. The quogs were so thick that Carlyle had not seen the landing party, Garrett, Hogan and Weiss. The sight of these men, his own kind, affected him powerfully. His sense of proportion was restored; he smiled and choked up, just as they all did. He felt as if he had returned from some other dimension, not a routine stint on AC14.

"Hey there!" cried Garrett. "Some welcome you got here, Lieutenant."

"Am I glad to see you!" said Carlyle.

They heaved him ashore; the quogs were whisked off the raft by hundreds of willing hands.

Carlyle turned back to the Chief.

"See the raft is made fast," he said.

The men of the landing party turned back and watched as the Chief and his off-siders tied up to a pillar of rock.

"Everything ship-shape!" said Dick Hogan.

"They know the ropes," said Carlyle.

The party ascended through an aisle of quogs, still hooting his name; Carlyle acknowledged the applause as modestly as he could. He was looking ahead eagerly . . . Yes, there was the landing module on the plateau, among the bushes and the stony burrows of the upland quogs. He was going upstairs, back to the station. His limbs began to ache in anticipation of a steam bath and a bunk.

"How's the head?" asked Hogan.

"Oh fine," said Carlyle. "It was just a simple concussion."

Garrett turned to him.

"You get it, don't you, Jim? You understand what you've discovered."

"I think so," said Carlyle. "I guess I knew all along. Or when they called out my name . . . Did you know it was my name?"

"We worked it out." They laughed and looked at Carlyle expectantly, waiting for him to bell the cat.

"The quogs are able to transmit pictures," said Carlyle. "They are natural telesends."

"The first in the Universe," said Garrett.

"There's more to it than that, Max," said Carlyle. "Some kind of group intelligence . . ."

"They had us on the hop upstairs!" put in Weiss.

"What way?" asked Carlyle.

"Reports of hallucinations," said Garrett. "Weiss here saw you on the raft. Hogan . . ."

"I saw Hogan," said Carlyle. "Spoke to him. I thought it was a dream."

He and Hogan exchanged glances, straight-faced; no one

said a word about Mary Long. The quogs certainly had a trick of embarrassing that girl.

"Communication can extend over vast distances," said Max Garrett.

He was smiling in an odd way; the men were still watching Carlyle closely. He couldn't read much in their faces, no pictures came to him; for a moment he wished they were quogs. Hogan dug him in the ribs.

"You got the prize, boy," he said.

Garrett cleared his throat.

"We had word. Commander Eva Magnussen put in a report. She has also requested a P.I.C. with Lieutenant Carlyle." A Personal Interplanetary Communication: something flashed from Earth to Armstrong Base to a chain of a hundred satellites. It was the spaceman's version of compassionate leave; marriages were contracted, births and deaths announced in this way. "She has requested a colonial posting."

Carlyle smiled foolishly and the men all shook him by the hand.

They were anxious to get him upstairs to sick bay; but Carlyle excused himself and turned aside. He bent down to the nearest quog.

"Where is my friend the Chief?"

There was an immediate response in the scattered groups of quogs returning up the sides of the plateau. A strong impulse, stronger perhaps because of the numbers involved, directed him to a low cave some distance away. He strode over and found the Chief, with his wives and children, being regaled with berries and limpets and sweet-bark. He realized that he had been aware for some time that the Chief was in fact a male; he found no difficulty in sexing quogs at a glance. The Chief knew that he was leaving.

"I'll come back after a few days," said Carlyle.

The pair of them stood in a clear space, looking out from the height of the plateau. The three giant causeways in the rock were explained, three great chutes that drained off the deluge of rain from the high ground. The purple sea spread out beneath them; the mee-haw trees marked the submerged islands. In a series of quick superimpositions Carlyle saw the great day when the flood receded altogether; when the star approached its apogee and the islands became dry land again.

"Yes," he said. "I'll be back to see that."

As he turned to rejoin the landing party Carlyle took in the scene. The three men beside their vehicle, tall visitors in regulation silversuits, and a fourth man, unkempt and hairy, in ragged coveralls, communing at a distance with the members of a new species. The men looked curiously towards Carlyle; their anxiety did not quite diminish as he came closer. The distance between Carlyle and the landing party could not be taken up in a few small steps. They saw tomorrow's man, who by some chance operation of goodwill, some accident of understanding, reached forward into new modes of being.

Death has been likened to an ocean. A talented writer tells us what it feels like to be swept along—

ON THE RIVER

by Robert F. Young

Farrell was beginning to think that he had the River all to himself when he saw the girl. He had been traveling downstream for nearly two days now—River days, that is. He had no way of knowing for certain, but he was convinced that River time had very little to do with real time. There were days and nights here, yes, and twenty-four hours elapsed between each dawn. But there was a subtle difference between time as he had known it once and time as he knew it now.

The girl was standing at the water's edge, waving a diminutive handkerchief. It was obvious that she wanted him to pole over to the bank. He did so, forcing the raft out of the sluggish current and into the shallows. Several yards from shore it nudged bottom, and he leaned on the pole, holding the raft in position and looking questioningly at the girl. It surprised him to discover that she was young and attractive, although it shouldn't have, he supposed. Assuming that he had created her, it was only logical that he would have made her pleasing to the eye; and assuming that he had not, it was illogical to conclude that merely because he had reached the age of thirty it was necessary for someone else to reach the age of thirty in order not to want to go on living. Her hair was only a shade less bright than the splash of afternoon sunlight in which she stood, and she wore it very short. A scattering of freckles lightly dappled the bridge of her delicate nose and the immediate areas on either side. She was willowy, and rather tall, and she had blue eyes.

"I'd like to share your raft," she said across the several yards of water that separated her from him. "My own broke loose during the night and drifted downstream, and I've been walking ever since dawn."

Her yellow dress was torn in a dozen places, Farrell noticed, and the slender slippers that encased her feet had already reached the point of no return. "Sure," he said. "You'll have to wade to get on board, though. This is as far in as I can get."

"I don't mind."

The water came to her knees. He helped her up beside him; then, with a strong thrust of the pole, he sent the raft back into the current. The girl shook her head as though her hair had once been long and she had forgotten that it had been cut, and wanted the wind to blow it. "I'm Jill Nicols," she said. "Not that it matters very much."

"Clifford," Farrell said. "Clifford Farrell."

She sat down on the raft and removed her shoes and stockings. After laying the pole aside, he sat down a few feet from her. "I was beginning to think I was the only one making the journey," he said.

The wind was moderate but brisk and was blowing upstream, and she faced into it as though expecting it to send her hair streaming behind her. The wind did its best, but succeeded only in ruffling the almost-curls that fringed her pale forehead. "I thought I was all alone, too."

"The way I had it figured," Farrell said, "the River was the product of my imagination. Now I see that it can't be—unless you're a product of my imagination also."

She smiled at him sideways. "Don't say that. I thought you were a product of mine."

He smiled back at her. It was the first time he had smiled in ages. "Maybe the River's an allegorical product of both our imaginations. Maybe this is the way you thought it would be, too. Drifting down a dark-brown stream, I mean, with trees on either hand and the blue sky above. Did you?"

"Yes," she said. "I've always thought that when the time came, it would be like this."

A thought struck him. "I took it for granted that because I'm here voluntarily, you are too. Are you?"

"Yes."

"Maybe," he went on, "two people visualizing an abstract idea by means of the same allegory can make that allegory come to life. Maybe, down through the years and without our being aware of it, we brought the River into existence."

"And then, when the time came, cast ourselves adrift on it? But where is the River? Surely, we can't still be on earth."

He shrugged. "Who knows? Reality probably has a thousand phases mankind knows nothing about. Maybe we're in one of them . . . How long have you been on the River?"

"A little over two days. I lost time today because I had to go on foot."

"I've been on it almost two days," Farrell said.

"I must have been the first to come—the first to cast myself adrift then." She wrung out her stockings and spread them on the raft to dry. She placed her bedraggled slippers beside them. She stared at the articles for some time. "Funny the way we do such things at a time like this," she said. "Why should it make any difference to me now whether my shoes and stockings are wet or dry?"

"I guess we're creatures of habit," he said. "Right up to the very end. Last evening, at the inn where I stayed the night, I shaved. True, there was an electric razor available; but why did I go to the trouble?"

She smiled wryly. "Last evening, at the inn where I stayed the night, I took a bath. I was going to put up my hair, but I caught myself just in time. It looks it, doesn't it?"

It did, but he didn't say so. Nor did he gallantly deny the fact. Somehow, small talk seemed out of place. The raft was drifting past a small island now. There were many such islands in the River—bleak little expanses of sand and gravel for the most part, although all of them had at least one tree. He glanced at the girl. Was she seeing the island, too? Her eyes told him that she was.

Still he was not convinced. It was hard to believe that two people—two people who did not even know each other, in fact—could have transformed the process of dying into an allegorical illusion so strong that it was indistinguishable from ordinary reality. And it was harder yet to believe that those same two people could have entered into that illusion and have met each other for the first time.

It was all so strange. He felt real. He breathed, he saw; he experienced pleasure and pain. And yet all the while he breathed and saw and experienced he knew that he wasn't actually on the River. He *couldn't* be on the River, for the simple reason that in another phase of reality—the *real* phase—he was sitting in his car, in his garage, with the motor running and the garage doors closed.

And yet somehow, in a way that he could not fathom, he *was* on the River; drifting down the River on a strange raft that he had never built or bought and had never even known existed until he had found himself sitting on it nearly two days ago. Or was it two hours ago? Or two minutes? Or two seconds?

He did not know. All he knew was that, subjectively at least, almost forty-eight hours had passed since he had first found himself on the River. Half of those hours he had spent on the River itself, and the other half he had spent in two deserted inns, one of which he had found on the River bank at the close of the first afternoon and the other of which he had found on the River bank at the close of the second.

That was another strange thing about the River. It was impossible to travel on it at night. Not because of the darkness (although the darkness did impose a hazard), but because of an insurmountable reluctance on his own part—a reluctance compounded of dread and of an irresistible desire to interrupt his ineluctable journey long enough to rest. Long enough to find peace. But why peace? he wondered. Wasn't it peace toward which the River was bearing him? Wasn't the only real peace the peace of oblivion? Surely by this time he should have accepted a truism as basic as that.

"It's beginning to get dark," Jill said. "There should be an inn soon." Her shoes and stockings had dried, and she put them back on.

"We'll watch for it. You keep an eye on the right bank and I'll keep an eye on the left."

The inn was on the right bank, built almost flush with the water's edge. A low pier protruded a dozen feet into the stream, and after securing the raft to it with the mooring line, Farrell stepped onto the heavy planking and helped Jill up beside him. So far as he could see, the inn—on the outside, at least—was not particularly different from the two he had already stayed overnight in. It was three-storied and square, and its tiers of windows made warm golden rectangles in the gathering dusk. The interior proved to be virtually identical too, give or take a few modifications—Jill's work, no doubt, since she must have collaborated on the creation. There was a small lobby, a bar, and a large dining room; a gleaming maple staircase curved upward to the second and third floors, and electric lights burned everywhere in the guise of counterfeit candles and imitation hurricane-lamps.

Farrell glanced around the dining room. "It looks as though you and I are slaves to American Colonial tradition," he said.

Jill laughed. "We do seem to have a lot in common, don't we?"

He pointed to a glittering juke box in the far corner of the room. "One of us, though, was a little mixed up. A juke box doesn't belong in an American Colonial setting."

"I'm afraid I'm the guilty party. There was a juke box just like that one in the inn where I stayed last night and in the inn where I stayed the night before."

"Apparently our inns vanish the minute we're out of sight. At any rate, I saw no sign of yours . . . I still can't help wondering whether we're the only force that holds this whole thing together. Maybe, the moment we're de—the moment we're gone—the whole business will disappear. Assuming of course that it has objective existence and *can* disappear."

She pointed to one of the dining-room tables. It was covered with an immaculate linen tablecloth and was set for two. Beside each place, a real candle—real, that is, to whatever extent it was possible for objects to be real in this strange land—burned in a silver candlestick. "*I* can't help wondering what we're going to have for dinner."

"The particular dish we happen to be hungry for most, I imagine. Last night I had a yen for southern-fried chicken, and southern-fried chicken was what I found waiting for me when I sat down."

"Funny, how we can take such miracles in our stride," she said. And then, "I think I'll freshen up a bit."

"I think I will too."

They chose rooms across the hall from each other. Farrell got back downstairs first and waited for Jill in the dining room. During their absence, two large covered trays and a silver coffee set appeared on the linen tablecloth. How this had been brought about, he could not fathom; nor did he try very hard. A hot shower had relaxed him, and he was permeated with a dream-like feeling of well-being. He even had an appetite, although he suspected that it was no more real than the food with which he would presently satisfy it would be. No matter. Stepping into the adjoining bar, he drew himself a short beer and drank it appreciatively. It was cold and tangy, and hit the spot. Returning to the dining room, he saw that Jill had come back downstairs and was waiting for him in the lobby doorway. She had repaired her torn dress as best she could and had cleaned her shoes, and there was a trace of lipstick on her lips and a touch of rouge on her cheeks. It dawned on him all of a sudden that she was positively stunning.

When they sat down at the table, the lights dimmed, and the juke box began to play. In addition to the two covered trays and the silver coffee set, the magic tablecloth had also materialized a mouth-watering antipasto. They nibbled radishes by candlelight, ate carrots Julienne. Jill poured steaming coffee into delicate blue cups, added sugar and cream. She had "ordered" sweet potatoes and baked Virginia ham, he had "ordered" steak and French fries. As they dined, the juke box pulsed softly in the ghostly room and the candle flames flickered in drafts that came through invisible crevices in the walls. When they finished eating, Farrell went into the bar and brought back a bottle of champagne and two glasses. After filling both glasses, he touched his to hers. "To the first day we met," he said, and they drank.

Afterward, they danced on the empty dance floor. Jill was a summer wind in his arms. "Are you a professional dancer?" he asked.

"I was."

He was silent. The music was dream-like, unreal. The big room was a place of soft lights and pale shadows. "I was an artist," he went on presently. "One of the kind whose paintings no one buys and who keep themselves going on scraps of hopes and crusts of dreams. When I first began to paint I thought that what I was doing was somehow noble and worthwhile; but a schoolboy conviction can't last forever, and finally I recognized and accepted the fact that nothing I would ever paint would justify my having gone without even so much as a single helping of mashed potatoes. But that's not why I'm on the River."

"I danced in night clubs," Jill said. "Not nice dances, but I was not a stripper."

"Were you married?"

"No. Were you?"

"Only to my work, and my work and I have been divorced for some time now. Ever since I took a job designing greeting cards."

"It's funny," she said, "I never thought it would be like this. Dying, I mean. Whenever I pictured myself on the River, I pictured myself on it alone."

"So did I," Farrell said. And then, "Where did you live, Jill?"

"In Rapids City."

"Why, that's where I lived too. Maybe that has something to do with our meeting each other in this strange land. I—I wish I had known you before."

"You know me now. And I know you."

"Yes. It's better than never having gotten to know each other at all."

They danced in silence for a while. The inn dreamed around them. Outside, beneath stars that had no right to be, the River flowed, dark-brown and brooding in the night. At length, when the waltz to which they were dancing came to an end, Jill said "I think we should call it a day, don't you?"

"Yes," Farrell said, looking down into her eyes, "I suppose we should." And then, "I'll wake at dawn—I know I will. Will you?"

She nodded. "That's part of it, too—waking at dawn, That, and listening for the falls."

He kissed her. She stood immobile for a moment, then drew away. "Good night," she said, and hurried from the room.

"Good night," he called after her.

He stood in the suddenly empty room for some time.

Now that she had gone, the juke box played no more and the lights had brightened and taken on a cold cast. He could hear the River, hear it whispering a thousand and one sad thoughts. Some of the thoughts were his, and some of them were Jill's.

At last he left the room and climbed the stairs. He paused in front of Jill's door. He raised his hand, knuckles turned toward the panel. He could hear her in the room beyond, hear her bare feet padding on the floor and the rustle of her dress as she slipped out of it for the night. Presently he heard the faint whisper of sheets and the muffled creak of springs. And all the while he heard these sounds, he heard the soft, sad susurrus of the River.

At length his hand fell to his side, and he turned and stepped across the hall and let himself into his own room. He closed the door firmly. Love and death might go together, but love-making and dying did not.

The sound of the River grew louder while he slept, and in the morning it was a steady murmur in his ears. Breakfast was eggs and bacon and toast and coffee served by ghosts, and gray words spoken in the gray light of dawn. With the rising of the sun he and Jill cast off, and soon the inn was far behind them.

A little past midday, they heard the roar of the falls.

It was a gentle roar at first, but it grew louder, decibel by decibel, and the river narrowed and began flowing between bleak gray cliffs. Jill moved closer to Farrell, and Farrell took her hand. Rapids danced around them, drenching them at sporadic intervals with ice-cold spray. The raft lurched beneath them, turned first this way and that at the whim of the River. But it did not capsize, nor would it, for it was the falls that stood for death—not the rapids.

Farrell kept glancing at the girl. She was staring straight ahead of her as though the rapids did not exist, as though nothing existed except herself, Farrell, and the raft. He had not expected death to come so soon. He had thought that life, now that he had met Jill, would linger on. But apparently this strange country which they had somehow brought into being had no function save to destroy them.

Well, destruction was what he wanted, wasn't it? A strange encounter in a strange land could not have changed that, any more than it could have changed it for Jill. A thought struck him, and, raising his voice above the gurgling of the rapids and the roar of the falls, he asked, "What did you use, Jill?"

"Gas," she answered. "And you?"

"Carbon monoxide."

They said no more.

Late in the afternoon, the River widened again, and the cliffs gradually gave way to gently sloping banks. Beyond the banks vague hills showed, and the sky seemed to have taken on a bluer cast. The roar of the falls was deafening now, but apparently the falls themselves were still a considerable distance downstream. Maybe this wasn't the last day after all.

It wasn't. Farrell knew it the minute he saw the inn. It was on the left bank, and it appeared a little while before the sun was about to set. The current was swift now, and very strong, and it required the combined efforts of both him and the girl to pole the raft in to the small pier. Breathing hard, and soaked to the skin, they clung to each other till they caught their breaths. Then they went inside.

Warmth rose up to meet them, and they rejoiced in it. They chose rooms on the second floor, dried their clothes, made themselves presentable, and joined each other in the dining room for the evening meal. Jill had a roast-beef dinner and Farrell had scalloped potatoes and pork chops. He had never tasted anything so delicious in all his life, and he savored every mouthful. Lord, but it was good to be alive!

Astonished at the thought, he stared at his empty plate. *Good* to be alive? Then why was he sitting in his car with the motor running and the garage doors closed, waiting to die? What was he doing on the River? He raised his eyes to Jill's, saw from the bewilderment in them that the face of all the world had changed for her, too, and knew that as surely as she was responsible for his new outlook, he was responsible for hers.

"Why did you do it, Jill?" he asked. "Why?"

She looked away. "As I told you, I used to dance in night clubs. Not nice dances, but I wasn't a stripper either—not in the strict sense of the word. But even though my act could have been far worse, it was still bad enough to awaken something in me that I didn't know existed. Anyway, one night I ran away, and not long after that I joined a convent."

She was silent for a while, and so was he. Then she said, looking at him now, "It's funny about a person's hair—what it can come to stand for, I mean. I wore my hair very long, and it was the most essential part of my act. The only decent part, because it covered my nakedness. Without my knowing what was happening, it came to symbolize for me the only really decent quality I possessed. But I didn't tumble to the truth until it was too late. With my hair, I had been able to live with myself. Without it, I felt unfit to live. I—I ran away again—to Rapids City this time—and I got a job in a department store and rented a small apartment. But a decent job wasn't enough—I needed something more. Winter arrived, and I came down with the flu. You know how it weakens you sometimes, how depressed you can feel afterwards. I—I—"

She looked down at her hands. They lay on the table before her, and they were slender and very white. The sad susurrus of the River filled the room, muting the throb of the juke box. Backgrounding both sounds was the roar of the falls.

Farrell looked down at his own hands. "I guess I was sick, too," he said. "I must have been. I felt empty. Bored. Do you know what true boredom is? It's a vast, gnawing nothingness that settles around you and accompanies you wherever you go. It comes over you in great gray waves and inundates you. It suffocates you. I said that my giving up the kind of work I wanted to do wasn't responsible for my being on the River and it wasn't—not directly. But my boredom was a reaction, just the same. Everything lost meaning for me. It was like waiting all your life for Christmas to come, and then getting up Christmas morning and finding an empty stocking. If I could have found something in the stocking—anything at all—I might have been all right. But I found nothing in it, absolutely nothing. I know now that it was my fault. That the only way anyone can expect to find something in his Christmas stocking is by placing something in it the night before, and that the nothingness I saw around me was merely a reflection of myself. But I didn't know these things then." He raised his head and met her eyes across the table. "Why did we have to die in order to live? Why couldn't we have met like other people—in a summer park or on a quiet street? Why did we have to meet on the River, Jill? Why?"

She stood up, crying. "Let's dance," she said. "Let's dance all night."

They drifted onto the empty dance floor and the music rose around them and took them in its arms—the sad and the gay and the poignant songs that first one of them and then the other remembered from the lifetimes they had cast aside. "That one's from my Senior Prom," she said once. "The one we're dancing to now," he said a short while afterward, "dates from the days when I was still a kid and thought I was in love." "And were you in love?" she asked, eyes gentle upon his face. "No," he answered, "not then. Not ever—until now." "I love you, too," she said, and the tune took on a softer note and for a long while time ceased to be.

Toward dawn, she said, "I hear the River calling. Do you hear it, too?"

"Yes," he said, "I hear it."

He tried to fight the call, and so did she. But it wasn't any use. They left the ghosts of themselves dancing in the dawnlight and went down to the pier and boarded the raft and cast off. The current seized them greedily and the roar of the falls took on a triumphant tone. Ahead, in the wan rays of the rising sun, mist was rising high above the gorge.

They sat close together on the raft, in each other's arms. The roar was a part of the air they breathed now, and the mist was all around them. Through the mist, a vague shape showed. Another raft? Farrell wondered. He peered into the ghostly vapor, saw the little trees, the sandy shore. An island . . .

Suddenly he understood what the islands in the River represented. Neither he nor Jill had truly wanted to die, and as a result the allegory which they had jointly brought to life and entered into contained loopholes. There might be a way back after all.

Springing to his feet, he seized the pole and began poling. "Help me, Jill!" he cried. "It's our last chance."

She, too, had seen the island and divined its significance. She joined him, and they poled together. The current was omnipotent now, the rapids furious. The raft lurched, heaved, wallowed. The island loomed larger through the mist. "Harder, Jill, harder!" he gasped. "We've got to get back—we've *got* to!"

He saw then that they weren't going to make it, that despite their combined efforts the current was going to carry them past their last link with life. There was one chance, and only one. He kicked off his shoes. "Keep poling, Jill!" he shouted, and, after placing the end of the mooring line between his teeth and biting into it, he leaped into the rapids and struck out for the island for all he was worth.

Behind him, the raft lurched wildly, tearing the pole from Jill's grasp and sending her sprawling on the deck. He did not know this, however, till he reached the island and looked over his shoulder. By then, there was just enough slack remaining in the line for him to belay it around a small tree and secure it in place. The tree shuddered when the line went taut, and the raft came to an abrupt stop several feet from the brink of the falls. Jill was on her hands and knees now, trying desperately to keep herself from being thrown from the deck. Gripping the line with both hands, he tried to pull the raft in to the island, but so strong was the current that he would have been equally as successful if he had tried to pull the island in to the raft.

The little tree was being gradually uprooted. Sooner or later it would be torn out of the ground and the raft would plunge over the falls. There was only one thing to do. "Your apartment, Jill!" he shouted across the whiteness of the rapids. "Where is it?"

Her voice was barely audible. "229 Locust Avenue. Number 301."

He was stunned. 229 Locust Avenue was the apartment building next to the one where he lived. Probably they had almost run into each other a dozen times. Maybe they *had* run into each other, and forgotten. In the city, things like that happened every day.

But not on the River.

"Hold on, Jill!" he called. "I'm going the long way around!"

To travel from the island to the garage required but the merest flick of a thought. He came to in his car, head throbbing with misted pain. Turning off the ignition, he got out, threw open the garage doors, and staggered out into the shockingly cold winter's night. He remembered belatedly that his hat and coat were in the back of the car.

No matter. He crammed his lungs with fresh air and rubbed snow on his face. Then he ran down the street to the apartment building next door. Would he be in time? he wondered. He could not have been in the garage more than ten minutes at the most, which meant that time on the River moved at an even faster pace than he had thought. Hours, then, had already passed since he had left the island, and the raft could very well have gone over the falls.

Or had there really been a raft? A River? A girl with sun-bright hair? Maybe the whole thing had been a dream —a dream that his unconscious had manufactured in order to snap him back to life.

The thought was unendurable, and he banished it from his mind. Reaching the apartment building, he ran inside. The lobby was deserted, and the elevator was in use. He pounded up three flights of stairs and paused before the door. It was locked. "Jill!" he called, and broke it down.

She was lying on the living-room sofa, her face waxen in the radiance of a nearby floor lamp. She was wearing the yellow dress that he remembered so well, only now it was no longer torn. Nor were her slender slippers bedraggled. Her hair, though, was just the way he remembered—short, and trying to curl. Her eyes were closed.

He turned off the gas in the fireless circulating heater that stood against the wall, and he threw open all of the windows. He picked her up and carried her over to the largest one and let the sweet-life-giving air embrace her. "Jill!" he whispered. "Jill!"

Her eyelids quivered, opened. Blue eyes filled with terror gazed up into his face. Slowly, the terror faded away, and recognition took its place. He knew then that there would be no more Rivers for either of them.

Before him lay the mesa of the Virgin's face, pale and poignant in the starlight. He was the only Earthman who had ever seen the Virgin as she really was; he had been only twenty at the time. Yet the intervening years were no more than a thin curtain, a curtain he had parted a thousand times.

In the moment of conquest, he forgot what a stoney heart must beat in a . . .

GODDESS IN GRANITE

by Robert F. Young

When he reached the upper ridge of the forearm, Marten stopped to rest. The climb had not winded him but the chin was still miles away, and he wanted to conserve as much of his strength as possible for the final ascent to the face.

He looked back the way he had come—down the slope of the tapered forearm ridge to the mile-wide slab of the hand; down to the granite giantess-fingers protruding like sculptured promontories into the water. He saw his rented inboard bobbing in the blue bay between forefinger and thumb, and, beyond the bay, the shimmering waste of the southern sea.

He shrugged his pack into a more comfortable position and checked the climbing equipment attached to his web belt—his piton pistol in its self-locking holster, his extra clips of piton cartridges, the airtight packet that contained his oxygen tablets, his canteen. Satisfied, he drank sparingly from the canteen and replaced it in its refrigerated case. Then he lit a cigarette and blew smoke at the morning sky.

The sky was a deep, cloudless blue, and Alpha Virginis beat brightly down from the blueness, shedding its warmth and brilliance on the gynecomorphous mountain range known as the Virgin.

She lay upon her back, her blue lakes of eyes gazing eternally upward. From his vantage point on her forearm, Marten had a good view of the mountains of her breasts. He looked at them contemplatively. They towered perhaps 8,000 feet above the chest-plateau, but, since the plateau itself was a good 10,000 feet above sea level, their true height exceeded 18,000 feet. However, Marten wasn't discouraged. It wasn't the mountains that he wanted.

Presently he dropped his eyes from their snow-capped crests and resumed his trek. The granite ridge rose for a while, then slanted downward, widening gradually into the rounded reaches of the upper arm. He had an excellent view of the Virgin's head now, though he wasn't high enough to see her profile. The 11,000-foot cliff of her cheek was awesome at this range, and her hair was revealed for what it really was—a vast forest spilling riotously down to the lowlands, spreading out around her massive shoulders almost to the sea. It was green now. In autumn it would be brown, then gold; in winter, black.

Centuries of rainfall and wind had not perturbed the graceful contours of the upper arm. It was like walking along a lofty promenade. Marten made good time. Still, it was nearly noon before he reached the shoulder-slope, and he realized that he had badly underestimated the Virgin's vastness.

The elements had been less kind to the shoulder-slope, and he had to go slower, picking his way between shallow gullies, avoiding cracks and crevices. In places the granite gave way to other varieties of igneous rock, but the overall color of the Virgin's body remained the same—a grayish-white, permeated with pink, startlingly suggestive of the hue of human skin.

Marten found himself thinking of her sculptors, and for the thousandth time he speculated as to why they had sculptured her. In many ways, the problem resembled such Earth enigmas as the Egyptian pyramids, the Sacsahuaman Fortress, and the Baalbek Temple of the Sun. For one thing, it was just as irresolvable, and probably always would be, for the ancient race that had once inhabited Alpha Virginis IX had either died out centuries ago, or had migrated to the stars. In either case, they had left no written records behind them.

Basically, however, the two enigmas were different. When you contemplated the pyramids, the Fortress, and the Temple of the Sun, you did not wonder *why* they had been built—you wondered *how* they had been built. With the Virgin, the opposite held true. She had begun as a natural phenomenon—an enormous geological upheaval—and actually all her sculptors had done, herculean though their labor had undoubtedly been, was to add the finishing touches and install the automatic subterranean pumping system that, for centuries, had supplied her artificial lakes of eyes with water from the sea.

And perhaps therein lay the answer, Marten thought. Perhaps their only motivation had been a desire to improve upon nature. There certainly wasn't any factual basis for the theosophical, sociological and psychological motivations postulated by half a hundred Earth anthropologists (none of whom had ever *really* seen her) in half a hundred technical volumes. Perhaps the answer was as simple as that . . .

The southern reaches of the shoulder-slope were less eroded than the central and northern reaches, and Marten edged closer and closer to the south rim. He had a splendid view of the Virgin's left side, and he stared, fascinated, at the magnificent purple-shadowed escarpment stretching away to the horizon. Five miles from its juncture with the shoulder-slope it dwindled abruptly to form her waist; three miles farther on it burgeoned out to form her left hip; then, just before it faded into the lavender distances, it blended into the gigantic curve of her thigh.

The shoulder was not particularly steep, yet his chest was tight, his lips dry, when he reached its summit. He decided to rest for a while, and he removed his pack and sat down and propped his back against it. He raised his canteen to his lips and took a long cool draught. He lit another cigarette.

From his new eminence he had a much better view of the Virgin's head, and he gazed at it spellbound. The mesa of her face was still hidden from him, of course—except for the lofty tip of her granite nose; but the details of her cheek and chin stood out clearly. Her cheekbone was represented by a rounded spur, and the spur blended almost imperceptibly with the chamfered rim of her cheek. Her proud chin was a cliff in its own right, falling sheerly—much too sheerly, Marten thought—to the graceful ridge of her neck.

Yet, despite her sculptors' meticulous attention to details, the Virgin, viewed from so close a range, fell far short of the beauty and perfection they had intended. That was because you could see only part of her at a time: her cheek, her hair, her breasts, the distant contour of her thigh. But when you viewed her from the right altitude, the effect was altogether different. Even from a height of ten miles, her beauty was perceptible; at 75,000 feet, it was undeniable. But you had to go higher yet—had to find the exact level, in fact—before you could see her as her sculptors had meant her to be seen.

To Marten's knowledge, he was the only Earthman who had ever found that level, who had ever seen the Virgin as she really was; seen her emerge into a reality uniquely her own—an unforgettable reality, the equal of which he had never before encountered.

Perhaps being the only one had had something to do with her effect on him; that, plus the fact that he had been only 20 at the time—20, he thought wonderingly. He was 32 now. Yet the intervening years were no more than a thin curtain, a curtain he had parted a thousand times.

He parted it again.

After his mother's third marriage he had made up his mind to become a spaceman, and he had quit college and obtained a berth as cabin boy on the starship *Ulysses*. The *Ulysses*' destination was Alpha Virginis IX; the purpose of its voyage was to chart potential ore deposits.

Marten had heard about the Virgin, of course. She was one of the seven hundred wonders of the galaxy. But he had never given her a second thought—till he saw her in the main viewport of the orbiting *Ulysses*. Afterward, he gave her considerable thought and, several days after planetfall, he "borrowed" one of the ship's life-rafts and went exploring. The exploit had netted him a week in the brig upon his return, but he hadn't minded. The Virgin had been worth it.

The altimeter of the life-raft had registered 55,000 feet when he first sighted her, and he approached her at that level. Presently he saw the splendid ridges of her calves and thighs creep by beneath him, the white desert of her stomach, the delicate cwm of her navel. He was above the twin mountains of her breasts, within sight of the mesa of her face, before it occurred to him that, by lifting the raft, he might gain a much better perspective.

He canceled his horizontal momentum and depressed the altitude button. The raft climbed swiftly—60,000 feet . . . 65,000 . . . 70,000. It was like focusing a telescreen—80,000 . . . His heart was pounding now—90,000 . . . The oxygen dial indicated normal pressure, but he could hardly breathe.

100,000, 101,000 . . . Not quite high enough. 102,300 . . . *Thou art beautiful, O my love, as Tirzah, Comely as Jerusalem, Terrible as an army with banners* . . .103,211 . . . *The joints of thy thighs are like jewels, the work of the hands of a cunning workman* . . . 103,288 . . .

He jammed the altitude button hard, locking the focus. He could not breathe at all now—at least not for the first, ecstatic moment. He had never seen anyone quite like her. It was early spring, and her hair was black; her eyes were a springtime blue. And it seemed to him that the mesa of her face abounded in compassion, that the red rimrock of her mouth was curved in a gentle smile.

She lay there immobile by the sea, a Brobdingnagian beauty come out of the water to bask forever in the sun. The barren lowlands were a summer beach; the glittering ruins of a nearby city were an earring dropped from her ear; and the sea was a summer lake, the life-raft a metallic gull hovering high above the littoral.

And in the transparent belly of the gull sat an infinitesimal man who would never be the same again . . .

Marten closed the curtain, but it was some time before the after-image of the memory faded away. When it finally did so, he found that he was staring with a rather frightening fixity toward the distant cliff of the Virgin's chin.

Roughly, he estimated its height. Its point, or summit, was on an approximate level with the crest of the cheek. That gave him 11,000 feet. To obtain the distance he had to climb to reach the face-mesa, all he had to do was to deduct the height of the neck-ridge. He figured the neck-ridge at about 8,000 feet; 8,000 from 11,000 gave him 3,000—3,000 feet!

It was impossible. Even with the piton pistol, it was impossible. The pitch was vertical all the way, and from where he sat he couldn't discern the faintest indication of a crack or a ledge on the granite surface.

He could never do it, he told himself. Never. It would be absurd for him even to try. It might cost him his life. And even if he could do it, even if he could climb that polished precipice all the way of the face-mesa, could he get back down again? True, his piton pistol would make the descent relatively easy, but would he have enough strength left? The atmosphere on Alpha Virginis IX thinned rapidly after 10,000 feet, and while oxygen tablets helped, they could keep you going only for a limited period of time. After that—

But the arguments were old ones. He had used them on himself a hundred, a thousand times . . . He stood up resignedly. He shrugged his pack into place. He took a final look down the nine-mile slope of the arm to the giantess-fingers jutting into the sea, then he turned and started across the tableland of the upper chest toward the beginning of the neck-ridge.

The sun had long since passed its meridian when he came opposite the gentle col between the mountains. A cold wind breathed down the slopes, drifting across the tableland. The wind was sweet, and he knew there must be flowers on the mountains—crocuses, perhaps, or their equivalent, growing high on the snow-soft peaks.

He wondered why he did not want to climb the mountains, why it had to be the mesa. The mountains presented the greater difficulties and therefore the greater challenge. Why, then, did he neglect them for the mesa?

He thought he knew. The beauty of the mountains was shallow, lacked the deeper meaning of the beauty of the mesa. They could never give him what he wanted if he climbed them a thousand times. It was the mesa—with its blue and lovely lakes—or nothing.

He turned his eyes away from the mountains and concentrated on the long slope that led to the neck-ridge. The pitch was gentle but treacherous. He moved slowly. A slip could send him rolling, and there was nothing he could grasp to stop himself. He noticed the shortness of his breath and wondered at it, till he remembered the altitude. But he did not break into his oxygen tablets yet; he would have a much more poignant need for them later.

By the time he reached the ridge, the sun had half completed its afternoon journey. But he wasn't dismayed. He had already given up the idea of assaulting the chin-cliff today. He had been presumptuous in the first place to have imagined himself capable of conquering the Virgin in a single day.

It was going to take at least two.

The ridge was over a mile wide, its curvature barely perceptible. Marten made good time. All the while he advanced he was conscious of the chin-cliff looming higher and higher above him, but he did not look at it; he was afraid to look at it till it loomed so close that it occulted half the sky, and then he had to look at it, had to raise his eyes from the granite swell of the throat and focus them on the appalling wall that now constituted his future.

His future was bleak. It contained no hand- or footholds; no ledges, no cracks, no projections. In a way he was relieved, for if no means existed for him to climb the chin-cliff, then he couldn't climb it. But in another way he was overwhelmingly disappointed. Gaining the face-mesa was more than a mere ambition; it was an obsession, and the physical effort that the task involved, the danger, the obstacles—all were an integral part of the obsession.

He could return the way he had come, down the arm to his inboard and back to the isolated colony; and he could rent a flier from the hard-bitten, taciturn natives just as easily as he had rented the inboard. In less than an hour after takeoff, he could land on the face-mesa.

But he would be cheating, and he knew it. Not cheating the Virgin, but cheating himself.

There was one other way, but he rejected it now for the same reason he had rejected it before. The top of the Virgin's head was an unknown quantity, and, while the trees of her hair might make climbing easier, the distance to be climbed was still over three times the height of the chin-cliff, and the pitch was probably just as precipitous.

No, it was the chin-cliff or nothing. The way things looked now, it was nothing. But he consoled himself with the fact that he had examined only a relatively small section of the cliff. Perhaps the outlying sections would be less forbidding. Perhaps—

He shook his head. Wishful thinking would get him nowhere. It would be time to hope *after* he found a means of ascent, not before. He started along the base of the cliff, then paused. While he had stood there, staring at the stupendous wall, Alpha Virginis had descended unobtrusively into the molten sea. The first star was already visible in the east, and the hue of the Virgin's breasts had transmuted from gold to purple.

Reluctantly, Marten decided to postpone his investigation till tomorrow. The decision proved to be a sensible one. Darkness was upon him before he had his sleeping bag spread out, and with it came the penetrating cold for which the planet was notorious throughout the galaxy.

He set the thermostat on the sleeping bag, then he undressed and crawled into the warm interior. He munched a supper biscuit and allotted himself two swallows of water from his canteen. Suddenly he remembered that he had missed his midday meal—and had not even known the difference.

There was a parallel there somewhere, an element of *déjà vu*. But the connection was so tenuous that he could not pin the other moment down. It would occur to him later, he knew, but such was the nature of the human mind that it would occur seemingly as the result of another chain of associations, and he would not remember the original connection at all.

He lay there, staring at the stars. The dark mass of the Virgin's chin rose up beside him, hiding half the sky. He should have felt forlorn, frightened even. But he did not. He felt safe, secure. For the first time in many years he knew contentment.

There was an unusual constellation almost directly overhead. More than anything else, it made him think of a man astride a horse. The man carried an elongated object on his shoulder, and the object could have been any one of a number of things, depending on the way you looked at the stars that comprised it—a rifle, perhaps, or a staff; maybe even a fishing pole.

To Marten, it looked like a scythe . . .

He turned on his side, luxuriating in his tiny oasis of warmth. The Virgin's chin was soft with starlight now, and the night slept in soft and silent splendor . . . That was one of his own lines, he thought drowsily—a part of that fantastic hodgepodge of words and phrases he had put together eleven years ago under the title of *Rise Up, My Love!* A part of the book that had brought him fame and fortune—and Lelia.

Lelia . . . She seemed so long ago, and in a way she was. And yet, in another way, a strange, poignant way, she was yesterday.

The first time he saw her she was standing in one of those little antique bars so popular then in Old York. Standing there all alone, tall, dark-haired, Junoesque, sipping her midafternoon drink as though women like herself were the most common phenomena in the galaxy.

He had been positive, even before she turned her head, that her eyes were blue, and blue they proved to be; blue with the blueness of mountain lakes in spring, blue with the beauty of a woman waiting to be loved. Boldly, he walked over and stood beside her, knowing it was now or never, and asked if he might buy her a drink.

To his astonishment, she accepted. She did not tell him till later that she had recognized him. He was so naïve at the time that he did not even know that he was a celebrity in Old York, though he should have known. His book certainly had been successful enough.

He had knocked it off the preceding summer—the summer the *Ulysses* returned from Alpha Virginis IX; the summer he quit his berth as cabin boy, forever cured of his ambition to be a spaceman. During the interim consumed by the voyage, his mother had remarried again; and when he found out, he rented a summer cottage in Connecticut as far away from her as he could get. Then, driven by forces beyond his ken, he sat down and began to write.

Rise Up, My Love! had dealt with the stellar odyssey of a young adventurer in search of a substitute for God and with his ultimate discovery of that substitute in a woman. The reviewers shouted "Epic!" and the Freudian psychologists who, after four centuries of adversity, still hadn't given up psychoanalyzing writers shouted "Death-wish!" The diverse appraisals combined happily to stir up interest in the limited literary world and to pave the way for a second printing and then a third. Overnight, Marten had become that most incomprehensible of all literary phenomena—a famous first-novelist.

But he hadn't realized, till now, that his fame involved physical recognition. "I read your book, Mr. Marten," the dark-haired girl standing beside him said. "I didn't like it."

"What's your name?" he asked. Then: "Why?"

"Lelia Vaughn . . . Because your heroine is impossible."

"I don't think she's impossible," Marten said.

"You'll be telling me next that she has a prototype."

"Maybe I will." The bartender served them, and Marten picked up his glass and sipped the cool blueness of his Martian julep. "Why is she impossible?"

"Because she's not a woman," Lelia said. "She's a symbol."

"A symbol of what?"

"I—I don't know. Anyway, she's not human. She's too beautiful, too perfect. She's a criterion, really."

"You look just like her," Marten said.

She dropped her eyes then, and for a while she was silent. Presently: "There's an ancient cliché that bears mentioning at this point," she said: " 'I'll bet you tell that to all the girls—' But somehow I don't think you do."

"You're right," Marten said. "I don't." Then: "It's so close in here, can't we go walking somewhere?"

"All right."

Old York was an anachronism kept alive by a handful of literati who doted on the prestige lent by old buildings, old streets and old ways of life. It was a grim, canyonesque grotesquerie compared to its pretty new cousin on Mars; but during the years, parts of it had taken on some of the coloring and some of the atmosphere once associated with the Left Bank of Paris, and if the season was spring and you were falling in love, Old York was a lovely place in which to be.

They walked through the dreaming desuetude of ancient avenues, in the cool shadows of buildings mellowed by the passage of time. They lingered in the wilderness of Central Park, and the sky was blue with spring, the trees adorned with the pale greenness of nascent leaves . . . It had been the loveliest of afternoons and, afterward, the loveliest of evenings. The stars had never shone so brightly, nor had the moon ever been so full, the hours so swift, the minutes so sweet. Marten's head had been light, seeing Lelia home, his footsteps unsteady; but it wasn't till later, sitting on his apartment steps, that he had realized how hungry he was, and simultaneously realized that he hadn't eaten a morsel of food since morning . . .

Deep in the alien night, Marten stirred, awakened. The strange star patterns shocked him for a moment, and then he remembered where he was and what he was going to do. Sleep tiptoed back around him and he turned dreamily in the warmth of his electronic cocoon. Freeing one arm, he reached out till his fingers touched the reassuring surface of the star-kissed cliff. He sighed.

Dawn wore a pink dress and crept across the land like a timid girl. Her sister Morning followed, dressed in blue, the sun a dazzling locket on her breast.

There was a tightness in Marten, a tightness compounded of anticipation and dread. He did not permit himself to think. Methodically he ate his concentrated breakfast, packed his sleeping bag. Then he began a systematic examination of the Virgin's chin.

In the morning light, the cliff did not seem nearly so awesome as it had the night before. But its pitch had not varied, nor had its sheer, smooth surface. Marten was both relieved and chagrined.

Then, near the western edge of the neck-ridge, he found the chimney.

It was a shallow fissure, perhaps twice the breadth of his body, created probably by a recent seismic disturbance. He remembered, suddenly, the other signs of recent seismic activity he had noticed in the colony but had not bothered to inquire about. A dozen or so ruptured dwellings were of little consequence when you were on the verge of resolving a complex that had plagued you for twelve years.

The chimney zigzagged upward as far as he could see, presenting, at least for the first thousand feet, a comparatively easy means of ascent. There were innumerable hand- and footholds, and occasional ledges. The trouble was, he had no way of knowing whether the holds and the ledges—or even the chimney itself—continued all the way to the summit.

He cursed himself for having neglected to bring binoculars. Then he noticed that his hands were trembling, that his heart was tight against his ribs; and he knew, all at once, that he was going to climb the chimney regardless, that nothing could stop him, not even himself—not even the knowledge, had it been available, that the chimney was a dead end.

He drew his piton pistol and inserted one of the dozen clips he carried in his belt. He aimed carefully, squeezed the trigger. The long hours he had spent practising, while awaiting transportation from the spaceport to the colony, paid off, and the peg, trailing its almost invisible nylon line, imbedded itself in the lofty ledge he had selected for his first belay. The sound of the second charge caromed down and joined the fading sound of the first, and he knew that the steel roots of the peg had been forced deep into the granite, guaranteeing his safety for the initial 500 feet.

He replaced the pistol in its self-locking holster. From now till he reached the ledge, the line would take in its own slack, automatically rewinding itself in the chamber in pace with his ascent.

He began to climb.

His hands were steady now, and his heart had resumed its normal beat. There was a song in him, throbbing soundlessly through his whole being, imbuing him with a strength he had never known before, might never know again. The first 500 feet were almost ridiculously easy. Hand- and footholds were so numerous most of the way that it was like climbing a stone ladder, and in the few places where the projections petered out, the walls were ideally spaced for opposite pressure. When he reached the ledge, he wasn't even breathing hard.

He decided not to rest. Sooner or later the thinness of the atmosphere was going to catch up with him, and the higher he got, while he was still fresh, the better. He stood up boldly and drew and aimed the piton pistol. The new peg soared forth, trailing the new line and dislodging the old, arrowing into the base of another ledge some 200 feet above the one on which he stood. The range of the pistol was 1,000 feet, but the narrowness of the chimney and the awkwardness of his position posed severe limitations.

He resumed his ascent, his confidence increasing with

each foot he gained. But he was careful not to look down. The chimney was so far out on the western edge of the neck-ridge that looking down entailed not only the distance he had already climbed, but the 8,000-foot drop from the ridge to the low lands. He did not think his new confidence quite capable of assimilating the shock of so appalling a height.

The climb to the second ledge was as uneventful as the climb to the first. Again he decided not to rest, and, sinking another peg into a third ledge approximately 250 feet above the second, he resumed climbing. Halfway to the third ledge the first pangs of oxygen starvation manifested themselves in a heaviness in his arms and legs and a shortness of his breath. He slipped an oxygen tablet into his mouth and went on climbing.

The dissolving tablet revived him, and when he reached the third ledge he still did not feel like resting. But he forced himself to sit down on the narrow granite shelf and he lay his head back against the chimney wall and tried to relax. Sunlight smote his eyes, and with a shock he realized that the speed of his ascent had been subjective; actually, hours had passed since he had left the neck-ridge, and Alpha Virginis was already at meridian.

Then he couldn't rest; there was not time. He had to reach the face-mesa before nightfall, else he might never reach it at all. In an instant he was on his feet, piton pistol drawn and aimed.

For a while the climb took on a different character. His confidence never diminished and the soundless song throbbed through him in ever-increasing cadence; but the heaviness of his limbs and the shortness of his breath recurred at more and more frequent periods, lending a dreamlike quality to the adventure, and this quality, in turn, was interspersed by the brief but lucid intervals that began immediately whenever he took an oxygen tablet.

The character of the chimney, however, varied only slightly. It grew wider for a while, but he found that by bracing his back against one wall and his feet against the other, he could inch his way upward with a minimum of effort. Then the chimney narrowed again and he returned to his original mode of ascent.

Inevitably he became bolder. Up to now he had been using three-point suspension, never moving one appendage till he was certain the other three were firmly placed. But as his boldness increased, his caution diminished. He neglected three-point suspension more and more often, finally neglected it altogether. After all, he reassured himself, what difference did it make if he did slip? The piton line would stop him before he fell two feet.

And it would have too—if the particular cartridge he had just discharged had not been defective. In his haste he did not notice that the nylon line was not rewinding itself, and when the chockstone, on which he'd just put his entire weight, gave way beneath his foot, his instinctive terror was tempered by the thought that his fall would be brief.

It was not. It was slow at first, unreal. He knew instantly that something had gone wrong. Nearby, someone was screaming. For a moment he did not recognize his own voice. And then the fall was swift; the chimney walls blurred past his clawing hands, and dislodged rubble rained about his anguished face.

Twenty feet down he struck a projection on one side of the chimney. The impact threw him against the other side, then the ledge that he had left a short while before came up jarringly beneath his feet and he sprawled forward on his stomach, the wind knocked from him, blood running into his eyes from a cut on his forehead.

When his breath returned he moved each of his limbs carefully, testing them for broken bones. Then he inhaled deeply. Afterward he lay there on his stomach for a long time, content with the knowledge that he was alive and not seriously hurt.

Presently he realized that his eyes were closed. Without thinking, he opened them and wiped the blood away. He found himself staring straight down at the forest of the Virgin's hair, 10,000 feet below. He sucked in his breath, tried to sink his fingers into the ungiving granite of the ledge. For a while he was sick, but gradually his sickness left him and his terror faded away.

The forest spread out almost to the sea, flanked by the magnificent precipices of the neck and shoulder, the nine-mile ridge of the arm. The sea was gold and glittering in the mid-afternoon sunlight, and the lowlands were a green-gold beach.

There was an analogy somewhere. Marten frowned,

trying to remember. Hadn't he, a long time ago, crouched on another ledge—or was it a bluff?—looking down upon another beach, a real beach? Looking down at—

Abruptly he remembered, and the memory set his face on fire. He tried to force the unwanted moment back into his subconscious, but it slipped through his mental fingers and came out and stood nakedly in the sun, and he had to confront it whether he wanted to or not, had to live it over again.

After their marriage, he and Lelia had rented the same cottage in Connecticut where *Rise Up, My Love!* was born, and he had settled down to write his second book.

The cottage was a charming affair, perched on a bluff overlooking the sea. Below it, accessible by a flight of winding stairs, was a narrow strip of white sand, protected from the prying eyes of civilization by the wooded arms of a small cove. It was there that Lelia spent her afternoons sunbathing in the nude, while Marten spent those same afternoons feeding empty words and uninspired phrases into the manuscript machine on his study desk.

The new book was going very badly. The spontaneity that had characterized the creation of *Rise Up, My Love!* was no longer with him. Ideas would not come, or, if they did come, he was incapable of coping with them. A part of his mood, he knew, could be ascribed to his marriage. Lelia was everything a bride should be, but there was something she was not, an intangible something that taunted him by night and haunted him by day . . .

The August afternoon had been hot and humid. There was a breeze coming in over the sea, but while it was strong enough to ruffle the curtains of his study window, it wasn't quite strong enough to struggle through the intervening expanse of stagnant air to the doldrums of the study proper where he sat miserably at his desk.

As he sat there, fingering words and phrases, grappling with ideas, he became aware of the soft sound of the surf on the beach below, and an image of Lelia, lying dark and golden in the sun, intruded repeatedly on his thoughts.

Presently he found himself speculating on the positions she might be lying in. On her side, perhaps . . . or perhaps on her back, the golden sunlight raining down on her thighs, her stomach, her breasts.

There was a faint throbbing in his temples, a new nervousness in the fingers that toyed with the correction pencil on the desktop before him. Lelia lying immobile by the sea, her dark hair spread out around her head and shoulders, her blue eyes staring up into the sky . . .

How would she look from above? Say from the height of the bluff? Would she resemble another woman lying by another sea—a woman who had affected him in some mysterious way and lent him his literary wings?

He wondered, and as he wondered his nervousness grew and the throbbing in his temples thickened and slowed till it matched the rhythmic beat of the surf.

He looked at the clock on the study wall: 2:45. There was very little time. In another half hour she would be coming up to shower. Numbly, he stood up. He walked slowly across the study, stepped into the living room; he walked across the living room and out upon the latticed porch that fronted the green lawn and the brow of the bluff and the sparkling summer sea.

The grass was soft beneath his feet and there was a dreaminess about the afternoon sunlight and the sound of the surf. When he neared the bluff he got down on his hands and knees, feeling like a fool, and crept cautiously forward. Several feet from the brow he lowered himself to his elbows and thighs and crawled the rest of the way. He parted the long grass carefully and looked down to the white strip of beach below.

She was lying directly beneath him—on her back. Her left arm was flung out to the sea and her fingers dangled in the water. Her right knee was drawn upward, a graceful hillock of sun-gold flesh . . . and the smooth expanse of her stomach was golden too, as were the gentle mountains of her breasts. Her neck was a magnificent golden ridge leading to the proud precipice of her chin and the vast golden mesa of her face. The blue lakes of her eyes were closed in peaceful sleep.

Illusion and reality intermingled. Time retreated and space ceased to be. At the crucial moment, the blue eyes opened.

She saw him instantly. There was amazement on her face at first, then understanding (though she hadn't understood at all). Finally her lips curved in a beckoning smile and she held out her arms to him. "Come down, darling," she called. "Come down and see me!"

The throbbing in his temples drowned out the sound of the surf as he descended the winding stairs to the beach. She was waiting there by the sea, waiting as she had always waited, waiting for him; and suddenly he was a giant striding over the lowlands, his shoulders brushing the sky, the ground shuddering beneath his Brobdingnagian footsteps.

Thou art beautiful, O my love, as Tirzah, Comely as Jerusalem, Terrible as an army with banners . . .

A breeze, born in the purple shadows between the mountains, wafted up to his eyrie, cooling his flushed face and reviving his battered body. Slowly he got to his feet. He looked up at the enigmatic walls of the chimney, wondering if they continued for the thousand-odd feet that still separated him from the summit.

He drew his piton pistol and ejected the defective cartridge; then he took careful aim and squeezed the trigger. When he replaced the pistol he experienced a wave of giddiness and he reached instinctively for the oxygen packet on his belt. Then he fumbled for the packet, frantically feeling every inch of the web surface, and finally he found the tiny rivets that had remained after the packet had been torn away during his fall.

For a while he did not move. He had but one logical course of action and he knew it: climb back down to the neck-ridge, spend the night there and return to the colony in the morning, then arrange for transportation to the spaceport, take the first ship back to Earth and forget about the Virgin.

He nearly laughed aloud. Logic was a fine word and an equally fine concept, but there were many things in heaven and earth that it did not encompass, and the Virgin was one of them.

He started to climb.

In the neighbourhood of 2,200 feet, the chimney began to change.

Marten did not notice the change at first. Oxygen starvation had decimated his awareness and he moved in a slow, continuous lethargy, raising one heavy limb and then another, inching his ponderous body from one precarious position to another equally precarious—but slightly closer to his goal. When he finally did notice, he was too weary to be frightened, too numb to be discouraged.

He had just crawled upon the sanctuary of a narrow ledge and had raised his eyes to seek out another ledge at which to point his pistol. The chimney was palely lit by the last rays of the sinking sun and for a moment he thought that the diminishing light was distorting his vision.

For there were no more ledges.

There was no more chimney either, for that matter. It had been growing wider and wider for some time; now it flared abruptly into a concave slope that stretched all the way to the summit. Strictly speaking, there had never been a chimney in the first place. *In toto,* the fissure was far more suggestive of the cross section of a gigantic funnel: the part he had already climbed represented the tube, and the part he had yet to climb represented the mouth.

The mouth, he saw at a glance, was going to be bad. The slope was far too smooth. From where he sat he could not see a single projection, and while that didn't necessarily rule out the possible existence of projections, it did cancel out the likelihood of there being any large enough to enable him to use his piton pistol. He couldn't very well drive a piton if there was nothing for him to drive it into.

He looked down at his hands. They were trembling again. He started to reach for a cigarette, realized suddenly that he hadn't eaten since morning, and got a supper biscuit out of his pack instead. He ate it slowly, forced it down with a mouthful of water. His canteen was nearly empty. He smiled wanly to himself. At last he had a logical reason for climbing to the mesa—to replenish his water supply in the blue lakes.

He reached for a cigarette again and this time he pulled one out and lit it. He blew smoke at the darkening sky. He drew his feet up on the ledge and hugged his knees with his arms and rocked himself gently back and forth. He hummed softly to himself. It was an old, old tune, dating back to his early childhood. Abruptly he remembered where he had heard it and who had sung it to him, and he stood up angrily and flicked his cigarette into the deepening shadows and turned toward the slope.

He resumed his upward journey.

It was a memorable journey. The slope was just as bad

as it had looked. It was impossible to ascend it vertically, and he had to traverse, zigzagging back and forth with nothing but finger-thick irregularities to support his weight. But his brief rest and his condensed meal had replenished his strength and at first he experienced no difficulties.

Gradually, however, the increasing thinness of the atmosphere caught up with him again. He moved slower and slower. Sometimes he wondered if he was making any progress at all. He did not dare lean his head back far enough to look upward, for his hand- and footholds were so tenuous that the slightest imbalance could dislodge them. And presently there was the increasing darkness to contend with too.

He regretted not having left his pack on the last ledge. It was an awkward burden and it seemed to grow heavier with each foot he gained. He would have loosened the straps and slipped it from his shoulders—if he had had hands to spare.

Repeatedly, sweat ran down into his eyes. Once he tried to wipe his wet forehead on the granite slope, but he only succeeded in reopening his cut, and the blood joined forces with the sweat and for a while he could not see at all. He began to wonder if the cliff was forever. Finally he managed to wipe his eyes on his sleeve, but still he could not see, for the darkness was complete.

Time blurred, ceased to be. He kept wondering if the stars were out, and when he found a set of hand- and footholds less tenuous than the preceding ones, he leaned his head back carefully and looked upward. But the blood and the sweat ran down into his eyes again and he saw nothing.

He was astonished when his bleeding fingers discovered the ledge. His reconnaissance had been cursory, but even so he had been certain that there were no lodges. But there was this one. Trembling, he inched his weary body higher till at last he found purchase for his elbows, then he swung his right leg onto the granite surface and pulled himself to safety.

It was a wide ledge. He could sense its wideness when he rolled over on his back and let his arms drop to his sides. He lay there quietly, too tired to move. Presently he raised one arm and wiped the blood and sweat from his eyes. The stars *were* out. The sky was patterned with the pulsing beauty of a hundred constellations. Directly above him was the one he had noticed the night before—the rider-with-the-scythe.

Marten sighed. He wanted to lie there on the ledge forever, the starlight soft on his face, the Virgin reassuringly close; lie there in blissful peace, eternally suspended between the past and the future, bereft of time and motion.

But the past would not have it so. Despite his efforts to stop her, Xylla parted its dark curtain and stepped upon the stage. And then the curtain dissolved behind her and the impossible play began.

After the failure of his third novel (the second had sold on the strength of the first and had enjoyed an ephemeral success), Lelia had gone to work for a perfume concern so that he could continue writing. Later on, to free him from the burden of household chores, she had hired a maid.

Xylla was an e.t.—a native of Mizar X. The natives of Mizar X were remarkable for two things: their gigantic bodies and their diminutive minds. Xylla was no exception. She stood over seven feet tall and she had an I.Q. of less than 40.

But for all her height she was well proportioned, even graceful. In fact, if her face had possessed any appeal at all, she could have passed for an attractive woman. But her face was flat, with big, bovine eyes and wide cheekbones. Her mouth was much too full, and its fullness was accentuated by a pendulous lower lip. Her hair, which, by contributing the right dash of color, might have rescued her from drabness, was a listless brown.

Marten took one look at her when Lelia introduced them, said, "How do you do?" and then dismissed her from his mind. If Lelia thought a giantess could do the housework better than he could, it was all right with him.

That winter Lelia was transferred to the West Coast, and rather than suffer the upkeep of two houses they gave up the Connecticut cottage and moved to California. California was as sparsely populated as Old York. The promised land had long since absconded starward, lay scattered throughout a thousand as yet unexploited systems. But there was one good thing about the average man's eternal hankering for green pastures: the pastures he left behind grew lush in his absence; there was plenty of space for the stay-at-homes and the stubborn; and Earth, after four centuries of opportunism, had finally settled down in its new role as the cultural center of the galaxy.

Lavish twenty-third century villas were scattered all along the California coast. Almost all of them were charming and almost all of them were empty. Lelia chose a pink one, convenient to her work, and settled down into a routine identical, except for a change from the morning to the afternoon shift, to the routine she had left behind; and Marten settled down to write his fourth book.

Or tried to.

He had not been naïve enough to think that a change in scene would snap him out of his literary lethargy. He had known all along that whatever words and combinations thereof that he fed into his manuscript machine had to come from within himself. But he *had* hoped that two failures in a row (the second book was really a failure, despite its short-lived financial success) would goad him to a point where he would not permit a third.

In this he had been wrong. His lethargy not only persisted; it grew worse. He found himself going out less and less often, retiring earlier and earlier to his study and his books. But not to his manuscript machine. He read the great novelists. He read Tolstoy and Flaubert. He read Dostoevski and Stendhal. He read Proust and Cervantes. He read Balzac. And the more he read Balzac, the more his wonder grew, that this small, fat, red-faced man could have been so prolific, while he himself remained as sterile as the white sands on the beach below his study windows.

Around ten o'clock each evening Xylla brought him his brandy in the big snifter glass Lelia had given him on his last birthday, and he would lie back in his lazy-chair before the fireplace (Xylla had built a fire of pine knots earlier in the evening) and sip and dream. Sometimes he would drowse for a moment, and then wake with a start. Finally he would get up, cross the hall to his room and go to bed. (Lelia had begun working overtime shortly after their arrival and seldom got home before one o'clock.)

Xylla's effect upon him was cumulative. At first he was not even conscious of it. One night he would notice the way she walked—lightly, for so ponderous a creature, rhythmically, almost; and the next night, the virginal swell of her huge breasts; and the night after that, the graceful surge of her Amazonian thighs beneath her coarse skirt. The night finally came when, on an impulse, or so he thought at the time, he asked her to sit down and talk for a while.

"If you weesh, sar," she said, and sat down on the hassock at his feet.

He hadn't expected that, and at first he was embarrassed. Gradually, however, as the brandy began its swift infiltration of his bloodstream, he warmed to the moment. He noticed the play of the firelight on her hair, and suddenly he was surprised to find that it was something more than a dull brown after all; there was a hint of redness in it, a quiet, unassuming redness that offset the heaviness of her face.

They talked of various things—the weather mostly, sometimes the sea; a book Xylla had read when she was a little girl (the only book she had ever read); Mizar X. When she spoke of Mizar X, something happened to her voice. It grew soft and childlike, and her eyes, which he had thought dull and uninteresting, became bright and round, and he even detected a trace of blueness in them. The merest trace, of course, but it was a beginning.

He began asking her to stay every night after that, and she was always willing, always took her place dutifully on the hassock at his feet. Even sitting, she loomed above him, but he did not find her size disquieting any more, at least not disquieting in the sense that it had been before. Now her vast presence had a lulling effect upon him, lent him a peace of sorts. He began looking forward more and more to her nightly visits.

Lelia continued to work overtime. Sometimes she did not come in till nearly two. He had been concerned about her at first; he had even reprimanded her for working so hard. Somewhere along the line, though, he had stopped being concerned.

Abruptly he remembered the night Lelia had come home early—the night he had touched Xylla's hand.

He had been wanting to touch it for a long time. Night after night he had seen it lying motionless on her knee and he had marveled again and again at its symmetry and grace, wondered how much bigger than his hand it was, whether it was soft or coarse, warm or cold. Finally the time came when he couldn't control himself any longer, and he bent forward and reached out—and suddenly her giantess fingers were intertwined with his pygmy ones and he felt the warmth of her and knew her nearness. Her lips were very close, her giantess-face, and her eyes were a vivid blue now, a blue-lake blue. And then the coppices of her eyebrows brushed his forehead and the red rimrock of her mouth smothered his and melted into softness and her giantess-arms enfolded him against the twin mountains of her breasts—

Then Lelia, who had paused shocked in the doorway, said, "I'll get my things . . ."

The night was cold, and particles of hoarfrost hovered in the air, catching the light of the stars. Marten shivered, sat up. He looked down into the pale depths below, then he lifted his eyes to the breathless beauty of the twin mountains. Presently he stood up and turned toward the slope, instinctively raising his hands in search of new projections.

His hands brushed air.

He stared. There were no projections. There was no slope. There had never been a ledge, for that matter. Before him lay the mesa of the Virgin's face, pale and poignant in the starlight.

Marten moved across the mesa slowly. All around him the starlight fell like glistening rain. When he came to the rimrock of the mouth, he pressed his lips to the cold, ungiving stone. "Rise up, my love!" he whispered.

But the Virgin remained immobile beneath his feet, as he had known she would, and he went on, past the proud tor of her nose, straining his eyes for the first glimpse of the blue lakes.

He walked numbly, his arms hanging limply at his sides. He hardly knew he walked at all. The lure of the lakes, now that they were so close, was overwhelming. The lovely lakes with their blue beckoning deeps and their promise of eternal delight. No wonder Lelia, and later Xylla, had palled on him. No wonder none of the other mortal women he had slept with had ever been able to give him what he wanted. No wonder he had come back, after twelve futile years, to his true love.

The Virgin was matchless. There were none like her. None.

He was almost to the cheekbone now, but still no starlit sweep of blue rose up to break the monotony of the mesa. His eyes ached from strain and expectation. His hands trembled uncontrollably.

And then, suddenly, he found himself standing on the lip of a huge, waterless basin. He stared, dumbfounded. Then he raised his eyes and saw the distant coppice of an eyebrow outlined against the sky. He followed the line of the eyebrow to where it curved inward and became the barren ridge that once had been the gentle isthmus separating the blue lakes—

Before the water had drained away. Before the subterranean pumping system had ceased to function, probably as a result of the same seismic disturbance that had created the chimney.

He had been too impetuous, too eager to possess his true love. It had never occurred to him that she could have changed, that—

No, he would not believe it! Believing meant that the whole nightmarish ascent of the chin-cliff had been for nothing. Believing meant that his whole life was without purpose.

He lowered his eyes, half expecting, half hoping to see the blue water welling back into the empty socket. But all he saw was the bleak lake bottom—and its residue—

And such a strange residue. Scatterings of gray, sticklike objects, curiously shaped, sometimes joined together. Almost like—like—

Marten shrank back. He wiped his mouth furiously. He turned and began to run.

But he did not run far, not merely because his breath gave out, but because, before he ran any farther, he had to know what he was going to do. Instinctively he had headed for the chin-cliff. But would becoming a heap of broken bones on the neck-ridge be any different, basically, from drowning in one of the lakes?

He paused in the starlight, sank to his knees. Revulsion shook him. How could he have been so naïve, even when he was 20, as to believe that he was the only one? Certainly he was the only Earthman—but the Virgin was an old, old woman, and in her youth she had had many suitors, conquering her by whatever various means they could devise, and symbolically dying in the blue deeps of her eyes.

Their very bones attested to her popularity.

What did you do when you learned that your goddess had feet of clay? What did you do when you discovered that your true love was a whore?

Marten wiped his mouth again. There was one thing that you did *not* do—

You did not sleep with her.

Dawn was a pale promise in the east. The stars had begun to fade. Marten stood on the edge of the chin-cliff, waiting for the day.

He remembered a man who had climbed a mountain centuries ago and buried a chocolate bar on the summit. A ritual of some kind, meaningless to the uninitiated. Standing there on the mesa, Marten buried several items of his own. He buried his boyhood and he buried *RiseUp, My Love!* He buried the villa in California and he buried the cottage in Connecticut. Last of all—wth regret, but with finality—he buried his mother.

He waited till the false morning had passed, till the first golden fingers of the sun reached out and touched his tired face. Then he started down.

What has universal currency but no price? A symbol. And who earns the symbol of highest value?

THE SEEKERS

by E. C. Tubb

The head was becoming too Byzantine in the exaggerated torment of the face. Intalgo leaned back, frowning as he studied his work. The torment belonged, certainly, the portrait was that of a man on a cross. Any man on any cross and from what he knew crucifixion was a most agonizing form of death. But he really knew so little. He had never seen the face of a crucified man and the work lacked that certain conviction which only experience could provide. Disconsolately he leaned farther back and closed his eyes.

Around him the control room whispered its muted, mechanical lullaby.

He heard it just beneath the level of his consciousness. It was a sound so familiar that, to him, it was silence, but, if the whisper should break, should falter, he would be immediately aware. But the whisper did not change. The ship hummed its smooth way across the void at a pace which left light crawling far behind. A mechanical ballet aimed at a distant star. Another star, another planet, another step on the path of total domination.

Intalgo abruptly opened his eyes, staring at the portrait as if at an enemy, hoping to capture the missing ingredient by sheer surprize. How did a man die on a cross? There would be the constriction of the chest, the pressure on the lungs, the terrible strain. Surely the head would fall forward or, no, the head would have to be thrown back in order to straighten the throat. But in that case the chin would be more prominent. And what about cyanosis?

The artist sighed and reached for his pigments. He wished that Delray was awake. The doctor should know.

Delray was fighting. He strode through barbarous halls, the sword in his hand red with blood, his near-naked body dappled with ruby flecks. He came to the hall with the throne and halted, eyes narrowed against the leaping glare of giant flambeaux. The light dimmed, and from the shadows, something advanced.

It was anthropomorphic and obscene. It yammered a challenge and he roared an answer, springing forward, the sword firm in his hand. Then it was a blur of cut and thrust and vicious slashing. Spurting blood filled the air with its familiar reek. And, above all, was the mad, red, exhilaration of the battle.

The thing died. The hall threw back the echoes of his footsteps as he marched to the throne. He tensed as something moved beside it, relaxing as the woman came towards him. She was tall, proud, her mouth a ruby smear. Blonde hair trailed the floor at her feet. White flesh gleamed in the dancing light.

He laughed and heard the sword tinkle at his feet. He reached towards her and laughed again as a dagger flashed in her hand. Contemptuously he knocked it aside and clamped his hands on warm, struggling flesh. His blood thrilled with the lust for conquest.

He opened his eyes and stared at the satin finish of the ceiling.

He swore and rose and swore again as his forehead hit the edge of the cap. A hell of a time for the thing to break down. His instinct was to hit out and he slammed his hand against the warm metal, furious at the disturbance of his favourite dream. A tell-tale lit with a cold, green glow and he arrested the movement of his hand poised for a second blow. Grumbling, he thrust his head into the field of the cap. The spool must be broken or the selector at fault, but he could fix neither. Malchus would have to do that.

The engineer sat cross-legged before the quiescent bulk of the power unit. The side-edges of his naked feet rested on the metal of the floor, the tips of his supporting fingers touched it to either side. His eyes were closed, but he was not asleep.

He sensed the vibration of the metal, the path of incandescent particles within the pile, extrapolating from observable data to the logical conclusion. There was a tiny hesitancy from one of the turbines. It was almost nothing but the slight imbalance would hinder the path of the bases, deflecting them a trifle to one side. There would be excessive erosion on a certain spot and a rise in temperature. The extra heat would affect the bore of a pipe and create a minor bottleneck. Pressure would tend to build.

Eventually a repair and adjustment would have to be made.

But not now. Not for a long time yet. They would have time to finish this tour before things reached the point where to ignore the trouble would be to court disaster. Then he would oversee the work and guide the rebuilding.

The corners of his mouth lifted in a smile.

To build!

Feldman could never appreciate the beauty of the thought. But the navigator was not an engineer.

Feldman was the man who sent the ship lunging at invisible targets, who checked the radiation of suns and the atmosphere of planets, who lived by the lines of a spectroscope and the immutable laws of science. He worshipped the cold beauty of an equation. He was writing a book.

It was a work of love, a hobby, and would be published, if at all, under a pseudonym. He would not risk the sneers of his contemporaries. He wrote:

> The greatest foreseeable problem of heterosexual crews, the strains and frustrations of thwarted sexual desire, have apparently been overcome by use of the dream-cap in which paradoxical dreams are encouraged with the consequent release of physical strain by the superimposition of erotic and exotic stimuli. A choice of dream-sequences is provided by varied tapes and, it is to be assumed, the synthetic world so provided compensates for the boredom of space flight and the lack of congenial company. By congenial I mean female and not incompatable types. Choice of crew-members is carefully governed both from the view-point of dual-attributes and . . .

He was wandering. He lifted the pen and sucked thoughtfully at the tip. The book was to be about the sexual tensions and problems in space, but, for some reason, he constantly veered from the subject. Now, for example, he was about to laud the Pentarch for their wisdom in crew-selection when, of course, it wasn't really wisdom at all but plain common sense. He really must stick to the point.

And yet—?

Was it really wise to write the book at all? A man in his position couldn't be too careful, and if the book were published and a whisper of the true identity of the author should leak out—?

He frowned and moved his hand to the release. A pressure and the surface was blank. Almost at once he regretted the total erasure—he should have printed it at least if only to make corrections. He could always destroy the thing before they landed. But perhaps if he tried a different approach?

The pen touched the surface and left a scrawl of thin lines. Hastily he jabbed the erase button again. He was sweating. He hadn't really meant to write that at all.

Intalgo took a smear of pigment on the tip of his thumb and wiped it beneath the staring eyes. He brushed a thin line at the corners of the mouth and touched the contour of a lip. Leaning back he looked at the result.

He frowned his disappointment. He had tried to portray resignation, acceptance, fortitude, the whole overlaid with a patina of pain. Instead he had added a new emotion. Now the face held hate.

He reached towards the erase then halted the movement of his hand. Was he so wrong? Wouldn't a man so tormented have cause to hate his tormentors? He had tried to picture an ideal and so had tried to achieve the impossible. Art could not deny reality.

Irritably he rose and paced the control room, wondering at his sombre thoughts. Death, torment, the ultimate in pain—why did his hands insist on creating such things? And why did that face hold a haunting tinge of familiarity?

Musing, he stared at his creation while around him the control room hummed its satisfaction. The hum gave the answer. The control room was too empty—something was missing. Something which, subconsciously, he had tried to replace.

The Pentarch had flung the ship like a challenging hand towards the stars. But now that hand was maimed.

The captain was dead.

Intalgo had loved that lonely man. Beneath the cold exterior he had sensed a warm personality and an imagination almost equal to his own. No artist, the captain, but a trained manipulator of men. But he had once likened the stars to camp fires burning in the fields of eternity and Intalgo could forgive many things to a man who had held thoughts of such poetic slant.

But he found it hard to forgive the manner of his death.

Such a man should not have died in such a fashion. For him was the noble ending, the song of trumpets, the heroic passing. Not a sharp edge drawn across a naked throat in the silence of his lonely watch. Often the artist wondered what had driven him to take his life. Had he, too, been crucified on the cross of duty and inclination?

Was that his face which looked back from the painted sheet?

Intalgo stared at it with sharpened interest, but it was not the captain. It was not anyone he knew and yet . . .

He sat, musing, looking at the painted face, remembering the dead.

They had often talked during the long, silent hours between the stars. They had talked of death and of life and the purpose of existence. They had talked of what they did and why they did it.

And the captain had shown his fear.

"Out here," he'd said, "we're irritating intruders, rats scuttling among the granary of the stars. What may we find? Other, older races, perhaps? Strange ways and strange customs and mysteries which we lack the mental equipment to solve. And yet we go on. We have no choice but to go on."

Then he would laugh without humour and his eyes would grow bleak.

"One day we will find something beyond us and, when we do, God help our ignorance."

He had not waited for that day to come.

* * *

They landed on a planet which drowsed beneath the ruddy glare of a dying sun. The ship was an alien harshness on a rolling plain of yellow dust. An enigmatic cube thrust its squat ebony finger towards the sky. It was the only sign of life the world possessed and it was old. Old beyond their limited imagination.

But they landed to stamp the seal of the Pentarch on a new acquisition of Man.

"We must be armed," said Delray.

"No need—the entire planet is dead," said Feldman.

"I must get into that building," said Malchus.

Intalgo said nothing—a recorder should not speak. But in the log he wrote:

> Inertia caused normal landing precautions to be taken, but from habit, not from a sense of responsibility. Neither is willing to take the orders of another—each claiming that he has equal right. I am watching the corrosive effects of Democracy and, while it is fascinating in its unexpected nuances of individualism, it can lead only to chaos. These journeys last too long.

Too long—and yet it was as easy to continue as to return and the Pentarch was stern when it came to dealing with failure. More than stern when it dealt with disobedience. Intalgo sighed and closed the log and went to breathe the alien air.

The place had a timeless, dreamlike quality as if a segment of creation had been frozen so that there could be no change, no alteration, no newness or passing away. The air was heavy, stagnant, flattering the echoes of their conversation. Like ants the three others wended their way to the titanic bulk of the mysterious building. They walked with arrogance but without harmony. They were individuals, not a team.

Intalgo sighed again. Now the challenging hand was more than maimed—it was clawing itself apart.

Malchus found it first. It was almost buried in the yellow dust and he kicked it free then squatted, looking at it.

It was the part of a machine.

It was tooled and finished in a way he had never seen

before but, now that he saw it, the reason was obvious. It glinted and shone with the rainbow pattern of refracted light and the scored surface was designed to eliminate friction. The eddy currents generated when the machine was in operation would keep the surfaces an atom apart.

It was—it must be—the central bearing of an engine which was—it could only be—the drive unit of a . . .

He blinked and settled himself more comfortably and concentrated his attention.

A pipe would run from there and meet a shaft which had to run from there and the junction would have to be —there! Then that hollow must hold a swivel-drive leading to . . .

He sat immersed in the joys of construction.

Feldman found it next.

He snorted at the engineer then stooped as he saw what rested on the sand. Squatting, he looked at it.

It was crystallized truth.

It was a model so intricate and yet so plain that it was as easy to read as a book. There was the basic structure of the atom and there were the logical extensions of the formulae propounded by Einstein and there—if he looked very close—were the equations of the three-body problem and those surely must appertain to time itself so that . . .

Feldman sighed with intellectual satisfaction and settled himself for his greater concentration.

Delray found it next.

He came shouting over to the others and glared at what rested between them.

It was naked satiation.

It was the euphoria of combat, the thrill of physical violence, the tease of mental struggle. It was his own deep, dark heritage of type and it opened before him like a flower within whose petals was to be found all he had ever sought. He sank into it and into an eternal enervating dream.

Intalgo found it the last of all.

He stood murmuring into the recorder, his eyes fastened on the three, distant shapes, frozen in a fresco of bone and flesh and pulsating blood. Around him the air hung like many folds of scented silk.

* * *

"They have not moved for hours and are obviously unaware of any form of physical discomfort. The thing is divided between them, but it must be some kind of snare. The builders of this monolith must have devized means to protect it from intruders such as ourselves. In a short while I will go across to them and try to restore their senses and recall their responsibility."

He hesitated, then switched off the instrument.

There was really nothing more he could say.

Say, but not think. The dead words of the dead captain came to him as he walked across the plain of yellow dust to where his companions sat in frozen concentration.

Rats scurrying among the granary of the stars.

Rats!

The Pentarch would not be amused, but he knew now why he had depicted Man as being suspended from a cross. Man with his own face. Man, tormented in his eternal search for . . .

He saw what the others had found.

It was pure art.

It was the thing he had sought all his life and it held so great a joy that he felt tears sting his eyes and overwhelming emotion fill his heart.

Sitting he stared at it.

Man lives by his search for Heaven. This thing was Heaven—for all of them.

They could never leave it.

4

•

Mars and Venus

LOVE AND WAR

In the 1850s, William Whewell published anonymously a book entitled *On the Plurality of Worlds.* Whewell did not believe in the possibility of life on Venus. He suggested that, because of the proximity of Venus to the sun, she "may have cooled more slowly and quietly, like glass which is annealed in the fire; and hence, may have a smooth surface, instead of the furrowed and pimpled visage which the Moon presents to us." It is an attractive idea. With the cult of nostalgia affecting even science fiction, a writer might do worse than seize on Whewell's Venerian model for a story background. I can see it now: "Witch-Ball World."

Venus and Mars are our nearest planetary neighbours, and so have been the most popular targets for imaginary populations, whatever purists might say. Mars has been the more popular by far. Mars is good to observe, it turns a marked face towards us—and there was that mistranslation of the Italian astronomer Schiaparelli's "canelli" into "canals" (instead of "channels"), which started erroneous but stimulating trains (or barges) of thought. Whereas Venus's proximity to the sun has made her difficult to observe, and clouds shroud her surface in any case.

Stories about Mars have been predominantly of a martial character, as if dedicated to the God of War. "Baleful" is the word that crops up when descriptions of the Red Planet are concerned. Martians traditionally feature as invaders of a nasty order, from the time of THE WAR OF THE WORLDS onwards. Venus has preserved the name of the Goddess of Love; stories about her tend to be visionary, like C. S. Lewis's *Perelandra.* She's a bit watery, and visitors from Venus to Earth tend to drop in with feeble pleas for help, instead of trying to take over, like the obstreperous Martians.

As for expeditions from Earth to our neighbours, the same rule applies: they've always been much less likely to make Love than War.

Reality—so often a swindle—turns out disappointing again in this case. Neither planet proves capable of supporting any life more animated than a handful of gravel.

Both planets are still capable of surprises, if of a low order. As I write this, the Viking orbiters have been using infra-red grating spectrometers on the North Pole of Mars. Results indicate that the ice caps are, in fact, frozen water, rather than the frozen carbon dioxide which has been the acceptable model for several years. Who knows: we might find a few frozen coelacanth yet.

It is fitting to have a section dedicated to these two familiar planets. In the sixties, I compiled, with the aid of Harry Harrison, a volume entitled *Farewell, Fantastic Venus!: A History of the Planet Venus in Fact and Fiction.* Avoiding the material I used there, I have selected a story by the late Cordwainer Smith. A very strange story it is.

No less remarkable is the novella by P. Schuyler Miller. Miller was an effective writer at a time when most science fiction was badly written and based on absurd premises, like "Moon of Mad Atavism," which I mentioned earlier. Miller had a feel for alien life, portraying it as definitely odd but in no way horrifying or comic. This comes through in such stories as "Trouble on Tantalus" and "The Cave." Since I have anthologized both stories in the past, I resist the impulse to repeat the performance here. So you get "The Titan" instead.

Science fiction, often called "the literature of the future," seeks out the ancient past. Our friend the Sack was four hundred thousand years old. It's the quest for distance. A feeling for antiquity permeates "The Titan." Its own bibliographical antiquity is not without complexity.

After several rejections by other magazines, Miller's novella began to appear as a serial in a semi-professional magazine entitled *Marvel Tales.* Unfortunately, *Marvel Tales* was not successful and ceased publication in 1935, with the final chapters of "The Titan" still unpublished. (A similar accident occurred to Poul Anderson's serial

"The Escape," when *Space Science Fiction* ceased publication in 1953.) Eventually, the complete novella was published in hardcover by Fantasy Press, in a limited edition in 1952. A couple of years later, it was published in this country by Weidenfeld and Nicolson, only to be remaindered. Well, here it is again, and this time you're bound to like it, vampirism and all . . .

If you see thousands and thousands of people drifting towards you, the mathematics may make you pause. That's what the weight of numbers is all about.

WHEN THE PEOPLE FELL

by Cordwainer Smith

"Can you imagine a rain of people through an acid fog? Can you imagine thousands and thousands of human bodies, without weapons, overwhelming the unconquerable monsters? Can you—"

"Look, sir," interrupted the reporter.

"Don't interrupt me! You ask me silly questions. I tell you I saw the Goonhogo itself. I saw it take Venus. Now ask me about that!"

The reporter had called to get an old man's reminiscences about bygone ages. He did not expect Dobyns Bennett to flare up at him.

Dobyns Bennett thrust home the psychological advantage he had got by taking the initiative. "Can you imagine showhices in their parachutes, a lot of them dead, floating out of a green sky? Can you imagine mothers crying as they fell? Can you imagine people pouring down on the poor helpless monsters?"

Mildly, the reporter asked what showhices were.

"That's old Chinesian for children," said Dobyns Bennett. "I saw the last of the nations burst and die, and you want to ask me about fashionable clothes and things. Real history never gets into the books. It's too shocking. I suppose you were going to ask me what I thought of the new striped pantaloons for women!"

"No," said the reporter, but he blushed. The question was in his notebook, and he hated blushing.

"Do you know what the Goonhogo did?"

"What?" asked the reporter, struggling to remember just what a Goonhogo might be.

"It took Venus," said the old man, somewhat more calmly.

Very mildly, the reporter murmured, "It *did?*"

"You bet it did!" said Dobyns Bennett belligerently.

"Were you there?" asked the reporter.

"You bet I was there when the Goonhogo took Venus," said the old man. "I was there, and it's the damnedest thing I've ever seen. You know who I am. I've seen more worlds than you can count, boy, and yet when the nondies and the needies and the showhices came pouring out of the sky, that was the worst thing that any man could ever see. Down on the ground, there were the loudies the way they'd always been—"

The reporter interrupted, very gently. Bennett might as well have been speaking a foreign language. All of this had happened three hundred years before. The reporter's job was to get a feature from him and to put it into a language which people of the present time could understand.

Respectfully he said, "Can't you start at the beginning of the story?"

"You bet. That's when I married Terza. Terza was the prettiest girl you ever saw. She was one of the Vomacts, a great family of scanners, and her father was a very important man. You see, I was thirty-two, and when a man is thirty-two, he thinks he is pretty old, but I wasn't really old, I just thought so, and he wanted Terza to marry me because she was such a complicated girl that she needed a man's help. The Court back home had found her unstable and the Instrumentality had ordered her left in her father's care until she married a man who then could take on proper custodial authority. I suppose those are old customs to you, boy—"

The reporter interrupted again. "I am sorry, old man," said he. "I know you are over four hundred years old and you're the only person who remembers the time the Goonhogo took Venus. Now the Goonhogo was a government, wasn't it?"

"Anyone knows that," snapped the old man. "The Goonhogo was a sort of separate Chinesian government. Seventeen billion of them all crowded in one small part of Earth. Most of them spoke English the way you and I do, but they spoke their own language, too, with all those funny words that have come on down to us. They hadn't mixed in with anybody else yet. Then, you see, the Waywonjong himself gave the order, and that is when the people started raining. They just fell right out of the sky. You never saw anything like it—"

The reporter had to interrupt him again and again to get the story bit by bit. The old man kept using terms that he couldn't seem to realize were lost in history and that had to be explained to be intelligible to anyone of this era. But his memory was excellent and his descriptive powers as sharp and alert as ever . . .

Young Dobyns Bennett had not been at Experimental Area A very long before he realized that the most beautiful female he had ever seen was Terza Vomact. At the age of fourteen, she was fully mature. Some of the Vomacts did mature that way. It may have had something to do with their being descended from unregistered, illegal people centuries back in the past. They were even said to have mysterious connections with the lost world back in the age of nations when people could still put numbers on the years.

He fell in love with her and felt like a fool for doing it.

She was so beautiful, it was hard to realize that she was the daughter of Scanner Vomact himself. The scanner was a powerful man.

Sometimes romance moves too fast, and it did with Dobyns Bennett because Scanner Vomact himself called in the young man and said, "I'd like to have you marry my daughter Terza, but I'm not sure she'll approve of you. If you can get her, boy, you have my blessing."

Dobyns was suspicious. He wanted to know why a senior scanner was willing to take a junior technician.

All that the scanner did was to smile. He said, "I'm a lot older than you, and with this new santaclara drug coming in that may give people hundreds of years, you may think that I died in my prime if I die at a hundred and twenty. You may live to four or five hundred. But I know my time's coming up. My wife has been dead for a long time, and we have no other children, and I know that Terza needs a father in a very special kind of way. The psychologist found her to be unstable. Why don't you take her outside the area? You can get a pass through the dome any time. You can go out and play with the loudies."

Dobyns Bennett was almost as insulted as if someone had given him a pail and told him to play in the sand pile. And yet he realized that the elements of play in courtship were fitted together and that the old man meant well.

The day that it all happened, he and Terza were outside the dome. They had been pushing loudies around.

Loudies were not dangerous unless you killed them. You could knock them down, push them out of the way, or tie them up; after a while, they slipped away and went about their business. It took a very special kind of ecologist to figure out what their business was. They floated two meters high, ninety centimeters in diameter, gently just above the land of Venus, eating microscopically. For a long time, people thought there was radiation on which they subsisted. They simply multiplied in tremendous numbers. In a silly sort of way, it was fun to push them around, but that was about all there was to do.

They never responded with intelligence.

Once, long before, a loudie taken into the laboratory for experimental purposes had typed a perfectly clear message on the typewriter. The message had read, "Why don't you Earth people go back to Earth and leave us alone? We are getting along all—"

And that was all the message that anybody had ever got out of them in three hundred years. The best laboratory conclusion was that they had very high intelligence if they ever chose to use it, but their volitional mechanism was so profoundly different from the psychology of human beings that it was impossible to force a loudie to respond to stress as people did on Earth.

The name loudie was some kind of word in the old Chinesian language. It meant the "ancient ones." Since it was the Chinesians who had set up the first outposts on Venus, under the orders of their supreme boss, the Waywonjong, their term lingered on.

Dobyns and Terza pushed loudies, climbed over the hills, and looked down into the valleys, where it was impossible to tell a river from a swamp. They got thoroughly wet, their air converters stuck, and perspiration itched and tickled along their cheeks. Since they could not eat or drink while outside—at least not with any reasonable degree of safety—the excursion could not be called a picnic. There was something mildly refreshing about playing child with a very pretty girl-child—but Dobyns wearied of the whole thing.

Terza sensed his rejection of her. Quick as a sensitive animal, she became angry and petulant. "You didn't have to come out with me!"

"I wanted to," he said, "but now I'm tired and want to go home."

"You treat me like a child. All right, play with me. Or you treat me like a woman. All right, be a gentleman. But don't seesaw all the time yourself. I just got to be a little bit happy, and you have to get middle-aged and condescending. I won't take it."

"Your father—" he said, realizing the moment he said it that it was a mistake.

"My father this, my father that. If you're thinking about marrying me, do it yourself." She glared at him, stuck her tongue out, ran over a dune, and disappeared.

Dobyns Bennett was baffled. He did not know what to do. She was safe enough. The loudies never hurt anyone. He decided to teach her a lesson and to go on back himself, letting her find her way home when she pleased. The Area Search Team could find her easily if she really got lost.

He walked back to the gate.

When he saw the gates locked and the emergency lights on, he realized that he had made the worst mistake of his life.

His heart sinking within him, he ran the last few meters of the way and beat the ceramic gate with his bare hands until it opened only just enough to let him in.

"What's wrong?" he asked the doortender.

The doortender muttered something which Dobyns could not understand.

"Speak up, man!" shouted Dobyns. "What's wrong?"

"The Goonhogo is coming back and they're taking over."

"That's impossible," said Dobyns. "They couldn't—" He checked himself. *Could* they?

"The Goonhogo's taken over," the gatekeeper insisted. "They've been given the whole thing. The Earth Authority has voted it to them. The Waywonjong has decided to send people right away. They're sending them."

"What do the Chinesians want with Venus? You can't kill a loudie without contaminating a thousand acres of land. You can't push them away without them drifting back. You can't scoop them up. Nobody can live here until we solve the problem of these things. We're a long way from having solved it," said Dobyns in angry bewilderment.

The gatekeeper shook his head. "Don't ask me. That's all I hear on the radio. Everybody else is excited too."

Within an hour, the rain of people began.

Dobyns went up to the radar room, saw the skies above. The radar man himself was drumming his fingers against the desk. He said, "Nothing like this has been seen for a thousand years or more. You know what there is up there? Those are warships, the warships left over from the last of the old dirty wars. I knew the Chinesians were inside them. Everybody knew about it. It was sort of like a museum. Now they don't have any weapons in them. But do you know—there are millions of people hanging up there over Venus, and I don't know what they are going to do!"

He stopped and pointed at one of the screens. "Look, you can see them running in patches. They're behind each other, so they cluster up solid. We've never had a screen look like that."

Dobyns looked at the screen. It was, as the operator said, full of blips.

As they watched, one of the men exclaimed, "What's that milky stuff down there in the lower left? See, it's—it's pouring," he said, "it's pouring somehow out of those dots. How can you pour things into a radar? It doesn't really show, does it?"

The radar man looked at his screen. He said, "Search me. I don't know what it is, either. You'll have to find out. Let's just see what happens."

Scanner Vomact came into the room. He said, once he had taken a quick, experienced glance at the screens, "This may be the strangest thing we'll ever see, but I have a feeling they're dropping people. Lots of them. Dropping them by the thousands, or by the hundreds of thousands, or even by the millions. But people are coming down there. Come along with me, you two. We'll go out and see it. There may be somebody that we can help."

By this time, Dobyns's conscience was hurting him badly. He wanted to tell Vomact that he had left Terza out there, but he had hesitated—not only because he was ashamed of leaving her, but because he did not want to tattle on the child to her father. Now he spoke.

"Your daughter's still outside."

Vomact turned on him solemnly. The immense eyes looked very tranquil and very threatening, but the silky voice was controlled.

"You may find her." The scanner added, in a tone which sent the thrill of menace up Dobyns's back, "And everything will be well if you bring her back."

Dobyns nodded as though receiving an order.

"I shall," said Vomact, "go out myself, to see what I can do, but I leave the finding of my daughter to you."

They went down, put on the extra-long-period converters, carried their miniaturized survey equipment so that they could find their way back through the fog, and went out. Just as they were at the gate, the gatekeeper said, "Wait a moment, sir and excellency. I have a message for you here on the phone. Please call Control."

Scanner Vomact was not to be called lightly, and he knew it. He picked up the connection unit and spoke harshly.

The radar man came on the phone screen in the gatekeeper's wall. "They're overhead now, sir."

"Who's overhead?"

"The Chinesians are. They're coming down. I don't know how many there are. There must be two thousand warships over our heads right here, and there are more thousands over the rest of Venus. They're down now. If you want to see them hit ground, you'd better get outside quick."

Vomact and Dobyns went out.

Down came the Chinesians. People's bodies were raining right out of the milk-cloudy sky. Thousands upon thousands of them with plastic parachutes that looked like bubbles. Down they came.

Dobyns and Vomact saw a headless man drift down. The parachute cords had decapitated him.

A woman fell near them. The drop had torn her breathing tube loose from her crudely bandaged throat, and she was choking in her own blood. She staggered toward them, tried to babble but only drooled blood with mute choking sounds, and then fell face forward into the mud.

Two babies dropped. The adult accompanying them had been blown off course. Vomact ran, picked them up, and handed them to a Chinesian man who had just landed. The man looked at the babies in his arms, sent Vomact a look of contemptuous inquiry, put the weeping children down in the cold slush of Venus, gave them a last impersonal glance, and ran off on some mysterious errand of his own.

Vomact kept Bennett from picking up the children. "Come on, let's keep looking. We can't take care of all of them."

The world had known that the Chinesians had a lot of unpredictable habits, but they never suspected that the nondies and the needies and the showhices could pour down out of a poisoned sky. Only the Goonhogo himself would make such a reckless use of human life. Nondies were men and needies were women and showhices were little children. And Goonhogo was a name left over from the old days of nations. It meant something like republic or state or government. Whatever it was, it was the organization that ran the Chinesians in the Chinesian manner, under the Earth Authority.

And the ruler of the Goonhogo was the Waywonjong.

The Waywonjong didn't come to Venus. He just sent his people. He sent them floating down into Venus, to tackle the Venusian ecology with the only weapons which could make a settlement of that planet possible—people themselves. Human arms could tackle the loudies, the loudies who had been called "old ones" by the first Chinesian scouts to cover Venus.

The loudies had to be gathered together so gently that they would not die and, in dying, each contaminate a thousand acres. They had to be kept together by human bodies and arms in a gigantic living corral.

Scanner Vomact rushed forward.

A wounded Chinesian man hit the ground, and his parachute collapsed behind him. He was clad in a pair of shorts, had a knife at his belt, canteen at his waist. He had an air converter attached next to his ear, with a tube running into his throat. He shouted something unintelligible at them and limped rapidly away.

People kept on hitting the ground all around Vomact and Dobyns.

The self-disposing parachutes were bursting like bubbles in the misty air a moment or two after they touched the ground. Someone had done a tricky, efficient job with the chemical consequences of static electricity.

And as the two watched, the air was heavy with people. One time, Vomact was knocked down by a person. He found that it was two Chinesian children tied together.

Dobyns asked, "What are you doing? Where are you going? Do you have any leaders?"

He got cries and shouts in an unintelligible language. Here and there someone shouted in English, "This way!" or "Leave us alone!" or "Keep going . . ." But that was all.

The experiment worked.

Eighty-two million people were dropped in that one day.

After four hours, which seemed barely short of endless, Dobyns found Terza in a corner of the cold hell. Though Venus was warm, the suffering of the almost-naked Chinesians had chilled his blood.

Terza ran toward him.

She could not speak.

She put her head on his chest and sobbed. Finally she managed to say, "I've—I've—I've tried to help, but they're too many, too many, too many!" And the sentence ended as shrill as a scream.

Dobyns led her back to the experimental area.

They did not have to talk. Her whole body told him that she wanted his love and the comfort of his presence, and that she had chosen that course of life which would keep them together.

As they left the drop area, which seemed to cover all of Venus so far as they could tell, a pattern was beginning to form. The Chinesians were beginning to round up the loudies.

Terza kissed him mutely after the gatekeeper had let them through. She did not need to speak. Then she fled to her room.

The next day, the people from Experimental Area A

tried to see if they could go out and lend a hand to the settlers. It wasn't possible to lend a hand; there were too many settlers. People by the millions were scattered all over the hills and valleys of Venus, sludging through the mud and water with their human toes, crushing the alien mud, crushing the strange plants. They didn't know what to eat. They didn't know where to go. They had no leaders.

All they had were orders to gather the loudies together in large herds and hold them there with human arms.

The loudies didn't resist.

After a time lapse of several Earth days, the Goonhogo sent small scout cars. They brought a very different kind of Chinesian—these late arrivals were uniformed, educated, cruel, smug men. They knew what they were doing. And they were willing to pay any sacrifice of their own people to get it done.

They brought instructions. They put the people together in gangs. It did not matter where the nondies and needies had come from on Earth; it didn't matter whether they found their own showhices or somebody else's. They were shown the jobs to do, and they got to work. Human bodies accomplished what machines could not have done—they kept the loudies firmly but gently encircled until every last one of the creatures was starved into nothingness.

Rice fields began to appear miraculously.

Scanner Vomact couldn't believe it. The Goonhogo biochemists had managed to adapt rice to the soil of Venus. And yet the seedlings came out of boxes in the scout cars, and weeping people walked over the bodies of their own dead to keep the crop moving toward the planting.

Venusian bacteria could not kill human beings, nor could they dispose of human bodies after death. A problem arose and was solved. Immense sleds carried dead men, women, and children—those who had fallen wrong, or drowned as they fell, or had been trampled by others—to an undisclosed destination. Dobyns suspected that the material was to be used to add Earthtype organic waste to the soil of Venus, but he did not tell Terza.

The work went on.

The nondies and needies kept working in shifts. When they could not see in the darkness, they proceeded without seeing—keeping in line by touch or by shout. Foremen, newly trained, screeched commands. Workers lined up, touching fingertips. The job of building the fields kept on.

"That's a big story," said the old man, "eighty-two million people dropped in a single day. And later I heard that the Waywonjong said it wouldn't have mattered if seventy million of them had died. Twelve million survivors would have been enough to make a spacehead for the Goonhogo. The Chinesians got Venus, all of it.

"But I'll never forget the nondies and the needies and the showhices falling out of the sky, men and women and children with their poor, scared Chinesian faces. That funny Venusian air made them look green instead of tan. There they were falling all around.

"You know something, young man?" said Dobyns Bennett, approaching his fifth century of age.

"What?" said the reporter.

"There won't be things like that happening on any world again. Because now, after all, there isn't any separate Goonhogo left. There's only one Instrumentality, and they don't care what a man's race may have been in the ancient years. Those were the rough old days, the ones I lived in. Those were the days *men* still tried to do things."

Dobyns almost seemed to doze off, but he roused himself sharply and said, "I tell you, the sky was full of people. They fell like water. They fell like rain. I've seen the awful ants in Africa, and there's not a thing among the stars to beat them for prowling horror. Mind you, they're worse than anything the stars contain. I've seen the crazy worlds near Alpha Centauri, but I never saw anything like the time the people fell on Venus. More than eighty-two million in one day, and my own little Terza lost among them.

"But the rice did sprout. And the loudies died as the walls of people held them in with human arms. Walls of people, I tell you, with volunteers jumping in to take the places of the falling ones.

"They were people still, even when they shouted in the darkness. They tried to help each other, even while they fought a fight that had to be fought without violence. They were people still. And they *did* win. It was crazy and impossible, but they won. Mere human beings did what machines and science would have taken another thousand years to do . . .

"The funniest thing of all was the first house that I saw a nondie put up, there in the rain of Venus. I was out there with Vomact and with a pale, sad Terza. It wasn't much of a house, shaped out of twisted Venusian wood. There it was. *He* built it, the smiling, half-naked Chinesian nondie. We went to the door and said to him in English, "What are you building here, a shelter or a hospital?"

"The Chinesian grinned at us. 'No,' he said, 'gambling.'

"Vomact wouldn't believe it: 'Gambling?'

" 'Sure,' said the nondie. 'Gambling is the first thing a man needs in a strange place. It can take the worry out of his soul.' "

"Is that all?" said the reporter.

Dobyns Bennett muttered that the personal part did not count. He added, "Some of my great-great-great-great-great-grandsons may come long. You count those greats. Their faces will show you easily enough that I married into the Vomact line. Terza saw what happened. She saw how people build worlds. This was the hard way to build them. She never forgot the night with the dead Chinesian babies lying in the half-illuminated mud, or the parachute ropes dissolving slowly. She heard the needies weeping and the helpless nondies comforting them and leading them off to nowhere. She remembered the cruel, neat officers coming out of the scout cars. She got home and saw the rice come up, and saw how the Goonhogo made Venus a Chinesian place."

"What happened to you personally?" asked the reporter.

"Nothing much. There wasn't any more work for us, so we closed down Experimental Area A. I married Terza.

"Any time later, when I said to her, 'You're not such a bad girl!' she was able to admit the truth and tell me she was not. That night in the rain of people would test anybody's soul, and it tested hers. She had met a big test and passed it. She used to say to me, 'I saw it once. I saw the people fall, and I never want to see another person suffer again. Keep me with you, Dobyns, keep me with you forever.'

"And," said Dobyns Bennett, "it wasn't forever, but it was a happy and sweet three hundred years. She died after our fourth diamond anniversary. Wasn't that a wonderful thing, young man?"

The reporter said it was. And yet, when he took the story back to his editor, he was told to put it into the archives. It wasn't the right kind of story for entertainment, and the public would not appreciate it any more.

The silence on Mars is deep and undisturbed. Nobody has given it more authentic voice than the author of "The Titan."

THE TITAN

by P. Schuyler Miller

Spring Night

Korul drew farther back into the shadow of the tapestry.

He had found a place close to the wall of the great hall, half-hidden by a hanging, where he could watch without being drawn into the saturnalia. As First Man of the Blood-Givers, he must rule there as nominal master of the revels—man over Master, here and in every city of Mur—but the spectacle of Masters and Blood-Givers wallowing in their own drunken lust brought a bitter taste to his mouth, and the old, black hatred back into his heart. The barriers were there, built up by blood and breeding for generations. Why must his people mock themselves and their servile place with this pretense that for one night, over half their dying world, Masters and Givers were equals.

Equality! That had ended long ago, farther than the oldest writing of the Searchers for Truth could reach. And yet, once it had been real. Once, they said—thousands of centuries ago, when the race was young and there were great cities where the crimson sands now lay—the two races had been one flesh and one blood. In that time the Masters came to the power that they had never lost. They looked upon themselves as a caste apart, born to rule, self-dedicated to contemplation and self-gratification while a servile breed worked to maintain the planetary culture they adorned. For thousands of years they lived as parasites, in ease and indulgence, and then those of them who still dabbled with science discovered a terrible thing!

In the blood of every man are certain substances, generated by the glands of his body to control its life-force and functions. Without them life seeps away or runs wild, uncontrolled and unpredictable. Somewhere, the Masters found, a germ of dissolution had found its way into their blood. Through centuries of inbreeding and inactivity, the vital glands were shriveling up or disappearing. The vital secretions were no longer generated, and in some of the most inbred strains subtle poisons were being created in their place. Men and women withered away in the prime of their years, if indeed they lived beyond infancy. Freaks were born in increasing numbers. And so the Blood-Givers were created.

Thanks to the labor to which they were born, the servile caste was physically as the gods had made it—strong, virile, with legs, arms, bodies, and minds created and trained to battle hostile Nature and to win. Their blood had not thinned; life and the love of living were still strong in them. And so the Masters decreed that these must be their lives as well.

Korul's long fingers crept up under his robe to the little platinum tube buried in the flesh at the base of his throat. At birth every Blood-Giver was branded with the mark of his servitude, the little valve cunningly inserted in the great vein of his throat where the pulse of blood was free and strong, and grafted into the flesh itself. With maturity, man and woman alike must carry the pouch containing a simple pump, a tube, and sterilizing materials. At intervals set by law he must pump his blood into the veins of one of the Masters, drawing the poisoned blood into his own body to renew the stuff of life. Only two days before, he, Korul, had been summoned to bleed for a paunchy, flabby woman who leered and fondled his bare skin, and made pointed jokes about his strength and manhood. There were some of his kind, he knew, who would have been glad of her favors. Out there in the Hall of Masters their kind and hers were locked in each others' arms in an orgy of unrestrained, drunken emotion.

All but one.

He had been watching her narrowly all that night. A few at a time they had gathered in the hall, the Masters rolling on their wheeled *tlornaks,* propped up among their silken cushions with their gaudy robes draped skillfully about them to hide the stumps or flabby tabs of flesh which passed for legs among their degenerate kind. In larger groups the Blood-Givers had straggled up from their dingy quarters, deep in the lower levels of the city. The men were naked to the waist, scrubbed and oiled to show the play of their muscles and the breadth of their shoulders to whichever woman of the Masters should claim them first. The women, girls just reaching maturity and matrons mated for many years, were more modestly and guilefully dressed in garments which would be put away after the night's revels to serve another year, when another Spring Night came and the polar sluices were again thrown open to send the waters of the melting ice-cap flooding through the ancient rock-hewn channels to bring new life and new beauty to half of Mur.

As First Man of the Blood-Givers, last of a line which reached back to the tribal chieftains who ranged the still-green uplands of a young planet, Korul was "master" of Spring Night. He had gone through the ancient ritual, coming to the hall with his little retinue, going through the ceremony of mock-brotherhood with the First of the Masters and "deposing" him, closing and locking the great book of the law—or what purported to be the law. When the signal came from the pole, it was Korul whose bare arm was raised to open the revels—then as the flutes shrilled, and the babble of voices and ring of crystal rose around him, he had slipped away to the place against the wall, where hidden by a tapestry he could see without being seen.

He had seen her soon. She was high-born, with the fragile beauty of her breed—only daughter of the First Master. Her great oval eyes—her soft red lips—her slender arms and delicate hands—even to him, with the black hatred of her kind cold in his heart, she was appealing. He might have taken her, under the law of Spring Night, but apart from the bitterness in his mouth there was an aloofness about her, a fastidious hauteur, that forbade it. Others had seen it that night—even Karak, who boasted that any woman of the Masters would come to him at any time—and they respected it.

She was a spot of pure scarlet amid a riot of raw color. Her *tlornak* was heaped with scarlet cushions, and a vivid scarlet robe was flung about her, hiding her body. It would be beautiful, Korul mused: these women of the Masters had time for beauty.

It was not long to dawn. By now, in all that great, gaudily decked hall, no one stirred. Drunken, exhausted by their debauchery, sprawled among the wine-stained cushions, they were sleeping. Only she, Thorana, sat proud and beautiful by herself, sipping her golden *tulla*. Then, with a little shudder, she sent the crystal beaker crashing across the floor and touched the controls of her machine. Swiftly it wound in and out among the sleepers, carrying her toward the corridors and the lifts. As she reached the outer archway, she turned and looked back. In the curve of her painted lips Korul read the same bitter scorn, the same mixture of pity and disgust, that lay in his own heart. Then she was gone.

As the silken hangings closed behind her, Korul sprang to his feet. Racing across the hall, he reached the corridor in time to see the winking fleck of red moving slowly around the circle—up, up past the levels which the Masters used, into the deserted upper regions of the city. Nobody went there now—neither Master nor Blood-Givers—yet the red dot crept up and up, level after level, until there were no more numbers, until, Korul knew, her lift must be at the topmost terrace of the city.

Turning from the lifts, Korul raced down the long corridor toward the ramps. There were secrets of the ancient city which the Masters had never known. Near the head of the ramp, which law and custom decreed must be used by the Givers, was a hidden lift far speedier than the ponderous things the Masters reserved for their own use. He found the panel quickly, brought the car to his level and stepped inside. As he stabbed with one finger at the control-stud, the car gathered speed. Its drone rose to a shrill scream; his legs buckled under him, and he found himself on his knees, his body a leaden mass forcing him to the floor. Then with a sickening swoop it stopped. He pushed aside the panel, and stepped out into a corridor from which the bitter cold of the outer night licked at his naked skin. There in the dust at his feet were the tracks of the *tlornak*, leading away from the lifts toward the last short ramp that led to the summit of the city.

It was an unbroken terrace of cut stone, worn and polished by the tread of many feet through the centuries when the city was young and full of life. Nobody had come here in ages, Korul knew, except an occasional Searcher studying the stars. Once it had been a highway of the people of Mur, running beside the great rift across the parched upland to the poles. Now the fine red dust of the desert covered it, rippled and curled in little drifts where a tendril of wind from the drylands had touched it.

He had never been so high before. Terrace on terrace the city fell away below him. Down there, quarried in the rock under the clinging city, were the warrens of his own kind.

Far down the terrace something moved. Crouching at the mouth of the ramp, Korul peered through the darkness. It was coming nearer, and he could hear the mutter of tires on the stone. It was the girl.

She was rolling along the inner edge of the terrace, where a wall twice a man's height rose to the steep rubble at the crest of the gorge. Korul drew down until only his head cleared the terrace. Whatever she was seeking, she was too deeply engrossed to see him there. The car rolled by, close against the wall, and he crept out of the ramp and followed in the darkness. Suddenly the *tlornak* darted ahead. The line of the wall was broken there, where a ramp or steps led up into the desert. As the machine stopped, Thorana sprang out and vanished in the opening.

By the gods, *she had legs!*

It was incredible. For centuries—for thousands of years—no Master had been able to walk. Long before their blood thinned, their legs had shriveled until they must roll on their soft-tired *tlornaks,* padded with pillows and swathed in draperies to protect their puny bodies from discomfort. And now—a woman of the Masters with legs? By the gods, it could not be!

A flight of steep steps led to the top of the wall, then there was only the rubble of the gorge's edge. Far above him Korbul heard the trickle of loosened pebbles as the woman climbed into the darkness. Throwing aside the embroidered robe of office which he had worn, Korul followed her.

* * *

The mists of the city had not yet risen with the coming of spring and the melting of the polar ice, to boil out of the gorge and moisten the upper slopes. Then, Korul knew, the red rock would grow soft and green with freshening vegetation. Now there was only a sere, crackling mat of brittle vines and fallen leaves underfoot, which caught at his plodding feet and flung him headlong among the boulders. He lay where he had fallen, cursing the whim that had brought him after the woman—then far above him sounded the broken clatter of her climbing feet. No woman—especially no woman of the Masters—would put Korul to shame!

Up and up they clambered—it seemed endlessly. The soft moccasins he wore were shredded and his feet bruised and bleeding. Suddenly he realized that the sound of her stumbling flight had ceased. He stopped, panting, to listen. There was no sound but the thud of his own heart, beating in his ears, and far away a soft, sibilant slithering. Where had she gone? What brought her here?

It was sand that he had heard. Pouring over the crest of the gorge, it had spilled down in a vast silken cascade over the uppermost ledges, over vines and stunted shrubs. In places it was hard-packed and rippled by the wind, as the dust on the terrace had been; in others he floundered and sank to his knees as the shifting grains slid away under his feet with that endless, secret whispering of grain on grain.

Thorana's footprints led still upward into the night, and Korul followed doggedly, slipping, falling, creeping on all fours. From the marks in the sand he knew that she, too, was having to struggle to keep her feet. Then, suddenly, the night opened out before him, and he knew that he had reached the top.

Beyond, beneath, stretching away into the night in great rolling waves of trackless sand, lay the red desert of Mur. Out of that desert his people had come, eons ago, to find shelter in the gorges which reached in a broad, dark band across the sandy waste for mile after desolate mile. Into that desert Thorana had gone, somewhere, for some purpose.

A faint breath of air touched his cheek, icy cold, scented with a raw taint that he had never known. The chill of the night began to bite into his naked body, but under the surface the sand still held the warmth of day. Korul crouched down, hugging his arms about him, and burrowed into it. He tipped his head back and let his gaze drive out and out . . .

He saw the stars.

The Desert

Once the people of Mur had lived by the stars. They were the guiding beacons which brought them safely over the desert wastes of their dying world, from oasis to oasis, to sheltered valleys in the parched red hills where some seepage kept a few miles of greenery alive. Their gods lived there, behind the velvet curtains of Nur-Atlaka, Land of Souls. Their names and stories had come down from mouth to mouth—Atta, the Seeker—the twins, Nurdok and Maltura—the Three Wanderers, Mulat, Mutaka, Maldruk.

At times they looked down into the depths of the city, to the Pit and the men and women who were penned there, peering through the mists of the upper gorge. From the Searchers, Korul knew that what he had seen there were planets, prisoners of Mur's own sun, and a handful of scattered suns like it. But nothing they had said had prepared him for the living reality of the desert night.

In hundreds and thousands they were strewn over the mighty vault of black—burning—living—diamonds, rubies, sapphires blazing against the sombre tresses of the infinite night. They were tiny watching eyes, the eyes of the gods of Mur themselves staring down through the half-drawn curtains of the Land of Souls.

In the east the sky was paling, the stars were disappearing until only the great golden eye of Tarkak, giant of the god-worlds, burned there. Korul rose to his feet and with quickening step went out to meet the dawn.

On he strode, and on, over the slow, soothingly monotonous rise and fall of the sand-waves, while in the heavens before him a cone of shimmering white rose slowly toward the zenith and the red world took form before his unseeing eyes. Then from behind the shoulder of the world was hurled the sun!

The desert reeled with color at its coming—raw and new and burning. The sky was a burnished bowl. Only the endless flaming sands ran out in limitless desolation under the cruel scourge of the climbing sun.

The wind ran before it, dry and hot, licking at his tender skin. Leaping, wavering phantoms of brilliance danced among the dunes, prying at his narrowed eyelids, mocking him. The magic of the night was gone out of the desert; only the fiery fury of the Pit itself remained, scourging his dark-loving body, lapping at the portals of his mind. Alone and lost among the scarlet dunes, Korul tottered and fell to his knees, flung back his head and screamed his rage and defiance at the savage sun. And out of that inferno came an answering cry—a woman's cry.

All thought of Thorana had slipped out of Korul's mind under the glory of the night, and in the growing torture of the desert morning. He crouched now, blind eyes buried in his bent arm, gathering his senses. If he had been trapped thus by the stars and the leering sun, what must she—weak—a woman—what must she be suffering out there in the burning sea?

He shouted again, and heard her answering whimper, far to his left where a comber of frozen fire swelled against the sky. From its crest he saw her, small, pitifully slender, swathed in her crimson silk, a red dot amid redness. Drifting before the wind, the soft sand was filling the folds of her gown, piling against her body, spilling over her outstretched legs, burying her alive.

With a last cry of encouragement Korul raced down the long slope of the dune to where she lay. Brushing the sand gently away, he raised her in his arms and peered into her face. It was thin and white—her lips were blue. Her blood was failing!

Korul had been bled two days before. By the Masters' own law he need not serve again for nearly fifty days. But without his blood this girl would die. Somehow, Master or no, he couuld not let her go.

Gently he searched for her valve. In the Blood-Givers it was in the throat, tapping the great vein, but the Masters placed theirs wherever their whim dictated. He found it beneath her heart, opening directly into the main artery—a perilous place, but one that many women chose. His back to the sun, shading her, Korul opened his pouch and drew out the little pump and tubes. Sterilizing them, he made the connection, opened the valves and started the pump. With each throb of his heart he felt the life gushing out of his body into hers, and in the pause drawn back by the pump. His blood into hers, and the mixture drawn back into his veins, carrying the body poisons that were draining off her life. He felt a giddiness creeping over him, and went down on all fours, his body arched over hers, braced by his two arms.

Then her eyelids fluttered; her great green eyes, cool as the polar ice, opened and looked up into his face. A pointed red tongue licked nervously at her lips.

"Where am I?" she whispered weakly. "When is it? Who are you?"

Korul found his voice grown husky. "Spring Night is past," he reassured her. "You came into the desert, and I followed. The sun overcame you, and you needed blood, so I gave it." His face hardened. "Is not that my duty to the daughter of the First Master?"

She seemed not to have heard. "It was my day yesterday," she murmured, "but I need less than the others, and I thought to wait." The green eyes searched his features. "You are Korul. You gave blood only two days ago—to Lula!"

"When I give blood and to whom is my own affair!" he snapped. "I gave it to you because I am strong, and because you needed it. I will give it again when I am ordered to."

A shadow slipped over her face, and she turned it aside. "I am not interested in your relations with Lula," she said petulantly. "She seemed to admire that strength of yours. She appreciates such things more than I. If you will disconnect us, I will go now."

Korul stopped the pump and slipped off the connecting tubes. A little blood dripped out on the sand, making a tiny mirror of red that quickly blackened to a hard crust. She stared at it, suddenly pale, then up at the giant dunes that hemmed them in on every side.

"Where is this?" she cried. "Where is the city?"

"Where indeed?" Korul's voice was dry and bitter. "This is the desert you found so enchanting by starlight. It has a different kind of beauty now, don't you think? We are lost, Thorana."

"Lost? How can I be? Last night I walked straight away from the gorge, over the sands. I can go back as I came."

His arm swept around the circle of unbroken sand. "How

did you come, Thorana? The stars circled and the sun came up. The wind has filled our tracks, and it will bury us when the time comes. Master and Blood-Giver—we'll die the same death."

She stared at him, her green eyes wide, then broke into sudden mocking laughter.

"How do the Blood-Givers choose their First?" she demanded. "For brute strength, isn't it? You are very strong, Korul, but you could use sharper wits. It is the sun that will kill you—then let the sun lead you home! Or stay here, if you like, and I will send men to fetch your body when you are dead."

With a swirl of her crimson robe she spun and stalked off up the side of the dune. Bewildered, Korul stared after her. Little fool! Let her die, if that was what she wanted; he had done his duty. Suddenly his eyes caught the black splotch of his shadow. It sprawled straight away, in the direction the girl had gone. Of course! The sun had risen in their faces—by keeping it at their backs, it would guide them back to the city.

Thorana was out of sight when Korul reached the top of the dune. Her footprints stretched away from him across the sands, straight away from the sun, each one a little black puddle of shadow against the crimson. The wind was filling them.

They had come a long way through the darkness, under the stars, and his shadow shortened. Korul trudged on through the shimmering scarlet sea, eyes closed to slits to shut out the glare. The girl was nowhere in sight, and a long time had passed since he had seen her tracks.

Hour followed hour. The red haze enveloped him now, he was floating in it, preceded by a dancing, wavering wraith of black that for some reason he must catch. However fast he stumbled after it, it evaded him.

Black beast, swimming in a red sea. The thought was funny! There had been no seas on Mur since the race was young. He began to laugh. That scared the black thing, and it scurried away, but he kept after it, almost on its tail, close enough to seize it if it were not so slippery. After a while it disappeared. Had it run away? He looked down, and it was hiding behind his feet. He kicked at it—almost fell—he ran shouting over the long dunes of fire, the blood singing in his ears, his head full of swirling, bursting lights. He slipped over the crest of a sandcliff and rolled in a rosy avalanche into the very middle of a streak of snowy white that licked out at its base.

He lay there for a long time. When he opened his eyes again, and swayed to his feet, the shadow-beast was crouching behind him. He turned and began to stalk it, swiftly and silently. It crept away, trying to escape, but there was nowhere to hide. This time he had it! And suddenly it seemed to rear up before him and he dove and caught it it in his hands.

It was the girl, Thorana, senseless and half buried in the drifting sand. Korul lay sprawled over her limp body. The red fog was clearing from his brain. That black thing —his shadow—it had crept between his legs, then behind him. But it was the sun that had moved! It was past midday, and the sun was in the west. For the gods alone knew how long he had been traveling away from the gorge and the city!

He gave her blood again. When she could walk they headed into the sun, clinging together, heads down, blinded by its white fire. Time seemed to be slowing; the beat of their hearts seemed heavier, wearier, pleading with them for rest, but they went on.

Korul could give no more blood. When Thorana collapsed again, he picked her up and wound her filmy scarf around his head. It shut out some of the sun, so that he could go on again.

Twice he found himself following the shadow, away from the city, into the desert. He began to chant, to keep his tired mind clear. "Into the sun! Into the sun! Into the sun!" He swung Thorna's slim body back and forth in a long, slow arc to the beat of the chant and the tread of his weary legs.

The scarlet scarf whipped loose in the singing wind. It fluttered away over the sand. He dropped the girl and ran after it. He caught it, and started on again. After a while he remembered Thorana. He started back, following his shadow again—or was it the sun he must follow? He found her, picked her up, began his chant again.

His eyes were closed now, caked and blackened by the sun. His throat was swollen with the dust; his lips were cracked and bleeding. Mad visions danced against the back of his eyes, in and out of his brain. But he held her tight against him and stumbled on over the sand—on and on and on . . .

The Elders

They came to the city again. For hours the search had been on, Masters and Blood-Givers ferreting through every level of the city, into every room. No one could have imagined that they would have ventured into the desert. Then, blind, blackened, bleeding Korul came plodding into the great hall with the girl cradled in his arms. The Masters took her from him; his own people led him away, down into their own levels where he could be given care.

He was strong, but the Masters were duly grateful. He had given blood to Thorana twice in the desert. He was excused from two givings.

As soon as he could stand, a messenger came to him from the Elders. Behind the facade of the Masters' law—behind the pattern of tradition which made Korul First of their race until some other man should drink his blood in fair combat—it was the Elders who ruled. The Masters knew nothing of them, but in every city two were chosen by the Givers—man and woman. Where they met and worked, deep in the secret vaults under the cities, was known only to a chosen few.

Korul came into the great hall, made in mocking imitation of that Hall of the Masters where the council of the ruling caste held its own deliberations, where the First Master sat in state and the orgy of Spring Nights took place. They lay on forbidden *tlornaks,* dressed in robes which mocked the Masters' finery, arrayed in circles around the central dais where their own chief sat.

There were cushions on the dais for Korul. As First of the Blood-Givers it was his right to sit there beside old Turun, First of their council and true First Man of Mur. Pages brought fine food, stolen from the Masters' own kitchens, and flagons of *tulla.* Nothing would be done until the ritual of food and drink was finished. The buzz of murmured conversation rose all about him.

Old Turun set down his cup. It was a signal; all through the Hall of the Givers the mutter of talk was quieted.

"Elders of Mur," he said, "here at my side sits Korul, son of Thandar, First Man as his father was before him. We have brought him here into our council because there are certain things that we have agreed must be said, through him, to the Blood-Givers of Mur."

He laid a bony hand on the young leader's shoulder. "Have you asked yourself why you are First of the Blood-Givers—why your father was—why some day some other young man of your people will challenge you, and drink your blood, and take your place here? We are an old people. We have built great cities. We carry water from the poles across half the world, and more. We draw heat out of the bowels of our planet, and make it warm our beds and turn the wheels of our machines. Then why—why—must our young men fight among themselves like the very beasts in their cages, why must they lap at each others' spilled blood like beasts?" The old voice took a mocking note. "Because it is the law, you'll say. The Masters' law—not ours. *They* make beasts of us!"

His arm swept the circuit of the hall. "We come from a dozen cities now, where once there were thousands. You know what is happening in those cities. By the law—the old law—the law of the Masters—a man of our people is bled every fiftieth day, and a woman every seventieth. Long ago the Searchers found that would keep the Masters alive, and would not kill us—so it became the law of Mur. The law says that except on two nights, when the waters of the poles are freed, no Blood-Giver may mate with a Master. That was *our* law—made to keep our race from weakening.

"But by the gods, Korul, the laws are not obeyed: Our women give their bodies and their blood to the Masters for food and comfort and pleasure which they cannot find in our life. Our children are born with blood like water and spindling, puny legs which will not hold their weight. Even our men give again and again, lusting after their painted women with their soft, perfumed flesh!

"Once there was force behind the laws the Masters made. Once they had power—weapons—knowledge with which to enforce their rule. But you know—we all know—that power is long gone. We are bound by habit, by tradition—by sand. And the time has come to sweep that sand away."

* * *

A shout went up from every mouth in the great hall. There was hysteria in it, and an ugly note of hunger. Offer food to the starving and they will eat sand, Korul thought wryly. But Turun's gaunt arms, upraised above his head, quieted them.

"There is one other thing, Korul. Tell him, Karak—tell us all."

Karak! The skin along Korul's nape tightened. The man was Elder in this city—his own. He stood half a head taller than Korul; his shoulders were nearly as broad. By sheer brute force he had driven himself into the Council of the Elders, and Korul knew that a time would come soon when he would try to drink the blood of the First Man.

Karak was on his feet, swaggering to the dais. There was a mutter of anticipation as he turned and looked slowly around over the faces of the Elders, then down at Korul who sat stiffly among his cushions.

"I am a big man," he said boastfully. "The women of the Masters like big men. They like to caress muscles like mine. They like me to tell them foolish things. And they tell me their secrets in return.

"Listen to this, Elders of Mur! There is a woman who has taken my blood many times. She is of a high family. Her mate is second to none but their First Man. What she has told me is true.

"They have their own Searchers for Truth—or for the kind of truth they want to find. Their Searchers have told them that a man can give blood every tenth day and still live—that a woman of our kind can be bled every twentieth day, and still work well. They have told them another thing—that their race is growing stronger and more numerous, while ours weakens and grows fewer.

"There will be a new law for the Blood-Givers of Mur to obey. There *is* a new law. Men will be bled each twentieth day—women each thirtieth. Twice as often as of old they will glut on our blood—and the poison in their veins will flow into ours and make our blood water. Their accursed seed will foul our race. And as we die—as they grow strong—the period will be shortened again, and again, and again!

"Get on your feet, Korul! Give us the word! *Death to the Masters! Death!*"

Their roar echoed from the vaulted roof as Korul rose. He stepped down from the platform and stood among them, Karak and old Turun looking down at him. He waited until the clamor subsided.

"The plan is ready," he told them. "We will use it. In every public place of Mur there are secret screens and speakers. In the walls of every city there are panels and lifts that lead to the quarters of the Masters. There are hidden cities beneath the cities, hewn out of the solid rock of Mur, where a race can live for an eternity.

"I will name a day, and the Blood-Givers of Mur will gather. I will speak the word, and they will hear me. We will seize the Masters and seal them in the hidden cells we have made for them. We will make the laws of Mur, and they will bow to them. *Our* Searchers will tell them what blood they can have—and they will get no more. Our Searchers will breed strength back into their flabby bodies—breed life into their blood again—and the time will come when Mur is ruled again by one race, one blood!"

Utter stillness answered him; then one mighty roar of rage and protest rose from every throat. Behind him old Turun was screeching at him, words he could not understand. Karak's bull-bellow roared out above the melee.

"Men and women of Mur," he shouted, "are we bloodless cowards to listen to such talk? So we will keep the Masters as our pets for a thousand years or two—or ten? So we will bleed for them whenever they whine prettily, and feed them well, and keep them strong and happy while we work and die? So we will let our Searchers make Masters of them again, strong and crafty as they once were, so that they can grind us back into the Pit? By the gods, we will not!

"We have had our fill of parasites. We have had enough of their luxuries. We have heard the last of this blasphemous myth of brotherhood and one-bloodedness that old women and *skulluts* teach! The Masters will die—to the last—and if there are so-called leaders among us who prefer to let their blood be licked up, by the gods there will be blood-letting among *them* and we will have men to lead us!"

Korul felt the blood draining out of his face. He knew that his ears had gone white with rage. With one hand he seized Karak by the shoulder and spun him in his tracks. He felt the giant wince in his grip.

"Who is First Man here?" he cried. "Who fought Narkul barehanded and tasted his blood? By the gods, Karak, what I do I do—and if you thirst for the honor, come and earn it. I offer it!"

Giant that he was, Karak had never willingly fought any man unless he was cornered. Redfaced, he pulled himself away from Korul's grip.

"Your Karak seems modest," Korul sneered. "He does not want high rank. He wants only to serve his people. Hear this, Elders of Mur—I am First Man, and what I plan the Blood-Givers of Mur will do. Who questions it?"

They were quiet now, Karak, all of them. There was fear in their faces. Then, at his back, the tired old voice of Turu spoke: "I question you, Korul, son of Thandar. I am First of these Elders as you are of the people. We *are* the people, Korul. The rest—they are *mattaks,* rushing after the first blustering bully to catch their fancy! They will fawn on Karak as well as you—and you know it. And if Karak is afraid to let your blood, then the Elders will do it for him and lead the people of Mur to mastery over your stripped bones!

"We want men over us, who will wipe the scourge of blood-giving off this world for all time. By the gods, if Thandar lived he would do it!"

Enheartened, Karak sprang to the dais again. His eyes were small with hate, and red as coals.

"I have given you one piece of news from the Masters' councils," he cried. "I can give you another. Who in all Mur does not know the story of what happened in the desert on Spring Night? Who does not know how our leader, Korul, met the painted witch Thorana under the stars and let her suck his blood—not once, but twice? A man will do foolish things on Spring Night, you tell me; let it be. But do you know, Elders of Mur, that by special decree of the First Master *this Korul will give blood to no one but Thorana from this day on?"*

With one blow Korul sent the mocking giant sprawling on the floor. "Listen!" he cried. "I cozen no women! I lap no Master's feet! They will die—but they will die when *I* give the word! Go to your cities—rally them—and when the time comes you will hear my word and blood-giving will end on Mur!"

He strode out of the hall. They parted to let him through. As the curtains fell behind him, he heard the buzz and gabble rise again, with Karak's bellow above it all.

There was a man to be watched—a man, it might be, to be feared.

Thorana

Korul's brain was whirling as he left the Council of the Elders. Was it true, what Karak had said? Thorana—only to Thorana? A picture of her shimmered in his mind—as he had seen her on Spring Night, in the Hall of the Masters, aloof and alone and beautiful—as she had been in the desert, soft and slender needing his strength, needing him.

A man—any man—could find a hundred sweet delights in the intimacies of giving blood to Thorana. But he was not any man; he was Korul, son of Thandar, First of the Blood-Givers. And the Masters—all the Masters—were to die!

Through the centuries the lower levels of the city had been honeycombed with passages and secret lifts which gave the Elders access to every public place, and to many less public. One led directly from the Hall of the Elders to the quarters allotted to the First Man. Chewing the black cud of his thoughts, Korul flung open the panel and was halfway across the room before he saw Thorana standing beside his table.

"What is that?" she demanded. "Where does it go?"

He dared not let her probe. "What brings a woman of the Masters to this place?" he countered savagely. "Surely there is nothing to amuse you here in the cattle-pens of my people. The smell of poverty must be too strong for your delicate nostrils."

Her green eyes grew darker and the color showed in her skin. Like Korul she used the ancient, formal tongue prescribed between Master and Giver. "It was not curiosity that brought me here," she said, "though I have never been in the lower city. I have not forgotten what you did in the desert, Korul. I wanted to thank you, and be sure that you are able again to give blood."

So Karak had the truth! It was his blood she wanted, like any scarlet-mouthed slut among them!

"When a Master is in need, our blood is his," he snapped. "That is the law, and I obeyed it. It seems that we Givers are blessed with more than our bodies need." He stared at her insolently, eyeing the soft body under her robe. "Tell me, Thorana—are you of the Masters in poor health? I have heard that we will be bled more, and oftener, for your benefit."

That gave her something to think about. The temper went out of her eyes and left her softer and somehow more appealing. "You must have been listening to the dust-gods, Korul. But—it is true. After Autumn Night, when the waters come again, my father will give you the new law."

He thought she hesitated. Certainly she was slipping out of the formal address. "There will be no more mingling of the races when the ice melts, Korul. I—we feel it is not seemly."

"No!" he jeered. "It might destroy the famous beauty of the Masters. It might put blood of their own into their veins, and grow them legs like the beasts they breed here in the Under-City!"

That had gone home! As Korul well knew, legs like Thorana's would bring her nothing but ridicule among her own flabby, bloodless kind. She'd covered them close enough on Spring Night, until she thought there was no one sober enough to watch! Her ear-tips were crimson with shame—or rage.

But when she answered, it was very softly. "I have a request."

Now it was coming! "You are feeling faint? The reek from that place makes you ill? A little blood for your health's sake—is that your request, Thorana?"

Her head was bent, hiding her eyes. She drew the fold of her robe away from her legs. Korul felt the pulse pounding in his neck as he stared. Gods! These weren't the pedestals of muscle on which the women of the Blood-Givers carried their chunky bodies. They were slim, smooth, the muscles swelling cunningly over the slender bones. This Thorana—she was like the women in the paintings of long ago which one of the Searchers had shown him!

"My—legs—Korul." He could barely hear her. "Only you among the Blood-Givers know how I am—deformed. Very few of my people know." Her head came up defiantly. "We Masters protect our monsters, Korul! What is your custom? The Pit, perhaps, where I can amuse the children and old men? Or do you slaughter your unfortunates because they are different from you?"

Korul gaped at her. "What are you talking about? What I know is in my head. Here, between these ears. If any man wants to spill it out, he must break the head open first—and I assure you, Thorana, it is a hard head to crack. Ask those who have tried—if you can teach dry bones to talk."

She shivered and let the crimson silk fall down again over her legs. "Is it true, Korul, that a man—a Giver—must kill you and drink your blood if he is to become First Man of your race?"

"A *man*—Giver or Master—proves that he is a man when he can drink my blood. It's not an old custom, Thorana. Your own kind made it law. You need a strong breed here in the Under-City, if you're to be fed and kept in comfort all your days. And the First Man of the Blood-Givers must be strongest of all if he's to breed strength in his sons."

The girl came toward him. She moved gracefully, like a wisp of mist along the rock-slopes of the gorges. "I want to know things like that, Korul. I want to see your people, how they live, what they do here in the depths. I want to know the thoughts they think when they are alone, and the dreams that come to them.

"Will you show them to me, Korul? You will find me grateful."

Grateful! The word grated in his ears. He seemed to hear Karak's mocking voice, raised over the clamor in the Hall of the Elders. She would be grateful!

"How do you plan to show this gratitude, Thorana?"

She hesitated. Her eyes turned away from him. "My father—he has said that hereafter you will give blood only to me."

Korul felt his neck swelling. The arrogance!

"A privilege indeed," he sneered. "I am sure any man

of the Givers would be proud to be at Thorana's call day and night for the rest of his life! For there would be nights, wouldn't there, Thorana? Nights when the warm blood would flow on and on and on in the perfumed darkness—when you would feel real life beating for the first time in your shriveled veins, as it drained out of the drugged, stupid clod in the cushions at your side! You must have great confidence in my strength, Thorana, to believe we could enjoy such moments often."

Every bit of colour had gone out of her face. She stood stiff and straight, taller than any woman he had ever seen.

"Keep your insolence to yourself!" she cried. "You may keep your savage's blood. I need none of it."

"No blood?" he mocked. "Have you forgotten the desert?"

She stared him down. "I remember. I am no brute beast like you, but I have blood of my own, and it's good blood. Once in a year I may need you—twice at the most, and maybe never. You see, Korul, I can read history as well as you. I know that we were once one race, with bodies and legs and blood like yours. We Masters have our own traditions of strength in our First Men, though we do not suck blood to prove it.

"I am proud to be a throwback to those old ones—proud to have blood and legs. But I think pride must be a stranger to your kind."

What kind of woman was this—one moment stiff with arrogance and the ingrown ignorance of her domineering breed, the next like this, soft, human? What was she after?

"If you are trying to do me a kindness, forget it," he said stiffly. "I am strong enough: choose someone weak or old who needs what help you can give him. I can find many such for you."

Her green eyes were searching his face again. "Korul," she said smiling, "you are learning more secrets than are good for you, but I will tell you another. There will be changes in the law of blood-giving—you know that, but what you have heard is only part of the truth. After Autumn Night the periods between givings will no longer be the same for everyone. You will come to our Searchers and be tested, your strength measured, every Spring Night. Those like you, Korul, who have blood to spare, will give it as often as it is needed—the sick and the old, never again."

Her eyes were shining. She put her hand on his bare arm. "We must work together in this plan, Korul—Masters and Givers together again! You will have to make a new work plan for your people, for now the whole burden of blood-giving will be on your young men and women. And it will help us to change. We aren't all fools and parasites, Korul—there are some of us, many of us, who know the story of the past and how we have made ourselves into a race of blood-sucking vermin.

"But we are one blood, Korul! We are one flesh. We can be one race again! Will you help?"

He turned the words slowly on his tongue. "One race? One blood? What then?"

"Show me your people. Help me to understand them. If we are to be one kind, Korul, we must know each other. The Pit is open to both races: will you meet me there—tomorrow? Will you teach me the things a Master must know, if he is to be a man?"

The words came with difficulty. "If you are telling the truth, Thorana, it seems one of the Masters is already a man. I will be in the Pit at mid-morning."

Karak

The cities of Mur clung to the sides of their gorges like a dry crust of rock-weed to the desert ledges. Along the terraced lips of the great clefts were crumbling walls of laid-up native stone, their roofs open to the sky, their halls deep in dust. Not all the power of the Pit would drive warmth so high.

Lower the city was carved out of the living rock, level after level of it reaching down and down into the perpetual mists of the deep. Below the abandoned levels were store-houses, libraries, the strange laboratories of the Searchers. Deeper still were the levels of the Masters, and under them in turn the warrens of the Blood-Givers in the dank, grumbling bowels of the city.

Deepest of all was the Pit. Circling up from it on every side were the sheer walls and retreating terraces of the city. The cages were there, penning up the strange beasts that were still to be found in forsaken wastelands of the planet, or that had roamed those wastes in the forgotten generations when Masters and Givers were one people. There were creatures in the Pit, one of the Searchers had said, whose pedigrees ran back farther and straighter than man's. Like the Blood-Givers they had been bred for strength, down through the centuries. Like Masters, they could no longer live outside their cages.

For a few hours each day during the Murian summer the sun rose clear of the gorges' rim, moved across the narrow strip of sky, and disappeared beyond the farther wall. Before its hot light cut through the mists of the gorge, Korul was hurrying through the lower corridors, surprising an occasional Giver. Thorana was there before him in a very small *tlornak* which could wheel silently through the narrowest passage of the Under-City.

So it began. They made an odd pair—the slim girl in her wheeled carriage, the bronzed Giver striding beside her. No Master had come into those levels in generations: no Master had a right there! Their faces spoke their distrust and hatred, but under the law—their law—Korul was First of their men and what he did and said was not to be questioned to his face unless the questioner was ready to try for his throat.

Korul knew the city as he knew the back of his spread hand. With him Thorana went into the very vitals of the city—the city within the city, where the great conduits rose like twisted entrails out of the bowels of the planet, where dynamos three levels high purred through the gloom, where the air machines hissed and bubbled, pumping warmed and perfumed breezes into the quarters of the Masters and cool, invigorating blasts into the shops and cells of the Givers.

She saw the shops of the Makers where *tlornaks* were built; the kitchens where the food of the Under-people was prepared; the hospitals where the weak and old came to recover from their blood-letting, where children were born and Givers died and she saw the dead fed into the furnaces which would burn away the semblance of life and leave a puff of clean ashes.

Holding Korul's arm, she went on her own feet down into the Pit beneath the Pit where the eternal fires of Mur smouldered, and sweating men tended the huge heat-pumps which kept the city alive.

What impressed her most, Korul thought, was his intimacy with his people. As leader of the Givers he knew hundreds of his folk by sight and name, and they knew and welcomed him. It startled her.

But what was most marked was the reception she had from them. Dressed quietly and unobtrusively, as she was from the first, and except for occasional traits of speech or attitude, Thorana might have been one of them—slight, weak-looking, finer than any of them in features and carriage, yet—human. She tried to fit into the life of the places Korul took her, to make friends with the people she saw there, but—she was a Master. Even the children in the great public nurseries shrank from her, as if by instinct.

They did not always explore the city. There were times when she had duties of her own, or when Korul had work of his own. Then they would come to the Pit at night, and talk.

Usually it was of the old times, when the races were one people. He forgot, then, that they were Master and Giver. Together, man and woman, they lived over the life of those old, good times. They remade the universe in their own pattern. like children, and in that made-over world, where the two races were again one blood and one flesh, they too would be one like their peoples. It was a pretty dream.

Korul had forgotten the Elders, and his pledge to them. They knew he had forgotten. That knowledge was in the whispers that followed them through the levels of the Under-City, in the eyes that watched their trysts in the Pit. It was in work hidden when he appeared.

All over Mur the preparations were under way. In the hidden shops men and women both were beating out slashing blades of steel and building ugly little bows that hurled steel bolts with deadly accuracy.

He should have seen. That was why he was First Man of all the Blood-Givers of Mur. The pulse and timbre of his people should have been his pulse, should have tightened his nerves. But—Korul was in love.

On the surface, everything was normal. Even before the Plan there had been muttered resentment and rebellious talk: the Masters expected it. Little overt acts of contempt

—mocking slowness in obeying an order—scrawled obscenities in the dust or on a wall—catch-words in the jargon of the Givers. The Masters expected it; their spies and supervisors saw it and reported it as usual. But now it was planned as carefully as the secret arsenals the Givers were building in every city of Mur. Now it was a screen for the soberer thoughts behind it.

Behind the screen, behind the secret bustle, was Karak.

Except in name, Korul was no longer First of his people. They let him keep the title as part of the screen. But it was Karak who carried the Elders' orders, who planned with them, who called the secret meetings and named their lieutenants. It was he who forged the lies which would keep the People's hate at fever-pitch, and who thundered out his warcry in the Hall of the Elders while men and women and half-grown children flung it back in savage frenzy:

"Death to the Masters! Death!"

Korul should have sat on the dais beside Turun at that meeting of his people. He sat in the Pit with Thorana, mooning over her fragile beauty, listening to her low, sweet voice, thinking her thoughts.

At another time Korul might have read a good deal in the strained attitude of the woman who brought him a summons from the Elders. As it was, he strode into the hall to see Karak standing in his place on the dais, beside Turun—and beside the banked controls of a transmitter which, Korul knew, would carry every detail of what happened to every corner of the city. There was an empty space before Turun's throne. It was the place decreed by the law of his people for those who came on trial before their Elders. And he stood there.

Old Turun looked down at him with pity behind the sadness in his eyes. "You have not been helpful, Korul," he said bitterly, "but the People have been strong without you. Tell him, Karak."

Karak swaggered forward to the edge of the dais. "You've been so busy with—things—Korul," he sneered, "that I was glad to help the Elders. I've cleared up some of the little details of organization that you'd have taken care of if you'd had the time."

The blusterer had to be deflated. "What details?" Korul

demanded. "What have you accomplished, that is so important?"

He had walked into Karak's trap. "Perhaps not important to you, or your new friends, Korul—but we have the sluices at both poles. Torkul is in command in the North, and Tatokin the South. I have found leaders in every city—strong leaders, without other distractions on their minds. And the People have weapons now, Korul."

"By the gods, Karak," he cried, "do you have a plan? Speak it out!"

The mockery went out of Karak's broad face. "It's very simple, Korul—and soon done. In two days the sluices will open, and the autumn flow begin. The Masters will be our equals for one night. It's to be the last, they tell me—and it *will* be the last, but we will make it so! Every man has been drilled in his part until he dreams it. Every woman knows her duty. In three breaths they will be cut down to the last one, and there will be no blood-giving on Mur."

"And my part, Karak? You've said nothing about that."

He was being sly again. "Oh, no, Korul!" he protested. "You are our First Man—you'll give the word that frees us. You will be at the feasting, I'm sure—in a very prominent place, no doubt. When you are quite ready, and have made your farewells to the old days, you will rise and give us the word."

He was holding out something that glistened: a knife, hammered out of steel, sharpened to a needle point and razor edge, with a handle of carved bone. "Take it, Karul—and strike the first blow for your people. The blood of the First Master and all his breed will drip from this blade when you're done."

And Turun's croak goaded him on. "Take it, Korul. Hold it up for the People to see. Then speak to them."

Slowly Korul's fingers closed over the carved hilt. It was a sweetly, wickedly made thing—and it would kill as quickly in Karak's hand as in his. If he refused now—if he hesitated in any way—the allegiance of the Givers would be lost. Karak would be First, then—and no woman's face swam before *his* eyes.

If he agreed, then he must smile and whisper and murmur love-words to Thorana and with his next breath slit her lovely throat—or see Karak do it for him.

At least, there were two days.

Every eye in the hall was on Korul as he stepped up on the dais beside Turun, in his rightful place, where the transmitter would carry face and voice to every city of Mur.

"People of Mur," he said hoarsely, "I will give you the word. The word is—*Death!*"

Behind him he heard Karak chuckling.

In The Pit

She was waiting for him there in the shadow of the great open cage of the Star-Beast, as she had waited so often. She rose as she heard his footsteps and stood slim and wonderful in the soft light that sifted down through the mists of the gorge.

Korul took her hands. He could not speak, or look at her. The knife, in its secret sheath at his side, seemed to burn into his flesh. In two nights that knife must slash across this lovely throat—must slip into this warm soft breast.

The warmth in his hands was suddenly the sticky warmth of fresh blood. Korul stepped quickly back; rubbed his open palms down his thighs.

Thorana reached out and drew him close again. "Tell me, Korul—what is it? I will not blame you."

It came pouring out then, in a flood of broken words—how he loved her—how he had betrayed her—how all her race were to be butchered at his word.

"Warn them!" he pleaded. "Tell them everything. There must be some stronghold—one of the abandoned cities, perhaps—where they can hide and give me time to reason with the People."

"It is too late for reasoning, Korul," she told him. "We could not live without your people. Who would tend the heat engines? Who would prepare our food? What should we do for blood? No—some of them have known it would come. We hoped, as we have always hoped, that it would be a little later—not in our own lifetime, but later. Instead, it is now."

Her fingers tightened on his arms. "Be true to them, Korul. Use the knife they gave you, and be quick and kind. Then they will trust you again; they will follow you as they used to. You can lead them in the way we've dreamed here so often, and keep it all from happening again in a thousand years or two thousand when the Givers of today have in their turn become Masters, and some other crushed-down race strikes back."

He stared at her. Kill her—that was what she was asking him. Drink her blood, as she had drunk his there in the desert. "I'll go with you—now," he insisted. "We'll use the secret lifts. There are places in the upper city that not even the Elders know. They don't need me now—they've proved that. Let the Elders care for the People."

Thorana pointed to the archway through which he had come into the Pit. There were shadows there, and as one moved he caught the glint of light on bare metal. Slowly he looked around him. Every entry was guarded.

Remembering, he heard Karak's mocking chuckle.

The girl drew him down beside her on the stone bench that ran across the front of the Star-Beast's cage. "We've been watched from the beginning, Korul: I thought you knew that. They know how it is with us. They knew you would betray them, to me. Karak has never intended that we would live out this night."

Korul went down on his knees at her side. How could he have been so stupid? *This* was Karak's real plan—to strike tonight. Everything was ready—the sluices taken—weapons distributed—only a word was needed, and why should that word wait for Autumn Night? No—his death, and Thorana's, here in the Pit, would be the signal for massacre.

Out of the darkness above him came a thundering voice, hoarse, savage, rasping!

"Korul!"

Korul's heart stood still. Was this some other mockery of Karak's? Gently he slipped the knife out of its hiding place and balanced it in his hand. Then it came again:

"Korul!"

Sweeping Thorana behind him, he leaped back into the open Pit. Above them, huge and repulsive, the Star-Beast clung to the bars of its cage and glared down at them with little, glittering eyes.

The thing's head and body were shaggy with tangled reddish hair. It's legs and arms were thick and crooked; its body squat and brutish. It had narrow, club-like feet and stubby fingers. There were little, crumpled ears half-hidden in its matted hair—flabby, slobbering lips—a nose which was a bulbous snout set between two tiny bloodshot eyes that glared palely out of the darkness. A foul animal reek came from the filth of its cage.

The Beast had come out of the desert, twenty years and more before. Thandar, Korul's father and First Man in his time, had trapped it among the high levels. They netted it, like any of the great carnivores in the Pit, and chained it—but it burst its chains and crushed its captors in its mighty arms. It ran wild in the upper city and broke into the Hall of the Masters, trampling them underfoot in its efforts to escape, beating off its pursuers with a metal shaft that it swung like a club.

Somehow the thing had found its way into the maze of corridors deep under the city where the water-conduits ran. It had lurked there for ten days, eluding the search parties with animal cunning, fighting savagely when cornered. Then it burst out into the secret cells of the Searchers, and with their cunning they made a gas that brought it down.

The thing was senseless when they brought it into the Pit and built this cage around it. They found it would eat flesh, and there they left it, raging and beating at its bars and bellowing its bestial gibberish at the stars.

Star-Beast they named it. When it had grown quiet and people came to look at it, it would mouth and mutter and gesture with its fore-paws at the mists above the Pit—and when they laughed, or shrank away, it would fly into a fury and shake the bars of its cage and roar. Then the novelty wore off, and only occasionally visitors came to see it—children, for the most part. When it roared and gibbered, they would mock and gibber back, and run off laughing.

The Beast grew sullen. Time and again it tried to leap on its keeper when he came with food, or to clean its cage. Finally no one would go into the cage, and it lay in its filth staring up through the mists of the gorge at the dim, haloed stars.

It had been docile enough during all the nights they had been meeting on the bench under its cage. It would pace to and fro as caged beasts do, or squat against the bars above them, staring down, listening, watching, mumbling or whining to itself. Thorana had grown fond of the thing; often she would bring food for it from the Masters' kitchen. It showed no inclination to harm her, but growled in pleasure and made half-hearted efforts to groom itself as other beasts do. Now it clung against the bars, huge, shaggy, monstrous, yet no longer repulsive. They were growing tolerant of life and its many forms, Korul thought, now that death was so near.

Thorana clutched his arm. "What was it?" she whispered.

"Up there, I think." Korul pointed to the lowest terrace, above them in the dark. Perhaps there are some who still consider Korul their First Man, he thought grimly. "Korul!" It came again, close to them. "Here!"

Thorana's fingers dug into his muscle. "Korul—*the Beast!* The Star-Beast!"

He stared at her. "It's true," she insisted. "I was watching it. I saw its lips move!"

Korul's grip tightened on his knife. What trickery was this? Was there a hidden speaker, an eavesdropping pick-up in the cage? Was one of Karak's bullies there in the cage spying on them, disguised in the Beast's flayed pelt?

He climbed up on the stone bench and peered at the Beast through the bars. It towered over him, fully a third again his height—huge, hairy, hideous, staring at him with eyes that seemed to try to speak. And its lips moved, clumsily, spewing out blurred, uncouth sounds that were somehow twisted into words:

"Korul! I—not—speak—good. I—hear. I—understand. I—sad." Then, hesitantly: "I—help!"

Gods above! Crudely, roughly, mouthing the syllables and ignoring the simplest rules of grammar, the Star-Beast was speaking in the ancient language of Mur!

Thorana was there beside him. "What are you?" she demanded. "How can you speak our tongue?"

"Slow. Slow," pleaded the Beast. "I—not—understand—good—too. Speak—slow. Slow."

Korul repeated what she had said.

"I—hear—you," the thing explained. "Many—days—I

—hear—you—speak. I—understand—your—words. I—learn—slow. Now—I—hear—your—trouble. I—will—help."

"But—what are you?" It was Thorana again. "How can you help us?"

"Stay—here—tonight. Speak—slow. Show—me—words. Stay—tomorrow. Tell—me—all. I—tell—you. Tomorrow—night—I help."

Weird, unnatural words from that hairy brute, caged here in the Pit as a montrosity, tormented by children and malicious men and women. Weirder still the story that he told.

All that night and the next day they sat by the cage, talking slowly, using simple words, illustrating with gestures. The guards at the archways were puzzled, and faces peered down curiously from the terraces that encircled the Pit. Perhaps Karak did not dare attack in daylight, in the open, with the People looking on. Perhaps it was Turun who remembered his old friendship with Thandar and Thandar's son. They were not molested.

The Beast was wonderfully quick to learn. From the beginning it had tried to remember words—couple them with gestures—understand their meanings. For half a year now it had spied on Korul and Thorana almost every night. It had had twenty years to lay the foundations of the language of Mur; now, in a day, they must raise the superstructure—grammar, pronunciation, distinctions of meaning.

The thing's throat and tongue were ill-fitted for their rapid, sibilent speech. It spoke ponderously. By straining it could make the words clear, if dull and heavy as an idiot child might speak them. But this beast from the stars was no idiot!

Jim-Berk it—he—was called, in his own tongue. He had come from a world nearer the sun than Mur, in a metal shell driven by explosives. He had lived twenty of his own years then. Here on Mur—*Mars,* he called it—the years passed twice as slowly.

Jim-Berk's shell had landed safely in the low hills beyond the desert, far to the North. From his world, Searchers had been able to see the straight clefts of the gorges that crisscrossed Mur, and watch them grow green in the spring as the first vapors boiled up out of them to moisten the clinging plants along the desert's edge. Such clefts must be the work of an intelligent race, they thought, and Jim-Berk had been sent to find that race.

He started for the nearest rift and was lost in the desert. Exhausted, starved, half mad with heat and thirst, he stumbled into the upper levels of the city. Far below, from the lip of the gorge, he had seen the lights of the living levels, smelled the warm mist, heard the twitter of voices and the throb of the heat pumps that beat through all the foundations of the city. Then he was found—a monster out of the desert. They attacked, and he fought back—and in the end was caged.

For a long time, he told them, he tried vainly to make someone understand, calling to curious sightseers in his own tongue or in what seemed to him to be theirs, flying into a blind rage when they ran away in horror from his bellowing. He tried to escape, beating at the bars, ambushing his jailer—all without avail. In the end he gave up hope and became the beast they thought him. Then Korul came with Thorana.

"You were young," he said painfully. "You weren't afraid like the others. You sat where I could hear you, and you talked a lot. Young people like you didn't talk so much when they were alone, on my world.

"Hearing the same voices helps when you are learning to talk. I got so I could understand a lot of what you were saying. Last night, when Korul told his story, I had to speak. On *Earth* we're more used to violence than you seem to be here on *Mars*. Maybe I can help."

"Why do you want to help, Jim-Berk?" Thorana asked. "Think how we have treated you through all these years—a beast, caged in the Pit for the curious to torment! My parents threatened me with you, and some of our young men use your name as a curse. That Erth of yours must be wonderful, Jim-Berk, to breed such as you!"

"I think so, Thorana," he rumbled softly. "Here in this cage with only the other animals for company—not even the stars at night, or a moon like Erth's—it was lonely. I used to lie back and try to look up through the mist at the bright spots where the stars would show through, and wonder if one of them was Erth, and if people there remembered me and were waiting for me to come back.

"Erth is a world you could never imagine, Thorana, you on this dry, dead ball of sand. Its deserts are rolling water, blue and green and gray, breaking against great cliffs and over white smooth sands. Its plains are green as your eyes, Thorana, and the forests that go up over the hills are darker green, and the sky as blue—well, as blue as my own eyes used to be. And now it's only a silver speck shining in the night, with the gray mist hiding it from me. But by Erth herself, I'm forgetting you two!"

"There's nothing you can do," Korul told him. "We're trapped here, all three of us, but if Turun will speak to me I'll tell him your story. He'll let you go, I'm sure—back to your Erth, away from our bleeding and our bickering."

"Don't cackle like an old woman!" he growled. "Who is First Man in this place if you're not? Who has the key to everything? I'm no more caged than your infernal Karak, if you'll take the trouble to unlock this cage. Listen to me—will they kill you if you come out alone?"

"There's nothing you can do."

"They might. Karak hates me, and they are his men. But he's afraid of Turun and the Elders, and I think he's been looking forward to seeing my knife in Thorana's throat. I think I could go free, for another night at least."

"Then do it, and leave Thorana here with the key. I'll promise to have her out of here in the wink of an eye, once it's dark enough. It's you they'll be watching anyway, not us. Now then, have you a map of the place anywhere?"

There was a mosaic on the floor of the Pit that showed the entire world of Mur. Thorana copied it on a bit of cloth torn from her mantle. Jim-Berk crumpled it in his big paw.

"What place is there you'll be safe?" he demanded.

"Torkul, our leader at the northern sluices, is like a brother," Korul told him. "But to him you're a wild beast, and Thorana one of the Masters, whom he's sworn to kill. Besides, it is too far . . ."

"That's my affair," he snapped. "I'm big enough, I think, to take care of myself and of her too. Where are there cities, now? We must keep away from them."

* * *

Korul pointed them out in dimming light. Jim-Berk's little eyes grew thoughtful. "Look here," he said finally. "I'll go the way I came, over the desert and through the hills—here—to where I left the ship. There'll be water there, and food, and clothes for me, though it makes little enough difference what I wear after twenty years of running naked in this zoo of yours! Then we'll follow the height of the land to your other rift, here, and follow it to the pole. Is that clear?"

"I can follow you," Korul assured him, "but how will you find the way? Mur is a strange world to you, and this map is no more than a scrawl copied from an artist's crude picture. There have been no surveys in the memory of man—we don't go into the desert, and haven't for centuries."

"So much the better!" he grunted. "There'll be no one there to see us. As for steering my way, there's the sun and the stars, and forty years haven't changed them beyond remembering. The skies are higher and older than you people dream, Korul. You've forgotten a lot that we on Erth never knew, perhaps, but I'll bet you were never the men for the open that we are. Little folk like you are safest close to home."

"Don't wait for me," Korul warned him. "I'll be watched for days after the—Change. Keep Thorana safe for me, and if I'm alive I will come to the sluices. I trust you, Jim-Berk."

"I'll keep her safe enough," he grinned, "and it'll give you something to come after, so you'll not forget. Unlock the cage now, and get out of here."

The cage door locked with a combination. Korul set the key and tugged, but nothing moved. He tried again, and still again. The master combination should open the lock, but the door had not been touched for years, since Berk had killed his keeper.

Then the Star-Beast grasped the bars. His rolling muscles swelled; water stood out on his hairy pelt in droplets, and dripped from the end of his snout. And the door moved! He shoved it open and slipped out into the night.

"Argh!" he grunted. "It's good to smell fresh air again!"

As far as Korul could see, he had no more air than before, and as for smell . . . But he was of a different world and another race: things would be different to him. With a squeeze of the hand he left Thorana and strode warily toward the nearest entry.

Two men with bows and arm-long knives stepped out of the shadows. "Karak wants to see you," growled one of them.

"I want to see Karak!" Korul snapped. "It has to do with the girl, Thorana. She will be kept here in the Pit, as he said. It should amuse our children to have one of the Masters caged with the other beasts. Let no one into the Pit without my word or Karak's. This woman is our affair. Now take me to Karak or Turun, quickly."

The Hunting of the Beast

By luck, it was Turun. His old eyes narrowed as he saw Korul. Karak's plan must have been plenty definite.

"Karak or no Karak," Korul told him when the guard had left, "I am First Man of Mur until someone lets my blood. What I do and think is my affair, unless the People are harmed by it.

"I've left the girl in the Pit. She can't leave or warn the Masters, and there is no need to kill her before the signal is given. I ask that you leave her there until the killing is over. If you grant me this, I will lead as you wish, and if the Elders still say she must die, I will take her life myself. Otherwise you may do as you please—without your First. I do not trust Karak!"

Turun was on his feet in a rage. "By the gods you talk boldly for a man who has betrayed his race! Be you First or last, you have no claim on the People or their Elders now. If Karak agrees, you may lead the attack. Until then, if you wish, the girl is safe where she is. Now go away. I want to remember Thandar, and forget he had a son!"

It suited Karak to have Korul as his puppet-leader. The Elders would reward him in any way he asked, when the time came—and a thrust from behind was as quick and quiet a way of letting a First Man's blood as open combat. In the hubbub of killing, who would say which Master had done it?

Korul read his thoughts, and swallowed his own fury. From the Hall of Elders, Karak's grinning face behind him, he explained the plan of attack to the people—knowing all the while that it had all been done, and done thoroughly, long before, while he and Thorana were wandering through each other's dreams.

Karak was feeling his power. "Turun's growing old," he boomed, "and he can't see beyond his nose. When it's all over, and the Givers are in the Master's halls, there'll be concessions for those who have cooperated with the Elders. As I recall this Thorana, she may be worth saving. I'll look her over tomorrow." Better the knife for Thorana, if Karak was taking an interest in her. But if he knew the man, there would be other beautiful daughters of the Masters safely spirited away when the killing started.

"What news from Torkul?" he asked, to change the subject.

Karak frowned. "None," he muttered, "nor from Tatok. They struck without my order, and we have rumors that they're holding the Masters prisoner and giving them blood when they need it." He glared suspiciously at Korul. "You know them pretty well don't you?"

"I know Torkul. We were young together. He was headstrong and dreamy—wanted to be a Searcher. Maybe he wants to experiment with the Masters a little before he lets them die."

That thought seemed attractive to Karak. "What about Tatok?" he demanded. "Wasn't his father a friend of your father and Turun?"

Korul let his eyes shift away. If Karak could see just far enough into a ruse, but not too far . . .

"I haven't heard from Tatok in a year," he insisted. "Our fathers were friends, but I never knew him well. You know yourself the story they tell—when a spy for the Masters caught him shirking, he ran away and hid for twenty days in the deserted levels. He had food only twice before they caught him. No—Tatok is loyal enough. The Masters may have been able to cut the signal lines before he killed them."

Tatok was a blustering bully very much like Karak himself, as Korul knew very well. If he refused to answer questions, it was probably because he had no fondness for taking orders from anyone when he had power of his own. If Karak's suspicions could be turned to him, and away from Torkul, perhaps he could be kept away from the nearer pole.

Whether the bluff had worked, Korul never knew. There

was a shout in the corridor outside and a guard flung open the door. It was the man from the Pit.

"The Star-Beast is loose!" he shouted. "It's got the girl!"

Karak's mouth hardened. He stared thoughtfully at Korul, then turned to the guard. "What happened?" he demanded. "Who's let the thing out?"

"I don't know," the man told him. "There wasn't a sound after Korul left. Then the thing showed up out of the shadows and strangled the guards at the other archway. The girl ran after him, and he picked her up and disappeared. We shot at them, but it was too dark to aim, and he was running very fast. You remember, they say that when he was captured he could jump very high and run faster than any man."

"This could be bad," Karak said slowly. "If the woman gets away, she may warn her friends and make the killing a bit messier than we'd planned. What do you suggest, Korul—find them first, or call the signal now?"

"Find them!" Korul snapped. "I've seen that thing close up. Let it run wild and it can kill more of our men than a score of the Masters can, warned or not. Remember your history, man—what happened when it was wild and scared of us? Now it's been caged for twenty years. It hates our blood and bones, and it will hunt us down as long as we leave it alive!"

He sensed Karak puzzling over what he said. Was it a bluff? Was there some scheme afoot delaying the Change—giving the Masters time to protect themselves, or escape?

"We'll use *ullas,*" Karak decided. "Whether it's gone down into the tunnels, as it did before, or headed back for the desert, they'll follow it. Zon, get three men who can handle the things and meet us in the Pit."

He wheeled to look at Korul again. "If your stomach won't stand for hunting this girl with *ullas*, perhaps you'd like to stay behind—under guard."

It would have taken more than Karak to make Korul stay behind, but he had been sure that the bully would see the irony of the situation and make him join the hunt. If he could protect Thorana, it would be there.

Zon and three like him met them with the *ullas*. There were six of the things, leashed two and two, ugly scaly things with their flat heads and frill of savage-looking spines. They were as vicious as they looked. Korul knew: men like Karak trained them to fight and hunt small creatures bred in the cages of the Pit.

The reek of the Star-Beast was strong in his cage, and the *ullas* were off like streaks on the trail. From the pit it led deep into the tunnels under the city, twisting back and forth, going ever deeper until the heat and stench of the Under-Pit was choking in their throats. Jim-Berk knew *ullas* well: he had been caged with them for two thirds of his life—but their scent was too keen for his tricks.

When the trail led to one of the secret lifts, Korul felt Karak's suspicious glare on his back. A beast using lifts?

They had no way of knowing where the lift would stop. The *ullas* were split into two packs, muzzled still, and set to scout out every level while Karak waited in the car. It was a stupid performance, but it gave the Beast and Thorana time to hide their trail.

At the very top of the city the creatures struck a hot scent.

The Star-Beast had scrambled straight up the wall to the rock slope above, trying to confuse the pursuit. The hissing *ullas* hurled themselves again and again against the wall, fell back and leaped again, until Zon's men clubbed them back and dragged them hissing and struggling, to the nearest steps.

From the wall, Berk's trail led raggedly up through the rocks to the desert. Where his hunters squirmed and struggled through crevices and over jagged boulders twice their height, the Star-Beast had climbed like a *zannak* in great, straddling leaps that carried him from block to block. Karak's temper was rising fast. He would never leave the trail now, Korul realized.

On and on they went over the swelling sand-sea of the dunes—up one great, sweeping, gentle slope, then down in a rushing slide—up again, then down. The glow of the gorge was sinking in the sky behind them when one of Zon's men stumbled and went down, dragging his *ullas* with him in a hissing, clawing tangle that rolled in a river of sand to the foot of the dune. When they reached him, he lay still, bleeding from the gashes of the monster's knife-sharp claws. They crouched over him, probing with their muzzled snouts, running out their forked tongues to lap at his oozing blood.

Karak sent him back, with a second man to help him. Zor and the remaining guard took the *ullas*. They were experienced hunters, Karak and Zor: they held their beasts to an easy, swinging pace that ate up the distance. But the great strides of the Star-Beast, clear in the sand before them, measured twice their paces. The *ullas* seemed less eager, too: the scent must be growing cold.

Karak was no fool. The Star-Beast's tracks were slowly filling with sand, with every breath of air that curled over the desert's face. He stopped them at the crest of one gigantic dune that rose above all the rest.

"You—Zor!" he demanded. "Can you follow a trail in the sand?"

"I have hunted with you," the man reminded him.

"Then let the *ullas* go, and follow as you can. We're losing ground."

Silently they bent over the straining beasts, plucking at the straps that muzzled them. Then like living shadows, the creatures leaped out on the Star-Beast's scent.

"Come on!" shouted Karak, "if you want to see the kill!"

Now they were running, with a stride that nearly matched the Star-Beast's—pace for pace on the track of the hunting beasts. As the darkness lightened and the dawn-cone thrust up before them, paling the watching stars, Korul saw that the character of the ground was changing and a fierce hope sprang up in him.

As the night passed they had seen the *ullas* from time to time, far ahead on the crest of some dune, skimming like shadows over the pale sand. Gradually they had drawn ahead, until Karak was following the trail of their clawed paws. Now the sand was giving way to a hard, gravelly plain, naked and flat, where the beast's claws left no trace. What marks there were in the thin dust, that overlaid the ancient, sun-baked clay would be gone as the dawn-wind rose. By the gracious gods, they might escape!

With the first arc of the sun above the far horizon, Karak stopped to stare ahead over the red expanse. It sloped down like a saucer before them, but in all that great waste nothing living moved. He grunted and ran on, Korul at his side matching stride for stride.

As the sun climbed in the sky, the red plain came alive

with flickering phantoms of the heat. Broad, shining lakes spread over the desert, like the seas of which Jim-Berk told, bordered with monstrous vegetable shapes. Weird, ruined cities hung against the distance, walls and towers that melted and changed as they looked and faded into a wash of crimson light.

Looking back, Korul saw the long vanished dunes hung huge and inverted in the heavens, while over them crept two black dots—Karak's men—and far behind another moving line, the reinforcements which the wounded man had sent. Then before them the plain suddenly swelled and rushed to meet them with awful speed, its every detail growing with incredible swiftness, cracks swollen into gorges, pebbles into phantom bolders twice their height—and caught up by the mirage, the *ullas,* running low and tirelessly on the track of their prey!

Karak cried out and pointed: the ghost-land shivered and was gone. But somewhere out there the hunting beasts were drawing closer to Jim-Berk and to Thorana.

Slowly another shape began to take form in the red haze before them, wavering, looming in moments of mirage, sinking again, yet steadier and more solid than the ghost-shapes of the heat. Ragged arms ran out from it on either side, closing out the horizon, then began to draw together, shutting them in.

Was this another trick of the desert and the heat, Korul wondered, or was it real? He saw uncertainty growing on Karak's flat face. What were these crazy crimson towers, these shadowed crevices, these tottering spires of scarlet that flickered like tongues of solid flames against the black sky? Were they another phantom swimming in their heat-warped brain? If so Karak saw them too.

Mirage or not, the heat in this rock-walled slot was terrible. Karak was tearing at his clothes, and his skin was beginning to redden and blister in the sun's fierce glare. Korul drew his own mantle closer about him.

The fine red dust that their plodding feet stirred up settled over them, sifting into the creases of their skin and between cloak and skin, setting their flesh on fire. Their sandals were thin: no protection for bruised and blistered feet. Remembering that other time, Korul knew what must come and hardened himself against it—but Karak ran tirelessly beside him along the wavering track of three-clawed feet. Karak was a man!

A man—yes, but a man who had loved soft things, and taken them when he found them: good food from the Masters' cupboards, wine from the Masters' flagons, women from the Masters' beds. As they came out of the broken land into a place of packed white sand, white as the snow-cap at the pole, Korul saw that the other's steps were beginning to waver. His breath rasped in and out of his open mouth in great, dry sobs. Slowly Korul began to draw ahead. There was a strangled command, then a scuff of gravel and a thump as Karak fell sprawling. Korul did not look back.

He had become a machine like Karak now, tireless and unfeeling, that raced on and on along that shimmering track while the sun climbed higher and the white sands blazed about him with almost ponderable heat. He narrowed his eye to slits, but still the white fire burned into his brain. He felt the skin of his face tightening and cracking.

Then far ahead, where the white sands melted again into red and rose in a vast, slow wave against the inky sky, he saw the *ullas* running on the track.

Somewhere they must have lost the trail—in the soft sands, perhaps—in the broken land. They were tiring too, running slower, and a savage satisfaction woke in Korul's throat as his dazed mind cleared and the thud of his pounding feet came crisper and faster from the packed white sand.

The skimming shapes grew in his vision until he could make out every detail of their long, lithe forms, glistening with tiny scales as black as night itself.

They vanished over the crest of the first sand-wave. Korul toiled up the slope behind them. From the top he saw a distant line of red hills, the sand rolling against their base. Halfway up the next slope raced the slim black shadows of the *ullas*—and at the very crest, silhouetted for an instant before he dropped into the hollow beyond, was the Star-Beast with Thorana cradled in his mighty arms!

Up that long slope, and down, and up again—the Beast, the *ullas* and Korul far behind. As he topped each reaching wave, Korul could see that the hunting beasts were gaining steadily. Their prey in sight, their great legs had taken new strength.

And the Star-Beast was stumbling—slowing—*stopping!*

The Star-Beast's Lair

Where the red sand-waves broke, against the base of the first range of hills, a flat-topped ridge, ran out into the plain. With a heave of his great shoulders Jim-Berk lifted Thorana to its top, then crouched with his back against the rock, waiting.

Far behind the racing *ullas* Korul raised one trembling arm and tried to shout. The Star-Beast saw him. His hand went up in a last salute; then the hunters were on him.

He had wedged his broad back into a crevice where they could not come at him from the back or sides. As the first beast sprang, his foot lashed out and caught it in the belly, hurling it back into the pack. Before he could recover, he swung a fragment of rock above his head and sent it smashing into their midst, bowling two of the brutes end over end. One lay twitching, its flat skull crushed; the other writhed with a broken spine. Then, low under his guard, the other four closed in.

For a moment he towered over them, his red mane and flashing eyes rising out of a heap of glittering black, then he was down and fighting for his life. One arm flung across his throat for protection, he fought them off with the other and with his feet. He lay on his back, one of them striking at his throat, the others circling for an opening. Coolly he seized the *ulla* by its skull, his blunt fingers sinking into its glassy eyes, and as it struggled back in agony he plucked it from his body and swung it, hard, against the rock.

As the other beasts closed in, Korul flung himself, knife in hand, on the back of the nearest. The keen steel ripped out the monster's throat. Then he too had his back to the rock and was fighting for his life.

Berk was on his feet again, and as the first beast leaped he reached out with his long arms and caught it under the shoulders, thrusting it away. Hissing with fury it raked him with its long hind claws until the blood ran in stripes down his chest and thighs. Grimly he turned and drove it back against the ledge. There was a horrible crunching of bones and the thing went limp in his hands. Then, shouting encouragement, he pounced on the beast that had Korul down.

The Murian had wrapped his forearm in the folds of his cloak and thrust it between the *ulla*'s ravening jaws. Striking under its grasping forepaws, he was stabbing at the creature's horny belly, feeling for a vital spot between the armor-plates. Then the Star-Beast had the thing by its lashing tail and swung it in a great arc around his head, crashing its life out against the rock.

Wearily Korul pushed himself to his feet. The *ulla*'s fangs had cut through the thin cloak and lacerated his arm. Jim-Berk's huge hand came down on his shoulder with a hearty pat that nearly drove him to his knees again.

"You're a man, Korul!" the Star-Beast boomed. "There's not one on Erth could run all day, then go for a beast like that."

Stooping, he picked up a block of stone half Korul's size and smashed the skull of the crippled thing that lay hissing with a broken back. "Dumb thing!" he muttered. "Killing is all it's ever known. It tried hard to do what it was trained for."

He turned back to Korul. "Do you think you can give blood now? The girl had more than she could take, and I had to carry her. She doesn't have the strength you Givers have."

"She should have water, too," Korul said worriedly.

"She'll have water. It's the reason we went down into the tunnels in the beginning. There's a flask up there on the rock with her, still half-full. You little people don't seem to have the need for water that we do on Erth."

Laying Thorana in the shadow of the ledge where the heat was less, they gave her a little water and then blood until her strength came back. Scrambling to the top of the rock, Korul stared back over the dunes.

"Karak is out there," he pointed out. "By this time his men will have caught up with him, and they may have *ullas* with them. We can't stay here."

"We won't—be sure of that," the Star-Beast told him grimly. "This is the way I came before, and my ship's not far away. We'll have food and shelter there, and if Karak and his *lizrds* haven't had their fill of me, there are weapons that will make 'em think again!"

Helping Thorana to her feet, Korul took her arm and stepped out of the shadow of the rock. As the sun struck him, a wave of sickness surged up through his vitals, leaving his legs weak and shaky. He took two steps, then the red haze swirled down on him and the world went black.

The hills rose high and rugged around them when Korul came to himself again. They were old and worn, their slopes gentled by time. They swayed and rocked with a smooth, jogging rhythm, and suddenly he realized that the Beast was carrying him.

By all the gods, it was shameful! Korul, First Man of Mur, carried like a child! Jim-Berk only laughed.

"Be still about it," he said. "I'm only a beast by your standards, and on Erth we have beasts trained to carry us. You and this girl have trained me well enough. We were in a hurry, and she objected to leaving you there, so I brought you with us."

Deeper they went and deeper into the red, worn hills, following a trail that not even twenty of Mur's years had erased from Jim-Berk's memory. From time to time he would point out landmarks—an oddly shaped pinnacle of rock that was like some thing of Erth—a parti-colored cliff—the opening of a cave. Legend had it that the ancients had a sense of direction like this Erth-thing's, Korul knew, but it had long since been bred out of the race. Without Jim-Berk he and Thorana would never find their way back to the cities of their race.

At last they came to a cliff of deep red rock from which queer, lighter-colored, rounded knobs protruded.

"We'll be there in a *jifi,*" Jim-Berk told them. "This is the first place I found after I left the *rokt*. There's many a Searcher back home on Erth would be glad of a look at those bones. Your own kind too, I've no doubt."

"What bones?" Korul demanded. "I see nothing."

"Maybe so," the Star-Beast admitted, "but no race would get where yours is without knowing about fossil bones. There's no time now to fool with them, but those knobs and humps you're looking at are the dead bones of beasts that lived here before Erth had a moon, like as not, and that were buried and turned to stone. Come on, now—

up through here to the top and we'll see what there is to see."

They climbed a winding crevice in the rock to the summit of the cliff of bones. A broad plateau stretched out before them, haunted with grotesque monsters of wind-carved stones. Everywhere lay the bones, bigger than a man and strangely shaped. True enough, Korul found, some of them lay together in the shape of some gigantic *ulla* or *ganak*—but how could Jim-Berk be so sure that these things were not fantasies like the wind-shaped spires of the plain?

The Star-Beast was not concerning himself with bones. As he came out of the cleft, Jim-Berk took to his heels. Seizing Thorana's hand, Korul raced after him. A moment later they rounded a spur of rock, and there in a little hollow was the ship!

There had been nothing like it in all the long history of the people of Mur, Korul thought. Or had there been a time, long ago when the races were one people, when they too had wandered among the stars?

It was long and blunt-nosed, fashioned out of steel. Terrible heat had scarred and blackened it, and pitted it like the stones that sometimes fell out of the sky. Here and there small, heavy windows were set in the steel. Jim-Berk was working at one of them. It swung open, and he squeezed through into the dark interior. For a moment the two Murians hesitated, then as bright white lights blazed from the ports they crept up to the open hatch and looked inside.

They looked into a room tipped over on its side. Furniture, instruments, books were tumbled together in confusion. In what was now a wall, a metal ladder disappeared into the base of the ship, where twelve huge tubular jets showed on the outside.

Tottering precariously on a metal table, Jim-Berk was fumbling with the fastening on a door set in the thickness of the ship above his head. It opened suddenly, deluging him with little metal cylinders. With a growl he tried another. Hanging in this compartment were a number of queer-shaped garments of coarse cloth.

"I'll be with you in a moment," he shouted. "After forty years it's a great feeling to have on a pair of *pantz* again!"

Perched on the rim of the hatchway, Korul and Thorana watched him dress. Two layers of heavy cloth covered his hairy body from head to foot. A peaked blue cap went on his head, and on his feet he tried to pull queer, stiff boxes. After forty Erth years of nakedness, his feet were beyond the wearing of these *shuz.*

A queerly human figure in his stiff, dark garments, with the little cap set on his shaggy mane and his hands plunged into pouches in the sides of his *pantz,* the Star-Beast confronted his two guests.

"Well," he asked, "what do you think of me now? Less like an animal, eh? Welcome to *Terra!*"

"Terra?" Thorana questioned, puzzled.

"It's the name I gave the ship," he explained. "There are hundreds of different languages on Erth, and 'Terra' means 'Erth' in one of them. What do you call yourselves as a lot—Masters and Blood-Givers together, I mean—the whole race?"

"There is no such word in our language today," Thorana said slowly. "We haven't been so ready to admit that the two peoples came from one stock. But I have seen a word in the old books . . ."

"Murtas," Korul told him. "Sons of Mur."

"It's a good name," Berk said. "Better than we have. Erth is a world with many races and many languages, and a different name in each one. *Mankind* we say—or *men* —or *man*—for the kind of animal we all are—but its different in every language.

"There's an old word, though, in the legends, that I've always liked. It's the name of a race of giants who were the sons of Erth. *Titans,* they were called, and there were some great men among them. One of them showed men how to make fire.

"Now that we're finding our way out here into the emptiness where the planets are, and the sun and stars, that's a name I'd be proud to have used for men and men like me. *Titan!* Sounds big and powerful, doesn't it—and that's the way we men from Erth are and always will be. Do you like it, you two—Titans? What do you say?"

"It is a good word," Thorana agreed. "Better than Star-Beasts. But for yourself, we must use your own name—Jim-Berk, the Titan."

"Not the whole of it," he pleaded. "Not Jim-Berk, run

together like it was a name out of the Good Book. Jim, my friends call me—only Jim. Will you do that?"

Little by little, the Titan managed to put the confusion of his ship into order. The two Murians were of little help. Korul was greatly interested in the apparatus with which the craft was propelled, while Thorana poured over his books. They were printed on a rough white fabric which the Titan said came from the matted fibers from the stems of the huge plants of his world. *Paypr* he called it.

Some of the books had *paypr* covers, and in them Thorana found pictures more wonderful than anything she had seen outside the museums of the Searchers. All the teeming life and civilization of Erth was there—people like Jim, dressed as strangely and gaudily as the little creatures he called *brdz*—towering buildings of stone and steel—machines that carried hundreds of people from place to place, as their *tlornaks* carried one or two. Once there had been such machines on Mur, Thorana knew, before the world grew dry and the People retreated to the gorges.

Erth was a world of beautiful strangeness to those two. They remembered what the Star-Beast had told them of the seas of Erth, and here they were in truth—seas, and deep blue lakes, and rivers that carved their way through mighty forested hills that raised snow-capped crests against the sky. To Thorana it was like opening the past, for all these things had been on Mur in ancient times. She begged Jim-Berk to leave these books behind, to show to the Searchers who knew about such things.

As the day passed, Korul was sure that Karak must have turned back or lost their trail. Autumn Night had come and gone: had the Change come with it? Were the Masters only an ugly memory now, on all the face of Mur, save only here in the Star-Beast's lair where Thorana lived and regained her strength?

They would know soon.

Jim's *rokt* had to be made ready for his return to Erth. With spades and powerful explosives they opened a pit under its base and toppled it in until the ship stood upright, its open hatchway at the level of the ground. Across the mountains, only a short distance away, was the second gorge. Now that the sluices had been opened there should be water there. While Korul and Thorana kept watch at the *rokt,* Jim-Berk set out across the plateau to the east. A day later he was back, flasks of water slung all around him with the news that the gorge-city was deserted.

After six days Jim had enough water to fill his empty reservoirs. He would never let Korul or Thorana accompany him. What he found in the abandoned city he did not say, nor did they ask him.

The books from Erth were a never ending source of fascination to Thorana. Jim showed them the key to his written language: twenty-six symbols which stood for twenty-six sounds in the tongue his people spoke. The same symbols, he said, could be used to write down the languages of other peoples, though not always as exactly as they would like. Some of them had symbols of their own. He drew a few from memory that seemed no more and no less arbitrary than the ones in which the books were written.

Thorana soon learned the sounds of these twenty-six symbols. She liked to sound out the words under the pictures, while Jim-Berk gave her the meanings in her own tongue. In a little time she was able to talk to him in his own rough *Inglis.*

Korul felt much neglected during these little colloquies. He would see a broad grin creeping over Jim-Berk's bearded face as he listened to Thorana stumbling through one of his uncouth phrases, then the Titan would burst into a great roar of laughter that rocked the ship and call her some outlandish name in his own tongue that brought the blood to the girl's face in confusion. Or they would talk about him—Korul—both of them laughing, until he brought the fire to Thorana's eyes and Jim-Berk's thunderous laughter roaring through the ship by using the secret code-talk of the Elders.

Thorana seemed content to ignore the revolt and what might be happening across the mountains and the desert, in the gorge cities of her people. Family ties meant very little to the Masters, except as an index of social position, and the girl had been a monster to most of her kind. Such children, Korul knew, were often killed at birth to save their parents from embarrassment when they grew up with legs and the other stigmata of atavism.

It was a pleasant life, there in the Titan's sky-ship, but it could not last. Berk and Thorana worked over the books and diagrams which told him when he must leave Mur. He brought out a small telescope, such as some of the Searchers had, and showed them Erth, his planet, a silvery, shadowed crescent against the night. Erth was Ulra—star and goddess of love to all the generations of Mur, Masters and Givers alike. To Korul it seemed an omen for good.

When the Erth crescent was of such-and-such a thinness Jim-Berk must leave Mur, they decided. That would be very soon. And he knew, as they knew, that without his help they would never reach the pole alone.

The books and instruments which he would not need were hidden in a crevice near the ship, where Korul could find them again. Food and water for five days were put into Berk's big pack. He wanted the Murtas to carry no more than their own weight, or at most a little water. They would travel fastest that way, he assured Korul.

A few days before they were to leave, he gave Thorana blood again. She objected, but Jim-Berk insisted. She would need all the strength her woman's body could hold.

The Polar Sluices

Jim-Berk seemed to know the way, and the going was easy after they left the hills. They went down to the nearer gorge, along the route he had followed in getting water. An ancient road followed the edge of the crevice from city to empty city, straight to the polar sluiceways. By common consent, they did not go down into the cities except at night, when they went far enough into the empty upper levels to protect themselves from the cold.

"It's an end to fighting that both our worlds need most, Korul," the Titan said wistfully one night. "With this trouble of yours done and over, and young men and thinkers making good laws to replace the bad old ones Mur can dig up what it has forgotten and fit it to the little bit of news that I've left you. You'll be a great, wise planet as we've always dreamed of you back on Erth. Not that you're not good enough for me as you are, but there's a lot you can learn and be the better for it.

"Then some day you'll see us dropping out of the sky again—me or my sons or their sons—real men you can talk to, and trust like you do me. There'll be the two of you here to spread the word about us, and I'll do as much for you back on Erth. This time there'll be no cages, and in no time at all there'll be great ships coming and going like bees between us, carrying the richness and sweetness of the one world to the other.

"Ah, the star-gazers I've known in my life that would give their souls and the taxpayers' riches a dozen times over for one of your clear, bright nights—and there'll be poets and painters among you who have longed down through the years for the rumble of the sea-waves on the rocks or the singing of the wind high up in the tall pines. Ah, there's a thousand things will bring them flocking down out of the skies to you, and you to us! It's the dream that was in my head all the years ago—and now I'm going back again, to see human faces and hear human voices, and to be under a blue sky with a bit of green under my feet."

"There will be someone waiting for you on Erth, Jim-Berk?" Thorana asked gently.

"After forty years? Small chance of that. I had a father and a mother there who thought me wild and a bit mad, and a girl who was sure I was touched in the head. For all that, they were mine and they'd wait and watch for me for a year, or maybe five—but then the days would come creeping on, and the hope in them begin to fade.

"The girl would go first, I'm thinking. She was a sensible piece, for all she'd taken up with me, and she could have her choice of the men once she'd made up her mind it was the thing to do. As for the others—well, what's twenty of your years are close to forty back on Erth, and it's not likely they'll be alive. You've taken good care of me in your infernal cage and the years have laid a light hand on me here, but better than sixty years is good living for one of our race on Erth.

"No, Thorana, there'll be no one to welcome me as close as you two are, but they'll be my own kind. I'll see to them, and you see to your own breed here so that when my grandchildren and yours meet again out there in the desert, there'll be no nonsense of Sky-Beasts and cages between them!"

As the days followed the nights, the road climbed above the rift-line and went winding through the low hills which closed in the polar basin. It came out at last high on a bare hillside, and there before them were the great dams and the ice.

Only scattered white patches of upland snow were left where the polar cap had been lying across the dark hills like the clouds of Erth that were in Jim's book. At their base was the dark network of swampland, green with new life, and far below where the waters reached the plain was the black line of the dam.

When the ancients knew that water and air were leaving Mur, they built their chain of dams at either pole to hold back the water of the melting frosts until, through the great sluices that run deep under the gorges, they could be pumped to every part of the dying planet. Korul remembered it as a place of solemn stillness, brooding with the lost wisdom of the past—but now the curving wall of the giant dam was swarming with the tiny black shapes of men, and steel flickered in the autumn sunlight. A dark wave surged up and broke against the breast of the dam, rose halfway to its crest, then dropped away as a net of shimmering silver wavered over it.

It was war!

Jim-Berk came out of his revery. "What's happening?" he demanded.

Korul told him. "Torkul, who keeps the sluices, is my friend. We wanted to bring back the old ways gently, with the help of the Searchers—not by killing and hate. And Karak is no man to stand differences of opinion among his leaders."

"With Torkul holding the gates, Mur will go without water for half a year if he chooses," Thorana pointed out. "If Tatok is with him, in the South, and Karak cannot break their defense, they hold Mur in the hollow of their palm."

"If your Torkul has the men and the will, he can hold that wall against an army," the Titan said. "Korul—if you're with him, and Karak knows it, there'll be more of the fear of the Lord in his black heart. Have you been here? How does the land lie?"

Korul pointed. "The plain is a maze of shallow gullies and ravines. You can see them as dark lines against the red, because the water follows them and plants grow there. They should give me cover enough to creep up in Karak's rear, then run for the dam when he next attacks."

"And be picked off by Torkul's best bowman, I have no doubt," the Titan said grimly. "Is there any signal that will let them know who you are?"

"By the gods, there is! Torkul and I used a cry when we were boys together that made the levels ring. 'Mur! Murata! *Mur!*' Gods, how the Masters hated it. He'll know it still."

"Come on then," the giant rumbled. "Keep to cover, and when I shout, run for the dam."

Thorana seized his sleeve. "Wait!" she cried. "You can't go with us! We may be penned up there for days, and you have barely time to get back to your ship. We owe you enough now, Jim-Berk—go back to Erth while you still can. This is our affair."

He shook her gently off. "But for that little tussle with the *ullas,* I've not had a good fight for upward of forty years," he said grandly. "I owe your friend Karak something from all three of us, and I have a little toy here at my hip that may come as a surprise to him. If it's the ship that's bothering you, it's well hidden and another year more or less won't matter to it. I'd like to see what your scientists make of me, anyway, now they know what they're looking at. Come on—if we wait much longer the sun will be down on us, and a day wasted is a day lost."

The Titan

The sun was well down in the west when they crept up through the scarred plain behind Karak's camp. All day they had been hammering the wall with those savage attacks, trying by brute force to break through Torkul's defense. Now they were gathering for what would be a last attack before night closed down and they took cover from the cold.

Karak himself led them. Peering from behind a pinnacle of crumbling clay, Korul decided that he looked less omnipotent than on the day when he had begged for Thorana's life. He was ranging back and forth among his men, bunching them into some sort of order. As the ranks took shape, his plan became evident. Swordsmen would charge under a barrage of arrows, and the bowmen would attack when the first wave fell back.

And then—they.

The gabble of Karak's forces faded away into deathly stillness, then with a shout the big man leaped forward toward the dam. With the twang of steel-bows behind them and the whistle of bolts over their heads, his swordsmen sprang after him.

It was as though two waves flowed together. Down from the top of the dam came Torkul's men to meet the advancing swordsmen. A little above the center they met with a clang of steel. The thin line of defenders held, perched on the sheer face where Karak's men must claw their way upward block by block. They held, then the attackers broke and fled—and at Karak's shout, out of the gullies poured his bowmen, their squat bows hurling buzzing death at the men who stood in a huddled mass halfway up the face of the great dam.

Up the black wall, striking a shower of fire from the stone, beat the hail of steel bolts, with Torkul's line retreating slowly before it. Higher they were driven—higher—then with a shout the bowmen drew their swords, and at the same moment Torkul and his men fell flat against the rock-face, while over them hurtled a barrage of flickering steel from hidden arches at the crest.

The black wave faltered—slowed—and tumbled back in wild confusion while Torkul and his swordsmen leaped behind them bringing quick death to the laggards. And at Jim-Berk's cry the three sprang from their shelter and raced toward the milling host.

One of the fugitives saw them, pounding through the half-light, and recognized the Titan's giant shape.

"The Beast!" he screamed. "The Beast!"

A startled hush fell over the fighters; then out of it came the Titan's roaring voice, thundering their battle-cry: "Mur! Murata! *Mur!*"

Korul's voice echoed it, and Thorana's shrilled above them both. And from where Torkul's men stood, puzzled, at the dam-front the answer came:

"Mur! *Mur!* MUR!"

Then they were at them.

In the Titan's hand appeared a squat weapon of blued steel with a stubby muzzle. As Karak's men turned on them, it roared with a battering death that tore into their bodies and sent them reeling out of the path. Into the gap raced the Titan, Korul behind him with Thorana close at his back. Then as Karak's howl of rage went up, they closed in with ready swords on every side.

There is a saying among the Givers: A dead man's sword will make more dead men. Korul and Thorana armed themselves, and as the Titan's weapon failed and he began to push new projectiles into its magazine, they raised a shield of darting steel behind him. Then the *gun* roared again over their heads, and Karak's men fell back.

They could not go far. The weight of rushing men behind them drove them on. Unable to retreat, they had to fight. With a shout of rage the Titan scooped up the two Murians, one under each arm, and plunged headlong at the line of steel that separated them from the dam.

The utter fury of it took them through. Torkul's defenders closed in around them, but hot on their heels pounded Karak's howling, cursing host in one irresistible bolt of certain death.

Over the din thundered the Star-Beast's voice: "Run! Up the dam if you like your life!"

And they ran, Jim-Berk clambering ponderously after them. They reached the line of the first stand, passed it, spilled over Torkul's barricades into a clamoring host that at Torkul's word sprang to their places and loosed a hail of steel on the attackers.

Korul looked around him. The Titan was not there!

His cry checked the bowmen and brought Torkul to his side at the top of the barricade. Halfway down the slope Jim-Berk was holding Karak's wedge of steel.

He had stopped behind the line of dead. Piling their bodies into a human breastwork, he loaded his weapon—then was up again, gigantic in the twilight, flame spitting from his roaring death-frail, crumpling them up in agony, choking the narrow ledges of the dam-face with lifeless bodies. Close-packed as through body after body, bringing them down in swaths.

Three times he rose and drove them back. The fourth time his *gun* roared twice and stopped. He hurled it in their faces, then dropped on his haunches behind his wall of dead while over him sang the steel hail of Karak's bows, sweeping the rock face and cutting off his retreat.

There in the shelter of the dead Jim-Berk garnered a sheaf of swords. Again they rushed the dam, and as Karak's barrage lifted to let them through he sprang to his feet and with deadly accuracy hurled them, one by one, into the faces of the attacking men. Ten men he brought down, spitted by ten swords: the last he kept, and with it charged down the dam-face at the climbing foe.

He was a giant, and his sword seemed to blaze with the white fire of Death itself, but they outnumbered him by hundreds. Thorana was screaming in his own strange tongue, and his own voice roared back in gleeful laughter. Snatching a sword Korul was over the top of the dam, Torkul at his side, the defenders screaming after them.

They were too late. Streaming, panic-stricken, Karak's men broke and fled from the attack of the Star-Thing, with the Titan, a bloody, grinning spectre of destruction at their heel. Behind them Karak stood with his bowmen, and as his swordsmen broke they swept the slope with a hail of death that beat fiercely about the giant figure of the Titan.

They saw the blood spurt where the heavy bolts plowed into his body. They saw his massive frame quiver as each bolt struck. But still he laughed, and still the momentum of his charge carried him after the fleeing swordsmen, slashed at them with a sword that ran red to the hilt.

Thorana screamed. The Titan's charge had stopped. He stood towering over the frightened faces of Karak's bowmen then slowly, like a falling monolith, he went down among them, dead.

They ran. Korul and Torkul left them scattered over the plain, hiding like rats in the gullies, shivering in the deepening night. As the cold deepened they crept out, whimpering for mercy, and got it or the sword according to the humor of the guard whom they approached.

Karak had escaped. His own men told how he had run from the last wild charge of the dying Star-Beast. They would help hunt him down. The fear of the Titan, and the memory of his awful laughter, lay on them like death.

They carried him back to the shelter of Torkul's barricade, his bearded lips still grinning at the sky where Ulra—his Erth—swam bright and clear among the cold, far stars. They watched beside him through the night, as was the old custom, while the greater moon of Mur rose out of the dying sky-glow and raced in silent fear across the wan river of the galaxy.

Above the black wall of the hills, a meteor burned and went out. Thorana snuggled close to Korul's side.

"That should have been he," she murmured. "Jim-Berk, going home to the Erth he loved. We must have been monsters to him, Korul, as he was to us. How did he see us—dwarfed, hairless, saucer-eyed, hideous things out of a fevered dream. But he, the Star-Beast whom we mocked and imprisoned and tormented for more than half his life, saw us and understood. He could have gone back, but he stayed to help us. We must be like that, Korul, when the new race grows strong. We must be ready when the Titans come again in their starships.

"They may have forgotten you on Earth, Jim-Berk, as you said they would. But Mur remembers you, and the people—the one People—of Mur will build truth into your dream. If they do not come to us, then some day we will go to Erth.

"How did he say it, Korul? 'Flocking down out of the skies to you—and you to us.' That is how it must be, for the Titan's sake."

5

•

Becoming More Alien

A UNIVERSAL HOME TRUTH

There are times when you are at an impressionable age when science fiction can scare the living daylights out of you.

On the last occasion that that happened to me, I was reading *The Possessors,* by an author for whom I have considerable respect, John Christopher. *The Possessors,* in case you have not had the pleasure of reading it, is a grand working out of the theme of aliens who can take over or exactly simulate human beings for their own malign ends. It is one of the most compelling of all sf themes, with a high terror quota.

A Freudian interpretation of the theme would be interesting; the idea implies, after all, a paranoid mistrust of one's fellow men. But such interpretation would be beside the point unless it was remembered that the height of the theme's popularity coincided with the depths of the Cold War—when, in fact, one half of mankind hated and sought to destroy the other half without actually resorting to outright war.

Many themes which find popular expression in sf share the same mixture of inwardness and outwardness; neither one is particularly effective without the other.

Sf writers and readers work on each other by stating and restating themes. There is now a clearer realization than ever before of man himself being no less strange than the guy on the next planet. The old Us and Them situation has softened into something much more ambivalent. It too has its rewards for a writer.

Hence the inclusion here of Bob Silverberg's most beautiful story, "Schwartz Between the Galaxies." A sort of dissolving has gone on. The modernity of the story holds great appeal for us now; I have no doubt that time will work its transformations on the story, as on "Brightside Crossing," for example; so that in another ten years we shall see it from another perspective—and undoubtedly still find it good.

Schwartz—oh yes, Schwartz is cosmopolitan. Cosmopolitan and alienated. The power of the story derives from Schwartz's feeling on the subject. I must apologize for the planet on which Frederik Pohl's cameo is set; I hope it is perilous enough to satisfy all tastes. Those dreadful people, Tandy and Howard are not at all cosmopolitan, not at all alienated. They uncomplicatedly enjoy life. And that's what makes "The Snowmen" a powerful story.

Some more awful people inhabit the narrow wastes of Spinrad's tale. You could claim that it takes place on Earth, and consequently should find no place here. But think, as you laugh, that there is something terribly universal about its home-truths.

Is that yet another definition of science fiction: a universal home truth? I leave the question with others, hastening to say of Damon Knight's "Four in One" that it contains a planet where the wild life is odd indeed. Yet the wild life functions much like society on Earth; it can digest you, make you, break you, or ultimately excrete you. The message is much more fun when set in Knight's madly imaginative terms. Home truths are often more amusing when not at home.

"Four in One" comes from the same epoch as Simak's "Beachhead." The situation is roughly the same. Simak's characters are dead ducks if they move outside the rugged military posture; Knight's, on the other hand, find salvation simple by moving out. Or falling out, one should say.

From this you may make your own deductions.

Just don't venture too far from the spaceship.

George realized he was lucky. He fell into something scientists dream of—he was able to become completely absorbed in his work!

FOUR IN ONE

by Damon Knight

I

George Meister had once seen the nervous system of a man—a display specimen, achieved by coating the smaller fibers until they were coarse enough to be seen, then dissolving all the unwanted tissue and replacing it by clear plastic. A marvelous job; that fellow on Torkas III had done it. What was his name? . . . At any rate, having seen the specimen, Meister knew what he himself must look like at the present moment.

Of course, there were distortions. For examples, he was almost certain that the distance between his visual center and his eyes was now at least thirty centimeters. Also, no doubt the system as a whole was curled up and spread out rather oddly, since the musculature it had originally controlled was gone; and he had noticed certain other changes which might or might not be reflected by gross structural differences. The fact remained that he—all that he could still call *himself*—was nothing more than a brain, a pair of eyes, a spinal cord, and a spray of neurons.

George closed his eyes for a second. It was a feat he had learned to do only recently and he was proud of it. That first long period, when he had had no control whatever, had been very bad. He had decided later that the paralysis had been due to the lingering effects of some anesthetic—the agent, whatever it was, that had kept him unconscious while his body was—

Well.

Either that or the neuron branches had simply not yet

knitted firmly in their new positions. Perhaps he could verify one or the other supposition at some future time. But at first, when he had only been able to see and not to move, knowing nothing beyond the moment when he had fallen face-first into that mottled green and brown puddle of gelatin . . . that had been upsetting.

He wondered how the others were taking it. There were others, he knew, because occasionally he would feel a sudden acute pain down where his legs used to be, and at the same instant the motion of the landscape would stop with a jerk. That could only be some other brain, trapped like his, trying to move their common body in another direction.

Usually the pain stopped immediately, and George could go on sending messages down to the nerve-endings which had formerly belonged to his fingers and toes, and the gelatinous body would go on creeping slowly forward. When the pains continued, there was nothing to do but stop moving until the other brain quit—in which case George would feel like an unwilling passenger in a very slow vehicle—or try to alter his own movements to coincide, or at least produce a vector with the other brain's.

He wondered who else had fallen in. Vivian Bellis! Major Gumbs? Miss McCarty? All three of them? There ought to be some way of finding out.

He tried looking down once more and was rewarded with a blurry view of a long, narrow strip of mottled green and brown, moving sluggishly along the dry stream bed they had been crossing for the last hour or more. Twigs and shreds of dry vegetable matter were stuck to the dusty, translucent surface.

He was improving; the last time, he had only been able to see the thinnest possible edge of his new body.

When he looked up again, the far side of the stream bed was perceptibly closer. There was a cluster of stiff-looking, dark-brown vegetable shoots just beyond, on the rocky shoulder. George was aiming slightly to the left of it. It had been a plant very much like that one that he'd been reaching for when he lost his balance and got himself into this situation.

He might as well have a good look at it, anyhow.

The plant would probably turn out to be of little interest.

It would be out of all reason to expect every new life-form to be a startling novelty; and George Meister was convinced that he had already stumbled into the most interesting organism on this planet. Something-or-other *meisterii,* he thought, named after him, of course. He had not settled on a generic term—he would have to learn more about it before he decided—but *meisterii* certainly. It was his discovery and nobody could take it away from him. Or, unhappily, him away from it. Ah, well!

It was a really lovely organism, though. Primitive—less structure of its own than a jellyfish, and only on a planet with light surface gravity like this one could it ever have hauled itself up out of the sea. No brain, no nervous system at all, apparently. But it had the perfect survival mechanism. It simply let its rivals develop highly organized nervous tissue, sat in one place (looking exactly like a deposit of leaves and other clutter) until one of them fell into it, and then took all the benefit.

It wasn't parasitism, either. It was a true symbiosis, on a higher level than any other planet, so far as George knew, had ever developed. The captive brain was nourished by the captor; wherefore it served the captive's interest to move the captor toward food and away from danger. *You steer me, I feed you.* It was fair.

They were close to the plant, almost touching it. George inspected it. As he had thought, it was a common grass type.

Now his body was tilting itself up a ridge he knew to be low, although from his eye-level it looked tremendous. He climbed it laboriously and found himself looking down into still another gully. This could probably go on indefinitely. The question was—did he have any choice?

He looked at the shadows cast by the low-hanging sun. He was heading approximately northwest, directly away from the encampment. He was only a few hundred meters away; even at a crawl, he could make the distance easily enough . . . if he turned back.

He felt uneasy at the thought and didn't know why. Then it struck him that his appearance was not obviously that of a human being in distress. The chances were that he looked like a monster which had eaten and partially digested one or more people.

If he crawled into camp in his present condition, it was a certainty that he would be shot at before any questions were asked, and only a minor possibility that narcotic gas would be used instead of a machine rifle.

No, he decided, he was on the right course. The idea was to get away from camp, so that he wouldn't be found by the relief party which was probably searching for him now. Get away, bury himself in the forest, and study his new body: find out how it worked and what he could do with it, whether there actually were others in it with him, and if so, whether there was any way of communicating with them.

It would take a long time, he realized, but he could do it.

Limply, like a puddle of mush oozing over the edge of a tablecloth, George started down into the gully.

Briefly, the circumstances leading up to George's fall into the Something-or-other *meisterii* were as follows:

Until as late as the mid-twenty-first century, a game invented by the ancient Japanese was still played by millions in the eastern hemisphere of earth. The game was called *go*. Although its rules were almost childishly simple, its strategy included more permutations and was more difficult to master than chess.

Go was played at the height of development—just before the geological catastrophe that wiped out most of its devotees—on a board with nine hundred shallow holes, using small gill shaped counters. At each turn, one of the two players placed a counter on the board, wherever he chose, the object being to capture as much territory as possible by surrounding it completely.

There were no other rules; and yet it had taken the Japanese almost a thousand years to work up to that thirty-by-thirty board, adding perhaps one rank and file per century. A hundred years was not too long to explore all the possibilities of that additional rank and file.

At the time George Meister fell into the gelatinous green-and-brown monster, toward the end of the twenty-third century AD, a kind of *go* was being played in a three-dimensional field which contained more than ten billion positions. The Galaxy was the board, the positions were star-systems, men were the counters. The loser's penalty was annihilation.

The Galaxy was in the process of being colonized by two opposing federations, both with the highest aims and principles. In the early stages of this conflict, planets had been raided, bombs dropped, and a few battles had even been fought by fleets of spaceships. Later, that haphazard sort of warfare became impossible. Robot fighters, carrying enough armament to blow each other into dust, were produced by the trillion. In the space around the outer stars of a cluster belonging to one side or the other, they swarmed like minnows.

Within such a screen, planets were safe from attack and from any interference with their commerce . . . unless the enemy succeeded in colonizing enough of the surrounding star-systems to set up and maintain a second screen outside the first. It was *go,* played for desperate stakes and under impossible conditions.

Everyone was in a hurry; everyone's ancestors for seven generations had been in a hurry. You got your education in a speeded-up capsulized form. You mated early and bred frantically. And if you were assigned to an advance ecological team, as George was, you had to work without proper preparation.

The sensible, the obvious thing to do in opening up a new planet with unknown life-forms would have been to begin with at least ten years of immunological study conducted from the inside of a sealed station. After the worst bacteria and viruses had been conquered, you might proceed to a little cautious field work and exploration. Finally—total elapsed time fifty years, say—the colonists would be shipped in.

There simply wasn't that much time.

Five hours after the landing Meister's team had unloaded fabricators and set up barracks enough to house its 2,628 members.

An hour after that, Meister, Gumbs, Bellis and McCarty had started out across the level cinder and ash left by the transport's tail jets to the nearest living vegetation, six hundred meters away. They were to trace a spiral path outward from the camp site to a distance of a thousand meters, and then return with their specimens—providing nothing too large and hungry to be stopped by machine rifle had previously eaten them.

Meister, the biologist, was so hung down with collecting boxes that his slender torso was totally invisible. Major Gumbs had a survival kit, binoculars and a machine rifle. Vivian Bellis, who knew exactly as much mineralogy as had been contained in the three-month course prescribed for her rating, and no more, carried a light rifle, a hammer and a specimen sack. Miss McCarty—no one knew her first name—had no scientific function. She was the group's Loyalty Monitor. She wore two squat pistols and a bandolier bristling with cartridges. Her only job was to blow the cranium off any team member caught using an unauthorized communicator, or in any other way behaving oddly.

All of them were heavily gloved and booted, and their heads were covered by globular helmets, sealed to their tunic collars. They breathed through filtered respirators, so finely meshed that—in theory—nothing larger than an oxygen molecule could get through.

On their second circuit of the camp, they had struck a low ridge and a series of short, steep gullies, most of them cloaked with the dusty-brown stalks of dead vegetation. As they started down into one of these, George, who was third in line—Gumbs leading, then Bellis, and McCarty behind George—stepped out onto a protruding slab of stone to examine a cluster of plant stalks rooted on its far side.

His weight was only a little more than twenty kilograms on this planet, and the slab looked as if it were firmly cemented into the wall of the gully. Just the same, he felt it shift under him as soon as his weight was fully on it. He found himself falling, shouted, and caught a flashing glimpse of Gumbs and Bellis, standing as if caught by a high-speed camera. He heard a rattling of stones as he went by. Then he saw what looked like a shabby blanket of leaves and dirt floating toward him, and he remembered thinking, *It looks like a soft landing anyhow . . .*

That was all, until he woke up feeling as if he had been prematurely buried, with no part of him alive but his eyes.

Much later, his frantic efforts to move had resulted in the first fractional success. From then on, his field of vision had advanced fairly steadily, perhaps a meter every fifty minutes, not counting the times when someone else's efforts had interfered with his own.

His conviction that nothing remained of the old George Meister except a nervous system was not supported by observation, but the evidence was regrettably strong. To begin with, the anesthesia of the first hours had worn off, but his body was not reporting the position of the torso, head and four limbs he had formerly owned. He had, instead, a vague impression of being flattened and spread out over an enormous area. When he tried to move his fingers and toes, the response he got was so multiplied that he felt like a centipede.

He had no sense of cramped muscles, such as would normally be expected after a long period of paralysis—*and he was not breathing.* Yet his brain was evidently being well supplied with food and oxygen; he felt clearheaded, at ease and healthy.

He wasn't hungry, either, although he had been using energy steadily for a long time. There were, he thought, two possible reasons for that, depending on how you looked at it. One, that he wasn't hungry because he no longer had any stomach lining to contract; two, that he wasn't hungry because the organism he was riding in had been well nourished by the superfluous tissues George had contributed.

Two hours later, when the sun was setting, it began to rain. George saw the big, slow-falling drops and felt their dull impacts on his "skin." He didn't know whether rain would do him any damage or not, but crawled under a bush with large, fringed leaves just to be on the safe side. When the rain stopped, it was night and he decided he might as well stay where he was until morning. He did not feel tired, and it occurred to him to wonder whether he still needed to sleep. He composed himself as well as he could to wait for the answer.

He was still wakeful after a long time had passed, but had made no progress toward deciding whether this answered the question or prevented it from being answered, when he saw a pair of dim lights coming slowly and erratically toward him.

* * *

George watched them with an attentiveness compounded of professional interest and apprehension. Gradually, as they came closer, he made out that the lights were attached to long, thin stalks which grew from an ambiguous shape below—either light organs, like those of some deep-sea fish, or simply luminescent eyes.

George noted a feeling of tension in himself which seemed to suggest that adrenalin or an equivalent was being released somewhere in his system. He promised himself to follow this lead at the first possible moment; meanwhile, he had a more urgent problem to consider. Was this approaching organism the kind which the Something *meisterii* ate, or the kind which devoured the Something *meisterii?* If the latter, what could he do about it?

For the present, at any rate, sitting where he was seemed to be indicated. The body he inhabited made use of camouflage in its normal, or untenanted state, and was not equipped for speed. So George held still and watched, keeping his eyes half closed, while he considered the possible nature of the approaching animal.

The fact that it was nocturnal, he told himself, meant nothing. Moths were nocturnal; so were bats—no, the devil with bats, they were carnivores.

The light-bearing creature came nearer, and George saw the faint gleam of a pair of long, narrow eyes below the two stalks.

Then the creature opened its mouth.

It had a great many teeth.

George found himself crammed into some kind of crevice in a wall of rock, without any clear recollection of how he had got there. He remembered a flurry of branches as the creature sprang at him, and a moment's furious pain, and nothing but vague, starlit glimpses of leaves and soil.

How had he got away?

He puzzled over it until dawn came, and then, looking down at himself, he saw something that had not been there before. Under the smooth edge of gelatinous flesh, three or four projections of some kind were visible. It struck George that his sensation of contact with the stone underneath him had changed, too. He seemed to be standing on a number of tin points instead of lying flat.

He flexed one of the projections experimentally, then thrust it out straight ahead of him. It was a lumpy, single-jointed caricature of a finger or a leg.

II

Lying still for a long time, George Meister thought about it with as much coherence as he could muster. Then he waggled the limb again. It was there, and so were all the others, as solid and real as the rest of him.

He moved forward experimentally, sending the same messages down to his finger-and-toe nerve-ends as before. His body lurched out of the cranny with a swiftness that very nearly tumbled him down over the edge of a minor precipice.

Where he had crawled like a snail before, he now scuttled like an insect.

But how? No doubt, in his terror when the thing with the teeth attacked, he had unconsciously tried to run as if he still had legs. Was that all there was to it?

George thought of the carnivore again, and of the stalks supporting the organs which he had thought might be eyes. That would do as an experiment. He closed his eyes and imagined them rising outward, imagined the mobile stalks growing, growing . . . He tried to convince himself that he had eyes like that, had always had them, that everyone who was anyone had eyes on stalks.

Surely, something was happening.

George opened his eyes again and found himself looking straight down at the ground, getting a view so close that it was blurred, out of focus. Impatiently, he tried to look up. All that happened was that his field of vision moved forward a matter of ten or twelve centimeters.

It was at this point that a voice shattered the stillness. It sounded like someone trying to shout through half a meter of lard. "Urghh! Lluhh! *Eeraghh!*"

George leaped convulsively, executed a neat turn and swept his eyes around a good two hundred and forty degrees of arc. He saw nothing but rocks and lichens. On a closer inspection, it appeared that a small green and orange larva or grub of some kind was moving past him. George regarded it with suspicion for a long moment, until the voice broke out again:

"Ellfff! Elffneee!"

The voice, somewhat higher this time, came from behind. George whirled again, swept his eyes around—

Around an impossibly wide circuit. His eyes *were* on stalks, and they were mobile whereas a moment ago he had been staring at the ground, unable to look up. George's brain clattered into high gear. He had grown stalks for his eyes all right, but they'd been limp, just extensions of the jelly-like mass of his body, without a stiffening cell-structure or muscular tissue, to move them. Then, when the voice had startled him, he'd got the stiffening and the muscles in a hurry.

That must have been what had happened the previous night. Probably the process would have been completed, but much more slowly, if he hadn't been frightened. A protective mechanism, obviously. As for the voice—

George rotated once more, slowly, looking all around him. There was no question about it; he was alone. The voice, which had seemed to come from someone or something standing just behind him, must in fact have issued from his own body.

The voice started again, at a less frantic volume. It burbled a few times, then said quite clearly in a high tenor, "Whass happen'? Wheh am I?"

George was floundering in enough bewilderment. He was in no condition to adapt quickly to more new circumstances, and when a large, dessicated lump fell from a nearby bush and bounced soundlessly to within a meter of him, he simply stared at it.

He looked at the hard-shelled object and then at the laden bush from which it had dropped. Slowly, painfully, he worked his way through to a logical conclusion. The dried fruit had fallen without a sound. This was natural, because he had been totally deaf ever since his metamorphosis. But he had heard a voice!

Ergo, hallucination or telepathy.

The voice began again. "Help! Oh, dear, I wish someone would answer!"

Vivian Bellis. Gumbs, even if he affected that tenor voice, wouldn't say, "Oh, dear." Neither would Miss McCarty.

George's shaken nerves were returning to normal. He

thought intently, *I get scared, grow legs. Bellis gets scared, grows a telepathic voice. That's reasonable, I guess—her first and only impulse would be to yell.*

George tried to put himself into a yelling mood. He shut his eyes and imagined himself cooped up in a terrifying alien medium, without any control or knowledge of his predicament. He tried to shout: "Vivian!"

He went on trying, while the girl's voice continued at intervals. Finally she stopped abruptly in the middle of a sentence.

George said, "Can you hear me?"

"Who's that? What do you want?"

"This is George Meister, Vivian. Can you understand what I'm saying?"

"What—"

George kept at it. His pseudo-voice, he judged, was a little garbled, just as Bellis's had been at first. At last the girl said, "Oh, George—I mean Mr. Meister! Oh, I've been so frightened. Where are you?"

George explained, apparently not very tactfully, because Bellis shrieked when he was through and then went back to burbling.

George sighed, and said, "Is there anyone else on the premises? Major Gumbs? Miss McCarty? Can you hear me?"

A few minutes later two sets of weird sounds began almost simultaneously. When they became coherent, it was no trouble to identify the voices.

Gumbs, the big, red-faced professional soldier, shouted, "Why the hell don't you watch where you're going, Meister? If you hadn't started that rock-slide, we wouldn't be in this mess!"

Miss McCarty, who had a grim white face, a jutting jaw, and eyes the color of mud, said coldly, "Meister, all of this will be reported. *All* of it."

It appeared that only Meister and Gumbs had kept the use of their eyes. All four of them had some muscular control, though Gumbs was the only one who had made any serious attempt to interfere with George's locomotion. Miss McCarty, not to George's surprise, had managed to retain a pair of functioning ears.

But Bellis had been blind, deaf and dumb all through

the afternoon and night. The only terminal sense-organs she had been able to use had been those of the skin—the perceptors of touch, heat and cold, and pain. She had heard nothing, seen nothing, but she had felt every leaf and stalk they had brushed against, the cold impact of every rain drop, and the pain of the toothy monster's bite. George's opinion of her went up several notches when he learned this. She had been terrified, but she hadn't been driven into hysteria or insanity.

It further appeared that nobody was doing any breathing and nobody was aware of a heartbeat.

George would have liked nothing better than to continue this discussion, but the other three were united in believing that what had happened to them after they got in was of less importance than how they were going to get out.

"We can't get *out,*" said George. "At least, I don't see any possibility of it in the present state of our knowledge. If we—"

"But we've got to get out!" Vivian cried.

"We'll go back to camp," said McCarty coldly. "Immediately. And you'll explain to the Loyalty Committee why you didn't return as soon as you regained consciousness."

"That's right," Gumbs put in self-consciously. "If you can't do anything, Meister, maybe the other technical fellows can."

George patiently explained his theory of their probable reception by the guards at the camp. McCarty's keen mind detected a flaw. "You grew legs, and stalks for your eyes, according to your own testimony. If you aren't lying, you can also grow a mouth. We'll announce ourselves as we approach."

"That may not be easy," George told her. "We couldn't get along with just a mouth. We'd need teeth, tongue, hard and soft palates, lungs or the equivalent, vocal cords, and some kind of substitute for a diaphragm to power the whole business. I'm wondering if it's possible at all, because when Miss Bellis finally succeeded in making herself heard, it was by the method we are using now. She didn't—"

"You talk too much," McCarty interrupted. "Major Gumbs, Miss Bellis, you and I will try to form a speaking apparatus. The first to succeed will receive a credit mark on his record. Commence."

* * *

George, being left out of the contest by implication, used his time trying to restore his hearing. It seemed to him likely that the Whatever-it-was *meisterii* had some sort of division of labor built into it, since Gumbs and he—the first two to fall in—had kept their sight without making any special effort, while matters like hearing and touch had been left for the latecomers. This was fine in principle, and George approved of it, but he didn't like the idea of Miss McCarty's being the sole custodian of any part of the apparatus whatever.

Even if he were able to persuade the other two to follow his lead—and at the moment this prospect seemed dim—McCarty was certain to be a holdout. And it might easily be vital to all of them, at some time in the near future, to have their hearing hooked into the circuit.

He was distracted at first by muttered comments between Gumbs and Vivian—"Getting anywhere?" "I don't think so. Are you?"—interspersed between yawps, humming sounds and other irritating noises as they tried unsuccessfully to switch over from mental to vocal communication. Finally McCarty snapped, "Concentrate on forming the necessary organs instead of braying like jackasses."

George settled down to work, using the same technique he had found effective before. With his eyes shut, he imagined that the thing with all the teeth was approaching in darkness—*tap; slither; tap; click.* He wished valiantly for ears to catch those faint approaching sounds. After a long time he thought he was beginning to succeed—or were those mental sounds, unconsciously emitted by one of the other three? *Click. Slither. Swish. Scrape.*

George opened his eyes, genuinely alarmed. A hundred meters away, facing him across the shallow slope of rocky ground, was a uniformed man just emerging from a stand of black vegetation spears. As George raised his eye-stalks, the man paused, stared back at him, then shouted and raised his rifle.

George ran. Instantly there was a babble of voices inside him, and the muscles of his "legs" went into wild spasms.

"Run, dammit!" he said frantically. "There's a trooper with—"

The rifle went off with a deafening roar and George felt a sudden hideous pain aft of his spine. Vivian Bellis screamed. The struggle for possession of their common legs stopped and they scuttled full speed ahead for the cover of a nearby boulder.

The rifle roared again. George heard rock splinters screeching through the foliage overhead. Then they were plunging down the side of a gully, up the other slope, over a low hummock and into a forest of tall, bare-limbed trees.

George spotted a leaf-filled hollow and headed for it, fighting somebody else's desire to keep on running in a straight line. They plopped into the hollow and crouched there while three running men went past them.

Vivian was moaning steadily. Raising his eye-stalks cautiously, George was able to see that several jagged splinters of stone had penetrated the monster's gelatinous flesh near the far rim. They had been very lucky. The shot had apparently been a near miss—accountable only on the grounds that the trooper had been shooting downhill at a moving target—and had shattered the boulder behind them.

Looking more closely, George observed something which excited his professional interest. The whole surface of the monster appeared to be in constant slow ferment, tiny pits, opening and closing as if the flesh were boiling . . . except that here the bubbles of air were not forcing their way outward, but were being engulfed at the surface and pressed down into the interior.

He could also see, deep under the mottled surface of the huge lens-shaped body, four vague clots of darkness which must be the living brains of Gumbs, Bellis, McCarty—and Meister.

Yes, there was one which was radically opposite his own eye-stalks. It was an odd thing, George reflected, to be looking at your own brain. He hoped he could get used to it in time.

The four dark spots were arranged close together in an almost perfect square at the center of the lens. The spinal cords, barely visible, crossed between and rayed outward from the center.

Pattern, George thought. The thing was designed to make use of more than one nervous system. It arranged them in an orderly fashion, with the brains inward for greater protection—and perhaps for another reason. Maybe there was even a provision for conscious cooperation among the passengers: a matrix that somehow promoted the growth of communiation cells between the separate brains. If that were so, it would account for their ready success with telepathy. George wished acutely that he could get inside and find out.

Vivian's pain was diminishing. Hers was the brain opposite George's and she had taken most of the effect of the rock splinters. But the fragments were sinking now, slowly, through the gelid substance of the monster's tissues. Watching carefully, George could see them move. When they got to the bottom, they would be excreted, no doubt, just as the indigestible part of their clothing and equipment had been.

George wondered idly which of the remaining two brains was McCarty's and which was Gumb's. The answer proved easy to find. To George's left, as he looked back toward the center of the mound, was a pair of blue eyes set flush with the surface. They had lids apparently grown from the monster's substance, but thickened and opaque.

To his right, George could make out two tiny openings, extending a few centimeters into the body, which could only be Miss McCarty's ears. George had an impulse to see if he could devise a method of dropping dirt into them.

Anyhow, the question of returning to camp had been settled, at least for the moment. McCarty said nothing more about growing a set of speech organs, although George was sure she was determined to keep on trying.

He didn't think she would succeed. Whatever the mechanism was by which these changes in bodily structure were accomplished, amateurs like themselves probably could succeed only under the pressure of considerable emotional strain, and then just with comparatively simple tasks which involve one new structure at a time. And as he had already told McCarty, the speech organs in Man were extraordinarily diverse and complicated.

It occurred to George that speech might be achieved by creating a thin membrane to serve as a diaphragm, and an air chamber behind it, with a set of muscles to produce the necessary vibrations and modulate them. He kept the notion to himself, though, because he did not want to go back.

George was a rare bird: a scientist who was actually fitted for his work and loved it for its own sake. And right now he was sitting squarely in the middle of the most powerful research tool that had ever existed in his field: a protean organism, with the observer *inside* it, able to order its structure and watch the results; able to devise theories of function and test them on the tissues of what was effectively his own body—able to construct new organs, new adaptations to environment!

George saw himself at the point of an enormous cone of new knowledge and some of the possibilities he glimpsed humbled and awed him.

He *couldn't* go back, even if it were possible to do it without getting killed. If only he alone had fallen in—No, then the others would have pulled him out and killed the monster.

There were, he felt, too many problems demanding solutions all at once. It was hard to concentrate; his mind kept slipping maddeningly out of focus.

Vivian, whose pain had stopped some time ago, began to wail again. Gumbs snapped at her. McCarty cursed both of them. George himself felt that he had had very nearly all he could take, cooped up with three idiots who had no more sense than to squabble among themselves.

"Wait a minute," he said. "Do you all feel the same way? Irritable? Jumpy? As if you'd been working for sixty hours straight and were too tired to sleep?"

"Stop talking like a video ad," Vivian said angrily. "Haven't we got enough trouble without—"

"We're hungry," George interrupted. "We didn't realize it, because we haven't got the organs that usually signal hunger. But the last thing this body ate was *us*, and that was a whole day ago. We've got to find something to ingest. And soon, I'd say."

"Good Lord, you're right," said Gumbs. "But if this thing only eats people—I mean to say—"

"It never met people until we landed," George replied curtly. "Any protein should do."

He started off in what he hoped was the direction they had been following all along—directly away from camp. At least, he thought, if they put enough distance behind them, they might get thoroughly lost.

III

They moved out of the trees and down the long slope of a valley, over a wiry carpet of dead grasses, until they reached a watercourse in which a thin trickle was still flowing. Far down the bank, partly screened by clumps of skeletal shrubbery, George saw a group of animals that looked vaguely like miniature pigs. He told the others about it, and started cautiously in that direction.

"Which way is the wind blowing, Vivian?" he asked. "Can you feel it?"

She said, "No. I could before, when we were going downhill, but now I think we're facing into it."

"Good. We may be able to sneak up on them."

"But we're not going to eat *animals,* are we?"

"Yes, how about it, Meister?" Gumbs put in. "I don't say I'm a squeamish fellow, but after all—"

George, who felt a little squeamish himself—like all the others, he had been brought up on a diet of yeasts and synthetic protein—said testily, "What else can we do? You've got eyes; you can see that it's autumn here. Autumn after a hot summer, at that. Trees bare, streams dried up. We eat meat or go without—or would you rather hunt for insects?"

Gumbs, shocked to the core, muttered for a while and then gave up.

Seen at closer range, the animals looked less porcine and even more unappetizing than before. They had lean, segmented, pinkish-gray bodies, four short legs, flaring ears, and blunt scimitar-like snouts with which they were rooting in the ground, occasionally turning up something which they gulped, ears flapping.

George counted thirty of them, grouped fairly closely in a little space of clear ground between the bushes and the river. They moved slowly, but their short legs looked powerful; he guessed that they could run fast enough when they had to.

He inched forward, keeping his eye-stalks low, stopping instantly whenever one of the beasts looked up. Moving with increasing caution, he had approached to within ten meters of the nearest when McCarty said abruptly:

"Meister, has it occurred to you to wonder just *how* we are going to eat these animals?"

"Don't be foolish," he said irritably. "We'll just—" He stopped, baffled.

Did the thing's normal method of assimilation stop as soon as it got a tenant? Were they supposed to grow fangs and a gullet and all the rest of the apparatus? Impossible; they'd starve to death first. But on the other hand—*damn* this fuzzy-headed feeling—wouldn't it have to stop, to prevent the tenant from being digested with his first meal?

"Well?" McCarty demanded.

That guess was wrong, George knew, but he couldn't say why; and it was a distinctly unpleasant thought. Or, even worse, suppose the meal became the tenant, and the tenant the meal?

The nearest animal's head went up, and four tiny red eyes stared directly at George. The floppy ears snapped to attention. It was not time for speculation.

"He's seen us!" George shouted mentally. *"Run!"*

One instant they were lying still in the prickly dry grass; the next they were skimming across the ground, with the herd galloping away straight ahead of them. The hams of the nearest beast loomed up closer and closer, bounding furiously; then they had run it down and vaulted over it.

Casting an eye backward, George saw that it was motionless in the grass—unconscious or dead.

They ran down another one. *The anesthetic,* George thought lucidly. *One touch does it.* And another, and another. *Of course we can digest them,* he thought, with relief. *It had to be selective to begin with or it couldn't have separated out our nervous tissue.*

Four down. Six down. Three more together as the herd bunched between the last arm of the thicket and the steep river-bank; then two that tried to double back; then four stragglers, one after the other.

The rest of the herd disappeared into the tall grass up the slope, but fifteen bodies were strewn behind them.

Taking no chances, George went back to the beginning of the line and edged the monster's body under the first carcass.

"Crouch down, Gumbs," he said. "We have to slide

under it . . . that's far enough. Leave the head hanging over."

"What for?" barked the soldier.

"You don't want his brain in here with us, do you? We don't know how many this thing is equipped to take. It might even like this one better than any of ours. But I can't see it bothering to keep the rest of the nervous system, if we make sure not to eat the head."

"Oh!" said Vivian.

"I beg your pardon, Miss Bellis," George said contritely. "It shouldn't be too unpleasant, though, if we don't let it bother us. It isn't as if we had taste buds or—"

"It's all right," she said. "Just please let's not talk about it."

"I should think not," Gumbs put in. "A little more tact, don't you think, Meister?"

Accepting this reproof, George turned his attention to the corpse that lay on the monster's glabrous surface, between his section and Gumbs's. It was sinking, just visibly, into the flesh. A cloud of opacity was spreading around it.

When it was almost gone and the neck had been severed, they moved on to the next. This time, at George's suggestion, they took aboard two at once. Gradually their irritable mood faded; they began to feel at ease and cheerful, and George found it possible to think consecutively without having vital points slip out of his reach.

They were on their eighth and ninth courses, and George was happily engaged in an intricate chain of speculation as to the monster's circulatory system, when Miss McCarty broke a long silence to announce:

"I have now perfected a method by which we can return to camp safely. We will begin at once."

Startled and dismayed, George turned his eyes toward McCarty's quadrant of the monster. Protruding from the rim was a stringy, joined something that looked like—yes, it was!—a grotesque but recognizable arm and hand. As he watched, the lumpy fingers fumbled with a blade of grass, tugged, uprooted it.

"Major Gumbs!" said McCarty. "It will be your task to locate the following articles as quickly as possible. One, a surface suitable for writing. I suggest a large leaf, light in color, dry but not brittle, or a tree from which a large section of bark can be easily peeled. Two, a pigment. No doubt you will be able to discover berries yielding suitable juice. If not, mud will do. Three, a twig or reed for use as a pen. When you have directed me to all these essential items, I will employ them to write a message outlining our predicament. You will read the result and point out any errors, which I will then correct. When the message is completed, we will return with it to the camp, approaching at night, and deposit it in a conspicuous place. We will retire until daybreak, and when the message has been read, we will approach again. Begin, Major."

"Well, yes," said Gumbs, "that ought to work, except—I suppose you've figured out some system for holding the pen, Miss McCarty?"

"Fool!" she replied. "I have made a hand, of course."

"Well, in that case, by all means. Let's see, I believe we might try this thicket first—" Their common body gave a lurch in that direction.

George held back. "Wait a minute," he said desperately. "Let's at least have the common sense to finish this meal before we go. There's no telling when we'll get another."

McCarty demanded, "How large are these creatures, Major?"

"About sixty centimeters long, I should say."

"And we have consumed nine of them, is that correct?"

"Nearer eight," George corrected. "These two are only half gone."

"In other words," McCarty said, "we have had two apiece. That should be ample. Don't you agree, Major?"

George said earnestly, "Miss McCarty, you're thinking in terms of human food requirements, whereas this organism has a different metabolic rate and at least three times the mass of four human beings. Look at it this way—the four of us together had a mass of about three hundred kilos and yet twenty hours after this thing absorbed us, it was hungry again. Well, these animals wouldn't weigh much more than twenty kilos apiece at one G—and according to your scheme, we've got to hold out until after daybreak tomorrow."

"Something in that," Gumbs agreed. "Yes, on the whole, Miss McCarty, I think we had better forage while we can.

It won't take us more than half an hour longer, at this rate."

"Very well. Be as quick as you can, though."

They moved on to the next pair of victims. George's brain was working furiously. It was no good arguing with McCarty. If he could only convince Gumbs, then Bellis would fall in with the majority—maybe. It was the only hope he had.

"Gumbs," he said, "have you given any thought to what's going to happen to us when we get back?"

"Not my line, you know. I leave that to the technical fellows like yourself."

"No, that isn't what I mean. Suppose you were the CO of this team, and four other people had fallen into this organism instead of us—"

"What? What? I don't follow."

George patiently repeated it.

"Yes, I see what you mean. So?"

"What orders would you give?"

Gumbs thought a moment. "Turn the thing over to the bio section, I suppose."

"You don't think you might order it destroyed as a possible menace?"

"Good Lord, I suppose I might. No, but you see, we'll be careful what we say in the note. We'll point out that we're a valuable specimen and so on. Handle with care."

"All right," George said, "suppose that works, then what? Since it's out of your line, I'll tell you. Nine chances out of ten, bio section will classify us as a possible biological enemy weapon. That means, first of all, that we'll go through a full-dress interrogation and I don't have to tell you what that can be like—"

"Major Gumbs," said McCarty strictly, "Meister will be executed for disloyalty at the first opportunity. You are forbidden to talk to him, under the same penalty."

"But she can't stop you from listening to me," George said tensely. "In the second place, Gumbs, they'll take samples. Without anesthesia. Finally, they'll either destroy us just the same, or they'll send us back to the nearest strong point for more study. We will then be Federation property, Gumbs, in a top-secret category, and since nobody in Intelligence will ever dare to take the responsibility of clearing us, we'll *stay* there.

"Gumbs, this *is* a valuable specimen, but it will never do anybody any good if we go back to camp. Whatever we discover about it, even if it's knowledge that could save billions of lives, that will be top-secret, too, and it'll never get past the walls of Intelligence . . . If you're still hoping that they can get you out of this, you're wrong. This isn't like limb grafts. *Your whole body has been destroyed,* Gumbs, everything but your nervous system and your eyes. The only new body we'll get is the one we make ourselves. We've got to stay here and—and work this out ourselves."

"Major Gumbs," said McCarty, "I think we have wasted quite enough time. Begin your search for the materials I need."

For a moment, Gumbs was silent and their collective body did not move.

Then he said: "Miss McCarty—unofficially, of course—there's one point I'd like your opinion on. Before we begin. That is to say, they'll be able to patch together some sort of bodies for us, don't you think? I mean one technical fellow says one thing, another says the opposite. Do you see what I'm driving at?"

George had been watching McCarty's new limb uneasily. It was flexing rhythmically and, he was almost certain, gradually growing larger. The fingers groped in the dry grass, plucking first a single blade, then two together, finally a whole tuft. Now she said: "I have no opinion, Major. The question is irrelevant. Our duty is to return to camp. That is all we need to know."

"Oh, I quite agree with you there," said Gumbs. "And besides," he added, "there really isn't any alternative, is there?"

George, staring down at one of the fingerlike projections visible below the rim of the monster, was passionately willing it to turn into an arm. He had, he suspected, started much too late.

"The alternative," he said, "is simply to keep on going as we are. Even if the Federation holds this planet for a century, there'll be places on it that will never be explored. We'll be safe."

"I mean to say," Gumbs went on as if he had only

paused for thought, "a fellow can't very well cut himself off from civilization, can he?" There was a thoughtful tone to his voice.

Again George felt a movement toward the thicket; again he resisted it. Then he found himself overpowered as another set of muscles joined themselves to Gumbs's. Quivering, crabwise, the Something-or-other *meisterii* moved, half a meter. Then it stopped, straining.

"I believe you, Mr. Meister—George," Vivian Bellis said. "I don't want to go back. Tell me what you want me to do."

"You're doing beautifully right now," George assured her after a speechless instant. "Except if you can grow an arm, I imagine that will be useful."

"Now we know where we stand," said McCarty to Gumbs.

"Yes. Quite right."

"Major Gumbs," she said crisply, "you are opposite me, I believe?"

"Am I?" asked Gumbs doubtfully.

"Never mind. I believe you are. Now is Meister to your right or left?"

"Left. I know that, anyhow. Can see his eye-stalks out of the corner of my eye."

"Very well." McCarty's arm rose, with a sharp-pointed fragment of rock clutched in the blobby fingers.

Horrified, George watched it bend backward across the curve of the monster's body. The long, knife-sharp point probed tentatively at the surface three centimeters short of the area over his brain. Then the fist made an abrupt up-and-down movement and a fierce stab of pain shot through him.

"Not quite long enough, I think," McCarty said. She flexed the arm, then brought it back. "Major Gumbs, after my next attempt, you will tell me if you notice any reaction in Meister's eye-stalks."

The pain was still throbbing along George's nerves. With one half-blinded eye, he watched the embryonic arm that was growing, too slowly, under the rim; with the other, fascinated, he watched McCarty's arm lengthen slowly toward him.

It was growing visibly, he suddenly realized, but it wasn't

getting any nearer. In fact, incredibly enough, it seemed to be losing ground.

The monster's flesh was flowing away under it, expanding in both directions.

McCarty stabbed again, with vicious strength. This time the pain was less acute.

"Major?" she asked. "Any result?"

"No," said Gumbs, "no, I think not. We seem to be moving forward a bit, though, Miss McCarty."

"A ridiculous error," she replied. "We are being forced *back*. Pay attention, Major."

"No, really," he protested. "That is to say, we're moving toward the thicket. Forward to me, backward to you."

"Major Gumbs, *I* am moving forward, *you* are moving back."

They were both right, George discovered. The monster's body was no longer circular; it was extending itself along the axis. A suggestion of concavity was becoming visible in the center. Below the surface, too, there was motion.

The four brains now formed an oblong, not a square.

The positions of the spinal cords had shifted. His own and Vivian's seemed to be about where they were, but Gumbs's now passed under McCarty's brain, and vice versa.

Having increased its mass by some two hundred kilos, the Something-or-other *meisterii* was fissioning into two individuals—and tidily separating its tenants, two to each. Gumbs and Meister in one, McCarty and Bellis in the other.

Next time it happened, he realized, each product of the fission would be reduced to one brain—and the time after that, one of the new individuals out of each pair would be a monster in the primary state, quiescent, camouflaged, waiting to be stumbled over.

But that meant that, like the common ameba, this fascinating organism was immortal, barring accidents. It simply grew and divided.

Not the tenants, though, unfortunately. Their tissues would wear out and die.

Or would they? Human nervous tissue didn't regenerate, but neither did it proliferate as George's and Miss McCarty's had done; neither did *any* human tissue build new cells fast enough to account for George's eye-stalks or Miss McCarty's arm.

There was no question about it: none of that tissue could possibly be human; it was all counterfeit, produced by the monster from its own substance according to the structural "blue-prints" in the nearest genuine cells. And it was a perfect counterfeit: the new tissues knit with the old, axones coupled with dendrites, muscles contracted or expanded on command.

And therefore, when nerve cells wore out, they could be replaced. Evenutually the last human cell would go, the human tenant would have become totally monster—but "a difference that makes no difference is no difference." Effectively, the tenant would still be human and he would be immortal.

Barring accidents.

Or murder.

Miss McCarty was saying, "Major Gumbs, you are being ridiculous. The explanation is quite obvious. Unless you are deliberately deceiving me, for what reason I cannot imagine, then our efforts to move in opposing directions must be pulling this creature apart."

McCarty was evidently confused in her geometry. Let her stay that way—it would keep her off balance until the fission was complete. No, that was no good. George himself was out of her reach already and getting farther away, but how about Bellis? Her brain and McCarty's were, if anything, closer together . . .

What was he to do? If he warned the girl, that would only draw McCarty's attention to her sooner.

There wasn't much time left, he realized abruptly. If some physical linkage between the brains actually had occurred to make communication possible, those cells couldn't hold out much longer; the gap between the two pairs of brains was widening steadily. He had to keep McCarty from discovering how the four of them would be paired.

"Vivian!" he said.

"Yes, George?"

"Listen, we're not pulling this body apart. It's splitting. That's the way it reproduces. You and I will be in one half. Gumbs and McCarty in the other," he lied convincingly. "If they don't give us any trouble, we can all go where we please."

"Oh, I'm so glad!" What a warm voice she had . . .

"Yes," said George nervously, "but we may have to fight them; it's up to them. So *grow an arm,* Vivian."

"I'll try," she said uncertainly.

McCarty's voice cut across hers. "Major Gumbs, since you have eyes, it will be your task to see to it that those two do not escape. Meanwhile, I suggest that you also grow an arm."

"Doing my best," said Gumbs.

Puzzled, George glanced downward, past his own half-formed arm. There, almost out of sight, a fleshy bulge appeared under Gumbs's section of the rim! The Major had been working on it in secret, keeping it hidden . . . and it was already better-developed than George's.

"Oh-oh," said Gumbs abruptly. "Look here, Miss McCarty, Meister's been leading you up the garden path. Deceiving you, you understand. Clever, I must say. I mean you and I aren't going to be in the same half. How could we be? We're on *opposite sides* of the blasted thing. It's going to be you and Miss Bellis, me and Meister."

The monster was developing a definite waistline. The spinal cords had rotated now, so that there was clear space between them in the center.

"Yes," said McCarty faintly. "*Thank* you, Major Gumbs."

"George!" came Vivian's frightened voice, distant and weak. "What shall I do?"

"Grow an arm!" he shouted.

There was no reply.

IV

Frozen, George watched McCarty's arm, the rock-fragment still clutched at the end of it, rise into view and swing leftward at full stretch over the bubbling surface of the monster. He had time to see it bob up and viciously down again; time to think. *Still short, thank God—that's McCarty's right arm, it's farther from Vivian's brain than it was from mine;* time, finally, to realize that he could not possibly help Vivian before McCarty lengthened the arm the few centimeters more that were necessary. The fission was only half complete, yet he could no more move to where he wanted to be than a Siamese twin could walk around his brother.

Then his time was up. A flicker of motion warned him, and he looked back to see a lumpy, distorted pseudo-hand clutching for his eye-stalks.

Instinctively he brought his own up, grasped the other's wrist and hung on desperately. It was half again the size of his, and so strongly muscled that although his leverage was better, he could not force it back or hold it away. He could only keep the system oscillating up and down, adding his strength to Gumbs's so that the mark was overshot.

Gumbs began to vary the force and rhythm of his movements, trying to catch him off guard. A thick finger brushed the base of one eye-stalk.

"Sorry about this, Meister," said Gumbs. "No hard feelings, you understand. Between us (oof) I don't fancy that McCarty woman much—but (ugh! almost had you that time) way I see it, I've got to look after myself. Mean to say (ugh) if I don't, who will? See what I mean?"

George did not reply. Astonishingly enough, he was no longer afraid, either for himself or for Vivian; he was simply overpoweringly, ecstatically, monomaniacally angry. Power from somewhere was surging into his arm. Fiercely concentrating, he thought *Bigger! Stronger! Longer! More arm!*

The arm grew. Visibly, it added substance to itself, it lengthened, thickened, bulked with muscle. So did Gumbs's, however.

He began another arm. So did Gumbs.

All around him the surface of the monster was bubbling violently. And, George realized, the lenticular bulk of it was perceptibly shrinking. Its curious breathing system was inadequate; the thing was cannibalizing itself, destroying its own tissues to make up the difference.

How small could it get and still support two human tenants?

And which brain would it dispense with first?

He had no leisure to think about it. Scrabbling in the grass with his second hand, Gumbs had failed to find anything that would serve as a weapon. Now, with a sudden lurch, he swung their entire body around.

The fission was complete.

That thought reminded George of Vivian and McCarty. He risked a split-second's glance behind him, saw nothing but a featureless ovoid mound, and looked back in time to see Gumbs's half-grown right fist pluck up a long, sharp-pointed dead branch and drive it murderously at his eyes.

The lip of the river-bank was a meter away to the left. George made it in one abrupt surge. Their common body slipped, tottered, hesitated, hands clutching wildly—and toppled, end over end, hurtling in a cloud of dust and pebbles down the breakneck slope to a meaty smash at the bottom.

The universe made one more giant turn around them and came to rest. Half-blinded, George groped for the hold he had lost, found the wrist and seized it.

"Oh Lord!" said Gumbs. "I'm hurt, Meister. Go on, man, finish it, will you? Don't waste time."

George stared at him suspiciously, without relaxing his grip. "What's the matter with you?"

"Paralyzed. I can't move."

They had fallen onto a small boulder, George saw, one of many with which the river-bed was strewn. This one was roughly conical; they were draped over it, and the blunt point was directly under Gumbs's spinal cord, a few centimeters from the brain.

"Gumbs, that may not be as bad as you think. If I can show you it isn't, will you give up and put yourself under my orders?"

"How do you mean? My spine's crushed."

"Never mind that now. Will you or won't you?"

"Why, yes," agreed Gumbs. "That's very decent of you, Meister, matter of fact. You have my word, for what it's worth."

"All right," said George. Straining hard, he managed to get their body off the boulder. Then he stared up at the slope down which they had tumbled. Too steep; he'd have to find an easier way back. He turned and started off eastward, paralleling the thin stream that flowed in the center of the watercourse.

"What's up now?" Gumbs asked after a moment.

"We've got to find a way up to the top," George said impatiently. "I may still be able to help Vivian."

"Ah, yes. Afraid I was thinking about myself, Meister. If you don't mind telling me, what's the damage?"

She couldn't still be alive, George was thinking despondently, but if there were any small chance—

"You'll be all right," he said. "If you were still in your old body, that would be a fatal injury, or permanently disabling, anyhow, but not in this thing. You can repair yourself as easily as you can grow a new limb."

"Stupid of me not to think of that," said Gumbs. "But does that mean we were simply wasting our time trying to kill one another?"

"No. If you'd crushed my brain, I think the organism would have digested it and that would be the end of me. But short of anything that drastic, I believe we're immortal."

"Immortal? That does rather put another face on it, doesn't it?"

The bank was becoming a little lower, and at one point, where the raw ground was thickly seeded with boulders, there was a talus slope that looked as if it could be climbed. George started up it.

"Meister," said Gumbs after a moment.

"What do you want?"

"You're right, you know—I'm getting some feeling back already. Look here, is there anything this beast *can't* do? I mean, for instance, do you suppose we could put ourselves back together the way we were, with all the—appendages, and so on?"

"It's possible," George said curtly. It was a thought that had been in the back of his mind, but he didn't feel like discussing it with Gumbs just now.

They were halfway up the slope.

"Well, in that case," said Gumbs meditatively, "the thing has *military* possibilities, you know. Man who brought a thing like that direct to the War Department could write his own ticket, more or less."

"After we split up," George offered, "you can do whatever you please."

"But dammit," said Gumbs in an irritated tone, "that won't do."

"Why not?"

"Because," said Gumbs, "they might find you." His

hands reached up abruptly, pried out a small boulder before George could stop him.

The large boulder above it trembled, dipped and leaned ponderously outward. George, directly underneath, found that he could move neither forward nor back.

"Sorry again," he heard Gumbs saying, with what sounded like genuine regret. "But you know the Loyalty Committee. I simply can't take the chance."

The boulder seemed to take forever to fall. George tried twice more, with all his strength, to move out of its path. Then, instinctively, he put his arms up straight under it.

It struck.

George felt his arms breaking like twigs, and saw a looming grayness that blotted out the sky; he felt a sledge impact that made the ground shudder beneath him.

He heard a splattering sound.

And he was still alive. That astonishing fact kept him fully occupied for a long time after the boulder had clattered its way down the slope into silence. Then, at last, he looked down to his right.

The resistance of his stiffened arms, even while they broke, had been enough to lever the falling boulder over, a distance of some thirty centimeters. The right half of the monster was a flattened, shattered ruin. He could see a few flecks of pasty gray matter, melting now into green-brown translucence as the mass flowed slowly together again.

In twenty minutes, the last remnants of a superfluous spinal cord had been absorbed, the monster had collected itself back into its normal lens shape, and George's pain was diminishing. In five minutes more, his mended arms were strong enough to use.

They were also more convincingly shaped and colored than before—the tendons, the fingernails, even the wrinkles of the skin were in good order. In ordinary circumstances this discovery would have left George happily bemused for hours. Now, in his impatience, he barely noticed it. He climbed to the top of the bank.

Thirty meters away, a humped green-brown body like his own lay motionless on the dry grass.

It contained, of course, only one brain. Whose?

McCarty's, almost certainly; Vivian hadn't had a chance.

But then how did it happen that there was no visible trace of McCarty's arm?

Unnerved, George walked around the creature for a closer inspection.

On the far side, he encountered two dark-brown eyes, with an oddly unfinished appearance. They focused on him after an instant and the whole body quivered slightly, moving toward him.

Vivian's eyes had been brown; George remembered them distinctly. Brown eyes wth heavy dark lashes in a tapering slender face. But did that prove anything? What color had McCarty's eyes been? He couldn't remember.

George moved closer, hoping fervently that the Something-or-other *meisterii* was at least advanced enough to conjugate, instead of trying to devour members of its own species . . .

The two bodies touched, clung and began to flow together. Watching, George saw the fissioning process reverse itself. From paired lenses, the alien flesh melted into a slipper-shape, to an ovoid, to a lens-shape again. His brain and the other drifted closer together, the spinal cords crossing at right angles.

And it was only then that he noticed an oddity about the other brain. It seemed to be more solid and compact than his, the outline sharper.

"Vivian?" he said worriedly. "Is that you?"

No answer. He tried again; and again.

Finally:

"George! Oh dear—I want to cry, but I don't seem able to do it."

"No lachrymal glands," George said automatically. "Uh, Vivian?"

"Yes, George?" That warm voice again . . .

"What happened to Miss McCarty? How did you—"

"I don't know. She's gone, isn't she? I haven't heard her for a long time."

"Yes," said George, "she's gone. You mean you don't *know?* Tell me what you did."

"Well, I wanted to make an arm, because you told me to, but I didn't think I had time enough. So I made a skull instead, and those things to cover my spine—"

"Vertebrae." *Now why,* he thought discontentedly, *didn't I think of that?* "And then?"

"I think I'm crying now," she said "Yes, I am. It's such a relief—And then, after that, nothing. She was still hurting me, and I just lay still and thought how wonderful it would be if she weren't in here with me. After a while, she wasn't. And then I grew eyes to look for you."

The explanation, it seemed to George, was more perplexing than the enigma. Staring around in a vague search for enlightenment, he caught sight of something he hadn't noticed before. Two meters to his left, just visible in the grass, was a damp-looking grayish lump, with a suggestion of a stringy extension trailing off from it.

There must, he decided suddenly, be some mechanism in the Something-or-other *meisterii* for disposing of tenants who failed to adapt themselves—brains that went into catatonia, or hysteria, or suicidal frenzy. An eviction clause in the lease.

Somehow, Vivian had managed to stimulate that mechanism—to convince the organism that McCarty's brain was not only superfluous but dangerous—"Toxic" was the word.

It was the ultimate ignominy. Miss McCarty had not been digested. She'd been excreted.

By sunset, twelve hours later, they had made a good deal of progress. They had reached an understanding very agreeable to them both. They had hunted down another herd of the pseudo-pigs for their noon meal. They had not once quarreled or even irritated each other. And for divergent reasons—on George's side because the monster's normal metabolism was unsatisfactory when it had to move quickly, and on Vivian's because she refused to believe that any man could be attracted to her in her present condition—they had begun a serious attempt to reshape themselves.

The first trials were extraordinarily difficult, the rest surprisingly easy. Again and again, they had to let themselves collapse back into an ameboid shape, victims of some omitted or malfunctioning organ, but each failure smoothed the road. They were at last able to stand breathless but breathing, swaying but stable, face to face—two preliminary sketches of self-made Man.

They had also put thirty kilometers between themselves and the Federation camp. Standing on the crest of a rise and looking southward across the shallow valley, George could see a faint funereal glow: the mining machines, chewing out metals to feed the fabricators that would spawn lethal spaceships.

"We'll never go back there, will we?" begged Vivian.

"No," said George confidently. "We'll let them find us. When they do, they'll be a lot more disconcerted than we will. We can make ourselves anything we want to be, remember."

"I want you to want me, so I'm going to be beautiful."

"More beautiful than any woman ever was," he agreed, "and both of us will have super-intelligence. I don't see why not. We can direct our growth in any way we choose. We'll be more than human."

"I'd like that," said Vivian.

"They won't. The McCartys and the Gumbs and all the rest would never have a chance against us. We're the future."

There was one thing more, a small matter, but important to George, because it marked his sense of accomplishment, of one phase ended and a new one begun. He had finally completed the name of his discovery.

It wasn't Something-or-other *meisterii* at all.

It was *Spes hominis*—Man's hope.

With a reckless laugh, Norman Spinrad here kicks aside the debris of misinformation surrounding Primitive Man, bores to the very roots of civilization, and gives a brief and funny insight into the way it really was, and is, and will be.

THE AGE OF INVENTION

by Norman Spinrad

One morning, having nothing better to do, I went to visit my cousin Roach. Roach lived in one of those lizard-infested caves on the East Side of the mountain. Roach did not hunt bears. Roach did not grow grain. Roach spent his daylight hours throwing globs of bearfat, bison-chips and old rotten plants against the walls of his cave.

Roach said that he was an Artist. He said it with a capital "A." (Even though writing has not yet been invented.)

Unlikely as it may seem, Roach had a woman. She was, however, the ugliest female on the mountain. She spent her daylight hours lying on the dirty floor of Roach's cave and staring at the smears of old bearfat, moldy bison-chips and rotten plants on the wall.

She used to say this was Roach's Soul. She would also say that Roach had a very big soul.

Very big and *very* smelly.

As I approached the mouth of Roach's cave, I smelt pungent smoke. In fact, the cave was filled with this smoke. In the middle of the cave sat Roach and his woman. They were burning a big pile of weeds and inhaling the smoke.

"What are you doing?" I asked.

"Turning on, baby," said Roach. "I've just invented it."

"What does 'turning on' mean?"

"Well, you get this weed, dig? You burn it, and then you honk the smoke."

I scratched my head, inadvertently killing several of my favorite fleas.

"Why do that?" I asked.

"It like gets you high."

"You don't seem any further off the ground than I am," I observed. "And you're still kinda runty."

Roach snorted in disgust. "Forget it, man," he said. "It's only for Artists, Philosophers and Metaphysicians, anyway. (Even though Philosophy and Metaphysics have not yet been invented.) Dig my latest!"

On the nearest wall of the cave, there was this big blob of bearfat. In the middle of it was this small piece of bisonchip. Red and green and brown plant stains surrounded this. It smelt as good as it looked.

"Uh . . . interesting . . ." I said.

"Like a masterpiece, baby," Roach said proudly. "I call it 'The Soul of Man'."

"Uh . . . 'The Sole of Man?' Er . . . it *does* sort of look like a foot."

"No, no, man! *Soul* not *sole!*"

"But Roach, spelling hasn't been invented yet."

"Sorry. I forgot."

"Anyway," I said, trying to make him feel a little better, "it's very Artistic. (Whatever that meant.)

"Thanks, baby," Roach said sulkily.

"What's the matter, Roach?" I asked. He really looked awful.

"We haven't eaten in a week."

"Why don't you go out and kill a bear or something?" I suggested.

"I don't have the time to waste on hunting," Roach said indignantly. "I must live for Art!"

"It appears that you are dying for Art," I replied. "You can't do very much painting when you are dead."

"Well, anyway," said Roach, in a very tiny voice, "I'm a pretty lousy hunter in the first place. I would probably starve even if I spent the whole day hunting. Or maybe a bear would kill *me*. This way, I'm at least like starving for a Reason."

I must admit it made a kind of sense. Roach is terribly nearsighted. Also amazingly scrawny. The original 90 pound weakling.

"Mmmmmmm . . ." I observed.

"Mmmmmmm . . . *what?*" asked Roach.

"Well, you know old Aardvark? He can't hunt either. So what he does is he makes spearheads and trades them for bears. Maybe you could . . . ?"

"Go into *business?*" Roach cried. "Become bourgeois? *Please!* I am an Artist. Besides," he added lamely, "I don't know how to make spearheads."

"Mmmmm . . ."

"Mmmmm . . ."

"I know!" I cried. "You could trade your paintings!"

"Cool, baby!" exclaimed Roach. "Er . . . only why would anyone want to trade food for a painting?"

"Why because . . . er . . . ah . . ."

"I guess I'll just have to starve."

"Wait a minute," I said. "Er . . . if I can get someone to trade food for your paintings, will you give me some of the food, say . . . oh, one bear out of every ten?"

"Sure," said Roach. "What've I got to lose?"

"It's a deal then?"

"Deal, baby!"

I had just invented the Ten-Pencenter.

So I went to see Peacock. Peacock lived in the weirdest cave on the mountain—all filled up with stuff like moose-skins dyed pink, stuffed armadillos, and walls covered with withered morning-glories. For some reason which I have not yet been able to fathom, the women of the more hen-pecked men on the mountain give Peacock bears to make the same kind of messes in their caves.

Peacock is pretty weird himself. He was dressed in a skin-tight sabertooth skin dyed bright violet.

"Hello sweets," Peacock said, as I entered his perfumed cave.

"Hello, Peacock," I said uneasily. "Heard about Roach?"

"Roach?" shrilled Peacock. "That dirty, dirty man? That beatnik with the positively *unspeakable* cave?"

"That's him," I said. "Roach the Artist. Very good Artist, you know. After all, he invented it."

"Well what about that dreadful, dreadful creature?"

"Well you know your friend Cockatoo—?"

"Please, sweets!" shrieked Peacock. "Do not mention that *thing* Cockatoo in my presence again! Cockatoo and I are on the outs. I don't know what I ever saw in him. He's gotten so unspeakably *butch*."

Cockatoo was this . . . uh . . . *friend* of Peacock's . . . or *was*. They . . . uh . . . invented something together. Nobody is quite sure what it was, but we've organized a Vice Squad, just in case.

"Yeah," I muttered. "Well anyway, Cockatoo is paying Roach twenty bears to do a painting in his cave. He says that having an Original Roach in his cave will make your cave look like . . . er . . . 'A *positive* sloth's den, bubby,' I think his words were."

"Oooooh!" shrieked Peacock. "Oooooh!" He began to jump around the cave, pounding his little fists against the walls. "That monster! That veritable *beast!* Oooh, it's *horrid*, that's what it is! What am I going to do, sweets, whatever am I going to do?"

"Well," I suggested, "Roach is my cousin, you know, and I do have some pull with him. I suppose I could convince him to do a painting in *your* cave instead of Cockatoo's. Especially if you paid *thirty* bears instead of twenty . . ."

"Oh, *would you* sweets? Would you really?"

"Well I don't know. I do kind of like you, Peacock, but on the other hand . . ."

"Pretty, pretty, *pretty* please?"

I sighed heavily. "Okay, Peacock," I said. "You've talked me into it."

So Peacock got his Original Roach for thirty bears. Next week, I went to see Cockatoo, and I told him the story.

I got *him* to pay *forty* bears. Forty and thirty is seventy. Which gave me seven. Not bad for a couple hours' work. I better watch out, or someone'll invent income tax.

I saw Roach last week, the ingrate. He has moved to a bigger cave on the *West Side* of the mountain. He has a fine new leopard skin and *three* new women. He has even invented the Havana cigar, so he can have something expensive to smoke.

Unfortunately, he has discovered that he no longer needs me to make deals for him. His going price is eighty bears a painting. I, like a dope, neglected to invent the renewable exclusive agency contract. Can't invent 'em all, I suppose.

Roach has become truly insufferable, though. He now talks of "art" with a small "a" and "Bears" with a capital "B." He is the first Philistine.

He is going to get his.

How do you like my fine new leopard skin? Would you like one of my Havana cigars? Have you met this new woman yet? Have you seen my new cave?

I can buy and sell Roach now. I am the first tycoon. How did I do it? Well . . .

Hog was the mountain bum. He never trimmed his beard. He didn't have a woman, not even an *ugly* one. He laid around his filthy cave all day, doing nothing but belching occasionally. A real slob.

But even a jerk like Hog can throw bearfat and bison-chips against a cave wall.

I made an Artist out of Hog. I did this by telling him he could make fifty bears a day just by throwing bearfat and bison-chips against the walls of other people's caves.

This appealed to Hog.

This time I did *not* neglect to invent the renewable exclusive agency contract. It was another ten percent deal.

Hog gets ten percent.

Then I went to Peacock's cave. I stared in dismay at Roach's painting. "What is *that?*" I sneered.

"That, sweets, is an Original Roach," Peacock crooned complacently. "Isn't it divine? Such sensitivity, such style, such grace, such—"

"Roach!" I snorted. "You *can't* be serious. Why that Neo-pseudo-classicalmodern stuff went out with the Brontosaurs. You're *miles* behind the times, Peacock," I said, thereby inventing the Art Critic. *"The* Artist today is of course the Great Hog."

"Hog?" whined Peacock. "Hog is beastly, beastly. A rude, stupid smelly thing, a *positive* slob. Why his whole cave is a wretched mass of slop!"

"Exactly," I answered. "That's the source of his greatness. Hog is the mountain's foremost Slop Artist."

"Oooooh . . . How much do the Great Hog's paintings cost?"

"One hundred bears apiece," I said smugly. "Cockatoo is already contracting to—"

"I told you never to mention that *creature* to me again!" Peacock shrieked. "He must not steal an Original Hog from me, do you hear? I simply couldn't *bear* it! But all this is getting so *expensive* . . ."

I gave Peacock my best understanding smile. "Peacock, old man," I said, "I have a little business proposition for you . . ."

Well, that's all there was to it. You guessed it, now when Peacock makes one of his messes in some henpecked caveman's cave, it always includes at least one Original Hog, or maybe a couple Original Treesloths—Treesloth being another jerk Artist I have under contract. I sell the painting to Peacock for a hundred bears, and he charges his suck—er, *client*, *two* hundred bears for the same mess of bearfat and bison-chips. Peacock calls this Interior Decorating.

I call it "Civilization." Maybe it'll last for a couple of months, if I'm lucky.

Science fiction's most acute writer reminds us how human ingenuity will be needed to conquer other planets—while it ruins this one.

THE SNOWMEN
by Frederik Pohl

Tandy said, "Not tonight, Howard. Why, I'm practically in bed already, see?" And she flipped the vision switch just for a second; long enough so I could get a glimpse of a sheer negligee and feathered slippers and, well, naturally, I couldn't quite believe that she *really* wanted me to stay away. Nobody made her flip that switch.

I said, "Just for a minute, Tandy. One drink. A little music, perhaps a dance—"

"Howard, you're *terrible.*"

"No, dearest," I said, fast and soft and close to the phone, "I'm not terrible, I'm only very much in love. Don't say no. Don't say a word. Just close your eyes, and in ten minutes I'll be there, and—"

And then, confound them, they had to start that yapping. *Bleep-bleep* on the phone, and then: "Attention all citizens! Stand by for orders! Your world federal government has proclaimed a state of unlimited emergency. All heatpump power generators in excess of eight horsepower per—"

I slammed down the phone in disgust. Leave it to them! Yack-yack on the phone lines at all hours of the day and night, no consideration for anybody. I was disgusted, and then, when I got to thinking, not so disgusted. Why not go right over? She hadn't said no; she hadn't had a chance.

So I got the Bug out, locked the doors and set the thermostats, and I set out.

It isn't two miles to Tandy's place. Five years ago, even, I could make it in three or four minutes; now it takes ten.

I call it a damned shame, though no one else seems to care. But I've always been more adventurous than most, and more social-minded. Jeffrey Otis wouldn't care about things like that. Ittel du Bois wouldn't even know—his idea is to bury his nose in a drama-tape when he goes out of the house, and let the Bug drive itself. But not me. I like to drive, even if you can't see anything and the autopilot is perfectly reliable. Life is for *living*, I say. *Live* it.

I don't pretend to understand this scientific stuff either—leave science to the people who like it, is another thing I say. But you know how when you're in your Bug and you've set the direction-finder for somebody's place, there's this *beepbeepbeepbeep* when you're going right and a *beep*-SQUAWK or a SQUAWK*beep* when you go off the track? It has something to do with radio, only not radio—that's out of the question now, they say—but with sort of telephoned messages through the magma of the Earth's core. Well, that's what it says in the manual, and I know because one day I glanced through it. Anyway. Excuse me for getting technical. But I was going along toward Tandy's place, my mind full of warm pleasures and anticipating, and suddenly the *beepbeepbeep* stopped, and there was a sort of crystal chime and then a voice: "Attention! Operation of private vehicles is forbidden! Return to your home and listen to telephoned orders every hour on the hour!" And then the *beepbeepbeep* again. Why, they'd even learned how to jam the direction-finder with their confounded yapping! It was very annoying, and angrily I snapped the DF off. Daring? Yes, but I have to say that I'm an excellent driver, wonderful sense of direction, hardly need the direction-finder in the first place. And anyway we were close; the thermal pointers in the nose had already picked up Tandy's temperature gradient.

Tandy opened the locks herself. "Howard," she said in soft surprise, clutching the black film of negligee. "You really came. Oh, naughty Howard!"

"My darling!" I breathed, reaching out for her. But she dodged.

"No, Howard," she said severely, "you mustn't do that. Sit down for a moment. Have one little drink. And then I'm going to have to be terribly stubborn and send you right home, dear."

"Of course," I said, because that was, after all, the rules

of the game. "Just one drink, certainly." But, damn it, she seemed to mean it! She wasn't a bit hospitable—I mean, not *really* hospitable. She seemed friendly enough and she talked sweetly enough, but . . . Well, for example, she sat in the positively-not chair. I can tell you a lot about the way Tandy furnished her place. There's the wing chair by the fire, and that's a bad sign because the arms are slippery and there's only room for one actually sitting in it. There's the love seat—speaks for itself, doesn't it? And there's the big sofa and, best of all, the bearskin rug. But way at the other end of the scale is this perfectly straight, armless cane-bottomed thing, with a Ming vase on one side of it and a shrub of some kind or other rooted in a bowl on the other, and that's where she sat.

I grumbled, "I shouldn't have come at all."

"What, Howard?"

"I said, uh, I couldn't come any, uh, faster. I mean, I came as fast as I could."

"I know you did, you brute," she said roguishly, and stopped the Martini-mixer. It poured us each a drink. "Now don't dawdle," she said primly. "I've got to get some sleep."

"To love," I said, and sipped the top off the Martini.

"Don't do that," she warned. I got up from the floor at her feet and went back to another chair. "You," she said, "are a hard man to handle, Howard, dear." But she giggled.

Well, you can't win them all. I finished my drink and, I don't know, I think I would have hung around above five minutes just to show who was boss and then got back in the Bug, and gone home. Frankly, I was a little sleepy. It had been a wearing day, hours and hours with the orchids and then listening to all nine Beethoven symphonies in a row while I played solitaire.

But I heard the annunciator bell tinkle.

I stared at Tandy.

"My," she said prettily, "I wonder who that can be?"

"Tandy!"

"Probably someone dull," she shrugged. "I won't answer. Now, do be a good boy and—"

"Tandy! How *could* you?" My mind raced; there was only one conclusion. "Tandy, do you have Ittel du Bois coming here tonight? Don't lie to me!"

"Howard, what a *terrible* thing to say. Ittel was *last* year."

"Tell me the truth!"

"I do not!" And she was angry. I'd hurt her, no doubt of it.

"Then it must be Jeffrey. I won't stand for it. I won the the toss fair and square. Why can't we wait until next year? It isn't *decent.* I—"

She stood up, her blue eyes smoldering. "Howard McGuiness, you'd better go before you say something I won't be able to forgive."

I stood my ground. "Then who is it?"

"Oh, darn it," she said, and kicked viciously at the shrub by her left foot, "see for yourself. Answer the door."

So I did.

Now, I know Ittel du Bois's Bug—it's a Buick—and I know Jeff Otis's. It wasn't either one of them. The vehicle outside Tandy's door parked next to mine was a very strange looking Bug indeed. For one thing, it was only about eight feet long.

A bank of infrared lamps glowed on, bathing it in heat: the caked ice that forms in the dead spots along the hull, behind the treads and so on, melted, plopped off, turned into water and ran into the drain grille. You know how a Bug will crack and twang when it's being warmed up? They all do.

This one didn't.

It didn't make a sound. It was so silent that I could hear the snip-snip of Tandy's automatic load adjuster, throwing another heatpump into circuit to meet the drain of the infrared lamps. But no sound from the Bug outside. Also it didn't have caterpillar treads. Also it had—well, you can believe this or not—it had windows.

"You see?" said Tandy, in a voice colder than the four miles of ice overhead. "Now would you like to apologize to me?"

"I apologize," I said in a voice that hardly got past my lips. "I—" I stopped and swallowed. I begged, "Please, Tandy, what is it?"

She lit a cigarette unsteadily. "Well, I don't rightly know. I'm kind of glad you're here, Howard," she confessed. "Maybe I shouldn't have tried to get rid of you."

"Tell me!"

She glanced at the Bug. "All right. I'll make it fast. I got a call from this, uh, fellow. I couldn't understand him very well. But . . ."

She looked at me sidewise.

"I understand," I said. "You thought he might be a mark."

She nodded.

"And you wouldn't cut me in!" I cried angrily. "Tandy, that's mean! When I found old Buchmayr dead, didn't I cut you in on looting his place? Didn't I give you first pick of everything you wanted—except heatpumps and machine patterns, of course."

"I know, dear," she said miserably, "but—hush! He's coming out."

She was looking out the window. I looked too.

And then we looked at each other. That fellow out of the strange Bug, he was as strange as his vehicle. He might be a mark or he might not; but of one thing I was pretty sure, and that was that he wasn't human.

No. Not with huge white eyes and a serpentine frill of orange tendrils instead of hair.

At once all my lethargy and weariness vanished.

"Tandy," I cried, "he isn't human!"

"I know," she whispered.

"But don't you know what this means? He's an alien! He must come from another planet—perhaps from another star. Tandy, this is the most important thing that ever happened to us." I thought fast. "Tell you what," I said, "you let him in while I get around the side shaft—it's defrosted isn't it? Good I hurried. At the side door I stopped and looked at her affectionately. "Dear Tandy," I said. "And you thought this was just an ordinary mark. You see? You *need* me." And I was off, leaving her that thought to chew on as she welcomed her visitor.

I took a good long time in the stranger's Bug. Human or monster, I could rely on Tandy to keep him occupied, so I was very thorough and didn't rush, and came out with a splendid supply of what seemed to be storage batteries. I couldn't quite make them out, but I was sure that power was in them somehow or other; and if there was power, the heatpump would find a way to suck it out. Those I took the opportunity of tucking away in my own Bug before I went back in Tandy's place. No use bothering her about them.

She was sitting in the wing chair, and the stranger was nowhere in sight. I raised my brows. She nodded. "Well," I said, "he was your guest. I won't interfere."

Tandy was looking quiet, relaxed and happy. "What about the Bug?"

"Oh, lots of things," I said. "Plenty of metal! And food —a lot of food, Tandy. Of course, we'll have to go easy on it, till I find out if we can digest it, but it smells *delicious*. And—"

"Pumps?" she demanded.

"Funny," I said. "They don't seem to use them." She scowled. "Honestly, dearest! You can see for yourself— everything I found is piled right outside the door."

"What isn't in your Bug, you mean."

"Tandy!"

She glowered a moment longer, then smiled like the sun bursting through clouds on an old video tape. "No matter, Howard," she said tenderly, "we've got plenty. Let's have another Martini, shall we?"

"Of course." I waited and took the glass. "To love," I toasted. "And to crime. By the way, did you talk to him first?"

"Oh, for *hours,*" she said crossly. "Yap, yap. He's as bad as the feds."

I got up and idly walked across the room to the light switch. "Did he say anything interesting?"

"Not very. He spoke a very poor grade of English, to begin with. Said he learned it off old radio broadcasts, of all things. They float around forever out in space, it seems."

I switched off the lights. "That better?"

She nodded drowsily, got up to refill her glass, and sat down again in the love seat. "He was awfully interested in the heatpumps," she said drowsily.

I put a tape on the player—Tchaikovsky. Tandy is a fool for violins. "He liked them?"

"Oh, in a way. He thought they were clever. But dangerous, he said."

"Him and the feds," I murmured, sitting down next to her. Click-click, and our individual body armor went on stand-by alert. At the first hostile move it would block us off, set up a force field—well, I *think* it's called a force field. "The feds are always yapping about the pumps too. Did I tell you? They're even cutting in on the RDF channels now."

"Oh, Howard! That's *too* much." She sat up and got another drink—and sat, this time, on the wide, low sofa. She giggled.

"What's the matter, dear?" I asked, coming over beside her.

"He was so *funny*. Ya-ta-ta-ta, ya-ta-ta-ta, all about how the heatpumps were ruining the world."

"Just like the feds." Click-click some more, as I put my arm around her shoulders.

"Just like," she agreed. "He said it was evidently extremely high technology that produced a device that took heat out of its surrounding ambient environment, but had we ever thought of what would happen when *all* the heat was gone?"

"Crazy," I murmured into the base of her throat.

"Absolutely. As though all the heat could ever be gone! Absolute zero, he called it; said we're only eight or ten degrees from it now. That's why the snow, he said." I made a sound of polite disgust. "Yes, that's what he said. He said it wasn't just snow, it was frozen air—oxygen and nitrogen and all those things. We've frozen the Earth solid, he says, and now it's so shiny that its libido is nearly perfect."

I sat up sharply, then relaxed. "Oh. Not libido, dear. Albedo. That means it's shiny."

"That's what he said. He said the feds were right . . . Howard. Howard, dear. Listen to me."

"Ssh," I murmured. "Did he say anything else?"

"But Howard! Please. You're—"

"Ssh."

She relaxed, and then in a moment giggled again. "Howard, wait. I forgot to tell you the funniest part."

It was irritating, but I could afford to be patient. "What was that, dearest?"

"He didn't have any personal armor!"

I sat up. I couldn't help it. "What?"

"None at all! Naked as a baby. So that proves he isn't human, doesn't it? I mean, if he can't take the simplest *care* of himself, he's only a kind of animal, right?"

I thought. "Well, I suppose so," I said. Really, the concept was hard to swallow.

"Good," she said, "because he's, well, in the freezer. I didn't want to *waste* him, Howard. And it isn't as if he was human."

I thought for a second. Well, why not? You get tired of rabbits and mice, and since there hasn't been any open sky for pasturing for nearly fifty years, that's about all there is. Now that I thought back on it, he was kind of plump and appetizing at that.

And, in any case, that was a problem for later on. I reached out idly and touched the button that controlled the last light in the room, the electric fireplace itself. "Oh," I said, pausing. "Where did he come from?"

"Sorry," her muffled voice came. "I forgot to ask."

I reached out thoughtfully and found my glass. There was a little bit left; I drained it off. Funny that the creature should bother to come down. In the old days, yes; back when Earth was open to the sky, you might expect aliens to come skyrocketing down from the stars and all that. But he'd come all the way from—well, from wherever—and for what? Just to make a little soup for the pot, to donate a little metal and power. It was funny, in a way. I couldn't help thinking that the feds would have liked to have met him. Not only because he agreed with them about the pumps and so on, but because they're interested in things like that. They're very earnest types, that's why they're always issuing warnings and so on. Of course, nobody pays any attention.

Still . . .

Well, there was no sense bothering my small brain about that sort of stuff, was there? If the heatpumps were dangerous, nobody would have bothered to invent them, would they?

I set down my glass and switched off the fireplace. Tandy was still and warm beside me; motionless but, believe me, by no means asleep.

Ultimately, we may have to invent the most perilously attractive planets . . .

SCHWARTZ BETWEEN THE GALAXIES
by Robert Silverberg

This much is reality: Schwartz sits comfortably cocooned —passive, suspended—in a first-class passenger rack aboard a Japan Air Lines rocket, nine kilometers above the Coral Sea. And this much is fantasy: the same Schwartz has passage on a shining starship gliding silkily through the interstellar depths en route at nine times the velocity of light from Betelgeuse IX to Rigel XXI, or maybe from Andromeda to the Lesser Magellanic.

There are no starships. Probably there never will be any. Here we are, a dozen decades after the flight of Apollo II, and no human being goes anywhere except back and forth across the face of that little O, the Earth, for the planets are barren and the stars are beyond reach. That little O is too small for Schwartz. Too often it glazes for him, it turns to a nugget of dead porcelain; and lately he has formed the habit, when the world glazes, of taking refuge aboard that interstellar ship. So what JAL Flight 411 holds is merely his physical self, his shell, occupying a costly private cubicle on a slender 200-passenger vessel which, leaving Buenos Aires shortly after breakfast, has sliced westward along the Tropic of Capricorn for a couple of hours and will soon be landing at Papua's Torres Skyport. But his consciousness, his *anima*, the essential Schwartzness of him, soars between the galaxies.

What a starship it is! How marvelous its myriad passengers! Down its crowded corridors swarms a vast gaudy heterogeny of galactic creatures, natives of the worlds of Capella, Arcturus, Altair, Canopus, Polaris, Antares—beings both intelligent and articular, methane-breathing or nitrogen-breathing or argon-breathing, spiny-skinned or skinless, many-armed or many-headed or altogether incorporeal, each a product of a distant and distinctly unique and alien cultural heritage. Among these varied folk moves Schwartz, that superstar of anthropologists, that true heir to Kroeber and Morgan and Malinowski and Mead, delightedly devouring their delicious diversity. Whereas aboard this prosaic rocket, this planetlocked stratosphere-needle, one cannot tell the Canadians from the Portuguese, the Portuguese from the Romanians, the Romanians from the Irish, unless they open their mouths, and sometimes not always then.

In his reveries he confers with creatures from the Fomalhaut system about digital circumcision; he tapes the melodies of the Achernarnian eye-flute; he learns of the sneeze-magic of Acrux, the sleep-ecstasies of Aldebaran, the asteroid-sculptors of Thuban. Then a smiling JAL stewardess parts the curtain of his cubicle and peers in at him, jolting him from one reality to another. She is blue-eyed, frizzy-haired, straight-nosed, thin-lipped, bronze-skinned—a genetic mishmash, your standard twenty-first-century-model mongrel human, perhaps Melanesian-Swedish-Turkish-Bolivian, perhaps Polish-Berber-Tartar-Welsh. Cheap intercontinental transit has done its deadly work: all Earth is a crucible, all the gene pools have melted into one indistinguishable fluid. Schwartz wonders about the recessivity of those blue eyes and arrives at no satisfactory solution. She is beautiful, at any rate. Her name is Dawn—O sweet neutral non-culture-bound cognomen!—and they have played at a flirtation, he and she, Dawn and Schwartz at occasional moments of this short flight. Twinkling, she says softly, "We're getting ready for our landing, Dr. Schwartz. Are your restrictors in polarity?"

"I never unfastened them."

"Good." The blue eyes, warm, interested, meet his. "I have a layover in Papua tonight," she says.

"That's nice."

"Let's have a drink while we're waiting for them to unload the baggage," she suggests with cheerful bluntness. "All right?"

"I suppose," he says casually. "Why not?" Her availability bores him: somehow he enjoys the obsolete pleasures of the chase. Once such easiness in a woman like this would have excited him, but no longer. Schwartz is forty years old, tall, square-shouldered, sturdy, a showcase for the peasant genes of his rugged Irish mother. His close-cropped black hair is flecked with gray; many women find that interesting. One rarely sees gray hair now. He dresses simply but well, in sandals and Socratic tunic. Predictably, his physical attractiveness, both within his domestic sixness and without, has increased with his professional success. He is confident, sure of his powers, and he radiates an infectious assurance. This month alone eighty million people have heard his lectures.

She picks up the faint weariness in his voice. "You don't sound eager. Not interested?"

"Hardly that."

"What's wrong, then? Feeling sub, Professor?"

Schwartz shrugs. "Dreadfully sub. Body like dry bone. Mind like dead ashes." He smiles, full force, depriving his words of all their weight.

She registers mock anguish. "That sounds bad," she says. "That sounds awful!"

"I'm only quoting Chuang Tzu. Pay no attention to me. Actually, I feel fine, just a little stale."

"Too many skyports?"

He nods. "Too much of a sameness wherever I go." He thinks of a star-bright top-deck bubble-dome where three boneless Spicans do a twining dance of propitiation to while away the slow hours of nine-light travel. "I'll be all right," he tells her. "It's a date."

Her hybrid face glows with relief and anticipation. "See you in Papua," she tells him, and winks, and moves jauntily down the aisle.

Papua. By cocktail time Schwartz will be in Port Moresby. Tonight he lectures at the University of Papua; yesterday it was Montevideo, the day after tomorrow it will be Bangkok. He is making the grand academic circuit. This is his year: he is very big, suddenly, in anthropological circles, since the publication of *The Mask Beneath The Skin*. From continent to continent he flashes, sharing his wisdom, Monday in Montreal, Tuesday Veracruz, Wednesday Montevideo. Thursday—Thursday? He crossed the International Date Line this morning, and he does not remember whether he has entered Thursday or Tuesday, though yesterday was surely Wednesday. Schwartz is certain only that this is July and the year is 2083, and there are moments when he is not even sure of that.

The JAL rocket enters the final phase of its landward plunge. Papua waits, sleek, vitrescent. The world has a glassy sheen again. He lets his spirit drift happily back to the gleaming starship making its swift way across the whirling constellations.

He found himself in the starship's busy lower-deck lounge, having a drink with his traveling companion, Pitkin, the Yale economist. Why Pitkin, that coarse, florid little man? With all of real and imaginary humanity to choose from, why had his unconscious elected to make him share this fantasy with such a boor?

"Look," Pitkin said, winking and leering. "There's your girlfriend."

The entry-iris had opened and the Antarean not-male had come in.

"Quit it," Schwartz snapped. "You know there's no such thing going on."

"Haven't you been chasing her for days?"

"She's not a 'her'," Schwartz said.

Pitkin guffawed. "Such precision! Such scholarship! *She's* not a *her,* he says!" He gave Schwartz a broad nudge. "To you she's a she, friend, and don't try to kid me."

Schwartz had to admit there was some justice to Pitkin's vulgar innuendos. He did find the Antarean—a slim yellow-eyed ebony-skinned upright humanoid, sinuous and glossy, with tapering elongated limbs and a seal's fluid grace—powerfully attractive. Nor could he help thinking of the Antarean as feminine. That attitude was hopelessly culture-bound and species-bound, he knew; in fact the alien had cautioned him that terrestrial sexual distinctions were irrelevant in the Antares system, that if Schwartz insisted on thinking of "her" in genders, "she" could be considered only the negative of male, with no implication of biological femaleness.

He said patiently, "I've told you. The Antarean's neither male nor female as we understand those concepts. If we happen to perceive the Antarean as feminine, that's the result of our own cultural conditioning. If you want to believe that my interest in this being is sexual, go ahead, but I assure you that it's purely professional."

"Sure. You're only studying her."

"In a sense I am. And she's studying me. On her native world she has the status-frame of 'watcher-of-life,' which seems to translate into the Antarean equivalent of an anthropologist."

"How lovely for you both. She's your first alien and you're her first Jew."

"Stop calling her *her,"* Schwartz hissed.

"But you've been doing it!"

Schwartz closed his eyes. "My grandmother told me never to get mixed up with economists. Their thinking is muddy and their breath is bad, she said. She also warned me against Yale men. Perverts of the intellect, she called them. So here I am cooped up on an interstellar ship with 500 alien creatures and one-fellow human, and he has to be an economist from Yale."

"Next trip travel with your grandmother instead."

"Go away," Schwartz said. "Stop lousing up my fantasies. Go peddle your dismal science somewhere else. You see those Delta Aurigans over there? Climb into their bottle and tell them all about the Gross Global Product." Schwartz smiled at the Antarean, who had purchased a drink, something that glittered an iridescent blue, and was approaching them. "Go *on,"* Schwartz murmured.

"Don't worry," Pitkin said. I wouldn't want to crowd you." He vanished into the motley crowd.

The Antarean said, "The Capellans are dancing, Schwartz."

"I'd like to see that. Too damned noisy in here anyway." Schwartz stared into the alien's vertical-slitted citreous eyes. Cat's eyes, he thought. Panther's eyes. The Antarean's gaze was focused, as usual, on Schwartz' mouth: other worlds, other customs. He felt a strange, unsettling tremor of desire. Desire for what, though? It was a sensation of pure need, nonspecific, certainly nonsexual. "I think I'll take a look. Will you come with me?"

The Papua rocket has landed. Schwartz, leaning across the narrow table in the skyport's lounge, says to the stewardess in a low, intense tone, "My life was in crisis. All my values were becoming meaningless. I was discovering that my chosen profession was empty, foolish, as useless as—as playing chess."

"How awful," Dawn whispers gently.

"You can see why. You go all over the world, you see a thousand skyports a year. Everything the same everywhere. The same clothes, the same slang, the same magazines, the same styles of architecture and decor."

"Yes."

"International homogeneity. Worldwide uniformity. Can you understand what it's like to be an anthropologist in a world where there are no primitives left, Dawn? Here we sit on the island of Papua—you know, headhunters, animism, bodypaint, the drums at sunset, the bone through the nose—and look at the Papuans in their business robes all around us. Listen to them exchanging stock-market tips, talking baseball, recommending restaurants in Paris and barbers in Johannesburg. It's no different anywhere else. In a single century we've transformed the planet into one huge sophisticated plastic western industrial state. The TV relay satellites, the two-hour inter-continental rockets, the breakdown of religious exclusivism and genetic taboo, have mongrelized every culture, don't you see? You visit the Zuni and they have plastic African masks on the wall. You visit the Bushmen and they have Japanese-made Hopi-motif ashtrays. It's all just so much interior decoration, and underneath the carefully selected primitive motifs there's the same universal pseudo-American sensibility, whether you're in the Kalahari or the Amazon rain forest. Do you comprehend what's happened, Dawn?"

"It's such a terrible loss," she says sadly. She is trying very hard to be sympathetic, but he senses she is waiting for him to finish his sermon and invite her to share his hotel room. He *will* invite her; but there is no stopping him once he has launched into his one great theme.

"Cultural diversity is gone from the world," he says. "Religion is dead, true poetry is dead, inventiveness is dead, individuality is dead. Poetry. Listen to this." In a high monotone he chants:

In beauty I walk
With beauty before me I walk
With beauty behind me I walk
With beauty above and about me I walk
It is finished in beauty
It is finished in beauty

He had begun to perspire heavily. His chanting has created an odd sphere of silence in his immediate vicinity; heads are turning, eyes are squinting. "Navaho," he says. "The Night Way, a nine-day chant, a vision, a spell. Where are the Navaho now? Go to Arizona and they'll chant for you, yes, for a price; but they don't know what the words mean, and chances are the singers are only one-fourth Navaho, or one-eighth, or maybe just Hopi hired to dress in Navaho costumes, because the real Navaho, if any are left, are off in Mexico City hired to be Aztecs. So much is gone. Listen." He chants again, more piercingly even than before:

> The animal runs, it passes, it dies. And it is the great cold.
> *It is the great cold of the night, it is the dark.*
> The bird flies, it passes, it dies. And it is—

"JAL FLIGHT 411 BAGGAGE IS NOW UNLOADING ON CONCOURSE FOUR," a mighty mechanical voice cries.

> —the great cold.
> *It is the great cold of the night, it is the dark.*

"JAL FLIGHT 411 BAGGAGE—"

> The fish flees, it passes, it dies. And—

"People are staring," Dawn says uncomfortably.

"—ON CONCOURSE FOUR."

"Let them stare. Do them some good. That's a Pygmy chant, from Gabon, in equatorial Africa. Pygmies? There are no more Pygmies. Everybody's two meters tall. And what do we sing? Listen. Listen." He gestures fiercely at the cloud of tiny golden loudspeakers floating near the ceiling. A mush of music comes from them: the current popular favorite. Savagely he mouths words: *"Star . . . far . . . here . . . near.* Playing in every skyport right now, all over the world." She smiles thinly Her hand reaches toward his, covers it, presses against the knuckles. He is dizzy. The crowd, the eyes, the music, the drink. The plastic. Everything shines. Porcelain. Porcelain. The planet vitrifies. "Tom?" she asks uneasily. "Is anything the matter?" He laughs, blinks, coughs, shivers. He hears her calling for help, and then he feels his soul swooping outward, toward the galactic blackness.

With the Antarean not-male beside him, Schwartz peered through the viewport, staring in awe and fascination at the seductive vision of the Capellans coiling and recoiling outside the ship. Not all the passengers on this voyage had cozy staterooms like his. The Capellans were too big to come on board; and in any case they preferred never to let themselves be enclosed inside metal walls. They traveled just alongside the starship, basking like slippery whales in the piquant radiations of space. So long as they kept within twenty meters of the hull they would be inside the effective field of the Rabinowitz Drive, which swept ship and contents and associated fellow travelers toward Rigel, or the Lesser Magnellanic, or was it one of the Pleiades toward which they were bound at a cool nine lights?

He watched the Capellans moving beyond the shadow of the ship in tracks of shining white. Blue, glossy green, and velvet black, they coiled and swam, and every track was a flash of golden fire. "They have a dangerous beauty," Schwartz whispered. "Do you hear them calling? I do."

"What do they say?"

"They say, *'Come to me, come to me, come to me!'* "

"Go to them, then," said the Antarean simply. "Step through the hatch."

"And perish?"

"And enter into your next transition. Poor Schwartz! Do you love your present body so?"

"My present body isn't so bad. Do you think I'm likely to get another one some day?"

"No?"

"No," Schwartz said. "This one is all I get. Isn't it that way with you?"

"At the Time of Openings I receive my next housing. That will be fifty years from now. What you see is the fifth form I have been given to wear."

"Will the next be as beautiful as this?"

"All forms are beautiful," the Antarean said. "You find me attractive?"

"Of course."

A slitted wink. A bobbing nod toward the viewport. "As attractive as *those?*"

Schwartz laughed. "Yes. In a different way."

Coquettishly the Antarean said, "If I were out there, you would walk through the hatch into space?"

"I might. If they gave me a spacesuit and taught me how to use it."

"But not otherwise? Suppose I were out there right now. I could live in space five, ten, maybe fifteen minutes. I am there and I say, *'Come to me Schwartz, come to me!'* What do you do?"

"I don't think I'm all that self-destructive."

"To die for love, though! To make a transition for the sake of beauty."

"No. Sorry."

The Antarean pointed toward the undulating Capellans. "If *they* asked you, you would go."

"They are asking me," he said.

"And you refuse the invitation?"

"So far. So far."

The Antarean laughed an Antarean laugh, a thick silvery snort. "Our voyage will last many weeks more. One of these days, I think, you will go to them."

"You were unconscious at least five minutes," Dawn says. "You gave everyone a scare. Are you sure you ought to go through with tonight's lecture?"

Nodding, Schwartz says, "I'll be all right. I'm a little tired, is all. Too many time-zones this week." They stand on the terrace of his hotel room. Night is coming on, already, here in late afternoon; it is midwinter in the Southern Hemisphere, though the fragrance of the tropic blossoms perfumes the air. The first few stars have appeared. He has never really known which star is which. That bright one, he thinks, could be Rigel, and that one Sirius, and perhaps this is Deneb over there. And this? Can this be red Antares, in the heart of the Scorpion, or is it only Mars? Because of his collapse at the skyport he has been able to beg off the customary faculty reception and the formal dinner; pleading the need for rest, he has arranged to have a simple snack at his hotel room, *à deux*. In two hours they will come for him and take him to the University to speak. Dawn watches him closely. Perhaps she is worried about his health, perhaps she is only waiting for him to make his move toward her. There's time for all that later, he figures. He would rather talk now. Warming up for the audience, he seizes his earlier thread:

"For a long time I didn't understand what had taken place. I grew up insular, cut off from reality, a New York boy, bright mind and a library card. I read all the anthropological classics, *Patterns of Culture* and *Coming of Age in Samoa* and *Life of a South African Tribe* and the rest, and I dreamed of field trips, collecting myths and grammars and folkways and artifacts and all that, until when I was twenty-five I finally got out into the field and started to discover I had gone into a dead science. We have only one worldwide culture now, with local variants but no basic divergences: there's nothing primitive left on Earth, *and there are no other planets.* Not inhabited ones. I can't go to Mars or Venus or Saturn and study the natives. What natives? and we can't reach the stars. All I have to work with is Earth. I was thirty years old when the whole thing clicked together for me and I knew I had wasted my life."

She says, "But surely there was something for you to study on Earth."

"One culture, rootless and homogeneous. That's work for a sociologist, not for me. I'm a romantic, I'm an exotic, I want strangeness, difference. Look, we can never have any real perspective on our own times and lives. The sociologists try to attain it, but all they get is a mound of raw indigestible data. Insight comes later—two, five, ten generations later. But one way we've always been able to learn about ourselves is by studying alien cultures, studying them completely, and defining ourselves by measuring what they are that we aren't. The cultures have to be isolated, though. The anthropologist himself corrupts that isolation in the Heisenberg sense when he comes around with his camera and scanners and starts asking questions; but we can compensate, more or less, for the inevitable damage a lone observer causes. We can't compensate when our whole culture collides with another and absorbs and obliterates it. Which we technological-mechanical people now have done everywhere. One day I woke up and saw there were no alien cultures left. Hah! Crushing revelation! Schwartz' occupation is gone!"

"What did you do?"

"For years I was in an absolute funk. I taught, I studied, I went through the motions, knowing it was all meaningless. All I was doing was looking at records of vanished cultures left by earlier observers and trying to cudgel new meanings. Secondary sources, stale findings: I was an evaluator of dry bones, not a gatherer of evidence. Paleontology. Dinosaurs are interesting, but what do they tell you about the contemporary world and the meaning of its patterns? Dry bones, Dawn, dry bones. Despair. And then a clue. I had this Nigerian student, this Ibo—well, basically an Ibo, but she's got some Israeli in her and I think Chinese—and we grew very close, she was as close to me as anybody in my own sixness, and I told her my troubles. I'm going to give it all up, I said, because it isn't what I expected it to be. She laughed at me and said, What right do you have to be upset because the world doesn't live up to your expectations? Reshape your life, Tom: you can't reshape the world. I said, But how? And she said, Look inward, find the primitive in yourself, see what made you what you are, what made today's culture what it is, see how these alien streams have flowed together. Nothing's been lost here, only merged. Which made me think. Which gave me a new way of looking at things. Which sent me on an inward quest. It took me three years to grasp the patterns to come to an understanding of what our planet has become, and only after I accepted the planet—"

It seems to him that he has been talking forever. Talking. Talking. But he can no longer hear his own voice. There is only a distant buzz.

"After I accepted—"

A distant buzz.

"What was I saying?" he asks.

"After you accepted the planet—"

"After I accepted the planet," he says, "that I could begin—"*Buzz. Buzz.* "That I could begin to accept myself."

He was drawn toward the Spicans too, not so much for themselves—they were oblique, elliptical characters, self-contained and self-satisfied, hard to approach—as for the apparently psychedelic drug they took in some sacramental way before the beginning of each of their interminable ritual dances. Each time he had watched them take the drug, they had seemingly made a point of extending it toward him, as if inviting him, as if tempting him, before popping it into their mouths. He felt bated; he felt pulled.

There were three Spicans on board, slender creatures two and a half meters long, with flexible cylindrical bodies and small stubby limbs. Their skins were reptilian, dry and smooth, deep green with yellow bands; but their eyes were weirdly human, large liquid brown eyes, sad Levantine eyes, the eyes of unfortunate medieval travelers transformed by enchantment into serpents. Schwartz had spoken with them several times. They understood English well enough—all galactic races did; Schwartz imagined it would become the interstellar *lingua franca* as it had on Earth—but the construction of their vocal organs was such that they had no way of speaking it, and they relied instead on small translating machines hung round their necks that converted their soft whispered hisses into amber words pulsing across a screen.

Cautiously, the third or fourth time he spoke with them, he expressed polite interest in their drug. They told him it enabled them to make contact with the central forces of the universe. He replied that there were such drugs on Earth, too, and that he used them frequently, that they gave him great insight into the workings of the cosmos. They showed some curiosity, perhaps even intense curiosity; reading their eyes was difficult and the tone of their voices gave no clues. He took his elegant leather-bound drugcase from his pouch and showed them what he had: learitonin, psilocerebrin, siddharthin, and acid-57. He described the effects of each and suggested an exchange, any of his for an equivalent dose of the shrivelled orange fungoid they nibbled. They conferred. Yes, they said, we will do this. But not now. Not until the proper moment. Schwartz knew better than to ask them when that would be. He thanked them and put his drugs away.

Pitkin, who had watched the interchange from the far side of the lounge, came striding fiercely toward him as the Spicans glided off. "What are you up to now?" he demanded.

"How about minding your own business?" Schwartz said amiably.

"You're trading pills with those snakes, aren't you?"

"Let's call it field research."

"Research? Research? What are you going to do, trip on that orange stuff of theirs?"

"I might," Schwartz said.

"How do you know what its effects on the human metabolism might be? You could end up blind or paralyzed or crazy or—"

"—or illuminated," Schwartz said. "Those are the risks one takes in the field. The early anthropologists who unhesitatingly sampled peyote and yage and ololiuqui accepted those risks, and—"

"But those were drugs that *humans* were using. You have no way of telling how—oh, what's the use, Schwartz? Research, he calls it. Research." Pitkin sneered. *"Junkie!"*

Schwartz matched him sneer for sneer. *"Economist!"*

The house is a decent one tonight, close to three thousand, every seat in the University's great horseshoe-shaped auditorium taken, and a video relay besides, beaming his lecture to all of Papua and half of Indonesia. Schwartz stands on the dais like a demigod under a brilliant noglare spotlight. Despite his earlier weariness he is in good form now, gestures broad and forceful, eyes commanding, voice deep and resonant, words flowing freely. "Only one planet," he says, "one small and crowded planet, on which all cultures converge to a drab and depressing sameness. How sad that is! How tiny we make ourselves, when we make ourselves to resemble one another!" He flings his arms upward. "Look to the stars, the unattainable stars! Imagine, if you can, the millions of worlds that orbit those blazing suns beyond the night's darkness! Speculate with me on other peoples, other ways, other gods. Beings of every imaginable form, alien in appearance but not grotesque, not hideous, for all life is beautiful; beings that breathe gases strange to us, beings of immense size, beings of many limbs or of none, beings to whom death is a divine culmination of existence, beings who never die, beings who bring forth their young a thousand at a time, beings who do not reproduce—all the infinite possibilities of the infinite universe!

"Perhaps on each of those worlds it is as it has become here: one intelligent species, one culture, the eternal convergence. But the many worlds together offer a vast spectrum of variety. And now: share this vision with me!

I see a ship voyaging from star to star, a spaceliner of the future, and aboard that ship is a sampling of many species, many cultures, a random scoop of the galaxy's fantastic diversity. The ship is like a little cosmos, a small world, enclosed, sealed. How exciting to be aboard it, to encounter in that little compass such richness of cultural variation! Now our own world was once like that starship, a little cosmos, bearing with it all the thousands of Earthborn cultures, Hopi and Eskimo and Aztec and Kwakiutl and Arapesh and Orokolo and all the rest. In the course of our voyage we have come to resemble one another too much, and it has impoverished the lives of all of us, because—" He falters suddenly. He feels faint, and grasps the sides of the lectern. "Because—" The spotlight, he thinks. In my eyes. Not supposed to glare like that, but it's blinding. Got to have them move it. "In the course . . . the course of our voyage—" What's happening? Breaking into a sweat, now. Pain in my chest. My heart? Wait, slow up, catch your breath. That light in my eyes—

"Tell me," Schwartz said earnestly, "what it's like to know you'll have ten successive bodies and live more than a thousand years."

"First tell me," said the Antarean, "what it's like to know you'll live ninety years or less, and perish forever."

Somehow he continues. The pain in his chest grows more intense, he cannot focus his eyes, he believes he will lose consciousness at any moment and may even have lost it already at least once, and yet he continues. Clinging to the lectern, he outlines the program he developed in *The Mask Beneath The Skin*. A rebirth of tribalism without a revival of ugly nationalism. The quest for a renewal sense of kinship with the past. A sharp reduction in nonessential travel, especially tourism. Heavy taxation of exported artifacts, including films and video shows. An attempt to create independent cultural units on Earth once again while maintaining present levels of economic and political interdependence. Relinquishment of materialistic technological-industrial values. New searches for fundamental meanings. An ethnic revival, before it is too late, among those cultures of mankind that have only recently shed their traditional folkways. (He repeats and embellishes this point particularly, for the benefit of the Papuans before him, the great-grandchildren of cannibals.)

The discomfort and confusion come and go as he unreels his themes. He builds and builds, crying out passionately for an end to the homogenization of Earth, and gradually the physical symptoms leave him, all but a faint vertigo. But a different malaise seizes him as he nears his peroration. His voice becomes, to him, a far-off quacking meaningless and foolish. He has said all this a thousand times, always to great ovations, but who listens? Who listens? Everything seems hollow tonight, mechanical, absurd. An ethnic revival? Shall these people before him revert to their loincloths and their pigroasts? His starship is a fantasy; his dream of a diverse Earth is mere silliness. What is, will be. And yet he pushes on toward his conclusion. He takes his audience back to that starship, he creates a horde of fanciful beings for them, he completes the metaphor by sketching the structures of half a dozen vanished "primitive" cultures of Earth, he chants the chants of the Navaho, the Gabon Pygmies, the Ashanti, the Mundugumor. It is over. Cascades of applause engulf him. He holds his place until members of the sponsoring committee come to him and help him down; they have perceived his distress. "It's nothing," he gasps. "The lights—too bright—" Dawn is at his side. She hands him a drink, something cool. Two of the sponsors begin to speak of a reception for him in the Green Room. "Fine," Schwartz says. "Glad to." Dawn murmurs a protest. He shakes her off. "My obligation," he tells her. "Meet community leaders. Faculty people. I'm feeling better now. Honestly." Swaying, trembling, he lets them lead him away.

"A Jew," the Antarean said. "You call yourself a Jew, but what is this exactly? A clan, a sect, a moiety, a tribe, a nation, what? Can you explain?"

"You understand what a religion is?"

"Of course."

"Judaism—Jewishness—it's one of Earth's major religions."

"You are therefore a priest?"

"Not at all. I don't even practice Judaism. But my ancestors did, and therefore I consider myself Jewish, even though—"

"It is an hereditary religion, then," the Antarean said, "that does not require its members to observe its rites?"

"In a sense," said Schwartz desperately. "More an hereditary cultural subgroup, actually, evolving out of a common religious outlook no longer relevant."

"Ah. And the cultural traits of Jewishness that define it and separate you from the majority of humankind are—?"

"Well—" Schwartz hesitated. "There's a complicated dietary code, a rite of circumcision for newborn males, a rite of passage for male adolescents, a language of scripture, a vernacular language that Jews all around the world more or less understand and plenty more, including a certain intangible sense of clannishness and certain attitudes, such as a peculiar self-deprecating style of humor—"

"You observe the dietary code? You understand the language of scripture?"

"Not exactly," Schwartz admitted. "In fact I don't do anything that's specifically Jewish except think of myself as a Jew and adopt many of the characteristically Jewish personality modes, which, however, are not uniquely Jewish any longer—they can be traced among Italians, for example, and to some extent among Greeks. I'm speaking of Italians and Greeks of the late twentieth century, of course. Nowadays—" It was all becoming a terrible muddle. "Nowadays—"

"It would seem," said the Antarean, "that you are a Jew only because your maternal and paternal gene-givers were Jews, and they—"

"No, not quite. Not my mother, just my father, and he was Jewish only on his father's side, but even my grandfather never observed the customs, and—"

"I think this has grown too confusing," said the Antarean. "I withdraw the entire inquiry. Let us speak instead of my own traditions. The Time of Openings, for example, may be understood as—"

In the Green Room some eighty or a hundred distinguished Papuans press toward him, offering congratulations. "Absolutely right," they say. "A global catastrophe." "Our last chance to save our culture." Their skins are chocolate-tinted but their faces betray the genetic mishmash that is their ancestry—perhaps they call themselves Arapesh, Mundugumor, Tchambuli, Mafulu, in the way that he calls himself a Jew, but they have been liberally larded with chromosomes contributed by Chinese, Japanese, Europeans, Africans, everything. They dress in International Contemporary. They speak slangy, lively English. Schwartz feels seasick. "You look dazed," Dawn whispers. He smiles bravely. Body like dry bone. Mind like dead ashes. He is introduced to a tribal chieftain, tall, gray-haired, who looks and speaks like a professor, a lawyer, a banker. What, will these people return to the hills for the ceremony of the yam harvest? Will newborn girl-children be abandoned, cords uncut, skins unwashed, if their fathers do not need more girls? Will boys entering manhood submit to the expensive services of the initiator who sacrifices them with the teeth of crocodiles? The crocodiles are gone. The shamans have become stockbrokers.

Suddenly he cannot breathe.

"Get me out of here," Schwartz mutters hoarsely, choking.

Dawn, with stewardess efficiency, chops a path for him through the mob. The sponsors, concerned, rush to his aid. He is floated swiftly back to the hotel in a glistening little bubble-car. Dawn helps him to bed. Reviving, he reaches for her.

"You don't have to," she says. "You've had a rough day."

He persists. He embraces her and takes her, quickly, fiercely, and they move together for a few minutes and it ends and he sinks back, exhausted, stupefied. She gets a cool cloth and pats his forehead, and urges him to rest. "Bring me my drugs," he says. He wants siddharthin, but she misunderstands, probably deliberately, and offers him something blue and bulky, a sleeping pill, and, too weary to object, he takes it. Even so, it seems to be hours before sleep comes.

He dreams he is at the skyport, boarding the rocket for Bangkok, and instantly he is debarking at Bangkok—just like Port Moresby, only more humid—and he delivers his speech to a horde of enthusiastic Thais, while rockets flicker about him, carrying him to skyport after skyport, and the Thais blur and become Japanese, who are transformed into Mongols, who become Uighurs, who become Iranians, who become Sudanese, who become Zambians, who become Chileans, and all look alike, all look alike, all look alike.

The Spicans hovered above him, weaving, bobbing, swaying like cobras about to strike. But their eyes, warm and liquid, were sympathetic: loving even. He felt the glow of their compassion. If they had had the sort of musculature that enabled them to smile, they would be smiling tenderly, he knew.

One of the aliens leaned close. The little translating device dangled toward Schwartz like a holy medallion. He narrowed his eyes, concentrating as intently as he could on the amber words flashing quickly across the screen.

". . . has come. We shall . . ."

"Again, please," Schwartz said. "I missed some of what you were saying."

"The moment . . . has come. We shall . . . make the exchange of sacraments now."

"Sacraments?"

"Drugs."

"Drugs, yes. Yes. Of course." Schwartz groped in his pouch. He felt the cool smooth leather skin of his drug-case. Leather? Snakeskin, maybe. Anyway. He drew it forth. "Here," he said. "Siddharthin, learitonin, psilocerebrin, acid-57. Take your pick." The Spicans selected three small blue siddharthins. "Very good," Schwartz said. "The most transcendental of all. And now—"

The longest of the aliens proffered a ball of dried orange fungus the size of Schwartz' thumbnail.

"It is an equivalent dose. We give it to you."

"Equivalent to all three of my tablets, or to one?"

"Equivalent. It will give you peace."

Schwartz smiled. There was a time for asking questions, and a time for unhesitating action. He took the fungus and reached for a glass of water.

"*Wait!*" Pitkin cried, appearing suddenly. "What are you—"

"Too late," Schwartz said serenely, and swallowed the Spican drug in one joyous gulp.

The nightmares go on and on. He circles the Earth like the Flying Dutchman, like the Wandering Jew, skyport to skyport to skyport, an unending voyage from nowhere to nowhere. Obliging committees meet him and convey him to his hotel. Sometimes the committee members are contemporary types, indistinguishable from one another, with standard faces, standard clothing, the all-purpose new-model hybrid unihuman, and sometimes they are consciously ethnic, elaborately decked out in feathers and paint and tribal emblems, but their faces, too, are standard behind the gaudy regalia, their slang is the slang of Uganda and Tierra del Fuego and Nepal, and it seems to Schwartz that these masqueraders are, if anything, less authentic, less honest, than the other sort, who at least are true representatives of their era. So it is hopeless either way. He lashes at his pillow, he groans, he wakens. Instantly Dawn's arms enfold him. He sobs incoherent phrases into her clavical and she murmurs soothing sounds against his forehead. He is having some sort of breakdown, he realizes: a new crisis of values, a shattering of the philosophical synthesis that has allowed him to get through the last few years. He is bound to the wheel; he spins, he spins, he spins, traversing the continents, getting nowhere. There is no place to go. No. There is one, just one, a place where he will find peace, where the universe will be as he needs it to be. Go there, Schwartz. Go and stay as long as you can. "Is there anything I can do?" Dawn asks. He shivers and shakes his head. "Take this," she says, and gives him some sort of pill. Another tranquilizer. All right. All right. It will help him get where he must go. The world has turned to porcelain. His skin feels like a plastic coating. Away, away, to the ship. To the ship! "So long," Schwartz says, and lets himself slip away.

Outside the ship the Capellans twist and spin in their ritual dance as, weightless and without mass, they are swept toward the rim of the galaxy at nine times the velocity of light. They move with a grace that is astonishing for creatures of such tremendous bulk. A dazzling light that emanates from the center of the universe strikes their glossy skin and, rebounding, resonates all up and down the spectrum, splintering into brilliant streamers of ultra-red, infra-violet, exo-yellow. All the cosmos glows and shimmers. A single perfect note of music comes out of the remote distance and, growing closer, swells in an infinite crescendo. Schwartz trembles at the beauty of all he perceives.

Beside him stands the seal-slick Antarean. She—definitely *she,* no doubt of it, *she*—plucks at his arm and whispers, "Will you go to them?"

"Yes. Yes, of course."

"So will I. Wherever you go."

"Now," Schwartz says. He reaches for the lever that opens the hatch. He pulls down. The side of the starship swings open.

The Antarean looks deep into his eyes and says blissfully, "I have never told you my name. My name is Dawn."

Together they float through the hatch into space.

The blackness receives them gently. There is no chill, no pressure at the lungs, no discomfort at all. He is surrounded by luminous surges, by throbbing mantles of pure color, as though he has entered the heart of an aurora. He and Dawn swim toward the Capellans, and the huge beings welcome them with deep glad booming cries. Dawn joins the dance at once, moving her sinuous limbs with extravagant ease; Schwartz will do the same in a moment, but first he turns to face the starship, hanging in space close by him like a vast coppery needle, and in a voice that could shake universes he calls, "Come, friends! Come, all of you! Come dance with us!" And they come, pouring through the hatch, the Spicans first, then all the rest, the infinite multitude of beings, the travelers from Formalhaut and Achernar and Acrux and Aldebaran, from Thuban and Arcturua and Altair, from Polaris and Canopus and Sirius and Rigel, hundreds of star-creatures spilling happily out of the vessel, bursting forth, all of them, even Pitkin, poor little Pitkin, everyone joining hands and tentacles and tendrils and whatever, forming a great ring of light across space, everyone looked in a cosmic harmony, everyone dancing. Dancing. Dancing.

AFTERWORD

The fair breeze blew, the white foam flew,
The furrow followed free;
We were the first that ever burst
Into that silent sea.

Or into that silent atmosphere, that other planet beyond reach of Ancient Mariner. New ocean, new atmosphere, new life—to these adventures the soul greatly responds, for they are part of everyone's fundamental experience, even when marred or muffled by suburban living.

I cannot claim to have fulfilled adequately the task I set myself in this volume; for that I would need much more space much more time. Yet these stories give a hint that one of the most stirring of science fiction adventures remains our first sight of Deneb IV. The science fiction adventure is more than merely an adventure. It stands for one of the fundamentals of the psyche, the quest for knowledge. What is unknown must be known. Though it brings disaster.

Brush aside the palsied claim that this sf or that is pessimistic. For there are dark riddles in our nature that must be faced. Many of the great life-giving legends concern the necessity for acquiring knowledge even if it brings disaster. The story of Adam and Eve, the story of Faust, of Frankenstein, of Dr. Jekyll, all embody this understanding. The knowledge always brings pain, and often degradation as well; yet still the journey into knowing must be made. One day, there will be a journey into knowledge that will bring a fairer reward—and then perhaps Mankind itself will be changed. The Sack need not always give a dusty answer.

Perhaps that redeeming knowledge will be found on another planet, though personally I doubt it (the journey to wisdom needs stillness, not action). Meanwhile, there remains the romantic excitement of viewing, at the end of the journey, another fragment of matter harbouring its own secrets, silences sea birds. The South African poet, Roy Campbell, said it precisely in the first verses of a poem celebrating his sight of Tristan da Cunha, as it stood out from the wastes of the South Atlantic:

> Snore in the foam; the night is vast and blind;
> The blanket of the mist about your shoulders,
> Sleep your old sleep of rock, snore in the wind,
> Snore in the spray! the storm your slumber lulls,
> His wings are folded on your nest of boulders
> As on their eggs the grey wings of your gulls.
>
> No more as when, so dark an age ago,
> You hissed a giant cinder from the ocean,
> Around your rocks you furl the shawling snow
> Half sunk in your own darkness, vast and grim,
> And round you on the deep with surly motion
> Pivot your league-long shadow as you swim . . .